My Brother's Keeper

By

John R. Dabrowski

My Brother's Keeper by John R. Dabrowski
Cover design by Jan Kostka
This edition published in 2023

Wrong Way Books is an imprint of

Winged Hussar Publishing, LLC
1525 Hulse Rd, Unit 1
Point Pleasant, NJ 08742

Copyright © Winged Hussar Publishing
ISBN 978-1-950423-92-7 PB
ISBN 978-1-958872-09-3 EB
LCN

Bibliographical References and Index
1. Historical Fiction. 2. World War II. 3. Thriller

Winged Hussar Publishing, LLC All rights reserved
For more information
visit us at www.whpsupplyroom.com

Twitter: WingHusPubLLC
Facebook: Winged Hussar Publishing LLC

What people are saying about, *My Brother's Keeper*

"As Franz Kafka's Metamorphosis turns Gregor Samsa into an intro-spective insect, John Dabrowski's *My Brother's Keeper* transforms the reader into an engaged, all knowing "Fly-on-the-Wall" who witnesses the inner workings of a plan hatched by two brothers during WWII. Dabrowski's knowledge of materiel and war strategy including the type of pipe Stalin smoked, exhibit his lifetime of service as a deco-rated Army colonel and respected Defense Department historian, but it is Dabrowski's life experiences as a storyteller which breath life and complexity into the characters he creates. Institutional memory and our collective consciousness may make it impossible for us to imagine the Catholic Church as anything but problematic during the Holocaust, but in Dabrowski's world order where he deftly mixes the fictional and nonfictional, we are able to suspend our institutional knowledge of World War II just enough to believe we were there ourselves wit-nessing history, albeit an alternate history. From a non-commissioned German soldier guarding the gates at headquarters to the rarified air enjoyed only by the elite at Hitler's Wolf's Lair, we are not passive readers but are transformed into a very lucky "you are there" who is hungry for even more intrigue and suspense Dabrowski-style. By cre-ating *My Brother's Keeper*, Dabrowski constructs not only a different history, but a kind of "Road to Damascus" where we are transformed from a passive reader to one who feels that we've landed right on the railing of Mussolini's balcony."

--Catherine Gong, author of *George's Kaddish: For Kovno and the Six Million*

"Historical fiction at its finest. *My Brother's Keeper* features a sweep-ing cast of memorable characters, many drawn from the pages of histo-ry and brought fully alive. The suspenseful and carefully woven plot--a clandestine attempt by Vatican officials to spirit 100 Jews in Estonia from the clutches of the SS to safety in Sweden--holds the reader's attention throughout. Highly recommended to military specialists, stu-dents of World War II in Europe, and all who relish a compelling mix of fact and fiction dramatically rendered."

---Edward G. Longacre, PhD, author of *War in the Ruins: The Amer-ican Army's Final Battle Against Nazi Germany*

Dedicated in loving memory to my mother, Concetta "Connie" Dabrowski

October 12, 1930 - March 5, 2020

My Brother's Keeper

By

John R. Dabrowski

Acknowledgments

I would like to take this opportunity to thank a number of individuals who assisted me in helping to bring this book into fruition. A big thank you to my dear friend Monsignor John J. Bendik, pastor emeritus of St. John the Evangelist Roman Catholic Church, Pittston, Pennsylvania for taking the time to read over the initial draft. His in-depth knowledge of Roman Catholic institutions and matters of the ecclesiastical nature, along with his critique were most welcome and appreciated. Thank you Father B.!

Dr. Edward G. Longacre, my friend and former colleague from our days as civilian Air Force Historians with the Air Combat Command History Office, was kind enough to review my manuscript and to offer his kind endorsement for this book. Ed is a prolific author in his own right, and although his field of expertise is the US Civil War, he has written a first-rate book on the Second World War as well (*War in the Ruins: The American Army's Final Battle Against Nazi Germany*, Westholme Publishing, 2009). My wish is that my book be as well received as his have been in the past.

My dear friend of over 45 years and college classmate, Bob Pangrazzi, reviewed for me a draft of my manuscript. Bob's in-depth critique and suggestions for possible changes in the main body of the work was most appreciated. I took Bob's advice and the result is a tighter-written and better-flowing story line.

My friend and former colleague with the US Department of Defense's Missile Defense Agency (MDA), Catherine Gong, an author in her own right (*George Kaddish For Kovno and the Six Million*, Xlibris Publications, 2009), was kind enough to review my manuscript and offer critical comments. Catherine's in-depth knowledge of the Holocaust and her previous research into that area have received accolades from well-known US Holocaust scholars. She too, was kind enough to offer an endorsement for my book.

My thanks to Allicyn Rosenthal, a retired educator and a dear friend of over 40 years. Allicyn's critical eye while reviewing my manuscript caught mistakes in grammar and syntax and once corrected, made for a better-flowing story line and I am most grateful for her assistance.

My thanks also to Deborah Crabtree of the Northwest Florida State College library who was kind enough to order a few hard-to-find books for me via interlibrary loan for research on this book; it is most appreciated.

Admittedly, I am a "technology-challenged" author and whenever I ran into any difficulties on my laptop, I relied heavily on my daughter, Christina, for assistance. As fate would have it, due to the COVID virus, Christina was able to telecommute from home, and was staying at our home in Navarre rather than at her apartment in Orlando, as I completed my draft. She was my "go to" on-site IT person whenever I had a computer related question, which was often. Christina also assisted in designing the front cover for this novel, using the limited software package that we had on my laptop. It was later much improved upon by the publishing company's designers.

My thanks to my son, Keith, who offered encouragement and support in my efforts. Years ago, when I wrote my first novel, *To Sup With the Devil*, Keith had been living with me in Carlisle, Pennsylvania and was my on-site IT person then - now it was his sister's turn to help out the "Old Man."

Finally, to my wife, Mary, who offered love and encouragement during the writing of this novel, I thank you for these last 37 years together and for your continued endurance with my fascination with all things strange.

On a more personal note - during the writing of this novel, my mother died in March 2020 as the result of complications from heart-valve replacement surgery. Months earlier, I had shown her an incomplete draft of this work and what she read, she thoroughly enjoyed. Most importantly, she was thrilled to see that I had dedicated the novel to her. I would hope that she would have enjoyed the completed version of this work. So, Mom, this one is for you!

My Brother's Keeper

John R. Dabrowski

Introduction

The actions taken by Pope Pius XII during the Second World War have, to date, been quite controversial. Many of Pius XII's detractors state that he had not done enough to save the Jews of Europe, let alone the Jews in Rome itself during the Nazi occupation of that city from 1943-44. Defenders of Pius XII point to the fact that thousands of Jews were saved by the Roman Catholic Church by providing them hiding places in churches, monasteries, convents, and other church properties, to include the pope's own summer residence at Castle Gandolfo, as well as issuing false baptismal certificates, all with the tacit approval of the pope himself. Individual clergy and other religious often risked their lives in assisting their Jewish friends and neighbors escape Nazi tyranny.

In 1963, a controversial play, *The Deputy* (in German, *Der Stellver-treter*), opened in West Berlin. Written by German playwright Rolf Hochhuth, it portrayed Pius as having taken little or no action in speaking out against the Holocaust and furthermore, painted the pontiff as being indifferent to the Nazi genocide that was going on all around him. More recent works, Guenter Lewy's *The Catholic Church and Nazi Germany* (1964) and John Cornwell's *Hitler's Pope: The Secret History of Pius XII* (1999) had only added further fuel to the controversy surrounding Pius XII. Until such time as the Vatican releases all of its wartime records surrounding Pius XII's pontificate, histori-ans, theologians and others will continue to debate what the pope should have or could have done during the war years.[168]

The novel you are about to read is of course, a work of fiction. While many of the characters in the book are factual historical figures from the time period, the two main characters, the brothers Bertram, are fictional. The story is written with the backdrop of historical wartime events occurring in the sum-mer of 1943, namely, the Holocaust, the invasion of Sicily/Italy, the overthrow and ultimate rescue of Benito Mussolini, the German occupation of Rome, and covers the critical months from June-September 1943. The reader will also note that the story takes place in various geographic locations - Berlin, Rome, Moscow, East Prussia, Estonia, the Vatican, Madrid, and other European lo-cales - and in some instances contains dual/multiple timelines, many occur-ing simultaneously, making it appear that some events occur out-of-sequence, which is not the case or intent.. One of the locales that factors prominently in this story is the *Via Tasso*, the wartime Gestapo headquarters/prison in Rome. Today it is The Historical Museum of Liberation. I had the opportunity to visit the museum in 2018 and would highly recommend those of you interested in the history of the Nazi occupation of Rome to visit this very moving and inter-esting historical site. In addition, I would also recommend to the reader a visit to the *Fosse Ardeatine*, or the Ardeatine Cave Memorial, the site of the worst wartime massacre of Italian civilians (March 24, 1944) perpetrated by the Nazis under the direct command of *Obersturmbannführer* Herbert Kappler, the main protagonist in this novel. The remains of all 335 victims of this massacre have been placed in a vast burial vault and a visit to it is a very moving and sobering experience, one which I can personally attest to.

The novel centers on the rescue of 100 Jews from the Klooga Concentration Camp in Estonia. Klooga was a real camp that would be liberated by the Red Army in September 1944. In the novel, these 'special' Jewish prisoners are rescued with the help of the German military - if this sounds so far-fetched as to be unbelievable, I will direct the reader to obtain a copy of Bryan Mark Rigg's excellent work, *The Rabbi Saved by Hitler's Soldiers* (University Press of Kansas, 2016). Rigg weaves a tale almost impossible to be true, that German soldiers, most of Jewish heritage, successfully rescued the ultra-orthodox Lubavitcher Jewish leader, *Rebbe* Joseph Schneersohn from German-occupied Warsaw in 1939. Surprisingly, playing central roles in the rescue effort was the head of German military intelligence (*Abwehr*), Admiral Wilhelm Canaris as well as Helmuth Wohlthat, chief administrator of Hermann Goring's Four Year Plan. The leader of the operation itself was a highly-decorated *Wehrmacht* officer, Ernst Bloch, who succeeded in spiriting The *Rebbe* and some of his followers out of Warsaw under the very noses of the Gestapo. Schneersohn and his followers would ultimately make their way safely to the United States as a result of the rescue effort. Mark Twain once wrote that "It's no wonder that truth is stranger than fiction. Fiction has to make sense."

The reader will also note that German, Spanish and Italian words are prevalent throughout the book and are *italicized* - I have made every effort to ensure the correct spelling of those words and hope I have not offended any of the native speakers of those languages if they are incorrect.

Where needed, I have placed informational footnotes for the reader for general historical fact and information. I hope the reader will enjoy this novel as much as I have enjoyed writing it.

John R. Dabrowski
Navarre, Florida
February 23, 2023

John R. Dabrowski

Dramatis Personae

(Characters with names in CAPS are historical, others fictional)

Abramovitz, Menachim	Rabbi, spokesman for Jewish prisoners at Klooga Concentration Camp
von ALTISHOFEN, HEINRICH PFYFER	Commander, Papal Swiss Guard
AUMEIER, HANS	Commandant, Vaivara Concentration Camp, Estonia
Bertram, Berthold	Son of Peter and Lydia Bertram
Bertram, Heidi	Daughter of Peter and Lydia Bertram
Bertram, Josef "Sepp"	Roman Catholic Monsignor, Vatican Foreign Office. Brother of Peter Bertram
Bertram, Lydia	Wife of Peter Bertram
Bertram, Peter	*SS Gruppenführer*, Deputy Higher SS and Police Leader for *Reichskomissariat Ostland.* Brother of Josef "Sepp" Bertram
BRANDT, RUDOLF	*SS Sturmbannführer* and adjutant to *Reichsfuhrer SS* Heinrich Himmler
von BRAUN, SIGISMUND	German Embassy Legation Secretary to the Vatican. Older brother of German

scientist Wehrner von Braun

Dahlerus, Arvid

Swedish foreign ministry official

Delgado, Maria

Roman prostitute

Denisov, Ivan

Red Army Captain, intelligence officer for the 12th Partisan Brigade

DOLLMANN, EUGEN

SS Standartenführer, Heinrich Himmler's personal representative in Rome

Davydova, Comrade

Female partisan agent, code-named "Tatiana"

EMMANUEL III, VITTORIO

King of Italy

ERFURTH, WALDEMAR

Wehrmacht general, senior liaison to Finnish military headquarters, (1941-44)

ESTEBAN-INFANTES, EMILIO

Commanding General, Spanish Blue Division, (1942-43)

FRANCO, FRANCISCO Y BAHAMONDE

Spanish head of State, (1939-75)

Fritz, Wilhelm

Wehrmacht officer assigned to the 517th Medical Battalion

Garcetti, Nicolo

Italian Air Force Colonel

Garcia, Jamie Chaplain

Spanish priest, assigned as a military

	chaplain to the Spanish "Blue Division" in Russia
Henrickson, Lars	Radio Sweden announcer
HIMMLER, HEINRICH	*Reichsführer SS*
HITLER, ADOLF	*Führer* of the German Reich, (1933-45)
JORDANA Y SOUZA, FRANCISCO GARCIA	Spanish Foreign Minister
KAPPLER, HERBERT	*SS Obersturmbannführer*, Chief of German Security Police in Rome
KNUPPEL, WILHELM	*Wehrmacht Oberstleutnant,* Chief, German Liaison to the Spanish Blue Division"
Koening, Hans	Luftwaffe officer-in-charge of German air force training detachment at Krasny Bor
Koening, Johannes	Head of the Reich Labor Office, Reval, Estonia
Kozlov, Vasilii	Red Army Colonel, commander 12th Partisan Brigade
Kuzin, Comrade	Head of local Communist partisan network in Reval. Codenamed "Walter"
LEHMANN, HANS	Swedish merchant and spokesman for the Or-

thodox Jewish community in Sweden

Loss, Willi — *SS Hauptsturmführer*, Commander of Klooga Concentration Camp, Reval, Estonia

MANNERHEIM, CARL GUSTAV — Finnish field marshal, commander of Finnish armed forces

MILAN DEL BOSCH, JAMIE — Captain, Spanish Blue Division

Mohl, Dieter — *Kripo Inspektor* in Reval, Estonia

MOLOTOV, VYACHESLAV M. — Soviet Foreign Minister

MONTINI, GIOVANNI — Monsignor, Vatican Assistant Secretary of State. Future Pope Paul VI, (1963-78)

MUSSOLINI, BENITO — Fascist leader and *Il Duce* of Italy, (1922-45)

O'FLAHERTY, HUGH — Irish Roman Catholic Monsignor assigned to the Vatican as the *Primo Notario*

PFEIFFER, PANKRAITIUS — Catholic clergyman, Superior General of the Salvatorian Order

PIUS XII — Born Eugenio Pacelli, Roman Pontiff, (1939-58)

PONOMARENKO, PANTILEIMON K. — Red Army Lieutenant General, Chief of Staff

	for the Soviet Partisan network
Prost, Willi	Former SS trooper, now a paid SS informant
PRIEBKE, ERICH	Gestapo officer assigned to Rome, directly subordinate to *Obersturmbannführer* Herbert Kappler
Punga, Aarne	Reich Labor Office employee, secretly a Soviet Partisan
Rauter, Alois	*Wehrmacht* officer
RONCALLI, ANGELO	Archbishop, Papal Nuncio in Istanbul. Future Pope John XXIII, (1958-63)
Roper, Hans	*Wehrmacht* officer assigned to the 517th Medical Battalion
Rudolph, Hans	*Wehrmacht* Major, Chief of *Feldgendarme* Office, 170th Division
Scavone, Giovanni	Italian Army Sgt, cousin to Fr. Giuseppe Scavone
Scavone, Giuseppe	Roman Catholic priest, pastor of San Antonio di Padua Church in Rome
Schobert, Maria	A *Volksdeutsche* from Estonia, housekeeper

to the Bertram family in Reval

STAHEL, RAINER

German General and military governor of Rome

STALIN, JOSEF V.

General Secretary, Communist Party, USSR

TARDINI, DOMENICO

Monsignor, Vatican Assistant Secretary of State

TISO, JOSEF

Roman Catholic cleric and President of the Republic of Slovakia, a Nazi puppet state (1939-45)

TISO, STEFAN

President of the Slovakia Supreme Court and cousin to Monsignor Josef Tiso

Weber, Viktor

Wehrmacht medical officer, Commander of the 517th Medical Battalion

Weiss, Peter

Deputy commander, Papal Swiss Guard

WEIZSÄCKER, ERNST VON

German Ambassador to the Holy See (1943-45)

WALLENBERG, JACOB

Co-owner of Enskilda Bank in Sweden with his brother, Marcus

WALLENBERG, MARCUS

Co-owner of Enskilda Bank in Sweden with his brother, Jacob

WOLFF, KARL

SS Obergruppen-führer and Highest SS and Police Leader (HSSPF) for all of Italy

Chapter I

"Only the Church protested against the Hitlerian onslaught…Up till then I had not been interested in the Church, but today I feel a great admiration for the Church"
--Albert Einstein, *Time* Magazine, 1940

Vatican Secretary of State's Office
Vatican City
June 20, 1943, 1045 Hours

Monsignor Domenico Tardini[1], one of two assistant Secretaries of State[2] for the Holy See, had just returned from a meeting with Pope Pius XII in the Holy Father's private apartments. The Pope was becoming more and more alarmed from the reports he was receiving from German-occupied Europe, particularly the Eastern Front, of the systematic liquidation of east European Jewry by the Nazis. If anything, the Holy See could pride itself as having one of the finest intelligence services in the world---countless clergy, missionaries, and layman who were scattered around the globe doing God's work, and who reported daily life under the Axis, both in Europe and in the Japanese-controlled regions of Asia and the Pacific. Since the Bolshevik Revolution of 1917, the Soviet Union had become xenophobic and atheistic, and over the years, established an almost impenetrable society - the Soviet secret police, the dreaded NKVD[3], saw to that. While there were very few, if any, Catholic missionaries left in Russia in 1943, there were numerous army chaplains serving with the German *Wehrmacht*.[4] It was these reports that were reaching the Holy See and which were greatly distressing the Holy Father.

Since 1939, Hitler had been carrying out his murderous conquest in the East, creating new areas of German *Lebensraum*, or living space, for German settlers that Hitler had so clearly defined in his book, *Mein Kampf*, written almost twenty years before in 1924. It made no difference to the Nazis that these areas were already inhabited by Slavic and Jewish people, whom according to Nazi racial doctrine, were considered *Untermensch* or sub-humans, and had to be physically exterminated. To carry out Hitler's plan, special mobile killing commando units known as *Einsatzgruppen*, followed behind the regular German Army units. Once an area was secured, the *Einsatzkommandos* would fulfill their deadly tasks---to eliminate Jews, Gypsies, Communists, Social Democrats, homosexuals, Soviet political commissars, and others deemed 'undesirable' by the Nazis. The Germans were very efficient in carrying out these mobile killings, to the point that by 1943, the Baltic States had been declared *Judenrein* or Jew-free by the Nazi officials governing the Baltics, now given the new administrative designation of *Reichskommissariat Ostland.*

Pius XII had confided to Monsignor Tardini that he was not appalled at the elimination of the godless and atheistic communists and Soviet political commissars by the Nazis.[5] As papal nuncio in Munich in the immediate aftermath of the First World War, Pius, then-Cardinal Eugenio Pacelli, witnessed first-hand communist intentions, especially towards the Christian churches. In 1918, the German state of Bavaria was briefly declared a Soviet republic amidst the chaos following the Great War. The Red Brigades desecrated church property, assaulted priests and nuns, and even attempted to seize the nuncio's automobile at gunpoint. Attempting to emulate Moscow, the communists wanted to make Germany an atheistic state, where God played no role whatsoever. It was only through force of the German *Reichswehr* and *Freikorps,* units of demobilized army veterans, that the communist revolution was put down and many of its leaders shot out of hand upon capture.[6]

The situation in Rome in June of 1943 was equally tense. Sources inside the Italian monarchy and Mussolini's own Fascist Grand Council reported that *Il Duce* could not retain his power if the Allies invaded Sicily, and then Italy itself. In May, Axis forces in North Africa had surrendered, some 250,000 men, one half of them Italians, and were taken into captivity by the Allies. It was now only a matter of time before Sicily would be invaded, and then, to quote British Prime Minister Winston Churchill, the "Soft Underbelly of Europe," Italy itself, would be threatened. For the time being, however, Mussolini was still blustering, and black-shirted Italian Fascist thugs still roamed the streets at will.

Pius XII had informed Tardini that while the Germans may have declared the Baltics Jew-free, Vatican intelligence reports contradicted the Nazi boasts. A German Army chaplain had sent photos as well as other documentation of a camp outside of Tallinn, (renamed Reval by the Germans) Estonia, housing some 100 Jews from the Baltic States. They were, in all probability, the very last surviving Jews in Estonia. These Jews were to be exterminated on August 30 in conjunction with a visit by *Reichsführer SS* Heinrich Himmler. The Germans were testing a new method of killing by a more potent poison gas, and a demonstration was being prepared in honor of Himmler's visit. The Deputy Higher SS and Police Leader ("*Höchster SS und Polizeiführer*" or HSSPF) for the area, was *Gruppenführer* (Major General) Peter Bertram, who was a rising star within the SS, and a close friend of Gotlieb Berger, an intimate of Himmler. Through his friendship with Berger, Bertram caught Himmler's attention in 1931, and after that it was a meteoric rise through the ranks of the SS. In 1942, Bertram was appointed Deputy Higher SS and Police Leader for *Ostland*. Bertram's efficiency in his new position again caught Himmler's attention, and it was believed that Himmler's impending visit to the area was to promote Bertram to the rank of *SS Obergruppenführer* (Lieutenant General) as well as giving him his own combat command within the *Waffen SS*. Bertram's promotions to the upper ranks of the SS often met resistance from the promotion board members, because Bertram's younger brother, Josef, known as "Sepp," was a Roman Catholic clergyman, assigned to the Vatican's Secretary of State. It was only through the direct intervention of Gotlieb Berger that Peter Bertram had risen as far as he had in the SS.

Monsignor Josef Bertram, was a rising star in his own right within the Holy See's diplomatic corps. Many referred to him as 'the Pope's troubleshooter' as he had embarked on missions just prior to the outbreak of hostilities in 1939, and even afterwards, having undertaken a particularly dangerous assignment in 1942 to the Independent State of Croatia,[7] where the government of Ante Pavelic, a Catholic, had embarked on a murderous campaign against his nation's Jews and Orthodox Serbs. The Croat *Ustashăs*, were operating a notorious concentration camp at Jasenovac,[8] near the Sava River, where brutality and murder were the order of the day. Even veteran SS and Gestapo officials visiting the camp were sickened by the camp's brutal conditions.[9] Josef Bertram, at the direction of the Vatican Secretary of State, had traveled to Croatia to negotiate the release of a number of Jews and Serbs being held at Jasenovac. The *Ustashă* were notoriously corrupt, and for the right price, could be easily bribed. With this in mind, some 250 Jews and Serbs were released, given false baptismal certificates, and then hidden at various monasteries and convents; with some even lucky enough to have reached Switzerland and freedom.

As Tardini sat at his desk and pondered the conversation he had with the Holy Father, he felt that Monsignor Bertram would be the man for the job. With his brother as deputy police leader, he could hopefully call on his brother's sense of decency and compassion (if he had any left) and possibly win the release of the 100 Jews in the camp at Reval. Arrangements could then be made to transport the freed personnel across to Finland. Even though Finland was fighting alongside Germany, it was only to recover the territory it had lost to the Soviets in the Winter War of 1939-40.[10] Finland's Marshal Karl Gustav Mannerheim had refused to hand over any of its Jews to the Nazis, as anti-Semitism was not part of Finnish domestic policy or culture. *Reichsführer SS* Himmler went so far as to travel to Helsinki in July 1942 to try and persuade the Finnish government to surrender its 2,000 or so Jews to the SS. Himmler was told in no uncertain terms that there was no 'Jewish Question' in Finland, and he promptly abandoned any further attempts at rounding up Finland's Jews. If Bertram could arrange for their release and safe passage through Finland and ultimately to Sweden, the Jews would be safe. It would be a small victory over the forces of evil, but a victory, nonetheless.

A small smile crossed Tardini's lips as he nodded and said to himself, "Yes, Josef Bertram is our man." Tardini arose from his desk and made his way to a small chapel. Once there, Tardini prayed for guidance in the hopes that he was making the right decision.

Vatican Secretary of State's Office
Vatican City
June 20, 1943, 1345 Hours

Monsignor Josef Bertram had been summoned to see Monsignor Tardini earlier in the day. Bertram's duties within the Secretariat was with the Congregation for Extraordinary Ecclesiastical Affairs.

"Sepp, so good of you to come," Tardini said, using Bertram's nickname.

"Excellency, it is always an honor to talk with you." Even though both men were monsignors, Bertram deferred to Tardini due to the high position he held within the Secretariat of State, and respectfully referred to him as 'Excellency.'

Tardini truly liked Bertram as he was an intelligent and honest individual, and told him what was on his mind, not like some of the 'yes men' who agreed with everything Tardini said. He was, Tardini thought with a smile, *'a straight shooter,'* as the Americans liked to say.

"Sepp, I met with the Holy Father yesterday, and he is deeply troubled about what your countrymen are doing in Eastern Europe, particularly to our Jewish brethren."

Bertram felt that this was an unintentional slight by Tardini, due to Bertram's German nationality. He knew of course, that there was no way that Tardini, or for that matter, the Pope himself, held Bertram personally responsible for the genocide taking place.

"Excellency, I know that our Jewish brethren are suffering terribly under that madman in Berlin. I pray every night for them."

"As do I, Sepp. But it is going to take a little more than prayers, I believe, to save them from certain death."

Both men were silent for a moment and then Tardini continued.

"Your brother is *Gruppenführer* Peter Bertram of the SS, correct?"

" Yes, Excellency."

"The Holy Father would like you to travel to see your brother in Estonia and to plead with him, if need be, to spare the lives of the remaining Jews held in a camp near Reval. Himmler himself will be traveling to Reval at the end of August to witness the execution of these poor innocents by a new method of poison gas. Your brother will be hosting him. Perhaps you can sway your

John R. Dabrowski

brother and talk him out of executing all those people."

Bertram looked at Tardini with a quizzical look then stated, "Excellency, I appreciate what the Holy Father is attempting to do, but my brother is a very dedicated SS man, and I'm sure if the Pope himself were to ask him, he would tell the Holy Father to take a flying leap! My brother and I are not particularly close. I, nor our parents, ever agreed with his politics and it nearly killed my parents the day he came home and told them he had joined the SS. My father, if I recall, slapped him across the face and told him to get out of the house. It is not a day I care to remember."

"How long has it been since you've seen your brother?"

"Not since our parents' funeral in Munich, Excellency. That was three years ago, and we hardly spoke. Despite my parents' disapproval of Peter's politics, they still loved him, and he loved them. He broke down at the funeral."

"Peter is married with a family, is he not, Sepp?"

"Yes, Excellency. His wife's name is Lydia, and she is or at least was a very fine woman, from a very good upstanding Catholic family in Bavaria. Her parents did not approve of Peter's politics either, and I believe she is estranged from her family because of it. Peter also has two children, Heidi and Berthold, whom I haven't seen in three years, as they were quite young at the time. I don't know if they'd recognize their Uncle Sepp," he said with a slight chuckle.

"Sepp, the Holy Father and I need you to visit your brother and to use all of your powers of persuasion to get him to release those people. We are working on a plan that if you can free those poor souls, we can get them to Finland and safely out of Hitler's clutches."

"I can talk until I'm blue in the face and Peter will ignore me. With Himmler's upcoming visit, I'm sure that his future in the SS will depend on putting on a bravo performance for Himmler while he is there."

"Sepp, you are no doubt familiar with the declarations made by the Allies earlier this year in Casablanca, not only for the Axis' unconditional surrender, but for their expectation to prosecute certain individuals for war crimes. No doubt they are documenting Hitler and his henchmen's crimes for the day they get them on the docket. You may want to use this reasoning with your brother. His career in the SS will be all for naught, especially if his head is in a noose."

Tardini let that thought settle in for a moment, and then continued.

"If your brother can assist us in getting those people out of the camp and into Finland, the Holy See will do everything in its power to see that your brother faces only a lenient sentence. I'm sure the Allies will insist that he is punished in some way, but we have our influence with the Allies and will make a strong case for Peter, that is if he decides to help us."

"Let's say he does this, Excellency; Himmler would have him shot on the spot once he found out. He'd have no escape."

"He will have a safe-haven. He would leave with the Jews to the safety of Finland then on to Sweden with the assistance of the papal nuncio in Helsinki. The Swedes would of course have him interned, as they are neutral, and he would remain there until war's end. This certainly beats a Soviet firing squad or the hangman."

Bertram knew that Tardini was blunt in articulating the limited choices left for Peter - continue on this murderous path and you'll meet your maker at the end of a rope; or redeem yourself, help your fellow man, and maybe, just maybe, live to a ripe old age.

"You love your brother don't you, Sepp?"

"Yes, Excellency, and I love Lydia and the children as well. They are all I have now."

"Perhaps your sister-in-law has some influence over your brother? She is a good daughter of the Church?"

"When I last saw her at my parents' funeral, she did take communion, while Peter did not. I assume she still has her Catholic faith."

"Talk to her, Sepp, and have her try and intercede for us."

"Very well, Excellency, when do you want me to leave?"

"As soon as possible. Another thing you need to be made aware of. Much like your earlier mission to Croatia, you'll be bringing with you false baptismal certificates, visas, and immigration certificates, this time enough for 100 people. The nuncios in Helsinki and Stockholm have been directed to contact those governments and request their assistance in this rescue operation."

"The Holy Father intends for this mission to succeed, doesn't he?" Bertram asked.

"Yes, he does, Sepp. And I know that you won't let him down."

Tardini smiled and gave Bertram a blessing and asked that he meet him again in two days' time in order to finalize preparations for his departure.

Vatican Secretary of State Office
Vatican City
June 22, 1943, 0950 Hours

Monsignor Bertram arrived at Monsignor Tardini's office at the appointed hour, knocked on the door and entered. To his surprise, another cleric, who looked vaguely familiar to him was seated across from Tardini. Both men stood as Bertram entered the room he was introduced to a chubby and cherubic smiling cleric.

"Sepp, I don't believe you have met Archbishop Angelo Roncalli[11], the papal nuncio in Istanbul."

Both men shook hands. "I have heard you are doing some wonderful things to help Jewish refugees escaping to Turkey, your Excellency," said Bertram.

"I have tried to do God's work the best I can," Roncalli answered.

Tardini then directed the men to sit down. "Sepp, I asked Archbishop Roncalli to meet with us today in preparation for your visit, we are very lucky that he had been recalled back to Rome at this time at the behest of the Holy Father. You are well aware that the archbishop has been dealing with the Jewish refugees as well as others fleeing the Nazis for the last couple of years now and has been quite successful with the assistance of the Turkish government as well as the German ambassador to Turkey himself, *Herr* Franz von Papen.

Sepp was duly impressed with Roncalli's accomplishments. He asked Roncalli, "How in heaven's name did you enlist the help of von Papen?"

"While von Papen may represent the German Reich, he is not a fan of *Herr* Hitler. You may recall, Monsignor Bertram, that *Herr* von Papen at one time was the German chancellor prior to the Nazi assumption of power in 1933 and was Hitler's vice-chancellor after January 30, 1933. Von Papen was lucky enough to escape with his life in the Nazi's purge of 1934. He was on the 'hit list' and only survived through *Reichsmarshal* Göring's personal intervention. When I first met *Herr* von Papen, he brazenly told me that with the German invasion of Russia underway, perhaps Germany could now obtain the moral support of the Holy Father, since Germany was battling atheistic Bolshevism."

"What was your response, your Excellency?" asked Bertram.

"I answered that I should well inform the Holy Father about the millions of Jews Germany was murdering in Poland and Russia.[12] *Herr* von Papen didn't respond. Von Papen is above all, an opportunist, he's a natural politician and is a very cautious man by nature. With the German defeat at Stalingrad and the loss of North Africa earlier this year, the prevailing winds are now blowing in from the side of the Allies. I think von Papen will do anything to ingratiate himself with the Allies, and if that means going against Hitler, so be it.[13] If he is brought up for war crimes as the Allies plan for the Nazi leadership after the war, I would certainly vouch for him for the assistance he has given to the Holy See. Von Papen is also a conservative Catholic, and Pius XI actually bestowed upon him the honorary title of Papal Chamberlain, which the present Pope, I am happy to report, did not renew. You may not be aware, but last year, von Papen actually survived an assassination attempt in Ankara, carried out by the Soviet NKVD."[14]

"Did your Excellency see von Papen after the attack?"

"Oh yes, indeed, I did. When I asked if both he and his wife were hurt, he said that they were both shaken, but uninjured. Von Papen seemed to be more upset and indignant of the fact that the attack had ruined a perfectly good suit that he was wearing at the time."

All three clerics got a good chuckle out of von Papen's cynical reply.

"Your Excellency's experiences in Greece, Turkey, and Bulgaria dealing with the refugees and escaping Jews really makes you the senior expert within the Vatican diplomatic corps, on such matters," Bertram said.

Roncalli let out a small chuckle, "My dear Bertram, it has taken the better part of two decades, well before the Nazis invaded the Balkans, to make the contacts and acquaintances of the Balkans' diplomats and clergy. It hasn't always been easy. I understand your mission is of great importance to the Holy Father. But you also have an 'ace' up your sleeve, and that of course is your brother. Unfortunately, I have no contacts in the Baltics, but your previous mission to Croatia and dealings with those *Ustashă* thugs should have given you plenty of experience. Trust in God, Monsignor, for He will guide you."

"I am going to let you gentlemen in on a little secret," Tardini stated. "In 1941, President Roosevelt sent his personal emissary, Mr. Myron C. Taylor, with a letter from the president, to meet with the Holy Father. In his letter, Mr. Roosevelt equated the evils of Nazism and Communism, but stressed that Hitler was more dangerous to humanity and religion than was Stalin."[15]

"How did the Holy Father respond to Mr. Roosevelt's letter?" asked Roncalli.

"The Holy Father, who of course witnessed the evils of Bolshevism first-hand after the First World War, didn't agree with Mr. Roosevelt's appeals that the Holy See take a less rigid stance against Stalin. He basically thought Roosevelt a fool who was falling for Stalin's 'charm offensive' with the West, and that Roosevelt had no idea of what lay in store if Bolshevism took hold in the rest of Europe. Let me just say this, that if Stalin conquers, he will be the lion devouring all of Europe."[16]

Tardini continued, "In his letter, Roosevelt told his Holiness 'Insofar as I know, some churches are open in Russia and that there was hope that after the war the Russian government would consent to religious liberty.'"[17] Tardini paused for a moment and stated, "Roosevelt is a fool if he thinks that Stalin will permit religious freedom. The Anglo-Americans have no idea of the evils of Bolshevism; at least Churchill had called for strangling Bolshevism in its cradle back in 1918."

Archbishop Roncalli then added, "Pius XI in his 1937 encyclical, *Divini Redemptoris,* clearly spelled out 'that Communism is intrinsically evil, and no one who wants to save Christian civilization can cooperate with it in any undertaking whatsoever.' That certainly puts the Anglo-Americans in a bind if they are providing Lend Lease and other aid to Stalin, doesn't it? It is the old question of the lesser of two evils—Hitler or Stalin? I know one thing for sure, that it is time to put an end to the distinction between the Red Army, which is now advancing West, and the Soviet State. The Red Army *is* the Soviet State insofar as it takes its orders from a godless tyrant—Stalin!"[18]

All three men shook their heads in agreement, and after a few moments of silence, Monsignor Tardini closed the meeting stating, "Monsignor Bertram, thank you for coming. Archbishop Roncalli has an audience with the Holy Father in about twenty minutes and I need to escort him to the Holy Father's private apartments. I will see you before your departure for Estonia. I have enlisted the aid of *Freiherr*[19] von Weizsäcker, the new German ambassador to the Holy See, and he will be meeting with you tomorrow at his office at two o'clock. Pay close attention to what he has to tell you."

With that, Tardini stood up, signaling that the talks were over, whereas both Bertram and Roncalli also stood up, shook hands and Bertram departed, leaving Tardini and Roncalli to discuss further ecclesiastical matters. As he walked through the marble halls, Bertram could not help but feel very vulnerable and frightened. He was literally going into the lions' den, and much like the prophet of the Old Testament, Daniel, he hoped to come out of the beasts' lair unscathed.

Chapter II

"The repeated interventions of the Holy Father on behalf of Jewish communities in Europe has evoked the profoundest sentiments of appreciation and gratitude from Jews throughout the world."

--Rabbi Maurice Perlzweig, World Jewish Congress, February 18, 1944

Office of the German Ambassador to the Holy See
Villa Napoleon Mission
Rome, Italy
June 23, 1943 1400 hours

Ambassador Ernst von Weizsäcker,[20] the recently appointed Reich Ambassador to the Holy See, greeted his fellow countryman warmly as Bertram entered his office.

"Monsignor Bertram, so very nice to finally meet you. I had the honor of meeting your brother in Berlin a few months back. The *Reichsführer SS* has great plans for your brother, you know. I wouldn't be surprised if he were made a corps commander shortly," he said with a grin. "Please, do sit down."

"Thank you, *Freiherr.*"

"Monsignor Tardini has informed me that you will be traveling to the *Reichskomissariat Ostland* on church-related matters, yes?"

"That is correct, *Freiherr.* I also hope to see my brother and his family in Reval."

"Yes, of course, I would do the same if I were in your shoes. I will send off a telex to your brother's headquarters announcing your arrival. Monsignor Tardini has already given me the particulars of your visit, dates, et cetera. I will arrange to have a *Luftwaffe* transport plane to take you to Reval. One rotator flight leaves Rome every week bringing diplomatic pouches, personnel, and supplies, to our forces in Russia. You'll be on that plane and take the return flight the following month. I'm sure a month will be more than enough time to complete your visit, Monsignor?"

"Yes, *Freiherr,* a month will be more than sufficient, thank you."

"You are aware, the *Reichsführer SS* will be in *Ostland* the same time as your visit, correct?"

"Yes, *Freiherr*, Monsignor Tardini informed me of it."

"I see the Vatican's intelligence sources have once more scored a major coup," von Weizsäcker said with a chuckle.

He then turned serious. "A word of warning, Monsignor; do not in any way attempt to undermine Himmler's visit; he is a very dangerous man, and that Roman collar you are wearing means nothing to him. He is ruthless and will stop at nothing to gain more power. I for one will not cross him and I avoid him whenever possible. He is always scheming and there is always some sort of intrigue, whether real or imagined, that he is involved with. He makes the Borgias look like choirboys."

Von Weizsäcker let his words sink in and then continued. "Cardinal Maglione and I have come to an arrangement of sorts. I will do everything in my power to respect the integrity of the Holy See and guarantee the personal safety and protection of the Holy Father. Since 1940, there has been talk of overrunning the Vatican and placing the Holy Father and the Roman Curia in 'protective custody' in either Liechtenstein or Bavaria.[21] I for one, do not wish to see that happen."

Bertram was taken aback by this revelation.

Von Weizsäcker continued, "I talked von Ribbentrop out of this insane idea and he in turn talked to the *Führer*, who dropped it, much over Himmler's protests, I may add. Remember, Monsignor, that there are many Catholics serving in the *Wehrmacht*, particularly units from Bavaria, and this would not sit well with them. I find it rather hard to believe that the hierarchy of the Third Reich, many of whom were baptized into the Church, now wish to destroy it. Hitler, Himmler, Goebbels, and others are all hell bent on the destruction of not only the Catholic Church but the other Christian churches as well."

"I cannot imagine the hatred inside their hearts," Bertram said.

"Unfortunately, I can, Monsignor, as I have been around them long enough to hear them spout their anti-Semitism and atheism. *If* Germany wins the war, Monsignor, it will not only be the death knell for the Jews but for all of Christianity as well, at least here in Europe."

"*Freiherr*, you sound as if you're not quite sure Germany will win this war after all? I know this must trouble you greatly since you lost a son in the opening days of the Polish campaign in '39."

For a moment, Von Weizsäcker was silent and reflected on the loss of his own son, Heinrich[22], then quickly recovered and continued, "With the defeats at Stalingrad and North Africa earlier this year, and now with the probability of the Anglo-Americans wresting Sicily from our forces, it will only be a matter of time before they are on the Italian mainland. I tell you; Mussolini cannot survive in power if this comes to pass."

"*Freiherr*, I will be very blunt with you, my mission to Estonia is to try and save some 100 Jews in a concentration camp outside of Reval. My brother is going to oversee the execution of these poor innocents, in order to seek favor with Himmler. I am going to do my very best to stop him."

Von Weizsäcker did not answer Bertram, but instead lowered his head and stared at his desk. Bertram used these few moments of silence to size up the German Ambassador. Bertram realized in their few minutes together that von Weizsäcker was an opportunist, like many of his peers serving the regime. With the recent military reverses suffered by Germany, von Weizsäcker wasn't so arrogant now, and perhaps, just perhaps, he began to have second thoughts about his role serving the Reich's foreign ministry.

Clearing his throat and looking up, von Weizsäcker said, "Monsignor, as I stated earlier, be very careful of Himmler, and I would be cautious of your brother as well. When I met him in Berlin, he appeared to me to be the personification of the perfect SS man. No doubt Himmler has got to him and I suspect that your brother, I'm sorry to say, probably hasn't a shred of decency left towards his fellow man. I hope I'm wrong. I don't envy you in your mission, but I will pray for your success."

With that, von Weizsäcker stood up and offered his hand to Bertram. "Good luck, Monsignor, and may God be with you and protect you."

"Thank you, *Freiherr*, I will need all the Divine assistance I can get."

"I will make the arrangements for your flight and send the telex to your brother's headquarters. The paperwork should take a few weeks to process. I will contact you when they are ready. Again, good luck."

With that, Monsignor Bertram turned and left the ambassador's office. Bertram still was unsure of where von Weizsäcker's allegiances truly lay.[23] There had been rumors that he was part of a growing anti-Nazi resistance, and Monsignor Tardini had told him that von Weizsäcker had personally intervened on the behalf of a number of Italian Jews, saving them from certain deportation and death. If anything, the German ambassador was playing a waiting game. Perhaps Germany's military fortunes would return once more, and then, von Weizsäcker, along with many other German officials, would show their true colors. Only time would tell.

Enskilda Bank
Blasieholmstorg 11
Stockholm, Sweden
June 29, 1943, 1020 Hours

The Wallenberg brothers, Jacob and Marcus, were the owners of one of Sweden's most successful banking firms, Enskilda Bank, and the scions of one of Sweden's wealthiest families. The Holy See had approached the brothers, who were very close to the Swedish royal family, in the hopes that they could act as intermediaries and arrange for the sanctuary of the Jews in the proposed rescue operation. This was a delicate matter, in that Sweden, while officially neutral, traded heavily with the Third Reich, supplying Hitler with most of his iron ore. The Swedes were very careful not to upset the uneasy alliance between their country and their powerful neighbor to the South. German forces were in neighboring Norway and Finland, and could, on orders from Berlin, march into Sweden. By 1943, however, German strength was waning, and it really didn't have the manpower to occupy another nation, particularly one as large as Sweden. Still, the Swedes walked a careful tightrope when dealing with Berlin as one never knew what surprises Hitler had up his sleeve.

Marcus Wallenberg carefully read the document he had received via diplomatic pouch from the Holy See's Secretary of State. While most Swedes claimed Evangelical Lutheranism as their religious preference, the country still maintained cordial relations with the Vatican.

"Jacob, you need to read this very carefully," Marcus told his brother. "The Vatican is requesting our assistance in rescuing over 100 Jews being held in Estonia and bringing them here for the duration of the war."

Jacob Wallenberg looked perplexed. "What? Help rescue Jews and bring them here to Sweden! That is the most preposterous thing I have ever heard of! The *Wehrmacht* would be on our doorstep within days—barring that the *Luftwaffe* would probably bomb Stockholm just for spite! Let me see that cable!" Marcus passed on the Vatican request to his brother and watched the expression on his face as he read it, his lips silently moving as he reviewed the document.

"If we go through with this, Marcus, it may mean the end of Swedish neutrality and maybe even our independence, you know that."

"I don't think so, Jacob," Marcus replied. "The Germans are stretched too thin now. They can't afford another conquest, particularly one the size of Sweden. Oh, there are Nazi sympathizers within the government and amongst the population, but Hitler would not be foolish enough to send in his armies. Look at the problems the Germans are having in the Balkans, Poland and Russia with the Partisan groups. If Hitler were crazy enough to send his armies into Sweden, he'd have another insurgency to deal with. He might, however, attempt to bomb the capital and some of our ports just for sport."

Both men were silent for a moment, lost in their own thoughts. Jacob was the first to speak up. "You know what this would do to Enskilda, don't you?" It had been long rumored that the Enskilda bank dealt in large black-market operations, money laundering and concealing German investments in the United States. If Sweden's neutral status were to change, that would all end, and the bank would be out of millions if not billions of Kroners[24].

"Jacob, we need to bring this to the attention of the prime minister and the king. Also, it is wise to contact Count Bernadotte[25] on this issue, after all he is vice chairman of the Swedish Red Cross, and nephew to King Gustav

V. Additionally, we should contact Hans Lehmann[26] and bring him in on the discussions."

"Lehmann? Ah, yes, I remember him now. He is the spokesman for Sweden's Orthodox Jewish community, correct?"

Marcus continued, "Also, Jacob, we need to include two individuals that have direct access to both German and American leaders."

"Whom might they be, Marcus?"

"Himmler's masseuse, Dr. Felix Kersten[27] and our old American friend, Abram Hewitt,[28] whom I understand is working directly for President Roosevelt."

"Not the same Hewitt that represented the International Match Company bankruptcy proceedings back in '32?"

"The one and the same."

"Very well, Marcus, if you want to include both Hewitt and Kersten, feel free to extend the invitation."

"Good. Then it's settled. I will contact them all and have them come by this evening and we shall discuss the Vatican proposal. I share your concern, Jacob, on how this may affect the future of Enskilda."

Enskilda Bank
Blasieholmstorg 11
Stockholm, Sweden
June 29, 1943, 1900 Hours

Count Bernadotte, Mr. Lehmann, Dr. Kersten, and Mr. Hewitt all joined the brothers in their conference room at the appointed hour.

"Gentlemen," Marcus Wallenberg said, "Thank you for coming on such short notice. Please make yourselves comfortable and help yourselves to the buffet." The men got up and heaped smoked salmon and other Swedish delicacies onto their plates along with an assortment of liquors from the bar. Once all were comfortably seated, Marcus Wallenberg got down to business.

"Gentlemen, these are dangerous times for Sweden as you know. Germany has had a number of battlefield reverses and it appears that the Allies are winning—but I would not count Hitler down and out just yet. He still might have a few Aces up his sleeve." He let his words sink in and then continued.

"We have received, via diplomatic pouch, a request from the Pope, asking that we accept 100 Jews who will hopefully be arriving here in the not-too-distant future. They evidently are being 'sprung' from a concentration camp in Estonia."

"What do you mean by 'sprung'?" asked Lehmann, whose knowledge of English-rooted idioms and terminology was somewhat limited.

"Escaped, *Herr* Lehmann. Escaped prisoners who will be trying to make their way to Sweden."

Bernadotte then spoke, "Marcus, how are they planning to escape? A mass breakout like that, I would have thought most of them would have been gunned down by their guards."

"They will have help," interjected Jacob. "It appears that a high-ranking SS man and his brother, who is a Roman priest and a Vatican representative, are behind it."

All were stunned at the revelation.

"Incredible!" exclaimed Lehmann. "You mean to sit there and tell me that a member of the SS is going to help 100 Jewish prisoners escape? It sounds like a well-laid trap if you ask me."

"I agree with *Herr* Lehmann," Bernadotte said. "It just doesn't make sense."

Marcus passed the Vatican document around for all the gathered men to read. "As you can see gentlemen, this operation has the full backing of the Pope himself. Pius has assembled a plan to rescue these Jews and bring them here."

Bernadotte then spoke. "The Vatican report matches what we have been receiving from our consul in Stettin, Karl Ingve Vendel, who confirms that Jews are being murdered in German killing centers in the East. Also, last August 20th, Baron Goran von Otter, Secretary to the Swedish Legation in Berlin, shared a train compartment with a young *SS Obersturmführer* (First Lieutenant) by the name of Kurt Gerstein. Gerstein related to von Otter during the trip that he had personally witnessed the execution of a number of Jews in Poland. Gerstein stated he was assigned to the German Institute of Hygiene, which gave him first-hand knowledge of the murders. This officer evidently has a conscience and told von Otter everything he had witnessed with the hopes he would tell the world of what he witnessed. Von Otter said that Gerstein broke down numerous times, sobbing uncontrollably. To his credit, Von Otter filed a report with the Foreign Ministry, but that is as far as it went. The officer also told von Otter that he had tried unsuccessfully to see the Papal Nuncio in Berlin and inform him as well, but to no avail."[29]

After a minute of silence and a sip of wine, Bernadotte cleared his throat and continued, "After our phone call earlier today, Marcus, I spoke to His Majesty and he agrees that we should do everything possible for these people to facilitate their stay in Sweden, *if* they make it." He continued, "His Majesty has spoken with Marshal Mannerheim in Helsinki. He will help facilitate the movement of the Jews if they reach Finnish territory, and only then, and not beforehand. He has also personally spoken with the papal nuncio here as well."

"But there are German forces in Finland; won't they hinder the movement of these Jews?" Lehmann asked excitedly.

"On the contrary, *Herr* Lehmann, Marshal Mannerheim has given me his word that if they make it, Finnish forces will guarantee their safety to the Swedish border. In talking with Mannerheim, His Majesty was under the impression that Mannerheim was not a very big fan of Hitler's and is only in this war to recapture the land the Soviets captured during the Winter War of '39."

Bernadotte continued, "What we must now do gentlemen is to ensure that by taking in these unfortunates, we do not provoke Hitler into doing something rash. I seriously doubt he has the manpower to spare for a full-blown invasion of Sweden, but with German troops in Finland, Norway, and Denmark, he could cause some border incidents or a minor incursion or just maybe even bomb the capital and some ports just for spite."

"Is it worth it, Bernadotte?" asked Jacob Wallenberg.

Bernadotte did not answer right away. He looked over at Lehmann, who, having lived in Germany and then fled after Hitler's assumption to power in 1933, and whose eyes pleaded with Bernadotte to do something.

"Yes, Jacob, I do believe it's worth the risk to Sweden to assist these Jews in every way possible.[30] I will recommend to His Majesty that we move forward with this. I know that Enskilda does business with the Reich, but I don't think our actions will have any effect on your business transactions with Germany, to be quite honest. The Germans are going to invest in either Swiss or Swedish banks, two of the closest neutral countries to Germany. Many of the Nazi bigwigs are starting to move large amounts of cash out of Germany in order to set themselves up for a nice post-war retirement, so to speak. *Reichsleiter* Bormann comes to mind."

The Wallenberg brothers were impressed with Bernadotte's inside knowledge of the Swedish banking system. Then again, he was after all, an aristocrat himself and related to the Swedish royal family. There was probably very little he didn't know about the circumstances inside wartime Sweden.

Bernadotte then turned to Lehmann. *"Herr* Lehmann, as a representative of the Orthodox Jewish community here in Stockholm, we will rely quite heavily upon you to assist the Jews if they safely reach Sweden. You of course, have some aid agencies set up already and you have been very instrumental in aiding your co-religionists out of occupied Europe, which I may say, is most commendable."

"Thank you, Count, for your very kind words. I do what I can to help."

"Gentlemen, I will report our discussions to His Majesty. You have the Crown's full support and I only pray that the Bertram brothers will pull this off."

"Bernadotte," Jacob asked, "What do you propose to do with the brother who is in the SS?"

"He will be interned like the rest of the warring parties who have fallen into our hands, and I assume his fate will be decided by the Allies after the war. Although I can't help but think that the Vatican will no doubt request some sort of immunity or leniency for him as he may be part of this rescue effort."

Jacob Wallenberg nodded in agreement.

As he emptied his wine glass, Bernadotte stated, "Gentlemen, the Army Chief of Staff will be informed of the Crown's decision and the Swedish Armed Forces will be responsible for the initial repatriation if these Jews enter Swedish territory. They will be housed, fed and given medical treatment by the Red Cross once under Swedish control."

With that, Bernadotte stood up, shook hands with the others and took his leave.

"There you have it, gentlemen," Marcus Wallenberg said, "I am afraid that Sweden's reputation and status as a non-belligerent may be at risk if these two brothers succeed with the rescue."

"Don't you mean *four* brothers, *Herr* Wallenberg?" Lehmann asked. "The Bertram brothers along with the Wallenberg brothers!" Lehmann said with a laugh.

Both Wallenberg siblings could only force a smile upon hearing Lehmann's comment.

Klooga Concentration Camp
Reval, Estonia
Reichskommissariat Ostland
June 30, 1943, 1330 Hours

Klooga Concentration Camp, a subcamp of the much larger Vaivara Camp System, was located 37 kilometers west of the city of Reval (Tallinn). It was here that *SS Gruppenführer* Peter Bertram was acting like a man possessed. With Himmler's visit later in the day and again in two months for a 'special demonstration', Bertram's nerves were frayed to the breaking point. He knew that these visits would either make or break him because he wanted a promotion and his own combat command. Bertram was a loyal party member and fulfilled all that was asked of him over the years. Now, in its third year of fighting the Soviets, the Germans were preparing to launch another offensive in early July. The *Führer* had promised that the new weapons rolling off the Reich's assembly lines would turn the tide against the Reds and allow Germany to regain the initiative once again in the East. The debacle at Stalingrad earlier in the year had shaken many to the core concerning Germany's invincibility on the battlefield, especially against the "subhumans" to the East. The loss of Stalingrad was partly avenged by the recapture of Kharkov by Field Marshal Erich von Manstein after von Paulus' surrender at Stalingrad.

He hoped that the loss of the entire Sixth Army and now the surrender of the *Afrika Korps* in May were not a harbinger of things to come.

Bertram's constant visits to Klooga were also fraying the nerves of the young SS officer in command of the camp. SS *Hauptsturmführer* (Captain) Willi Loss was not used to high-ranking officers hovering above him. A former officer in the *Einsatzgruppen*, Loss had suffered a nervous breakdown. Loss personally participated in the mass executions of Soviet Jews, and it finally affected him. After six weeks in a sanitarium on the Baltic Sea, he was declared fit for service and ordered to return to the East. Before his departure from the sanitarium, he had confided to a Catholic chaplain about the atrocities in the East. Loss was not a Catholic, so his testimonial was not a confession. However, it was this chaplain, who relayed Loss' account back to the Holy See. Additionally, Loss left the chaplain photographic images of the executions taken by some of his men. Many of the SS men in the photos were smiling and laughing and had shown no signs of remorse for their deeds. Many of the photos were considered "brag" photos, validating the SS efficiency in creating *Lebensraum* in the East. This chaplain sent these photos to Rome as well.

"Loss, we have approximately two months before the demonstration for the *Reichsführer,* I trust all is in order?"

"*Jawohl, Herr Gruppenführer,*" Loss responded. "As directed, we are preparing the guest house as well as having ordered the *Reichsführer's* favorite wine and cigars to be on hand for his visit."

"Very good, Loss. I am holding you personally responsible for the survival of our Jewish "guests" until the *Reichsführer's* arrival. I promised him 100 Jews and I intend to show him that 100 Jews can be eliminated with this new gas. Is that understood?"

"*Jawohl, Herr Gruppenführer*. As per your previous directive, I have increased the prisoners' daily rations and that *should* keep them alive until the end of August," he said with a smile.

"I don't want your assurance of *should,*" he thundered. "You *will* keep them alive by whatever means necessary, understood?" Bertram did not even bother to wait for a reply from Loss, who was left stammering something as Bertram turned and walked out of the commandant's office.

As Bertram walked across the courtyard to his waiting staff car, a young SS NCO ran up to him, saluted and said, *Herr Gruppenführer*, this telex just arrived for you, sir."

Bertram nonchalantly returned the salute, thanked the sergeant and read the telex.

> *Gruppenführer Peter Bertram...Monsignor Josef*
> *Bertram, Vatican Foreign Office to arrive at Reval*
> *airfield on 25 July 43. Request all courtesies be ex-*

*tended to Monsignor Bertram during his visit to Re-
ichskommissariat Ostland. Visit is of a diplomatic
nature and request to meet privately with Gruppenführer Bertram. Signed Freiherr Ernst von Weizsäcker, Ambassador to the Holy See.*

"*Mein Gott in Himmel!*" declared Bertram, as he crumpled the telex in his hand.

"Something wrong, sir," asked Bertram's aide-de-camp, SS *Sturm-bannführer* (Major) Heinz Wolfe.

"My brother, that no-good Jesuit, is coming for a social visit of sorts," Bertram said with a bit of disgust in his voice.

"Your brother is a priest, sir? I was unaware of it."

"It's not something I like to advertise, Heinz. He is with the Vatican Foreign Service, and there really isn't anything I can do about his visit. It has already been cleared through the Reich Foreign Ministry, and if I raise a stink, it may sour our relations with the Holy See and Italy as well. And need I remind you, Heinz, at this moment in time, the Reich needs all the friends it can get. His visit could not have come at a worse time, especially with the *Reichsführer's* impending visit."

"Sir, may I ask when you saw your brother last?"

"Heinz, it was back in '40 at our parents' funeral. Our parents had been killed in a freak auto accident outside of Munich. Sepp, that is my broth-er, was too devastated to say the funeral Mass. I must confess, I was shaken by their loss as well."

Realizing that he was exhibiting a bit of sentiment to a subordinate, Bertram quickly brought his thoughts back to the present. "Well, Heinz, I guess we'll have to make the monsignor comfortable. He will of course stay at my quarters with Lydia and the children. I'm sure the children will no doubt be happy to see their Uncle Sepp."

"Sir, I will arrange for transport from the Reval airfield to your quar-ters."

"Thank you, Heinz. Let's get back to my office and go over the *Re-ichsführer* itinerary again, I want to ensure nothing goes wrong during his visit." With that *Sturmbannführer* Wolfe closed the passenger door, ran around to the other side, got in, and Bertram's driver took them both back to their headquarters in downtown Reval.

Reval-Ulemiste Military Airfield
Reval, Estonia
Reichskommissariat Ostland
June 30, 1943, 1830 Hours

The Reval-Ulemiste military airfield was a combined airport and sea-plane station located some five kilometers east-southeast of the Reval city with the *Luftwaffe* having taken over the airfield in the summer of 1941 after the Red Army had been driven out of Estonia.

Reichsführer SS Heinrich Himmler arrived in his own transport plane with an escort of five *Luftwaffe* fighters, just in case the Red Air Force appeared. As Himmler's aircraft was taxiing to the terminal, *SS Gruppenführer* Bertram along with his staff waited for the aircraft to park and for the engines to power down before marching over to the plane and welcoming Himmler as he disembarked from the aircraft.

"*Reichsführer,* an honor and pleasure to see you again," Bertram stated after rendering the Nazi salute.

Himmler returned the salute and then shook Bertram's hand. "Good to see you again, my dear Bertram. I hear you are doing some great things for the Reich in *Ostland.*"

Bertram felt himself puff up with pride. "Very kind of you to say, *Reichsführer.* May I also present my aide, *Sturmbannführer* Wolfe."

Himmler acknowledged Wolfe with a nod, and then the party proceeded toward the terminal where the staff cars awaited. While enroute, Himmler and Bertram engaged in small talk.

"*Gruppenführer,* a word in private if you don't mind?" asked Himmler.

"*Jawohl, Herr Reichsführer,*" he stated as both men walked over to the terminal commander's office, which the commander, a *Luftwaffe* Major, quickly vacated so that both men had some privacy.

Himmler spoke first. "*Gruppenführer,* I understand your brother, the Monsignor, is due for a visit shortly. I trust it is for a social visit only?" Himmler asked pointedly.

Bertram was initially taken aback by Himmler's question.

Himmler continued, "The Vatican is not the only one with a good intelligence, Bertram, I can assure you. Your brother's visit here hopefully has nothing to do with my upcoming visit later this summer and the liquidation of the camp, does it Bertram?" Himmler's gaze was piercing enough to make anyone break out into a cold sweat.

"*Nein, nein, Herr Reichsführer,* my brother Sepp's visit is completely social. We have not seen each other since our parents' death three years ago and he needs to meet with me regarding the disposition of our parents' property in Munich. Also, some bank accounts need to be closed. My parents made Sepp the executor of their estate in the event anything happened to them." Bertram was telling a bold-faced lie, and he prayed that his poker face would hold up in line with Himmler's questioning.

"Yes, I recall your parents' death a few years back, auto accident wasn't it? A pity." Himmler continued, "If I recall from your file my dear Bertram, you are the older brother, is that not so?"

"*Jawohl, Herr Reichsführer.*"

"It is normally the custom that the eldest handle the affairs of one's parents when they pass on. Your parents evidently did not deem it necessary in your case. Why is that Bertram?"

Before he could answer, Himmler continued. "Your parents did not approve of National Socialism, nor did they approve of your party membership and then the SS, did they?"

"*Nein, Herr Reichsführer,* they did not."

"Again, a pity, as their eldest son was destined to do great things for the party and for the Fatherland, and you have done so, my dear Bertram. Your parents were practicing Catholics, were they not? And I suppose they were most proud of your brother the Monsignor? Well, I guess it is best that they were elim…., er, no longer here. I know that may be a cruel thing to say, but if they were still alive today, they would no doubt have stood in the way of your career advancement within the party and SS."

Himmler had caught himself but not before Bertram had heard it. It sounded as though Himmler meant to say that his parents had been *eliminated. This couldn't be true, could it*, Peter thought to himself? Now was not the time to worry, but to get through this visit and the next couple of days would either make or break his career. Still, in the back of his mind, he wondered if his beloved SS had been responsible for the death of his parents.

Officers Kasino
Reval, Estonia
Reichskommissariat Ostland
June 30, 1943, 2000 Hours

A sumptuous dinner had been prepared in honor of Himmler's visit at the German Officer's Kasino, a former Estonian Officer's Club taken over by the *Wehrmacht* in 1941. Nothing was spared, and generous portions of meat, fish, cheese, wine, schnapps, brandy, and pastries awaited Himmler's official party when they arrived.

When the official party arrived at the club, Himmler remarked, "Fabulous, absolutely fabulous, *Gruppenführer*, everything looks wonderful, and that smell coming out of the kitchen can only mean that *Wiener schnitzel* is on the menu."

"You are absolutely correct, *Reichsführer*, and we certainly hope you enjoy the meal that we have prepared for you and your staff. Our cook was the former chef to the Estonian president until 1940 when the Russians came. He fled to the woods and in 1941, joined the Estonian uprising against the retreating Reds. One of my men personally saw him hack to death a wounded NKVD officer who was left behind, so we have no questions as to where his loyalty lies."

"I'd like to meet him," Himmler replied.

"After dinner, sir, I will personally introduce you. And may I add, we have another treat for you. We were able to 'liberate' from a movie theater in 1941 a copy of the film *King Kong*. The troops love it and I thought you might enjoy it as well."

"Ah, yes, one of the *Führer's* favorite films, believe it or not. The story of a gigantic ape running amok in New York City. It is a pity that such a creature doesn't really exist, we could certainly use such a beast in the fight against the Americans," Himmler said with a chuckle.

Himmler continued, "*Gruppenführer*, after dinner and the film tonight, I want to meet with you privately and go over a planned speech I will be giving to the senior leadership of the SS. The date, time and location have yet to be determined, but I need a good sounding board, and with your record, I choose you to be the first to hear it."

Bertram, beaming with pride, replied, "*Reichsführer,* I will be honored to hear your speech. Nothing will give me greater pleasure."

"Good, said Himmler. "First, we will eat, drink and then watch this giant ape wreak havoc on New York City." Both men laughed as they were escorted to their seats by SS orderlies.

Officers Kasino
Reval, Estonia
Reichskommissariat Ostland
June 30, 1943, 2230 Hours

After the evening festivities were over, both Himmler and Bertram retired to a side room off the main dining room and Himmler told his orderly that they were not to be disturbed. Both men sat at a small table opposite each other, and Himmler spoke first.

"My dear Bertram, let me say again that tonight's festivities were first rate—my staff and I do appreciate all the courtesies extended to us. The meal, brandy and cigars, all first rate. I will have to tell the *Führer* we viewed *King Kong*. He was always of the opinion that Leni Riefenstahl would have played a much better 'Ann Darrow' than Faye Wray." Both men laughed at Himmler's remark.

Himmler then turned serious. "My dear Bertram, these are very trying times for the Reich, as you know. We are being assaulted on all fronts, apart from the West and I predict within a year, the Allies will be in France. Stalin is pressuring Roosevelt and Churchill to open a second front with a cross-channel invasion. We are still strong in France, but military exigencies dictate that we pull men out of France to shore up the East. There are rumblings coming out of Italy and there may be a coup against the *Duce*. Those duplicitous Italians are capable of anything. I believe it is only a matter of time. Along with the military situation, there is of course, the question of the Jews."

Bertram hung on Himmler's every word. He believed he knew what Himmler was going to say next, and his guess was correct.

Himmler continued, "The *Führer* feels, and I totally agree, that the situation with the Jews goes hand-in-hand with the military goals set forth by the *Führer*. The extermination of Judeo-Bolshevism is the number one priority of the SS and *Wehrmacht*. With that said, I am drafting a speech for the higher leadership of the SS that I alluded to earlier. I have with me a draft, a very rough draft mind you, that I would like for you to read and comment upon."

Bertram, again, puffed with pride that Himmler would solicit his feedback on such an important speech.

"I would be honored, sir."

Himmler then pulled from an inside tunic pocket several folded pages and slid them across the table to Bertram. "This draft was typed up by *Untersturmführer* Wenn on my staff. It should take you about fifteen minutes or so to read. I'll be back in thirty minutes, and I would like your honest assessment, based upon your vast experiences here in the East in dealing with these *Untermensch*."

Before Bertram could respond, Himmler got up and headed out to join his party, who were still seated in the main dining room and enjoying schnapps and cigars, per Himmler's orders.

Once Himmler left the room, Bertram unfolded the papers and discovered twenty typewritten pages, double-spaced, along with marginal notes, most likely written in Himmler's own hand. In his outline of the course of the war in Russia, Himmler commented on the deaths of millions of Soviet POWs. He noted how the elimination of the Slavs was also a historical and natural necessity. It read in part:

> One basic principle must be the absolute rule for the SS men: We must be honest, decent, loyal and comradely to members of our own blood and to nobody else. What happens to a Russian, to a Czech, does not interest me in the slightest. What other nations can offer in the way of good blood of our type, we will take, if necessary, by kidnapping their children and raising them here with us. Whether nations live in

prosperity or starve to death interests me only so far as we need them as slaves for our culture; otherwise, it is of no interest to me. Whether 10,000 Russian females fall down from exhaustion while digging an anti-tank ditch interests me only insofar as the anti-tank ditch for Germany is finished.[31]

Bertram wholeheartedly agreed with Himmler's comments and world-view. The Eastern peoples were to be Germany's slaves in order that Germany could colonize the East with farmers and soldier-settlers (*Wehrbauern)* in order to make Russia a satellite of Germany. The vast breadbasket of the Ukraine, along with the oil rich Caucuses would belong to Germany after the victory over the Bolsheviks. This very idea of course had been laid out by Hitler years before in *Mein Kampf.* Himmler's next paragraph caught Bertram entirely off guard as it revealed a policy not previously acknowledged in public by a high-ranking member of the Reich; it had only been spoken in whispers and in back rooms, but here it was in print:

I am now referring to the evacuation of the Jews, the extermination of the Jewish people. It's one of those things that is easily said. 'The Jewish people are being exterminated' says every party member, 'this is very obvious, it's in our program, elimination of the Jews, extermination, we're doing it, a small matter.' But of all those who talk this way, none had observed it, none had endured it. Most of you here know what it means when 100 corpses lie next to each other, when 500 lies here or when 1,000 are lined up. To have endured this and at the same time to have remained a decent person--with exceptions due to human weaknesses--had made us tough. This is a page of glory never mentioned and never to be mentioned. We have the moral right, we had the duty to our people to do it, to kill these people who wanted to kill us.[32]

Bertram lay the papers down on the table and rubbed his eyes. It had been a long day and coupled with the amount of alcohol he consumed during dinner, his eyelids were heavy, and he was ready for sleep. Yet, what he held in his hands was vindication that he and his men were executing state policy for two years in the East. Every good National Socialist had read *Mein Kampf* (or at least lied and said they did) and knew Hitler had outlined his plans for subjugation of the East for Germanization and *Lebensraum.* As he was trying to get his thoughts together of what to tell Himmler, the thirty minutes had passed and Himmler, ever punctual, returned.

Bertram attempted to rise from his seat as Himmler entered, but the *Reichsführer SS* waved him to stay seated—just as well, he thought to himself, he was feeling a bit lightheaded from all the alcohol and may have fallen over.

"Well, Bertram, what do you think? Will the senior leadership of the SS agree with me? More importantly, do *you* agree with me?"

Bertram collected his thoughts for a few seconds and then spoke. "*Herr Reichsführer*, I believe your words capture the essence of what we as good SS men and standard bearers for the *Führer* ought to be. While the mission here in the East has been difficult, the men know what they must do for the *Führer und Sieg!*"[33]

"All very well and good, my dear Bertram, but your answer sounds like one that I would expect to hear from an officer-cadet at Bad Tolz.[34] What about moral scruples, Bertram? Have you gotten your 'hands dirty,' so to speak? How many Jews or commissars have you personally shot?"

Bertram's head was beginning to spin, the alcohol was taking its effect, but he managed. "None, sir. I have been present during many *kommando aktions*, but I have not personally shot a single Jew or Partisan."

"And why do you think that is, Bertram? Your good Catholic upbringing perhaps? Tell me, Bertram, are you bothered by nightmares, or suffer bouts of illness or depression while serving here?"

"No, *Herr Reichsführer*, no to both questions (he was lying, of course)."

Himmler then asked, "I believe you know *Brigadeführer* (Major General) von dem Bach-Zelewski?[35] Well, he's been hospitalized at least twice that I know of for stomach ulcers while serving as my chief of anti-Partisan warfare here in the East. He also claims he suffered from hallucinations connected with the shooting of Jews. Von dem Bach is a good man, a good soldier, but I can't have one of my senior commanders absent himself from his troops for such long periods of time while he convalesces. To me, it's a sign of weakness."[36]

Himmler continued his verbal onslaught, "What I am trying to say Bertram is that my senior commanders are not getting involved enough to deal with the Jewish Question. I understand the hardships that the SS man endures, particularly here in the East. He sees and does things that he would not even consider in peacetime. But we are not at peace, Bertram, we are at war with a cunning and ruthless Judeo-Bolshevik enemy that must be annihilated at all costs. For if we fail, we will then have opened the floodgates of Central and Western Europe to these Mongolian savages from the East."

Bertram could only nod in agreement to Himmler's reasoning. Himmler then continued,

"I am ordering that the senior leadership of the SS take a more direct role and participate in these *aktions* against the Jews. I am sure that after you kill the first few of these vermin, the rest will be much easier to deal with. With the elimination of the camp in the near future, *Gruppenführer*, I do believe I would like for *you* to lead by example. Your promotion to *Obergruppenführer* may very well depend on it."

Chapter III

"We were convinced that a fiery protest by Pius XII against the persecution of the Jews…would certainly not have saved the life of a single Jew. Hitler, like a trapped beast, would react to any menace that he felt directed at him, with cruel violence."
--Albrecht von Kessel, German Embassy official to The Holy See

Villa Savoia
Via Salaria
Rome, Italy
July 25, 1943, 1700 Hours

Benito Mussolini, prime minister and *Il Duce* of Italy since 1922, strode into the royal residence after being summoned for an audience by King Vittorio Emmanuel III, Italy's constitutional monarch. It had always bothered Mussolini that he had to answer to the diminutive king, who stood barely five-foot-tall, and who was married to a woman, Queen Elena, who towered over her husband. Mussolini always chuckled when he saw the royal couple to-gether as they looked like the characters from the American comic strip *Mutt and Jeff*, which he had seen from captured copies of the American *Stars and Stripes* newspaper, which he read at every opportunity.[37] Today though, would be no laughing matter for Mussolini, for unbeknownst to him, the king was about to dismiss him as prime minister, and sue for peace with the Western Allies.

The first six months of 1943 had seen the monumental defeats of Ital-ian arms. The Italian Eighth Army and the *Corpo di Spedizione Italiano in Russia*[38] had suffered horrendous casualties at Stalingrad along with their Ger-man, Romanian, and Hungarian allies. Then of course was the surrender in North Africa in May and the loss of Italy's North African colonies. Mussoli-ni's dreams of an Italian Mediterranean lake, a *Mare Nostrum* ('Our Lake'), as he called it, were now just that, dreams and nothing more.

Mussolini was escorted to the king's private study where it was now just himself and the king, with no other courtiers' present.

"*Duce*, so good of you to come on such short notice," Vittorio Em-manuel said. "Please, do sit down."

The king continued, "My dear *Duce*, things don't work anymore. Italy has gone to pieces. The army is morally prostrated. The soldiers no longer want to fight. The vote of the Fascist Grand Council is dreadful. You certainly don't entertain any illusions about the Italians' state of mind?"

Mussolini sat in silence. The king continued, "My dear *Duce*, right now, I'm sorry to say, you are the most hated man in Italy." The king then let that sink in. He then continued, "You cannot trust a single friend. You have only one friend, me. Therefore, I tell you that you need not worry about your personal safety, which I shall take care to protect. I think the man for the present situation is Marshal Badoglio.[39] He can begin by forming a cabinet of caretakers who will manage the administration and go on with the war."

Mussolini then blurted out, "This means my complete collapse!"

The king replied, "I am sorry, my dear *Duce,* but everybody expects a change."[40]

With that, the king stood up, signaling that the meeting was over. He motioned to his now former prime minister, the door. Both men shook hands upon leaving and could now only comment to each other about the dreadful July heat in Rome.

When Mussolini left the king's residence, he noticed that his car and driver were gone. Instead, a *Carabinieri*[41] captain approached him, saluted, and motioned to a Red Cross ambulance parked in the courtyard, and asked him to get in. He was assured that it was for his own protection and much safer to travel by ambulance because his car was so easily recognizable by the populace. Thus, Mussolini was quietly placed under arrest without incident, effectively ending twenty-one years of Fascist rule and dictatorship. In the immediate aftermath of his overthrow, the military attaché to the German Embassy in Rome, Friedrich-Karl von Plehwe, stated "Seldom in history has the overthrow of a government been more overdue and less prepared for than that of 25 July 1943 in Italy."[42]

Reval-Ulemiste Military Airfield
Reval, Estonia
Reichskommissariat Ostland
July 26, 1943, 1600 Hours

The *Luftwaffe* Junkers JU-52 trimotor taxied toward the terminal where a small party of SS personnel awaited. SS *Gruppenführer* Peter Bertram, his aide, along with Bertram's wife and two children watched as the aircraft moved toward them. Bertram was not at all happy with his brother's visit, and he was quite surprised when he broke the news to his wife of Sepp's impending visit that she was in fact delighted. Lydia for the most part felt isolated here in Reval and missed life in Berlin. Her husband's high rank saw that they had been invited to dinner parties and other soirees given by the Nazi hierarchy. She had even met the *Führer* on two separate occasions, and Hitler, ever the gentleman, had kissed her proffered hand both times.

As the aircraft shut down its engines, a movable stairway was rolled to the aircraft door by *Luftwaffe* ground personnel and the door then opened. Alighting from the aircraft were military and civilian personnel returning to duty or arriving on official business. The last passenger off the plane was Sepp Bertram.

"Look children, there is your Uncle Sepp!" exclaimed Lydia. "Go and greet him!"

Taking their cue from their mother, Berthold, aged 10 and dressed in his Hitler Youth uniform, and Heidi, aged 7, and carrying a bouquet, ran towards the stairwell and met their uncle as he hit the tarmac.

"Berthold, Heidi, you've both gotten so big," he said as he embraced them both.

"Uncle Sepp, these flowers are for you," said Heidi, as she thrust them into her uncle's hands.

"Thank you my dear, they are very nice. Did you pick them yourself?"

"Yes, I did!" she exclaimed.

Turning to young Berthold, Sepp stated, "You look very handsome in your uniform, Berthold."

"Thank you, Uncle Sepp. I want to grow up to be a soldier just like father and serve the *Führer*!" he exclaimed.

Sepp could only smile weakly at the statement and patted the boy's head. "Let's go say hello to your parents." As he held his niece and nephew close, the three walked from the planeside over to where Peter and Lydia were waiting.

"Sepp, so good to see you!" Lydia said, hugging him tightly and kissing his check. "You look well."

Turning to his brother, Sepp held out his hand, "Hello, Peter, it is certainly good to see you."

Peter smiled and shook his brother's hand. "You look well yourself, Sepp, working at the Holy See appears to agree with you."

Sepp could hear the strain in his brother's voice and could not help but notice his tense body language.

"I want to thank you both for permitting me to stay with you during my visit, I hope I won't be too much of an inconvenience to you," stated Sepp.

As Peter was about to speak, his wife broke in, "Nonsense, Sepp! You're family and you are always welcome!" Taking her brother-in-law's arm, she began walking toward the staff car that would take them back to their quarters.

Peter's aide, Heinze Wolff was standing by holding the door open for the family. Lydia made the introductions.

Sturmbannführer Wolff, this is my brother-in-law, Monsignor Josef Bertram.

The two men shook hands, "The pleasure is all mine, Monsignor," stated Wolff, making a half-bow in the process.

"It is indeed a pleasure, *Herr Sturmbannführer*, thank you," stated Sepp who also made a half-bow.

As the entire Bertram family entered the staff car, for a brief moment at least, it appeared to Lydia that there existed a sense of normalcy, that there was no war, and that this visit by a beloved family member was just a regular happy event. She tried to put out of her mind the mission that her husband had been given by Himmler. While Peter never discussed his work with Lydia, there was an unspoken understanding that Lydia knew exactly what and who her husband was involved with—however much she tried to put it out of her mind and not think about it. However, it was getting harder and harder to ignore the signs that her husband was beginning to crack under the strain. His mood swings, and above all, his nightmares and night sweats, were becoming all too frequent.

For the time being at least, while Uncle Sepp was here, she thought back to happier times, before this dreadful war had started.

Villa of the Deputy HSSPF
Reval, Estonia
Reichskommissariat Ostland
26 July 1943 1830 Hours

With the Bertram family back in their quarters and Sepp given time to freshen up after his long journey, Sepp, Peter and Lydia gathered in the small study at Sepp's behest.

"I want you both to know that I am very happy to see both you and the children, it has been a long three years."

"Yes, it has, Sepp, since your parents' funeral back in '40" said Lydia.

Peter spoke next. "The cable I received from the Foreign Ministry stated that you were here on official Vatican business. May I inquire as to just what that business might be, dear brother?"

Before Sepp could speak, there was a knock on the study door.

"Enter," Peter ordered.

An SS orderly, bearing a tray with three glasses of schnapps, entered and served drinks to the Bertram's'.

"Thank you, Johann, and please see that we are not disturbed," ordered Peter.

The orderly left and quietly shut the study door behind him.

"*Prost!*" They all said in unison, with Lydia adding, "To happier days ahead."

Sepp began, "As I was about to say before we were interrupted, I have been sent here directly by the Holy Father to deal with a very delicate issue—to wit—to stop the execution of these last Jews here in Estonia. I know about the demonstration that you are planning to put on for Himmler during his visit and I am asking you to halt that operation."

Peter glared at his brother, "I see you get right to the point, don't you? Same old Sepp, thinking that he is better than everyone else just because he's wearing that collar. How dare you enter my home and ask me to spare those Jewish *schwein*. Let me tell you something, brother—those Jews are going to die on 30 August, and I plan to put on one hell of a show for the *Reichsführer SS* and neither you nor that Jew-lover of a Pope can stop me!"

Peter then downed what was left of his schnapps and threw the glass into the fireplace exclaiming "That's what I think of you and your Pope and your church. After this war is over, the *Führer* will deal with the church as well!"

Sepp responded, "Like he's dealing with the Jews?"

"Precisely!"

Lydia was becoming visibly upset and attempted to mediate.

"Peter, Sepp, please don't argue, for the sake of the children, please!"

Both men nodded in agreement and lowered their voices.

"Peter, you've got to realize what you are doing is wrong, not only in the eyes of the church but legally as well. It goes against the Geneva Convention, of which I may remind you, Germany is a signatory. You are attempting to annihilate an entire group of people."

"The *Führer* wills it," replied Peter.

"The *Führer* along with Himmler and the rest are all mad, can't you realize that by now, Peter? The war has turned against Germany—Stalingrad, then North Africa, and now the Allies are poised to invade Italy. Mussolini has just been overthrown and it is now only a matter of time—maybe a year, two, five years, who knows, but Germany cannot win this war!"

"The *Führer* has promised us *Wunderwaffen* to win the war."

"Those promises of 'wonder weapons' are pipedreams, Peter, nothing but pipedreams."

All were silent for a moment and Sepp continued.

"Peter, the Holy Father has asked me to plead with you to save these last Jews that you are currently holding in Klooga and ensure their passage to Sweden. You have the power, Peter, *you have the power*, to do this. For the love of God, please, please help these people. We are talking about killing one hundred people!"

"I see the Vatican's intelligence collection is still first-rate, Bravo!" he said, slowly clapping his hands in a mock applause. "Do you think for one minute that I would risk my life and those of my family to help a bunch of Jews escape? You must be out of your mind. Himmler would have me, and my entire family shot instantly."

"Peter, I can see that the SS has changed you. You are not the kind, caring brother that I knew all those years ago."

"You are correct, brother, I have changed. I am a firm believer in the *Führer's* destiny for Germany, and not that mumbo-jumbo Judeo-Christian ethic that was forced down our throats as children. I see that you bought it hook, line and sinker, but not I dear brother, not I!"

"Peter, Hitler is leading Germany to destruction and into an abyss! You are aware of the declaration by the Allies to prosecute those guilty of war crimes? To my knowledge, you are not on the Allies list *yet*. However, if you go through with this experiment or whatever you want to call it on 30 August, you will hang, trust me. If so, what of Lydia and the children? Do they go through the rest of their lives as a widow and fatherless?"

Sepp had obviously struck a nerve with his last comment.

Peter could only stare blankly back at his brother and slowly began to shake and then to openly sob, collapsing into a chair, his hands covering his face.

Lydia and Sepp raced over to his chair and attempted to comfort him.

"Sepp," Lydia said, "Peter has had these terrible nightmares and I know it's from the work he is doing at the camp. You were right, the SS has changed him so much—this is not the man I fell in love with and married."

Turning to her husband, Lydia spoke, "Peter, please let Sepp help us. I can no longer watch you destroy yourself. Sepp is right—if you go through with this planned *aktion* when Himmler arrives, you'll be branded a war crim-inal. If they hang you, what will become of the children and I?"

Peter sprung from the chair in a rage, "Lies, lies, all of it! Listen to you both—defeatist both of you! I can have you shot for such talk!"

Realizing that he had just threatened his own wife and brother, he suddenly turned and left the study, slamming the door on his way out.

Lydia began to cry, and Sepp grabbed her by her shoulders telling her, "Lydia, you must try and talk some sense into Peter. He will not listen to me, but perhaps he will listen to you. He has been so brainwashed by the SS that I seriously doubt he can even remember his Christian upbringing. You must make him see that by helping these Jews he is doing the right thing."

"What if he were to help them, Sepp, how would we escape?"

"The papal nuncios in Helsinki and Stockholm are standing by to assist us. Even though Finland is fighting alongside Germany, it does not have any anti-Semitic laws in place and Mannerheim will not surrender Finland's Jews to the Reich, even with pressure from Berlin. Sweden of course is neutral, so once you make it there, you will be safe. Peter of course will be interned, but he will be safe. The Holy See will do everything in its power to see that Peter will not be punished too severely after the war. But we must act quickly, Lydia. Himmler's visit is a month away and if Peter goes through with this *aktion* against the Jews, he is as good as dead."

Sepp let his last comment sink into his sister-in-law's head and then continued. "If need be, Lydia, I can get you and the children to Sweden, and you can sit out the war in relative comfort. I know it is destroying you on the inside to watch Peter destroy himself. But I also know that you love your husband very much and believe that a wife's place is at her husband's side. I'm giving you a chance to save your family, *my family* as well, from certain destruction. You are all that I have left."

Tears were now running down Sepp's cheeks and he reached for his handkerchief to wipe them away.

"Please think very carefully about what I've asked you—if Peter will listen to anyone, it will be you."

With that, Sepp kissed his sister-in-law on the cheek, giving her a weak smile and left the study, leaving her alone with her thoughts and fears about the future.

Villa of the Deputy HSSPF
Reval, Estonia
Reichskommissariat Ostland
July 26, 1943, 2000 Hours

Lydia slowly made her way up the steps towards the master bedroom where her husband had gone after leaving the study. She very slowly opened the door to find her husband seated in a chair in a darkened corner of the bedroom. All that could be seen was the glow of the lit cigarette in his right hand. As she approached him, he spoke.

"So, you've come up here to do the Jesuit's bidding for him, eh?"

"Peter, Sepp is correct—if you carry out this *aktion*, you will be branded a war criminal and hang. You've got to realize what you've been doing is wrong. I have tried to put it out of my head that this special treatment of the Jews is needed, but I can no longer justify it in my own mind."

"These people are vermin! They will, if given the chance, Bolshevize not only Germany but the rest of the world. We in the SS are the bulwark against these hordes from the East! They need to understand who the master is and who is the slave!"

"You actually believe that propaganda from Goebbels, don't you? I feel so sorry for you."

She turned to leave, when in a low voice he said, "Wait, don't go. Please sit here with me for a while."

Lydia sat on the floor at the foot of her husband's chair, holding his hand.

"Lydia, I love you and the children very much, I think you know that. I also love my brother no matter how self-righteous he can be at times. I must confess to you that I am frightened at being labeled a war criminal and have wracked my brain thinking of ways on how to get out of taking part in the *aktion* during Himmler's visit. There is just no way out!"

Lydia gazed at her husband with sympathetic eyes. He continued.

"If I were to back down from this assignment, I would be drummed out of the SS, my rank, salary, all thrown away, and for what? For the lives of a few Jews?

"One hundred, Peter, not just a few."

"Yes, yes, ok, one hundred. Rumor has it that Himmler is also coming to promote me and give me a combat command in the *Waffen SS*. Wouldn't that make you proud, Lydia?"

"No, Peter, it would not. If these killings continue, why should I be proud? Listen to me, please. We can leave this behind, and Sepp can help us to make it to Sweden and we can wait there until war's end. The Vatican will ensure that you are not given a long prison term. Oh Peter, please, please, for mine and the children's sake, please don't go through with this."

Lydia began to sob quietly, and Peter held her close and stroked her hair gently.

"Let me give it some thought. I'll talk to Sepp further about it."

"You will! Oh, darling thank you," she said, kissing him on the cheek. "Look at me, I must look like a mess," she said between sniffles and stood up, straightened her blouse and her hair in the process, and said, "I will leave it to you then, to talk to your brother about this. I have your word, Peter?"

"You have my word as an SS officer."

With that, Lydia turned and left the room, heading toward the kitchen to oversee the preparation of the evening meal with the SS orderly assigned to them.

Villa of the Deputy HSSPF
Reval, Estonia
Reichskommissariat Ostland
July 26, 1943, 2230 Hours

After a sumptuous meal of *Jagerschnitzel* with all the trimmings, Peter and Sepp withdrew to the study for some brandy and cigars, while Lydia and the children retired upstairs. Peter had dismissed his SS orderly for the evening, as he wanted no one to know of the treasonous plan that he was now contemplating. The two men sat in two comfortable chairs opposite each other, both lost in their own thoughts and for a time not saying anything, not knowing where to begin. Finally, it was Sepp who spoke first.

"A fine meal, Peter, thank you for having me. I know that my visit comes at an inopportune time, with Himmler's impending visit, and I know that you are annoyed with me for bringing the request from the Holy Father. I just wanted to let you know that while I do not agree with your mission here in the East, you are my brother and I do love you. I only hope that you will consider what I've asked of you. I know it's dangerous, but I do believe that it can be done. We have the mechanisms in place to save these Jews. You would be surprised at the amount of people within the *Wehrmacht*, Foreign Ministry, and yes, even the SS, who want to see Hitler gone and this war ended."

"And of course, the Holy See, knows all of these individuals you speak of?"

"Not all of them, of course, but many have approached the Holy See with offers to assist in saving the Jews."

"Sepp, Lydia and I had a long talk earlier and for her sake and the sake of the children, I will help you. I must confess to you, dear brother, that the nightmares that I have been suffering as of late, are coming more and more frequently. In these dreams, I see Jews that were shot by our forces---mowed down by machine gun fire into pits and made into mass graves. I myself, have not shot a single person—I know it's hard to believe, but I have not. I have witnessed these executions, but I could not force myself to actively participate. The other dream I have is of me mounting the gallows steps and a noose being placed around my neck. Just before the trap door opens, I awake, sometimes screaming."

Peter took a long puff on his cigar and continued.

"Sepp, the war has turned against the Reich, I can see that the writing is on the wall and the Allies will show us no mercy whatsoever. With Mussolini's overthrow yesterday, it's only a matter of time before the Allies drive into Germany proper."

"I'm glad you realize that the war is lost. I will do everything in my power to see that you and your family are safe. But we need to act quickly now. Can you feasibly move those Jews from the camp and get them to Finnish territory? It will take some logistical planning and the assistance of trusted personnel. Is this possible, without someone turning you in?" Peter's shoulders sagged as if a great weight was taken off them.

"It just so happens, Sepp, that there is a *Wehrmacht* medical unit stationed not too far from Klooga. I have met the unit commander, an *Oberst Doktor* Weber, who seems to be a very decent chap. He once expressed some concerns over the prisoners, and I told him quite bluntly to mind his own business. Based on talking with him he is neither a party member nor is he too thrilled with Hitler. I think if I approach him with this plan now, he may think it is some sort of trap—possibly to test his loyalty to the regime. Perhaps, Sepp, you can accompany me when I meet with him?"

"I can do that."

"If I remember correctly, the unit did have a number of ambulances and other vehicles that we could use to get these Jews out. In that case, Lydia, the children and I could join up in the convoy and make it to safety as well. Let's meet with the good doctor in the next few days and see if he will help us."

Chapter IV

"The people of Israel will never forget what His Holiness and his illustrious delegates, inspired by the eternal principles of religion, which form the very foundation of true civilization, are doing for our unfortunate brothers and sisters in the most tragic hour of our history, which is living proof of Divine Providence in this world."

--Rabbi Isaac Herzog, Chief Rabbi of the British Mandate of Palestine, March 1945

The Kremlin
Moscow, Russia
July 27, 1943, 1500 hours

The clock on the Kremlin's Spasskaya Tower struck three o'clock as Soviet Foreign Minister Vyacheslav M. Molotov and Red Army General Pantileimon K. Ponomarenko, chief of staff for the Soviet Partisan network, met with Josef Stalin, the General Secretary of the Communist Party of the Soviet Union. The ever-paranoid Stalin had received first-hand information from a spy[43] within the Holy See that a Vatican diplomat had been sent to the Baltics, now currently under German control. Even though the Baltics were temporarily free of Moscow's control, Stalin still demanded to know why a Vatican diplomat was being dispatched to Soviet territory. Was it to re-establish Catholicism in an area officially devoid of religion since the Soviets forcibly annexed the Baltic States in 1940? Stalin demanded answers and had summoned his foreign minister and the chief of staff for the Partisan network.

"Vyacheslav Mikhailovich," Stalin addressed his foreign minister, "We have a problem. The Pope has sent an emissary to the Baltics. Now why would he do that? The area, before the Revolution, was overwhelmingly Evangelical Lutheran apart from Lithuania. What does the Pope have in mind, I want to know.[44] Alert the Partisan bands in the area to focus their attention on an SS officer by the name of Bertram, and his brother, a Roman cleric by the same name. I need to know the connection. Perhaps, the Pope has thrown in his lot with the Hitlerites to forcibly convert our peace-loving Soviet peoples to Catholicism! Remember Marx's statement that religion is the opiate of the people!"

Molotov, who also saw conspiracies behind every bush, agreed with Stalin, that the Vatican had to be up to no good if they were sending a diplomat to deal with the Germans.

"Josef Vissarianovich, no doubt the Pope sees an opportunity to gain a foothold on Soviet territory while the Hitlerites are occupying it. After all, Pius XII is the same individual who dealt with Hitler back in 1933 when Germany and the Vatican signed the Concordat. Pius has made no secret of his hatred of our political system, and from the reports we have received, he has quietly hoped for, some say even prayed for, a German victory in the East. He was the papal nuncio in Bavaria in 1918 when the Soviet revolution broke out in Munich. Evidently, he sees Hitler as the lesser of two evils, Soviet Communism being the other."[45]

"Ha! How many divisions has the Pope?"[46] Stalin sarcastically mused.

"None, Josef Vissarianovich—but he could use the Germans as proxies to do his bidding for him and try to destroy everything Lenin worked so hard to establish. Only two years ago our security forces arrested a Polish-American Jesuit priest, Father Walter Ciszek[47], who entered our beloved Motherland illegally using false papers. He is currently re-thinking his crime in Lubyanka." Stalin then stated, "All through history Jesuits have been notorious plotters and the right hand of the Pope!"[48]

Molotov then continued, "You may remember, Josef Vissarianovich, in the early days of our beloved socialist republic; there were trials held against some Orthodox and Catholic clergymen who spoke out against us and resisted nationalization of the church properties. One of them was a Catholic Archbishop, a Pole by the name of Cieplak,[49] whom the People's Court sentenced to death, but later commuted due to international protests. We deported him to Poland and he later left for America, where he died."

"Ha! Another miserable Pole! Good riddance to him and his kind! Find out what this cleric Bertram is doing there, also have our people interrogate this American-born priest you speak of and see if he knows something. Get one of our people into the SS officer's house as a maid[50] or domestic servant, so that she can report back to us on Bertram's movements. I want to know everything that is going on!"

With that, Stalin dismissed both men with a wave of his hand and returned to his desk where he was reviewing execution orders needing his approval. Lighting up one of his favorite Dunhill pipes, Stalin began humming an old Georgian folk song while boldly signing, with his trademark thick blue pencil, his signature to all the orders stacked before him.

Adolf Hitler Platz
Reval, Estonia
Reichskommissariat Ostland
July 29, 1943, 1000 Hours

Frau Maria Schobert, a *Volksdeutsche*[51] from Estonia, and housemaid to *Gruppenführer* and Mrs. Bertram, was strolling down Adolf Hitler *Platz* in Reval. The *platz* had been renamed by the Germans in July 1941 in honor of their *Führer*. Maria, like most of the *Volksdeutsche* living in Estonia in 1941, had welcomed the *Wehrmacht* as liberators from Soviet oppression and was lucky enough to receive employment from the German occupation forces. Since she spoke fluent German, she applied for, and was selected to be a housekeeper for the new Deputy Higher SS and Police and SS Leader for *Ostland, Gruppenführer* Bertram. *Frau* Schobert got along very well with her new employers, and over the last two years had been given tasks of ever-increasing responsibility. Today happened to be *Frau* Schobert's day off, and since she had a bit of money saved up, she longed to buy a new dress. Unbeknownst to her, she was being closely watched by members of a local Partisan organization, who had received a direct order from General Ponomarenko that they were to find some way to infiltrate the Bertram household. Comrade Kuzin, code-named "Walter," and head of the local communist Partisan network in Reval, took personal charge of the operation. His plan was to eliminate *Frau* Schobert and, in her stead, replace her with a Partisan member who would masquerade as a household domestic and be placed inside the Bertram household. Kuzin's reasoning was that if Schobert went missing, or turned up dead, no doubt the Bertram's would be looking for a replacement maid. The Partisans would see to it that a female member of their network would be hired and placed on the "inside;" as a decoy she would grant them unfettered access to the inner workings of the Bertram household. As *Frau* Schobert made her way towards a desolate street, the opportunity now afforded itself to spring into action. Kuzin, along with a female Partisan, Comrade Davydova, code-named "Tatiana," pretended to be a couple, slowly strolling arm-in-arm, looking at the shop windows and generally trying to blend in. *Frau* Schobert was oblivious to their presence and as the couple closed in on their quarry, Tatiana reached into her purse for a knife. *Frau* Shobert had stopped ahead, looking at some dresses in a store window. Now was their chance. Tatiana would approach *Frau* Schobert alone, engage her in conversation, and then stab her. Kuzin would be the look-out. If the murderous ruse went according to plan, it would be over within minutes and the couple would escape undetected.

As the last moments of *Frau* Schobert's life ticked away, she admired a dress in the window. *Frau* Schobert wondered how she would look in it— and planned on wearing it when her fiancé, Rudi, was home on leave. Rudi was stationed in Norway, which, thank heaven, was relatively quiet for the time being. She then turned a corner and began walking slowly down a side alley, off the main Adolf Hitler *Platz* thoroughfare. Tatiana now saw her chance to strike. Schobert, momentarily lost in her thoughts, suddenly became aware of someone following her in the alley. Stopping, she turned to see a smiling, young, attractive woman coming from behind. Before she could react, Tatiana pulled the knife from her purse, lunged, and stabbed *Frau* Schobert in the chest. As she crumpled to the pavement, Tatiana heard her murmur, "Rudi, Rudi." And then she fell silent.

Kuzin ran over to his Partisan partner and said, "Ok, let's get out of here." Tatiana nodded in agreement, and both briskly walked in the opposite direction away from the body on the pavement. No doubt the police would find *Frau* Schobert's body in a short period of time; inquiries would be made, the body identified, and shortly, there would be a notice that the Bertram's would be seeking a new maid. Until that time, Kuzin's group would lay low and begin preparing Tatiana for her new role as a maid to the Deputy Higher SS and Police Leader of *Ostland* and his household.

Gonsiori Street 2
Reval, Estonia
Reichskommissariat Ostland
July 29, 1943, 1100 Hours

Kuzin and Tatiana returned to a nearby flat that the Partisans used as a "safe house." Tatiana was shaking—this was the first time she had ever killed a person, let alone a woman. Kuzin pulled out a bottle of vodka and poured two glasses. "Here, drink this, it will make you feel better."

Tatiana gulped down her glass, and nodding toward the bottle demanded, "Let me have another." Kuzin poured another glass and Tatiana gulped it down, this time coughing after downing the second drink.

"You did well for killing a person for the first time, Tatiana," Kuzin said. He then added, "Don't worry, the next time, it will be easier. Now we need to wait and see what will happen in the Bertram household when they find out their servant is dead. More than likely, they will need a replacement and that's where you come in. We should have some false papers for you in a day or so. The fact that you too are a *Volksdeutsche* and speak fluent German will no doubt help you get the position."

Tatiana was still shaking, although the vodka had taken some of the edge off. "Comrade, what if they don't look for another housekeeper, or import one in from Germany, what then?"

Kuzin was silent for a moment and then answered, "Then we will just have to find another way into the household, that's all."

Tatiana shook her head slowly, knowing that you just didn't walk into the home of the Deputy Higher SS and Police Leader and strike up pleasantries with the family. There was bound to be intense scrutiny on her security and background checks. "Comrade, I have a bit of a headache, I am going to lie down," she said wearily. With that, Tatiana went into the small bedroom and closed the door and laid down for a much-needed rest.

Off in the distance, police sirens could now be heard coming from the area where Tatiana killed *Frau* Schobert. Kuzin looked at his watch and thought *it hadn't taken long for the body to have been discovered and for someone to call the authorities.* Soon the area would be swarming with *Kripo*,[52] Gestapo and Military Police personnel, all investigating Schobert's death. Perhaps door-to-door searches would be carried out—one never knew what the Germans would do, but Kuzin was sure that no one had seen them, therefore no descriptions could be given and then circulated. The newspapers would read that "unknown assailants" had killed Schobert, and her demise would be described as just another unsolved murder on the police blotter.

Villa of the Deputy HSSPF
Reval, Estonia
Reichskommissariat Ostland
July 29, 1943, 1400 Hours

The *Kripo Inspektor*, a Lieutenant Dietrich Mohl, had informed *Gruppenführer* Bertram and his wife that *Frau* Schobert was murdered on the streets of Reval in broad daylight. Identity papers and a work permit found in Schobert's purse made it very easy for the *Kripo* to track down the Bertrams as the dead woman's employers.

"Who would do such a thing, *Herr Inspektor*?" asked Lydia, her voice laced with a bit of fear.

"We don't know, *Frau* Bertram, but our men are taking this very seriously. *Frau* Schobert was a *Volksdeutsche*, not just some Slav or Jew, but one of our own."

Peter chimed in, "Do you have leads, *Herr Inspektor*? Any witnesses perhaps?"

"None yet, sir," Mohl answered.

Peter continued, "A much more important question, *Herr Inspektor*; Do I need to be concerned for the safety of my family, or was this just some random killing? Were the assailants trying to get to me?"

Mohl could not honestly answer Peter's question. "I won't lie to you, sir. Since the woman was in your employ, whoever did this could be sending you a message; and then again, it could just be a random killing, although no valuables seem to have been taken. There was still money in her purse, and she was wearing some cheap costume jewelry." After pausing a moment, Mohl continued, "Sir, we will have a police guard placed around your home for additional security."

Showing signs of strain and aggravation, Petrer testily replied, "I expect nothing less, *Herr Inspektor*. See to it." With that, he turned on his heel and left his wife alone with the inspector.

"You will have to forgive my husband, *Herr Inspektor*, he has been under tremendous strain, especially with *Reichsführer SS* Himmler's impending visit."

"No need to apologize, *Frau* Bertram, I completely understand, and I can assure you we will have a cordon of security in place to protect you and your family. Your husband is very important to the Reich's implementation of the *Führer's* plans in *Ostland*."

"Thank you, *Herr Inspektor*, that is very kind of you to say."

"I will have men posted around the villa, along with men from the *Gruppenführer's* command as well. You are in good hands."

"Thank you, *Herr Inspektor*, and please keep us informed on your investigation."

"I will, *Frau* Bertram. Good day." With that, Mohl left the villa, and Lydia closed and locked the door behind her. It had been a long afternoon. She was shocked by Schobert's death and had cried. The children were informed, and they cried as well: *Frau* Schobert was, to them, a beloved family member, not just a mere household servant.

Lydia slowly made her way up the steps towards the master bedroom, where, as usual, Peter was sitting in a chair in the corner smoking a cigarette. The lights in the room were off, and as Lydia walked in, all she saw was the glow from Peter's lit cigarette.

"The police have finally left, Peter," Lydia said quietly.

"I can't help but think that Schobert's murder was a warning message to us, me in particular," Peter said.

"Or it could be a random killing. Nonetheless, we'll have to hire someone else, don't you think, Peter?"

"Yes, I suppose you are right. This house is much too big for you to run alone. You'll need help. I'll talk to the head of the local Reich Labor office tomorrow to find a replacement. Now let's get some sleep; it's been a long day and hopefully tomorrow will be a brighter day for all of us."

Reich Labor Office
Roosikrantsi 2
Reval, Estonia
Reichskommissariat Ostland
July 30, 1943, 0900 Hours

Herr Johannes Koening had just received a phone call from the Deputy SS and Police Leader for *Ostland, Gruppenführer* Peter Bertram, requesting that a suitable replacement be found for his late housekeeper, *Frau* Schobert. Koening had heard about Schobert's murder and expressed his condolences to the *Gruppenführer*, promising him that a candidate would be found by day's end. Hanging up the phone, Koening dabbed his sweaty brow with his handkerchief, and shouted to his assistant, Aarne Punga, to come to him. Punga, a native Estonian and a former Estonian civil servant during the brief Soviet occupation of his country from 1940-1941, came running in from the next room.

"Yes, *Herr* Koening, you called for me?"

"Punga, I just received a call from *Gruppenführer* Bertram with regards to finding a housekeeper for him. You probably heard that his housekeeper, *Frau* Schobert was brutally murdered yesterday, and he needs a woman to take her place. If I remember correctly, you had placed *Frau* Schobert with the Bertram family two years ago, correct?"

"Yes, Sir, I did."

"Good. Then you know the requirements. Young, attractive, diligent, oh, and she needs to be a *Volksdeutsche* and of course fluent in German. Do we have anyone suitable?"

"Yes, Sir, I believe we do. I will get the file and bring it to you shortly."

"Good, see to it, man" and with a wave of his hand, Koening dismissed his underling and returned to the pile of paperwork on his desk.

Reich Labor Office
Roosikrantsi 2
Reval, Estonia
Reichskommissariat Ostland
July 30, 1943, 1000 Hours

Unbeknownst to *Herr* Koening, his assistant Punga, was in fact working for the communist Partisans. In the last two years since the German invasion, the Soviets had been very successful in infiltrating agents into key positions within the German armed forces and other Reich organizations in the occupied areas. It was believed the Soviets even had a source within Hitler's inner circle who was providing intelligence on upcoming military operations. Punga had been a member of the pre-war and outlawed Estonian Communist Party. When the Soviets forcibly annexed the Baltic States in 1940, Punga welcomed the occupying Red Army with open arms. He was rewarded for his loyalty with an appointment to a civil service position in Tallinn. When the Soviets retreated after the German invasion in June 1941, Punga stayed behind in Tallinn and began to slowly organize a pro-Soviet Partisan network in the city. For his efforts, he was given the rank of Major in the Red Army and was in touch with Ponomarenko's Partisan headquarters via clandestine radio. Punga had received the order to kill Schobert directly from Ponomarenko.

Punga already had Tatiana's (Viktoria) file ready and pulled it out. He reviewed it carefully, ensuring that the paperwork looked authentic enough to pass the closest of scrutiny. The Partisan forgers were working overtime, producing authentic looking but nonetheless very fake identifications, work permits, and other documentation required by the German occupation authorities. Satisfied that Tatiana's file was in good order, Punga brought the file out to *Herr* Koening for review.

"Sir, I believe this exceptional woman qualifies," he said while handing the file over to Koening.

Koening took the file and reviewed it carefully, as he read every word in the file. Upon completion, he closed the file and said, "I think *Gruppenführer* Bertram will be quite happy with this young lady, *Frau* Viktoria Kessel. A rather pretty name, don't you think, Punga?"

"Yes, indeed, sir. And quite a pretty young woman as well; she made a real impression on me when she came in to fill out her paperwork."

"Very well. I will contact the Bertram household to see what time would be suitable for an interview. I will personally bring *Frau* Kessel to the villa."

"Whatever you say, *Herr* Koening. Please let me know what time will be agreeable and I will then contact *Frau* Kessel and inform her of her upcoming interview."

Koening grunted, nodded, waved Punga away, and went back to his paperwork.

A small smile came across Punga's face as he walked back to his office—so far, the plan to infiltrate the Bertram household was working—now hopefully Tatiana, correction, *Frau Viktoria Kessel,* would impress the Bertrams and be hired on as their housekeeper.

Villa of the Deputy HSSPF
Reval, Estonia
Reichskommissariat Ostland
July 31, 1943, 1000 Hours

Herr Koening and *Frau* Kessel arrived promptly at ten o'clock as re-quested by Lydia Bertram. *Herr* Koening showed his and *Frau* Kessel's iden-tification papers to the police guard at the villa's gates, and their names were checked against a daily list of visitors provided by the Bertrams. From a field telephone at the guard post, a plainclothes detective rang up to the house and informed *Frau* Bertram of her visitors. Lydia told the detective to let them pass and that she would meet them at the entrance.

As Koening and Kessel made their way up the steps to the front door, it opened, and Lydia met her two visitors. "*Herr* Koening, how nice to see you again," she said, offering her hand as Koening took it and gallantly kissed it.

"*Frau* Bertram, so kind of you to see us on short notice. May I present *Frau* Viktoria Kessel." The two women smiled and nodded at each other, and Lydia then invited her guests into a cozy sitting room off to the left of the vil-la's entrance.

Lydia offered her guests some real coffee rather than the tasteless *er-satz* that most of her countrymen were now drinking back in the Reich.

"I am very sorry that my husband could not be here with me to meet *Frau* Kessel and to participate in the interview, but then again, he told me that the hiring of a housekeeper was a woman's job," Lydia said with a slight chuckle. Her guests smiled at her attempt at humor.

"*Frau* Bertram, here is *Frau* Kessel's file for you to review, as you can see, she has solid references from some of the pre-war families living here."

Lydia opened Viktoria's file and reviewed it carefully—this was not the first time she had interviewed domestic help and knew what she was look-ing for in a candidate. She slowly reviewed the file, her lips moving silently as she read every line on the application. Both Koening and Kessel sat in silence but carefully studied Lydia's facial features as she reviewed the file; a slight smile, the arch of an eyebrow, a frown, a nod of the head, were all mentally noted.

Headquarters, 517ᵗʰ Medical Battalion
Reval, Estonia
Reichskommissariat Ostland
July 31, 1943, 0915 Hours

The Bertram brothers drove to the Headquarters of the 517ᵗʰ Medical Battalion of the German Army, located approximately five kilometers from the city center. Peter Bertram drove himself, foregoing his usual driver and by doing so, ensuring that no one else was privy to the attempted rescue plan. As the staff car drew up to the medical unit, it was halted by a posted sentry.

"Your papers please, *Herr Gruppenführer*," the soldier asked politely.

Peter presented his identification and those of his brother to the young corporal who scrutinized them carefully. Peering into the vehicle, the NCO saw that Sepp was not a soldier, but a cleric, his collar prominently displayed.

"Monsignor Bertram is here at the invitation of the Foreign Ministry; here are his travel orders and Vatican passport."

The young corporal, who was used to strictly looking at official documents such as soldier's paybooks and military orders, was a bit confused, but since the priest was travelling with a SS *Gruppenführer*, there was no way he was going to challenge the vehicle's occupants.

"Thank you, *Herr Gruppenführer, Heil Hitler!*" he stated as he waved them through.

As the staff car continued on its way, small wooden signs interspersed along the road pointed to various units of the battalion that were spread out over a few kilometers. They continued to drive slowly until they saw a sign reading *Hauptquartier* (Headquarters) and turned down a path following it until they came to an old farmhouse, which had been commandeered by the Germans for their use.

Another sentry at the door came to attention and rendered the Nazi salute. Peter returned the salute asking, "Where can I find the commander, *Oberst Doktor* Weber?"

The sentry then turned to a field telephone on a small table next to him and cranked the handle and awaited a response.

"*Herr Leutnant*, I have a SS *Gruppenführer* here who wishes to see *Herr Oberst*."

With that, the line went dead and within a matter of seconds, a young *Oberleutnant* (First Lieutenant) by the name of Hans Roper was at the door adjusting his tunic to ensure he was presentable to this high-ranking visitor.

"*Heil Hitler!*" Roper greeted his two visitors. "I am *Oberleutnant* Roper, the battalion adjutant, and I welcome you to the 517ᵗʰ Medical Battalion. I understand you wish to see *Oberst* Weber. If you gentlemen will please follow me."

With that, the young officer led the way through the old, but spotless farmhouse, whose many rooms were converted into offices for the various staff officers of the battalion. The commander's office was located on the second floor of the building as the Bertram brothers were led up the steps, they were then met by Weber himself.

"*Heil Hitler!*" Weber stated raising his arm in the Nazi salute.

Peter weakly returned the salute and made the introductions.

"*Herr Doktor*, we would like to talk with you on a very delicate matter if you don't mind. May we go to your office for a chat?"

Weber was mystified and a bit concerned. He remembered his first and only meeting with Peter and that had been rather strained to say the least. Now he shows up with this priest—he wondered what could this SS officer and this priest want from him?

"Hans, I don't wish to be disturbed," Weber told his young adjutant.

"*Zu befehl,*[53]" came the response as Roper closed the door behind him.

Weber directed his two visitors to some chairs and then asked, "How may the 517th Medical Battalion be of service to you gentlemen?"

There was a long pause before Peter spoke first. "First, *Herr Oberst*, I want to apologize for my rudeness towards you the last time we met."

Again, a moment of awkward silence.

"No need to apologize sir, it has been forgotten (which it had not)."

"At the time you had expressed some concern about the Jews being held at Klooga."

"Yes, sir, I did express concern, mainly with regards to a typhus outbreak amongst the prisoners and how it might affect our troops and civilians in the area."

Weber was only partially truthful. In fact, Weber had a genuine humanitarian concern for the Jews—for unbeknownst to many, his wife was part-Jewish, but they had been successful so far in hiding that information from the authorities. By volunteering for service as a *Wehrmacht* medical officer Weber assumed that his military service would prove his unwavering loyalty to the regime and eliminate any suspicions that the authorities may have concerning his wife's Jewish identity.

"*Herr Doktor*, my brother is with the Vatican Foreign Office and has been sent here by the Pope himself to help move the Jews being held in my camp. What do you think of that?"

Weber was dumbfounded and could not find the words to answer Peter's cynical question.

Peter continued, "No need to answer, *Herr Doktor*, I would be speechless as well if I were presented with the same question. The fact remains, I am going to try and get those Jews to freedom before Himmler's arrival. Using the cover of medical evacuations could assist us in moving the Jews unharmed. From there, they will be moved to Sweden and onto freedom."

Again, Weber was speechless. Here was an officer of the SS, the sworn enemy of the Jews, who was now asking his assistance in helping them escape certain death.

Having the courage to speak his mind to a senior officer of the SS, Weber retorted "If this is some sort of trick, *Herr Gruppenführer*, to test my loyalty to the *Führer*, I am not amused. I will report this at once to the Inspector General's office."

The Bertram brothers looked at each other and then at Weber. Sepp spoke next.

"*Herr Oberst*, I know how this must sound to you and I can appreciate your being careful as not to fall into some sort of trap that the Gestapo and SS are so good at springing on unsuspecting citizens of the Reich. However, what my brother says is the truth. The Holy Father has charged me with trying to rescue those Jews in Klooga to freedom. What my brother is doing is treason and will be shot if found out. He came to you because at your first meeting, he came away with the impression that you were a decent man and more than likely not a party member. Is that true?"

"Monsignor, it is no secret that I am not a party member. Many people have not joined the NSDAP,[54] yet faithfully serve the Reich and the *Führer*."

"No one is questioning your loyalty, *Herr Oberst*, on the contrary you have shown humanitarian qualities as a physician and we believe that you can be trusted to assist us in rescuing these poor innocents," Sepp said.

Weber was still wary and remained non-committal.

Peter then told Weber of his plan. "While the shortest route to Finland would be by boat, it would be too risky. The *Kriegsmarine* patrols are too heavy, and we would no doubt be intercepted by an S-boat.[55] Additionally, a Baltic crossing will put us at risk by Soviet submarines and naval vessels based out of Kronstadt. Also, due to a lack of buoys, many a ship has run aground. It is a shame that we failed in permanently knocking out the Soviet naval base back in '41. And the question begs to be asked, where are we going to find a boat to hold a hundred people without raising suspicion?"

"How many vehicles are assigned to your battalion, *Herr Oberst*?" asked Peter.

"One hundred, sir."

"And all are clearly marked with the Red Cross?" asked Sepp.

"Yes, Monsignor, all have Red Cross marking in compliance with international law."

"Good. How difficult is it to transport one hundred people in those marked Red Cross vehicles to the Finnish border?" asked Sepp.

Weber directed the Bertram brothers' attention to the map on the wall showing the disposition of German military units in the Baltic and Northern Fronts.

"We are here, and the nearest Finnish garrison would be here at Terijoki."[56] Weber stated. Before he could continue, Peter stepped up to the map and said, "Perhaps, there may be an even easier way than transporting one hundred people in a vehicle convoy. There is a weekly troop train between here and Krasny Bor, near the Leningrad front, subject of course to the Partisans not blowing up part of the railway line. It brings in supplies, reinforcements, mail, et cetera, and on the return trip transports the wounded. We will put them on the train—with proper uniforms and identification, they should not arouse suspicion."

"You've hit the nail right on the head *Herr Gruppenführer.*"

Peter continued, "Our plan is to place the younger male prisoners in *Wehrmacht* uniforms and the female prisoners as nurses or auxiliaries, while the older prisoners can be passed off as Finnish civilians, or maybe even as civilian members of the Red Cross making an inspection."

"With regards to uniforms, *Herr Oberst*, I am sure you can supply the *Wehrmacht* uniforms to the younger male prisoners as you have a warehouse full of them; we have already received confirmation of that. They may not fit the best, but most of the time these folks will be on a train, sitting down, so they really won't raise any suspicion at all."

"I see *Herr Gruppenführer*, that you have done your homework concerning my unit. Your plan sounds brazen enough that it just might actually work," Weber stated.

Peter continued, "After checking with the *Reichsbahn* troop train schedules, the train's final destination will be at Krasny Bor, which is currently occupied by the Spanish. It just so happens that my brother knows the division chaplain there and plans to enlist his aid with this mission."

Peter looked at Weber and said quite bluntly, "*Herr Oberst*, you know what we are doing is considered treason and that the penalty is death."

"I know sir, and I am willing to take that chance. One hears rumors about the camps in the East. As a medical officer, I've treated some SS men who served as camp guards. Many of them have talked while delirious or while heavily sedated. One can easily put two and two together and realize what is happening to the Jews and others in the East. I will be quite blunt, *Herr Gruppenführer*, my wife is part-Jewish, and I could not imagine her dying in one of those camps. That is why I am doing this."

Peter was taken aback by Weber's revelation of his wife's religious background.

"You look surprised, *Herr Gruppenführer*. Well, don't be, for I have first-hand knowledge of many officers themselves, some of them of general officer rank, being of Jewish ancestry. Most of them received special dispensation from the *Führer* himself."[57]

Sepp heard those rumors, but here was proof that even soldiers of Jewish descent were faithfully serving Hitler's *Wehrmacht.*

Villa of the Deputy HSSPF
Reval, Estonia
Reichskommissariat Ostland
July 31, 1943, 1300 Hours

The Bertram brothers returned to Peter's villa after their visit to the medical unit. Upon entering the villa, Lydia greeted them.

"Peter, Sepp, I have some very good news. This morning I interviewed a young woman to take poor Maria's place. Her name is Viktoria Kessel, and she is *Volksdeutsche* living here in Reval. I hired her, and she is currently upstairs changing and should be down in a moment."

Just then all three heard one of the upstairs bedroom door close.

"I think she's done changing...ah, here she comes now."

As Viktoria came down the steps she was greeted by Lydia and the Bertram brothers standing at the foot of the stairway.

"Viktoria, allow me to introduce you to my husband, *Gruppenführer* Bertram, and his brother, Monsignor Bertram."

Peter took Viktoria's hand, clicked his heels, and bowed slightly. "A pleasure, *Frau* Kessel."

Sepp simply bowed slightly and said "A pleasure indeed, *Frau* Kessel. You will be very happy working for the Bertram family."

"Thank you, *Gruppenführer* and Monsignor, I think I will be most happy here. I am looking forward to meeting the children."

"You settled into your room?" Lydia asked.

"Yes, *Frau* Bertram, I am settled in, thank you."

"Good, then come with me and I will show you where to start and explain some of the duties."

With that, both women disappeared into the other part of the house. As Lydia escorted Viktoria to one of the front parlors, Viktoria innocently asked, "Is the Monsignor assigned to a local parish here in Reval?"

"No, he is here visiting us from Rome. He is with the Vatican Diplomatic Corps."

"Oh, I see," Viktoria said. She thought about asking more probing questions but did not want to raise suspicions. In due time, Viktoria thought to herself, she would, through the course of daily conversations, piece together what the Monsignor was doing in Reval. Perhaps it was just an innocent family visit, one brother visiting another brother and his family. However, if this raised Comrade Stalin's suspicions then something must be terribly wrong. She would certainly find out. Perhaps when she was alone with the children, they would be able to give her more information—albeit small pieces at a time.

Villa of the Deputy HSSPF
Reval, Estonia
Reichskommissariat Ostland
July 31, 1943, 1600 Hours

While Viktoria watched her two young charges play in the villa's gardens, she felt a certain calm fall over her and could for a moment at least, forget that there was a world at war. Viktoria delighted in listening to the giggles and laughter from two young children—and quite frankly she had not had much to laugh about over the last two years, ever since the German invasion. Viktoria's parents, both dedicated Socialists, were deported to Germany as forced labor in early 1942 and were presumed dead. Her younger brother, Erich, had joined the Partisans, and only God knew if he was dead or alive. Viktoria had not seen or heard from Erich in over a year, and she hoped that his unit had at least been reassigned to another sector of the front and not wiped out by the Germans in one of their many anti-Partisan sweeps. Just before he disappeared, Erich had persuaded her to join the small Soviet-sponsored Partisan network in Estonia. Most Estonians wanted nothing to do with the Soviets or Communists; instead, many young men had flocked to join German-sponsored auxiliaries and created the *Omakaitse* (Home Guard) in order to keep the Reds at bay. She had been introduced to Punga by her brother, and in turn, Punga had introduced her to Comrade Kuzin, and the two ultimately became lovers. Kuzin and she worked well together, hence their teaming up for the current assignment. Just over the last couple of hours when Viktoria was alone with the children, she learned from them that their Uncle Sepp was a priest (that, of course she knew), and that he was visiting from a far-away place called the Vatican, and that is where the Pope lived. The children could not tell her how long the monsignor had intended to stay or the purpose of his visit (maybe it was just a family visit—but in wartime and in an active theater of operations?). Unfortunately, she would have to do a bit more digging on her own to find answers.

"Children, let's go back inside the house, shall we?" she cried out to the Bertram children.

"Do we really have to, *Frau* Kessel?" asked Berthold.

"Yes, I'm afraid so, Berthold."

With that, both Bertram children ran through the large French doors leading to the villa's garden. As soon as the children were down for their naps, she would search the Monsignor's room for any shred of evidence justifying his visit.

Chapter V

"What the Vatican did will be indelibly and eternally engraved in our hearts. Priests and even high prelates did things that will forever be an honor to Catholicism."
--Eugenio Zolli, former chief rabbi of Rome and later a convert to Catholicism, 1948

Headquarters
571ˢᵗ Medical Battalion
Reval, Estonia
Reichskommissariat Ostland
July 31, 1943, 1230 Hours

Oberst Weber met with his adjutant, *Oberleutnant* Roper as soon as the Bertram brothers left the headquarters.

"Hans," stated Weber, "You will never guess what that meeting with the SS *Gruppenführer* and the priest was all about."

"I have no idea, sir," Roper replied.

"Hans, I'm going to let you in on a little secret. I feel I can trust you and what I am about to tell you goes no further than this room, understood?"

"Perfectly, sir."

"The SS officer and the priest are brothers. They are about to embark on a plan so brazen that it just might work. It also reeks of high treason and if caught, both brothers face an automatic death sentence. Both have taken me into their confidence and now I'm taking you into mine. In past conversations we shared you and I have criticized Reich's treatment of the Jews."

Roper looked at his commander with a perplexed look.

"Now, don't deny it, Hans. I am disgusted and know only too well what the 'resettlement' and 'relocation' of Europe's Jews means here in the East. They are being systematically murdered, Hans—pure and simple."

Weber let that last statement sink into the young officer.

He continued, "Hans, the Bertram brothers plan on saving the camp's inmates here in Reval, which, by the way, the *Gruppenführer* is overseeing now. They plan on securing a train, and head East to the Leningrad sector, whereupon the priest hopes to contact a friend of his serving with the Spanish infantry division. From there, they will make their way to Finland and then on to Sweden."

Roper sat dumbfounded while his commander revealed his grand plan which bordered on insanity.

"Well, Hans, do you have anything to say?"

Roper blinked his eyes as if coming out of a trance. "Sir, this is unbelievable! This is treason and we will all be shot!"

"Yes, Hans, this is treason, but it is also the right thing to do. Now, I cannot order you to assist me, and if you don't want to, that is fine, I understand completely. But I ask you to keep this conversation between us. Do I have your word?"

"Yes, sir, of course. You have my word as an officer of the *Wehrmacht*."

"Good. Think it over and let me know tomorrow; we have a lot of work to do if you decide to help."

With that, Weber stood up, signaling that the meeting was over and shook his adjutant's hand. "Thank you, Hans, I know you will let your conscience be your guide."

Roper saluted, executed an about-face, and left Weber's office. Weber then slumped in his chair and felt the world's weight on his shoulders. He then stood up, and walked to his wall map, traced with his finger the route that the train would have to take to the Leningrad front and then on to Finland. Even there, he surmised, the danger would not be over as German troops were stationed in Finland and could somehow interfere with the repatriation. While Marshal Mannerheim gave his word that Finland would assist the Jews once they reached Finland, anything was possible, particularly if protests came from Berlin. As Weber was studying at the map, he heard a knock on his door.

"Enter," Weber ordered.

Roper returned, saluted, and shut the office door. "Sir, concerning our earlier conversation; you can count me in."

"Hans, how did you make your decision so quickly?"

"Sir, before the war, while attending university, I fell in love with a beautiful Jewish girl by the name of Hannah. This was before the Nuremberg Laws were passed in '35. Thereafter, my parents forced me to stop seeing Hannah; it was the hardest thing I ever had to do in my life. We tried to see each other secret, but to no avail. With the laws further restricting the Jews with their movements, etc., it became impossible. The last I saw Hannah was early 1937, six years ago."

"Do you know what became of her, Hans?"

"No, sir, I don't. Just before reporting for military duty in 1939, I walked past her home in Stuttgart, but another family was living there. I asked them where Hannah and her family might be, but they didn't know. They bought the house cheap because it was appropriated by the government."

Roper went quiet momentarily, lost in thought, back to happier times and his lost love.

"Maybe she and her family left Germany, Hans."

"I've often thought of that, sir. Hannah had family in America, New York, to be exact and I do remember meeting one of her American relatives in 1934. I've always prayed that she and her family got out safely. Now you know why I'll assist you and the Bertram brothers, sir."

Straightening up, Roper stated, "I am at your orders, sir."

A smile crept across Weber's face, and he walked around his desk and took his adjutant's hand and shook it. "Hans, thank you and welcome to the fight."

The young officer stood there for a moment, not really knowing what to say. The silence was broken with a knock on the door.

"Enter," Weber ordered.

A young sergeant entered, saluted and handed a dispatch to Weber. Moments later, Weber reviewed it, signed it, and gave it back to the sergeant, who then left, closing the door behind him.

"Now, Hans, we have lots to do. I will need to collect military uniforms, identity papers, rations, and a million other things before we can execute this plan. Is there someone you can trust to assist us?"

Roper thought for a moment and said, "Yes, sir, there is an officer whom we can trust emphatically. His name is *Hauptmann* Wilhelm Fritz. Fritz is the *Wehrmacht* liaison to the *Reichsbahn* and coordinates most of the train traffic coming into Reval. We met in the officers' *kasino* about a month ago and he appears to be a decent chap. Fritz told me his father was a Lutheran minister, who had spent some time at Dachau after delivering some homilies against the Nazis ill treatment of the Jews. When he was finally released, he was a broken man and died soon after. Based on our conversation, I don't think he is too keen on the regime and will help us."

"Hans, see if you can arrange to have *Hauptmann* Fritz report here later today to discuss his joining our little cabal of conspirators," Weber said.

"Yes, sir!" Roper replied. He saluted, did an about-face, and left Weber's office. Weber could only shake his head and ask himself, "Where do we get such brave men?"

Villa of the Deputy HSSPF
Reval, Estonia
Reichskommissariat Ostland
August 1, 1943, 1500 Hours

With the children down for their afternoon naps and Mrs. Bertram attending a local Nazi Party function, Viktoria had the villa to herself. The SS orderly normally assigned was on leave and would not return from Germany for another week. As Viktoria made her way to the guest bedroom where Monsignor Bertram was staying, she became nervous at the prospect of going through the priest's personal belongings. *Strange*, she thought to herself, that she was more nervous doing this than she had been in killing *Frau* Schobert.

Viktoria quietly entered the guest room's closet and began checking the pockets of Sepp's cassock. Almost immediately Viktoria found Sepp's papers from the Reich Foreign Ministry authorizing his travel to *Ostland*. Quickly scanning the document, Viktoria saw that he was permitted to stay for up to one month. Viktoria carefully refolded the papers and returned them to the cassock. Moving to the bureau drawers, she carefully removed some shirts, undergarments and socks, but found nothing. When Viktoria was done searching the drawers, she spotted over near the nightstand a small leather briefcase, which she hoped would contain further information. To Viktoria's relief, the briefcase was unlocked. Opening the briefcase, she looked through several sheets of paper with Vatican letterhead. Most of the papers were unfortunately written in Latin. She did, however, discover a small envelope with the Papal seal on the back. The letter had already been opened; holding her breath, Viktoria deftly removed the letter from the envelope. It was hand-written in German[58] and read:

> *Sepp, the mission you are about to undertake is absolutely critical in the Holy See's efforts to save the Jews in the East. I know that this mission will be fraught with danger, but I know that I have selected the right man for the mission. I pray to Our Savior, Jesus Christ, that you come through unscathed May Our Lord bless and keep you during these trying times, and bring you back safely to us.*
>
> *Pius pp. XII*

Viktoria finally found what she was looking for—the reason for Sepp's visit. She could now report back to her superiors in Moscow and report that the priest was here to rescue Jews at the Pope's behest. *But why?* she thought to herself. The monsignor's brother was in the business of killing Jews, so why come here to save them, unless, of course, *Gruppenführer* Bertram was involved as well.

Headquarters
571ˢᵗ Medical Battalion
Reval, Estonia
Reichskommissariat Ostland
August 1, 1943, 1530 Hours

Hauptmann Wilhelm Fritz followed his friend *Oberleutenant* Roper as they climbed the steps to Weber's office on the second floor of the battalion headquarters building. Roper had gone to the *kasino* for lunch and as fate would have it, Fritz was there as well. Fritz motioned Roper to join him and the two talked. During lunch Roper mentioned that his battalion commander asked if Fritz would not mind stopping by battalion headquarters for an informal talk about the *Reichsbahn* schedules with reference for the reception of wounded troops being treated by the 571st. It was an innocuous enough request that would not raise any objections or suspicions. Fritz readily agreed and returned to the battalion headquarters with Roper.

Prior to Roper knocking on Weber's office door, both men adjusted their tunics. Roper knocked.

"Enter," Weber ordered.

Both officers entered, stopped and saluted.

Roper made the introductions. "*Oberst* Weber, may I present *Hauptmann* Wilhelm Fritz.

Weber rose from his desk and shook hands with the young captain.

"Very good of you to come on such short notice, Fritz. Please sit down."

Weber offered both officers a cigarette, which both declined. "As a doctor, I shouldn't even have these damn cigarettes in my office, but some of the higher-ups smoke, and it wouldn't be cordial not to offer." They all chuckled at Weber's remark. He continued, "You know the Reich has initiated some pretty interesting programs with regards to educating the public about the dangers of smoking and its link to cancer. I'm glad neither of you smoke."

"Sir," Fritz spoke, "Hans mentioned that you asked me here to discuss the *Reichsbahn* timetables so that you can better coordinate the reception of the wounded coming from the East, correct?"

"*Herr Hauptmann*, that is *partially* what I wanted to discuss with you today," looking over towards Roper and nodding.

Roper picked up the conversation. "*Herr Hauptmannn*, what we are about to tell you is a delicate matter and cannot go beyond this room."

"You have my word of honor as an officer, that whatever is discussed here will not be divulged."

Weber nodded toward Roper to continue. In the next ten minutes, Roper explained to Fritz the meeting that had transpired with the Bertram brothers and the plan they had to rescue the Jews held in Reval and get them to freedom in Sweden. A train would be needed and the Jewish prisoners, disguised as troops, nurses and civilians would head East toward Finland, where they would be aided by the Finnish government in their bid to freedom.

Much like Roper only hours earlier, Fritz sat dumbfounded. After briefing Fritz, Roper asked, "Well, what do you think?"

Fritz, stammered, "This...this is treason! We can all be shot!"

Weber added, "*Hauptmann* Fritz, this is a lot to comprehend in such a short time. What Hans is telling you is no fairy tale—this is real, and we need to act quickly if we are going to succeed. We need the *Reichsbahn* for transporting Jews from Reval to the Leningrad Front. We need train schedules, and your *Reichsbahn* contacts. Will you please help us?"

Fritz stood up and walked to the window, pulling out a handkerchief to dab the perspiration forming on his forehead and upper lip.

"Gentlemen, this is suicide and has no chance of succeeding whatsoever."

"I beg to differ," said Weber. The man leading this plan is none other than an SS *Gruppenführer.*

"SS you say? Then it must be some sort of trap. I want no part of it."

"*Hauptmann*, please sit down. Hans told me about your father's imprisonment at Dachau and subsequent death from mistreatment there. He was put there in the first place because he took a stand against the Nazis treatment of German Jews, was he not?"

The mention of his father brought back sad memories for Fritz—he had been very close to his father and hoped someday to follow in his footsteps and enter the ministry. That all changed with his father's death, and with the Nazis in power, organized religion was greatly frowned upon. National Socialism was to be the new "religion" of the Reich and Hitler was its new "messiah."

"You can help finish the job your father started and help save these Jews. He would be very proud of you fighting against this evil."

"Gentlemen," Fritz said, "Are you not forgetting our personal oaths that *we all took* to the *Führer*?

"No, I haven't, my dear Fritz," Weber responded. "On the contrary, it weighs quite heavily on my conscience, but sometimes there is a 'higher calling' than one's duty to a country or leader."

Fritz sat silently for what seemed to be an eternity to both Weber and Roper. Finally, he spoke. "What you say is true, *Herr Oberst*, the Nazis were responsible for my father's death after being interned at Dachau. My mother's heart broke, and she was never the same again; none of us were. So, in memory of my father, I will assist you. If it is successful, perhaps we can all sit out this damn war in Sweden. I am at your orders, sir."

"Splendid, Fritz, absolutely splendid," as Weber jumped up to shake the young captain's hand. Roper joined in to congratulate his new fellow conspirator.

"Now, gentlemen," Weber stated, "I will contact *Gruppenführer* Bertram and let him know that we are backing his plan. In the meantime, I'd like you both to make some discreet inquiries with reference to our earlier discussion concerning the obtaining of identity papers, uniforms, etc. Fritz, I'll leave it up to you to use your contacts within the *Reichsbahn* to confirm availability of train transport, timetables, the works."

In unison, both junior officers answered, "*Jawohl, Herr Oberst*," to Weber's directive.

Weber closed the meeting by stating, "Gentlemen, I believe it was the American Benjamin Franklin, who during their war for independence stated that 'We can either hang separately or together.' For what we are about to embark on, may God give us protection and carry us through to success."

With that, Weber dismissed both officers and returned to his wall map to further study the route to Leningrad.

Headquarters
571ˢᵗ Medical Battalion
Reval, Estonia
Reichskommissariat Ostland
August 6, 1943, 1600 Hours

Roper, and Fritz met in Weber's office again to discuss the transportation and logistical issues involved with the rescue. Weber opened the discussion.

"We have 100 Jews that need safe passage from the camp in Reval to the train depot, five kilometers away. For the sake of appearances, let's transport them using our Opel Blitz 2x4 ambulance trucks. Under the guise of evacuating personnel and staff from a typhus outbreak at the camp, we will transport the Jews on our East-bound train and get them to rendezvous with Monsignor Bertram's Spaniards."

Roper crisply answered, "Sir, we've got plenty of transports for the operation. It will take about 10 trucks, with 10 passengers each to get to the train. Each of the vehicles will be marked with Red Crosses, so that should eliminate suspicion from the Gestapo and SS. Additionally, we have uniforms, both military and nursing that will be used. Since one has a habit of losing weight in a concentration camp, most of the uniforms will be quite big."

"I am told that the prisoners are healthy and are being fed a good diet in anticipation of Himmler's visit," Weber interjected.

"Fattening them up for the slaughter, I suppose," Roper said with disgust.

Hauptmann Fritz then added "I can lay on a hospital train for the mission. It consists of two cars for patients as well as a separate car for medical staff. Gentlemen, if we pull this off, this will look like an ordinary hospital train with "patients" and "medical staff" on board, heading East."

"Very well, gentlemen," Weber said, "Continue to coordinate. We will need to set up a meeting with *Gruppenführer* Bertram and the good monsignor to finalize our plans. Remember, secrecy will be paramount to the success of this operation. Any questions?"

Neither officer had any, so Weber dismissed them.

Headquarters
571ˢᵗ Medical Battalion
Reval, Estonia
__Reichskommissariat Ostland__
August 7, 1943, 0915 Hours

"Welcome *Herr Gruppenführer*, Monsignor," Weber shook both men's hands as he ushered them into his office, "Please do have a seat."

Both Bertram brothers took their seats opposite Weber.

"Gentlemen, I am happy to report that our plans are falling into place. The two officers I selected have organized transport and secured uniforms for our passengers. We can be ready to leave in two days' time. I am at your orders, *Gruppenführer*, just tell me when you need to move the prisoners and we will have transportation."

Both Bertrams were surprised by the medical unit's swiftness in securing the materiel and transport for the escape.

"These two officers you speak of, *Herr Oberst*; are they trustworthy?" asked Peter.

"Yes, I trust them with my life, *Herr Gruppenführer.*"

"That, unfortunately, is an understatement," Sepp said. "Given the graveness of the situation, we can all lose our heads if they don't keep their mouths shut."

"They know of our situation gentlemen I can assure you. I need at least 48 hours' notice to get my people into place. Also, the situation in the East is very fluid—the Russians have become more active lately after the failure of our latest offensive at Kursk. If so, the rolling stock may not be available when we most need it."

The Bertrams pondered the medical battalion commander's words carefully. "You say you will need at least 48 hours warning before we can begin our operation?" Peter asked.

"Yes, *Herr Gruppenführer.*"

"Very well, you shall have it," Peter said. With that he stood up, followed by Sepp, and both men shook Weber's hand and left.

As they entered Peter's staff car and slowly drove away, Sepp asked his brother, "Peter, can we be ready in time? Weber said that with the situation in the East rapidly changes, so we may not have the trains at our disposal."

Peter did not immediately answer because his mind was already racing at 100 mph, he did not think that Weber and his men could deliver in time.

He thought he had more time. His major concern now was the safety of Lydia and the children—to get them to safety, hopefully Sweden, where they could sit out the war in relative comfort.

"Peter, did you hear what I said," Sepp asked.

"Sorry, Sepp, I was lost in thought for a moment. Yes, Weber has done an outstanding job in getting things ready for our mission. Sepp, I need you to contact the Papal Nuncio in Stockholm, as I intend to send Lydia and the children there for safety."

"You will be joining them as well, correct, Peter?"

"Eventually. I will send them on ahead and will join them later. There are a few loose ends I need to tie up before I head to Sweden."

"Peter, you need to leave immediately! Once you are implicated, Himmler will have you shot!"

"That's the chance I am willing to take, Sepp. Please don't argue with me, my mind is made up. All I ask is that you contact the Nuncio and let them know to expect my family."

Sepp was saddened at his brother's decision not to join his family in fleeing to Sweden, but he understood his logic. "Very well, Peter, I will do as you ask."

The brothers drove on in silence, each lost in his own thoughts about the upcoming days ahead.

Chapter VI

"Death, you know keeps secrets better even than a guilty Roman."
--Lew Wallace, *Ben Hur: A Tale of the Christ*

Reich Labor Office
Roosikrantsi 2
Reval, Estonia
Reichskommissariat Ostland
August 8, 1943, 1200 Hours

On the first day that she had free to herself, Tatiana made her way down to the Reich Labor Office to see Punga in order to pass on the information that she had discovered concerning Sepp Bertram's visit. She still could not reason why a senior SS officer would willingly assist in saving the lives of Jews condemned to death. Perhaps it was to save his own neck? Do something good and perhaps the Allies would be lenient? This made no sense to Tatiana. Perhaps it was for a more nefarious reason? Perhaps the Germans were changing their tune with regards to Jews in order to win the sympathy of the Western Allies—then they would sign a separate peace[59] and turn on the Soviet Union? *That must be it*, she thought to herself, *otherwise Comrade Stalin would not have ordered the Partisan network to carry out this mission.*

At noon, Tatiana arrived at the office—Punga had told her that *Herr* Koening would be at lunch at a local café with some other employees and that they would have the entire place to themselves.

Tatiana entered the Reich Labor Office at exactly noon and Punga met her in the alcove.

"Your message said it was important," Punga said. "Let's go to my office in the back, where we won't be disturbed."

He guided Tatiana back through some alcoves stacked with boxes containing personnel records, forms, and other materials needed to run the office. Entering Punga's office, he gestured for her to sit down and offered her a glass of vodka, which she gladly accepted. In a mock toast, she said "*Na Zdorovie*"[60] and downed her drink.

"Comrade Punga, the priest has been sent by the Vatican to save the Jews that are in the camp outside of Reval. I don't know where or when, but it was in a letter signed by the Pope himself."

Punga had a surprised expression. "What are you talking about? The Pope has ordered a priest to save Jews here in Reval. Are you sure?"

"Yes, Comrade, it was in the letter."

"And of course, you read Latin, right?" Punga asked mockingly.

"No, I don't Comrade. The letter was written in German, in which I am fluent, as is the Pope" she answered back smugly.

"Where will these Jews go? They are surrounded by enemy territory. Do you know where they will be taken?"

"No, Comrade, I do not. Their location was not mentioned. The priest also has travel documents permitting his stay in Reval for one month. Whatever is in the works will have to occur soon because the priest has already been here for two weeks."

"Good, Tatiana, you have done well. I will report this information back to Moscow and await further orders. Maintain your position in the Bertram household until further notice. Are there any questions?"

"No, Comrade."

"Very well. Please go before *Herr* Koening and the rest return from lunch. I will be in contact."

Tatiana got up and along with Punga exited the Reich Labor Office. As Tatiana melted into the busy pedestrian traffic, her thoughts were a million miles away.

The Kremlin
Moscow, Russia
August 9, 1943, 1410 Hours

Punga's message about Tatiana's discovery was transmitted to Partisan leadership in Moscow. This missive prompted General Ponomarenko to contact Molotov, who then phoned Stalin, who called for an immediate meeting.

"So, the Vatican wants to save the lives of Jews in Estonia and the Pope has sent a priest to carry out his little rescue. Now this priest is the brother of the Deputy Higher SS and Police leader for that area occupied by the Hitlerites who are killing the Jews," Stalin pondered this irony aloud as he puffed on his Dunhill pipe.

Molotov and Ponomarenko stood by silently and meekly as Stalin paced the room. They knew better than to interrupt "the Boss" while he was deep in thought.

Stopping in front of a map of Europe, Stalin continued, "Where can these Jews find refuge in a war zone? I venture a guess: neutral Sweden, eh, gentlemen?" he said pointing to the map with his pipe's mouthpiece.

"Sweden has to be their final destination, there is no other outlet! To get to Sweden, they must either cross the Gulf of Finland, which will be too risky, or..." Stalin stopped short and traced an overland route with the tip of his pipe from Estonia across to Leningrad and then added. "Make an overland route to the Leningrad area and then attempt to enter Finland." What do you think, gentlemen?"

Clearing his throat, Molotov spoke first. "Josef Vissarianovich, what you say is probably true. This priest will probably attempt the long route, rather than the more direct one and head for Finland first. Once there, the Finns will naturally offer assistance."

General Ponomarenko then chimed in, "The logistics behind this are much too complicated—there has to be more than one individual behind this escape plan."

Stalin exploded, "Of course there are you idiot! Do you think one lowly priest could organize such an escape route? There are others, probably the bulk of them within the German armed forces who have offered to assist him because, quite frankly, they are sick and tired of Hitler's leadership and his treatment of the *Zhyds*[61]. Now, if they happen to succeed and word gets out that the German armed forces are now in the business of saving the Chosen People, that will have an effect in the areas of the Motherland still occupied by the Hitlerites. We know that from the past two years, there have been many Soviet citizens who have flocked to join the Hitlerites in their attempt to overthrow the government of the Soviet Union. We cannot allow any more of these traitors to join their ranks if there is a drastic change of heart with regards to the Hitlerites occupation policy."

What Stalin had stated was an open secret, at least among the leading Politburo members. Over one million Soviet citizens had joined the Germans, either assisting as auxiliaries, HIWIs (helpers) or outright joining the *Wehrmacht*. An entire Cossack Corps was under German command, and one high-ranking Soviet general, Andrei Vlaslov, now a German POW, was pleading with Hitler to allow him to form an anti-Soviet army[62] out of the millions of Soviet POWs in order to fight Stalin. Stalin purposely held troops back, particularly the dreaded NKVD divisions, to ensure stability behind the front lines. Regime survival was first and foremost on Stalin's ever-more paranoid mind.

"Ponomarenko, get back to your agent in Estonia and tell her she must find out how these *Zhyds* will be moved. Once we know their mode of transport overland, we can then get word to the Partisan bands to attack either the convoy or railway which they will be traveling by. Make it clear that none of these *Zhyds* is to survive the attack. You have your orders; let me know once you hear back from your agent. You are dismissed, Ponomarenko. Vyacheslav Mikhailovich, I need you to stay a while longer, as I need to discuss something with you."

After Stalin's dismissal, Ponomarenko headed to his own office within the walls of the Kremlin to execute the next phase of the operation.

Villa of the Deputy HSSPF
Reval, Estonia
Reichskomissariat Ostland
August 10, 1943, 1030 Hours

After receiving word from the Partisan network ordering her to find out further intelligence on the planned escape of the Jews, Viktoria mentally prepared to dig deeper into the Bertram brothers' plans, which would not be an easy task. Her window of opportunity was closing because Lydia Bertram was often home. However, there was a sliver of hope. For the next few days, Lydia would be busy with some Nazi Party functions being held in Reval, and would be gone most of the days, only returning in the early evening hours. The same was true for the Bertram brothers, who, unbeknownst to the female partisan, were meeting with their fellow conspirators. The brothers would be gone most days, returning only late in the evening. Now, she found herself once again alone in the house, except for the Bertram children playing outside. She slipped away unnoticed and crept upstairs to Sepp's room and once again began to look through his belongings, which she spread out across the bed. Silently, young Berthold snuck upstairs and was watching from the hallway as she rummaged through Sepp's personal effects. She did not hear Berthold's footsteps behind her.

"Why are you going through Uncle Sepp's things?" Berthold asked.

Startled, she quickly turned around. "Berthold, you scared me. I didn't hear you come up. Why aren't you outside with your sister? You should never leave her alone. I am looking for papers your Uncle Sepp said he needed, and he asked me to look for them." She had no time to think of an elaborate excuse, and this was the fastest she could come up with.

"Oh, alright," Berthold said laughing, and turned to go back outside.

She stopped him by grabbing his arm gently and said, "Berthold, let's just keep this between us, don't tell your parents about this, alright? It will be our little secret. You like secrets, don't you?"

Berthold just smiled and nodded in agreement; he made his way down the stairs and back outside to join his sister.

Not wanting to tempt fate further, Viktoria replaced Sepp's belongings and returned everything back in the closet; she would have to wait for another opportunity and soon, as Moscow was now demanding answers.

Villa of the Deputy HSSPF
Reval, Estonia
Reichskomissariat Ostland
August 10, 1943, 2330 Hours

The Bertram brothers returned late evening after spending the day finalizing plans with the 517th Medical Battalion. It was 11:30 PM by the time they entered the villa, and both dead tired from the events of the day.

"Good night, Sepp," said Peter.

"Good night, Peter, sleep well."

As both men climbed the steps to the family bedrooms, Peter stopped outside of the children's bedrooms and realized that since Sepp's arrival, he had not spent much time with his children. Both children were normally fast asleep by the time he arrived home most evenings.

As Peter entered Heidi's room, he looked down on the little blond-haired girl fast asleep, her favorite doll held closely. He bent down and kissed her on the forehead, and she stirred lightly.

Leaving her room, and closing the door quietly, he then went to Berthold's room. Looking down at his son, he realized how big the boy had gotten just in the last year. He's going to be a strapping young man, he thought to himself. He also thought the sooner this war ended, Berthold would not have to serve the Fatherland in the military and his generation could grow up without knowing the horrors of war.

Peter bent down to kiss his son's forehead and as he did the boy stirred and awoke.

"Papa, you're home!" The boy sat up immediately and became animated.

"Shhhh, or you will wake your sister, Mama and *Frau* Kessel," Peter said sternly but with a smile.

"*Frau* Kessel told me a secret today, Papa," the boy blurted out.

"What secret might that be, son?" Peter asked innocently.

"Well, I am not supposed to tell you, but this afternoon *Frau* Kessel was looking through Uncle Sepp's suitcase for some papers he said he needed, and she went looking for them."

Peter sat straight up on the edge of the boy's bed. "What papers was she looking for, Berthold? What kind of papers?"

"Papers for Uncle Sepp, Papa."

His suspicions now deeply aroused, Peter stood up, kissed his son on the head and told the boy to go back to sleep.

Peter left Berthold's room and quietly walked down the hallway toward the master bedroom, passing Viktoria's room on the way. Peter stopped for a minute in front of Viktoria's door, staring as if trying to bore through it with x-ray eyes to see who and what were lurking on the other side. Peter's biggest fear of course was a spy among them. An enemy agent planted in the household of the third most powerful man in *Reichskomissariat Ostland* was unthinkable, but *Frau* Kessel could be an embedded Soviet spy or even a Gestapo agent. It would not be beneath Himmler to place a spy in a senior SS officer's home. If true, it could spell disaster for the plans in rescuing the

Jews and getting them out of harm's way. Turning on his heel, he walked to his bedroom where he found Lydia fast asleep. He would deal with *Frau* Kessel in the morning and hopefully his worst fears would be for naught.

Kriminalpolizei Headquarters
Reval, Estonia
Reichskomissariat Ostland
August 11 1943, 0945 Hours

SS Gruppenführer Peter Bertram strode into the *Kripo* headquarters like a man on a mission. As he was in full uniform, the desk sergeant sprung to his feet shouting, "Heil Hitler!"

Peter weakly returned the salute and asked if *Inspektor* Lieutenant Dietrich Mohl was available.

The desk sergeant, a former police detective from Munich, gladly offered to escort Peter back to Mohl's office.

Upon arriving, they found Mohl's office door closed, which meant he was either out, working diligently, or asleep at his desk. "Thank you, sergeant, I will take it from here," Peter said.

Taking a deep breath, Peter turned the door handle and there was Mohl, busy at his desk, a mound of paperwork requiring his attention. Upon seeing Peter standing in the doorway, Mohl almost fell out of his chair.

"*Herr Gruppenführer,* what a pleasant surprise; I am honored that you are here. I didn't know you were in the building."

"No need to apologize, Mohl, I was in the area and thought I might stop by and have a little chat with you. It is a delicate matter that I wish to discuss with you, if you have the time."

Even if Mohl didn't have the time, he was not going to refuse a senior SS officer, who on a whim, could probably send Mohl to the Russian Front as a lowly private.

"How may I be of assistance, *Gruppenführer?*"

"Our housekeeper, *Frau* Viktoria Kessel, has been with us since the unfortunate death of our former housekeeper, *Frau* Schobert, if you recall."

"Yes, tragic indeed, and unfortunately, we still have no clues into *Frau* Schobert's murder. Her case is still an open investigation."

"No doubt you and your men are doing the best you can, Mohl, and I appreciate it. Now, for the purpose of my visit to you. I would like *Frau* Kessel investigated as I believe she may be an enemy agent," Peter said bluntly.

"A spy? Well, *Gruppenführer,* spies fall under the realm of the Gestapo, not the *Kriminalpolizei,"* he said with a smile.

"I am aware of that, Mohl. I want you to investigate because I think she may be an agent for the Gestapo, or possibly the Reds."

Mohl was dumbfounded at Peter's statement.

"You see, Mohl, I know that the Gestapo and *Kriminalpolizei* are at odds half the time, and I trust *you* to conduct an honest and impartial investigation."

"May I ask, *Herr Gruppenführer*, what makes you think that she is an agent?"

"I have it on good authority, Mohl, that she was seen rummaging through my brother's personal items while the family was out." Peter purposely omitted to tell the inspector that the 'good authority' was his ten-year old son - had he done so, Mohl may not have taken him seriously.

"Your brother, *Herr Gruppenführer?* "

"Yes, Mohl, my younger brother, Monsignor Josef Bertram, who is a Vatican diplomat."

Mohl was startled by the news. "He is here, *Herr Inspektor* on personal business, nothing official, just a family visit."

Mohl seemed satisfied at Peter's explanation.

"Why, *Herr Gruppenführer,* would *Frau* Kessel be rummaging through a priests' belongings? What would she hope to steal, rosary beads, perhaps?" Mohl asked in a futile attempt at humor.

"As I stated, my brother is a Vatican diplomat; maybe she was looking for diplomatic correspondence between the Reich and the Holy See?"

Mohl pondered that notion for a moment. It was no secret that the xenophobic Soviets feared the Catholic Church because it was a bulwark against the spread of communism in Europe.

"You may be correct, *Herr Gruppenführer.* If you would like, I can bring *Frau* Kessel in for questioning."

"That is fine, Mohl. Tomorrow sometime, would be fine. Try not to make a scene, as I don't want to upset the children. Better yet, pick her up outside the villa—I know she will be shopping tomorrow, and you can simply pick her up off the street."

"Very well, sir. Consider it done."

"Thank you, *Herr Inspektor,* " Peter said as he stood up and offered his hand to the detective. "I will see to it that your superiors are informed of your splendid work so far here in Reval."

Mohl, ever the opportunist, was greatly pleased at Peter's compliment. Perhaps, with the *Gruppenführer's* recommendation, he could even be posted to Berlin—that's where the real action was.

Villa of the Deputy HSSPF
Reval, Estonia
Reichskomissariat Ostland
August 11, 1943, 1115 Hours

Peter returned to the villa and found his wife upstairs in their bedroom, getting ready to attend a Nazi party function for some of the senior officers' wives. It was a duty she enjoyed in the early years before the war; now of course, with the knowledge of the horrors of the Holocaust and open secret, she no longer had the stomach for it.

"Peter, you are home, what a surprise!" she said kissing him on the cheek.

"Lydia, I need to talk to you alone. Where are *Frau* Kessel and the children?

"She took them to the park. We are alone."

"Good. Lydia, I have reason to believe that *Frau* Kessel has been spying on us. Berthold told me he saw her rummaging through Sepp's luggage the other day. When Berthold asked Viktoria, she said it was nothing, and asked him to keep it a secret, just between the two of them. She is either spying for the Reds or the Gestapo."

"Peter, you can't be serious?"

"I'm afraid I am. If she finds out our plans for the prisoners, it will all be over. That is why, you and the children need to leave for Sweden within the next 48 hours."

"You are coming with us, right, Peter?" Lydia asked nervously.

"Yes, of course, but not right away. I have some things to finish here before I join you. Of course, you know that once I join you, I will be interned, and I am sure, Berlin will put a lot of pressure on the Swedes to have me sent back."

"Oh, Peter, would the Swedes really do that, send you back?"

"I know of no cases where they have turned away Germans seeking asylum or pilots who have crashed landed on Swedish soil. They are there for the duration of the war."

Peter continued, "*Frau* Kessel will be picked up for questioning by *Inspektor* Mohl tomorrow sometime. It will get her out of our way and give us time to get you and the children to Sweden. There is a weekly Swedish *Aerotransport* airline that services Reval with a direct flight to Stockholm. Sepp will make arrangements for the Papal Nuncio there to meet you and provide for your safety and comfort."

Lydia took this all in stoically; she had learned to do so a long time ago as the wife of an up and coming SS officer.

"Whatever you say, Peter, we will be ready."

"Good. When *Frau* Kessel and the children return, you are to act naturally. I don't want her to be suspicious, and we are to carry on normally during supper."

With that, Peter and Lydia heard the front door open and the squeals of delight from their children echoing through the house. They knew it would be the last time they both would enjoy the sounds of their children's laughter in the villa.

Adolf Hitler Platz
Reval, Estonia
Reichskommissariat Ostland
August 12, 1943, 0950 Hours

Frau Kessel began her day by heading to a market located on *Adolf Hitler Platz*, just a few minutes' walk from Bertrams' villa. Viktoria was unaware that following her at a discrete distance by car was *Inspektor* Mohl along with one of his men, a detective by the name of Schaumburg, who before the war, was a police officer in Vienna.

Frau Kessel slowly made her way up the street, stopping occasionally to view displays in the store windows. With wartime rationing now the norm for most Germans, many featured goods were hard to come by, except if one worked in the household of the deputy HSSPF for *Ostland*.

"That's her up ahead," Mohl told his subordinate, "Just a bit longer now, we don't want to make a scene on a busy street."

Ironically, *Frau* Kessel was nearing the spot where she had killed *Frau* Schobert only weeks before, an act she felt was a lifetime ago.

"OK, pull over and let's get her," Mohl ordered his driver. The Opel Admiral automobile, confiscated by the Germans upon their occupation in 1941 and given to the *Kriminalpolizei* for their exclusive use, sped ahead and then jumped the curb, blocking Kessel's further movement.

Mohl leapt out of the auto's passenger side and immediately displayed his *Kripo* Warrant Disk, which identified the bearer as a member of the criminal police.

"Frau Kessel, I am *Inspektor* Mohl of the *Kriminalpolizei,* will you please come with us to the station for some questioning." It was more of an invitation than an order.

"What have I done?" Kessel asked, obviously shocked at being stopped by the police. "I am in the employ of *Gruppenführer* Bertram, call him if you have any questions."

"Please, *Frau* Kessel, come with us now, and I assure you we will have this matter cleared up in no time." Kessel reluctantly entered the back seat with Mohl sitting next to her, in the event she would try to escape. Mohl had used the old Gestapo playbook of letting their victims guard down, telling them that everything would be straightened out within a short while and that she would be on her way. Little did she know that it was Bertram who ordered Mohl to interrogate her and place her into police custody.

Headquarters, *Kriminalpolizei*
Hermann Goring Strasse, 58
Reval, Estonia
Reichskommissariat Ostland
August 12, 1943, 1015 Hours

Inspektor Mohl arrived at police headquarters with Kessel and immediately escorted her into the interrogation room, which was nothing more than an overhead light along with a table and two chairs.

Ever courteous, Mohl asked politely, "*Frau* Kessel, please be seated. May I get you water or coffee?" Kessel was shocked when Mohl offered her coffee; wartime rationing made coffee as scarce a commodity as gold.

"Thank you, coffee would be nice."

Mohl directed an Estonian policeman to fetch the drinks, which he did and then left the room.

"May I ask what this is all about, *Herr Inspektor?*"

Mohl stared at her for a moment before answering. "We received a report that you may be involved in activities directed against the Reich."

"This is preposterous! I am a loyal German!" she declared.

"That may be so, but we will have to keep you here for 48 hours until we can clear this up. I assure you, *Frau* Kessel, that you will be treated well and that no harm will come to you. You have my word."

Mohl was unlike many of his colleagues in the German security forces--he had never tortured or roughed up handcuffed prisoners, he thought that it was beneath him has a professional to resort to such tactics. Mohl's colleagues in the Gestapo would have a field day with Kessel, who was young and attractive; the very thought of her being brutalized by the Gestapo made him ill.

"I am going to step out for a minute, *Frau* Kessel, and will return shortly."

Mohl left and the Estonian policeman entered the interrogation room. When he saw that Mohl had left the immediate area, he whispered, "*Frau* Kessel, I too work for Punga. Here, take this and hide it."

Unbeknownst to *Frau* Kessel, the policeman was part of the Partisan network which had infiltrated many of the German organizations that used local labor. The officer had given Kessel a cyanide capsule in the event she was tortured.

"There are a few of us here working in the police station" said the officer, who identified himself only as Karl.

"Thank you, Karl," Kessel said as she hid the vial ampule in her bra.

"The matron who will receive and search you is one of us. She will 'overlook' the cyanide pill. Is there anything you need to pass on to Comrade Punga, tell me now."

"Tell him that the Bertram brothers are planning to rescue the Jews from Klooga by transporting them to Sweden. They will be heading *East* within the next few days on a German troop train bound for the Leningrad Front. That is all I know."

Before Karl could question her further, he heard Mohl's footsteps which signaled his return to the interrogation room.

Mohl dismissed the Estonian, "Thank you, Karl, that will be all." With that, Karl slightly bowed his head, turned and left.

Mohl continued, *"Frau* Kessel, if you will please come with me, we will get you in-processed."

Both policeman and prisoner walked down the long hallway where an Estonian matron awaited her new charge. *"Frau* Neilson will take charge of you from here. I will speak to you tomorrow morning. Have a pleasant evening." With that, Mohl turned and headed back to his office on the second floor of the building.

Frau Neilson gently guided her charge into the in-processing room where she was searched, and as promised, the cyanide capsule was 'overlooked.' To Viktoria's surprise, she was not photographed or fingerprinted, leading her to believe that she would be released after the 48 hours were up.

"We will do everything we can to make you comfortable, Comrade," Neilson said with a slight smile. "It has taken us a long time to penetrate the security forces and we cannot do anything rash which will blow our cover."

"I understand, Comrade Neilson. I too serve the Soviet Union and Comrade Stalin and I will risk my life for our common cause."

Neilson then escorted Kessel to her cell--it looked more like a dorm room and at first glance, appeared quite comfortable, until of course the door was closed and locked behind her. The police station was an old building, dating back to the 19th Century, and the cell doors were made of thick oak with a small, barred window towards the top.

Kessel looked around at her new surroundings for a few seconds then sat at the end of her cot. She could do nothing until morning, when, she feared, Mohl would take off his 'kid gloves' only to reveal a mailed fist, waiting to slam her into the ground.

Reval-Ulemiste Military Airfield
Estonia
Reichskommissariat Ostland
August 12, 1943, 1230 Hours

After receiving a call from *Inspektor* Mohl that Kessel was in custody, both Bertram brothers swiftly transported the Bertram family to the airfield in order to ensure they were on the plane bound for Sweden and freedom. As the family of a high-ranking SS officer, authorization for travel to another country, was not difficult. As a neutral country, Sweden accepted both Allied and Axis personnel, if the paperwork was in order. Stockholm, much like other neutral capitals during the war, were hotbeds of intrigue, with Allied and Axis spies oftentimes sitting across from each other at the same bars and hotel lobbies.

Bertram drove himself as was often his custom, foregoing his SS driver this time to ensure secrecy so that his plan would not be compromised.

The family reached the terminal. Each member packed lightly and carried their own bags in order to not arouse too much suspicion. Once in Sweden, the Papal Nuncio would take care of their housing, food, and personal amenities.

The aircraft was scheduled to depart at 1400 hours local time and the flight time was approximately two hours with a good tailwind.

Peter was saddened to see his family leave but knew that he had crossed the point of no return with his treasonous activity; he wanted to make sure his family was safe. Peter felt that this departure would be the last time he would see his family.

A *Luftwaffe* sergeant checked his family's paperwork and declared all documents to be in order. The NCO then escorted them to a VIP lounge, where military personnel with the rank of Colonel and above, were invited to wait for their flights in relative comfort. The Bertrams' were the only passengers in the VIP lounge, so they felt a bit more at ease.

Sepp spoke first, "Remember, Lydia, that the name of the man who will meet you in Stockholm is Monsignor Michael Rosselli. He is an old friend and can be trusted emphatically."

Lydia joked, "Well if you can't trust a priest, who can you trust, Sepp?"

"You would be surprised how many clerics are spying for the Soviets. We have uncovered several agents within the walls of the Vatican. One cannot be too careful these days."

Peter knelt and embraced both of his children tightly, not wanting to ever let them go. "I love you both so very much. Berthold, you are the man of the house now, so I want you to look after Momma and Heidi."

"I will, Papa, I promise," the boy said.

Peter stood up and moved to a corner of the lounge and spoke softly to his wife, while Sepp kept the children occupied.

"Lydia, if I don't make it out of this alive, I want you to know that I love you and the children so very much. I have been an absolute fool all these years--like so many others, I was hypnotized by Hitler and followed him blindly. He has led the German people like the Pied Piper of Hamlin led rats."

Lydia was crying softly, dabbing her eyes with a handkerchief the children had given her for her last birthday. It even had her monogrammed initials on it.

"You must be strong for the children's sake, Lydia. What Sepp and I must do, well, it's bigger than all of us. When this war is over, and when we Germans are put on trial for the unspeakable crimes that we have committed, at least someone can point to the actions of the Bertram family, who tried to do what was right in the world. It will let the world know that not all Germans were bad or that they were fanatical Nazis."

He kissed his wife gently on the lips just as the terminal's public address system announced the boarding of their Stockholm flight. Based on their senior military status, the Bertram family boarded first. Lydia gave her brother-in-law a long hug, whispering in his ear, "Watch over him, Sepp, please."

"I will, Lydia. God be with you all." Sepp then hugged his niece and nephew and blessed them as they left the terminal. Sepp's gaze followed his family's short walk onto the tarmac and their ascending the steps into the aircraft.

With typical German punctuality, the stairs were rolled away from the aircraft at precisely 1400 hours and the plane's engines began turning. Within minutes, the engines had reached almost maximum RPMs and began to taxi down the runway and ready for takeoff.

Sepp and Peter stood by the window in the VIP lounge which faced the runway and within a minute the plane was airborne, winging its way to Sweden and freedom. Sepp placed his arm around his brother's shoulder, and said, "They'll be fine, Peter. The Nuncio will contact us by telex when they have arrived. You have done a very brave thing and I am so very proud of you."

Peter's mind drifted while he watched the plane vanish into the clouds and out of sight. He had crossed his Rubicon and was prepared to face the consequences, whatever they may be.

Reich Labor Office
Roosikrantsi 2
Reval, Estonia
Reichskommissariat Ostland
August 12, 1943, 1730 Hours

Karl, the Estonian policeman, headed towards the Reich Labor Office to meet with Comrade Punga to pass on Kessel's message to be forwarded up the chain of the Partisan command. Karl had served with the Estonian police force prior to the outbreak of the war in 1939 and had served during the brief Soviet occupation and annexation of his country from 1940-41. He had always sympathized with the communists, and once the Soviets occupied the country, he became a card-carrying member of the Communist Party. Being a Party member had its benefits--preferential jobs and pay as well as access to hard-to-find foodstuffs. With the Nazi invasion in 1941, Karl was about to flee with the occupying Red Army when he was ordered to stay behind and join the nascent Partisan network. Karl knew nothing about espionage or guerrilla warfare—his position in the police department afforded him accessibility to the occupier's security forces and their plans; Karl's position made him important in the eyes of the Communist Party and Moscow. For the past two years, Karl's professionalism impressed his superiors, earning him promotions as well as German decorations. Mohl and the other German officers trusted him and suspected nothing.

Karl walked into the Labor Office and found it mostly deserted. *Herr* Koening, the director, was in Berlin for a conference leaving Punga in charge until Koening's return. Karl quietly walked to the back of the building where Punga had his office. Knocking on the door, he entered.

"Comrade Punga," he said. "I have news from *Frau* Kessel—she has been arrested."

"Tatiana, arrested? When? Why?"

"She was brought in today by *Inspektor* Mohl of the *Kriminalpolizei* on suspicion of activities against the Reich."

"Did she tell you anything?"

"Tatiana asked me to tell you about the Bertram brother's mission. They are taking 100 Jews East by train towards Leningrad with hopes of getting to Sweden. This will take place within the next few days, no specific date given."

"That's all, Karl, are you sure?"

"Yes, Comrade Punga."

"She has cyanide, just in case, Karl?"

"Yes, I gave it to her myself. Also, Comrade Neilson in-processed her and made sure to 'overlook' the pill when searched."

"This inspector, Mohl, what is he like? A real thug, or what?"

"No, Comrade, he is unlike those Gestapo thugs we have seen. I think he is a different breed of policeman. He was a civilian cop in Germany before the war."

"Alright, keep me posted on Tatiana, and keep an eye on her at all times during your shift. If it looks like she is going to break, then you can terminate her."

"What do you mean terminate her, comrade?"

"Kill her, Karl. Tatiana will be useless to us and will jeopardize the mission if she talks. Comrade Stalin has taken a personal interest in this matter."

The invocation of Stalin's name injected fear into even the most dedicated communists. Karl's police uniform would offer him no protection from the wrath of the Soviet dictator, especially since he routinely ordered the execution of field marshals and generals. One lowly policeman added to the list would mean nothing.

"I serve the Soviet Union, Comrade Punga!"

"Good. Now be on your way, Karl, I have to contact Moscow with your update."

Reich Labor Office
Roosikrantsi 2
Reval, Estonia
Reichskommissariat Ostland
August 12, 1943, 1750 Hours

When Karl left the building, Punga quickly locked the door behind him and placed the 'Closed' sign in the door's window. The office would not re-open until 9:00 the next morning.

At Punga's disposal, he had a transmitter with enough range to contact Partisan Headquarters located deep inside the Soviet Union. The transmitter was hidden behind a false wall in the back of a supply closet that only he had access to; *Herr* Koening not wanting to bother with minor irritants such as office supplies - thus Punga was given the only key.

Now, Punga was alone and took his time to set up the radio and to encode the message to Moscow. He informed them that the Jewish prisoners would be heading East towards Leningrad within the next few days and that Partisan units should be given this information. Punga had also received another bit of information from a Party member who worked at the Reval railway station. This source had seen a German request for the *Sondertransport* but did not know the exact date it was needed, only that it be large enough to hold 100 plus passengers. Punga added this information as well. It took over an hour to encode and send out the message, then place the transmitter securely back to its hiding place. His job was now done - he had informed his higher command with the intelligence that they so desperately needed. Although incomplete, the leaders in Moscow could come to their own conclusions on what he sent them. Now he had to wait and see if the information he sent would be acted upon by the thousands of Partisans active against the Hitlerite invaders.

Headquarters, *Kriminalpolizei*
Hermann Goring Strasse 58
Reval, Estonia
Reichskommissariat Ostland
August 13, 1943, 0900 Hours

Mohl returned to the police headquarters promptly at 0900 hours and ordered *Frau Kessel* to be brought before him.

"Good morning, *Frau* Kessel, I hope you found your quarters acceptable under the circumstances."

Viktoria nodded her head affirmatively.

"I have some good news: *Frau,* you are free to leave. There was a mix-up with another woman fitting your description. On behalf of my office, I apologize for any inconvenience you may have experienced. *Frau* Nielson will return your personal items and you may leave."

Viktoria stood there dumbfounded; she had expected the worst but now she was being released, a simple case of mistaken identity, so she was told.

"Thank you, *Herr Inspektor*. I was treated well by your staff, no complaints on my part," she said forcing a weak smile.

The jail matron came in and handed her a bag with personal items which she signed for.

"Good day, *Herr Inspektor*," Viktoria said as she turned and left his office and then the building. She was relieved to be out of police custody and quickened her steps back to the Bertram villa. Her thoughts returned to working for the family so as to continue her mission.

She received a rude awakening when she arrived at the villa only to find it locked, with no sign of life whatsoever. She knocked on the front door, and receiving no answer, moved to the side of the house, knocking on the French doors and then moving on to the back door. All locked, and no sign of the family.

The partisan realized that her true identity may have been discovered, hence her arrest and detention so she began worrying. She immediately headed to the safe house to link up with Kuzin and inform him of what had transpired.

Viktoria found Kuzin sitting on a small sofa and drinking a glass of vodka, despite it being still morning.

"Tatiana! You are free!" Kuzin rejoiced, jumping up and hugging her tightly.

"I knew you had been detained, because the Estonian policeman, Karl, informed Punga, who then told me. I was worried sick, but thankfully you are alright. Did they hurt you?"

"No, they did not, I was well treated—I think however the Bertram family grew suspicious of me. When I went to the villa, no one was there. Everything locked up. I don't recall them saying they were going anywhere. What do you think this means?"

"I don't know, but at least you are safe. We will both talk to Punga later and see if they know anything more. But first, come here and let me hold you." They held each other close, for as the war had proven, you could be taken at a moment's notice. Like the millions of those caught in Hitler's snare during World War II, Viktoria and Kuzin vowed early on to live each day as it if were their last.

Chapter VII

"Whosoever saves a single life, saves an entire universe."
--Inscription on the Medal of the Righteous Among the Nations
Chassidei Umot HaOlam

Klooga Concentration Camp
Reval, Estonia
Reichskommissariat Ostland
August 14, 1943, 1045 Hours

SS Hauptsturmführer Willi Loss, the camp commandant was not happy to see *Gruppenführer* Peter Bertram's staff car drive through the camp's main gate.

"*Mein Gott in Himmel,* not Bertram again," he said to himself, but loud enough that his secretary heard him through his office door. Adjusting his tunic and grabbing his cap and pistol belt, Loss headed out to meet Bertram as the staff car pulled up to the front of his office building.

Loss opened the door for his superior and then saluted Bertram, "*Heil* Hitler!"

Peter returned the salute weakly and then motioned to Loss that they move inside to speak in private.

Moving into the office, Peter asked Loss to dismiss his secretary. Taking Peter's cue, Loss ordered his secretary to take an early two-hour lunch, which she gratefully accepted. With the building secure and with only two occupants, Peter and Loss could now get down to business.

"Loss, I want to thank you for doing a splendid job in preparing the camp for *Reichsführer* Himmler's upcoming visit. I know I was a bit rough on you and your men in the beginning, but I want to make it up to you and your men. Therefore, I am ordering you and your SS contingent to take a mandatory week's leave in Germany. I will take temporary command of the camp and take the necessary measures for a security force to guard it."

Loss was stunned by Peter's order - he was certainly happy at the prospect of returning to Germany, but something did not sound right. Why order the entire SS contingent to take mandatory leave, especially with Himmler's upcoming visit?

"*Herr Gruppenführer,* this is very kind of you to offer my men and I leave, but sir, if I may ask, isn't the timing off, especially in light of the *Reichsführer's* scheduled visit?"

Peter studied his subordinate carefully—Loss was no fool; he suspect-ed something. Any SS man or soldier with a pulse would jump at the chance to take home leave, especially if he was serving on the Eastern Front, and at a concentration camp.

"Loss, I appreciate your dedication to duty, but those are my orders, understood? Go home, enjoy yourself, and come back rested and ready to tackle the challenges that lay ahead for all of us."

"Sir, may I ask what unit will be replacing my men and I?"

"I have arranged with the commander of a nearby unit to send a de-tachment to guard the camp," Peter answered.

Loss knew that there were no other SS formations close by and asked, "Are regular *Wehrmacht* troops going to be guarding the camp?"

Peter answered in the affirmative, adding, "Don't worry, Loss, I have requested that only good National Socialists be given the honor of guarding the camp."

Loss was not happy with his superior's response but there was nothing he could do but to comply.

"Your leaves start at midnight tonight. I have arranged transportation for you and your men to the railway and secured passage for you and your men on the *Reichsbahn*. Enjoy yourself, Loss, you have earned it." He then shook his subordinate's hand and told him to inform his men of the decision.

"You and your men are to be ready to leave at 2000 hours tonight--the unit relieving you will have Opel Blitzes to take you and your men to the station. Good luck and safe travels."

With that, Peter left the office and headed straight to his staff car, where his driver had been waiting. Once seated, the staff car left the camp and went back to Peter's villa. He could only hope and pray that Loss would take his orders like a good SS man should and clear out of the camp by the appointed hour. What Loss did not know was that the unit relieving he and his men were troops of the 517th Medical Battalion, most who would unknowingly help facilitate the escape of the camp prisoners.

Klooga Concentration Camp
Reval, Estonia
Reichskommissariat Ostland
August 14, 1943, 2000 hours

Four Opel Blitz trucks of the 517th Medical Battalion rolled into the camp carrying personnel who would relieve the SS from their duties at the camp. This of course was highly irregular as the regular German Army did not guard concentration camps - that was the purview of the SS alone. The *Wehr-*

macht did assist the SS at times in roundups and cordoning off villages so that the SS and other security forces could go about their dirty work, but to guard a concentration camp was simply unheard of.

The trucks were led by a staff car containing the 517th's commander, *Oberst* Weber and his driver. Weber had been fully briefed on the plan and his role and those of his men were key to the success of the mission.

Peter had arrived earlier to ensure that Loss and his 20-man contingent were preparing to leave. Peter worried that Loss could be a problem and was prepared to go to extremes in making sure he was not present when the operation began, to the point of killing Loss if the situation arose.

As the small convoy of vehicles pulled up in front of Loss's administration building, Weber's vehicle came to a halt, and Loss opened the door for the *Wehrmacht* colonel.

"*Heil* Hitler!" Loss shouted, raising his right arm in the Nazi stiff-armed salute.

Weber, while not a Nazi, played the part to the hilt and dramatically returned the salute as well as giving his own salute to Peter, who realized at that moment just how good an actor the medical officer was.

After some brief introductions and last-minute wishes for a safe travel back to the Fatherland, Loss's troops boarded the now empty Opels, having disgorged the replacement troops and their equipment. Loss rode in the cab of the lead Opel as the vehicles left the camp headed to the local railway station which served the community. With any luck, within 24-hours, all the men would be back in Germany enjoying their leaves.

No sooner had the last truck passed through the gates when another vehicle drove in carrying Sepp Bertram. The vehicle pulled up to the administration building and Sepp exited the vehicle. He greeted Weber and Peter warmly and the three men entered the building and into Loss's office. Peter had taken the additional step of giving Loss's secretary the week off, with pay, which made her very happy. Weber also gave orders to his senior noncommissioned officer to post his guards in order to ensure that operations appeared to be normal. The Bertram brothers and Weber could now plan and carry out their operation with no fear of outside interference - or so it was hoped.

As the three men settled into their seats, Peter was the first to speak.

"*Oberst*, thank you for getting the men here on time—absolutely flawless," Peter said with a smile.

"Thank you, *Gruppenführer.* We will have to act quickly of course. The train will be at the station at 0200 hours, so we can carry out everything under the cover of darkness. The personnel I have with me are anti-Nazi. Once we get to the station you will be joined by some of my nurses who volunteered to accompany your precious cargo."

Sepp was the next to speak up. "Thank you, *Herr Oberst*, for all that you have done. Now, let's talk about these prisoners. They have no idea of what is going on. They all still believe they are under sentence of death. We need to tell them that we are here to get them to safety. Peter, if you would lead the way to the barracks, we can talk to the senior prisoner."

Peter responded, "The prisoners had elected a rabbi as their spokesman in dealing with the camp administration. His name is Menachim Abramovitz and he oversaw one of the local *Yeshivas*[63] up until the time of the invasion in '41. He's an old man, probably close to 70, and of course well-respected by the Jews. Sepp, I think it will be best if you talk to him initially; he probably would not believe a word I said and would think we are leading them into some sort of trap."

"Yes, it may be best if another clergyman speaks to him—although I don't know how much these Eastern Jews will trust Catholics—the history between Jews and Catholics up until this point has not been the best. They are of course, 'the Christ-killers.'"

With that, all three men walked over to the barracks where the prisoners were held. The Jewish prisoners here were not like their brethren in some of the more notorious camps throughout the Reich. Additionally, these were 'special prisoners' who were to be human guinea pigs for the pleasure of the *Reichsführer SS*. Because of their special status, they were well-fed and not mistreated as were other camp prisoners.

Peter was the first to enter the men's barrack. The first prisoner to see him called the room to attention. "*Achtung!*" All the prisoners jumped to attention and lined up in front of their bunks. Unlike most prisoners, they were permitted to keep their civilian clothing, and could forego the striped prison uniforms worn by most concentration camp inmates.

Peter walked up directly to Rabbi Abramovitz. "Come with me," he ordered.

The rabbi slowly followed Peter out of the barrack. The other prisoners, noticing Sepp in his clerical garb standing in the background began to murmur in Yiddish, "Iz *az a katholik galekh?*" (Is that a Catholic priest?)

The prisoners feared the worst for their beloved rabbi, but there was little they could do. After the men left, the prisoners settled down once again, awaiting their own fates along with the sound of pistol shots, which to their relief, never came.

The four men walked back to the administration building and into a small conference room off to the side of Loss's office.

"Please sit down, Rabbi Abramovitz," Peter said in a gentle tone. "I would like to introduce you to *Oberst* Weber, commander of the 517th Medical Battalion, and my brother, Monsignor Josef Bertram of the Vatican Foreign Office."

Abramovitz could only stare dumbfounded at the trio standing before him—a priest, a *Wehrmacht* colonel, and a senior SS officer, whom only days before, was planning his murder.

"I, I don't understand," Abramovitz stammered, his knees shaking.

Sepp then took over the meeting. "Rabbi, we are here to get you and your flock to safety. *Oberst* Weber and his men will supply you and your people German uniforms and nurses' uniforms for the women. We will then put you on a train heading East with the hope of getting you to neutral Sweden. This trip is fraught with danger, for all of us," he said, gesticulating with his hand. We have purposely gotten rid of the SS contingent guarding you and replaced them with regular troops, many who are anti-Nazi and are willing to help. You are now under the protection of the *Wehrmacht*."

Sepp thought about what he had just said--to these Jews, there really was no difference between the SS and regular Army, both were symbols of tyranny and death.

Abramovitz could just stare at Sepp in utter amazement. Then he spoke.

"Monsignor, I thank you for your explanation, however I find this very hard to believe that you three are our saviors, especially you," as he pointed to Peter.

Regaining his nerve, the rabbi continued. "You, *Gruppenführer,* stand before me and expect me now to believe that you have had a change of heart, that you are now a friend to the Jews?"

Peter could not answer because he knew the rabbi was correct. He had a conversion and while he may not have become and instant friend to the Chosen People, he realized that Hitler's genocide was sheer insanity.

Sepp then stepped in. "Rabbi, you have to believe me when I tell you that my brother has undergone a conversion, much like Paul on his way to Damascus. He has put his life and that of his family in jeopardy, as has *Oberst* Weber, whose wife, by the way, is Jewish."

Abramovitz looked at Weber with shock, and Weber nodded in silent agreement to Sepp's revelation.

The rabbi then asked, "What do you want me to do?"

Sepp answered, "We will go back to the barracks, and you will tell your flock on what we plan on doing. We leave tonight. Take what little in the way of clothing and toiletries, you will be traveling light. We will provide you with food, mainly soldier's rations and water. You may be hesitant to wear German uniforms and we can understand your reluctance, but it is part of the ruse and we need to fool as many of the authorities as we can. The uniforms will help facilitate that. The soldiers driving you to the station tonight will not harm you, so tell your people not to worry. I will be traveling with you, as well as with a couple of *Oberst* Weber's officers."

Sepp continued, "The trip is not without its dangers. Partisans regularly attack the rail lines, and because of the secrecy of this mission, we did not want the 221st Security Division [64]personnel accompanying the train. A few of *Oberst* Weber's men have volunteered to accompany the train, but they are not infantrymen, just mainly medical personnel and clerks. Yet, they too want to see you free and have put aside their own personal safety to accompany the transport."

The rabbi could only nod and offer a brief smile. He still was unsure that this whole ruse was nothing, but an elaborate trap set by the Germans, something that they had excelled in so as to let their victims' guard down and put them at ease.

Taking a slight bow, the rabbi said, "Very well, gentlemen, our lives are in your hands."

Sepp then said, "You and your people have been given a reprieve on life. As God is my witness, I will die trying to ensure you make your way to freedom."

The four men, led by Sepp, then left the conference room for the barracks where the rabbi would have to persuade his people that a rescue operation was being put into effect in order that they may live.

Klooga Concentration Camp
Reval, Estonia
Reichskommissariat Ostland
August 14, 1943, 2030 Hours

Rabbi Abramovitz had a tough time convincing the other 99 prisoners of the Germans' sincerity in rescuing them from the camp. Heated debate arose among the prisoners, and they raised good questions, such as "Is that really a Catholic priest with them or a disguise?" or "This is just another German trick to get us on the train without fighting back, the same way they emptied the ghettos at the beginning of the war."

The rabbi heard them out and then said, "Look, the SS men have been removed and replaced with soldiers from a medical unit no less! Why would they give us German military uniforms to wear? Have you ever heard of such a thing? No, my children, I believe these men want to help. If we stay here, we know we die; if we leave then there is a chance we live. I say we take that chance."

One of the younger men, a man named Zimmerman, shouted, "I say we fight!"

"With what?" asked the rabbi. "We have no weapons. Don't be a fool, Efram, you cannot fight Goliath this time."

The other prisoners murmured their agreement to the rabbi's retort.

"Rabbi, we will follow you and do as you ask. We are all in this together. It beats waiting around like sheep for the slaughter for that pig, Himmler," said a voice from the back of the barrack. Again, the group all murmured their agreement.

The door to the barrack was opened and three *Wehrmacht* soldiers stood in the entrance. This made the group automatically step back in fear, a sign of a people who have been terrorized for far too long. However, to the surprise of the prisoners, they saw that the soldiers were unarmed, and instead, carried large boxes filled with German military and nurses' uniforms. Two more soldiers then entered and carried with them boxes of boots and shoes.

The noncommissioned officer-in-charge, a sergeant by the name of Strauss, then spoke, "In these boxes you will find uniforms and footwear of various sizes. Try them on. They do not have to be a perfect fit but try and find one that comes as close as possible. We will be leaving the camp at one AM, so please be ready. One of my men will be bringing you food and water shortly, so eat up." With that, Strauss and his men exited the building and left the prisoners to their own devices.

Klooga Concentration Camp
Reval, Estonia
Reichskommissariat Ostland
August 15, 1943, 0100 hours

After receiving confirmation that Loss and his men had boarded their train and left the station at midnight, ten Opel trucks left the camp on time for the 5-kilometer drive to the railway station, where a special train, a *Sonder-transport,* which had been requisitioned by the 517th Medical Battalion, awaited them. The drive down the dark narrow roads frightened the prisoners, who had not been outside the camp wire for over six months. The fear of the unknown gripped them as it did the Bertram brothers, Weber, and all the others that had been so involved in this operation. They knew the consequences for failure - instant death or languishing in a concentration camp.

As the small convoy drew closer to the station, those who could, were able to make out the silhouette of a locomotive and a number of cars - not box cars, but regular passenger cars with real seats! Due to wartime blackout regulations, the station was surrounded by complete darkness, with only a small red glow coming from the train engineer's control panel. Because of his age and position among the prisoners, Rabbi Abramovitz was driven to the station in Peter's staff car, along with Sepp. Sepp could only imagine what was going through the rabbi's mind. *A trick of some sort? Are we really going to live?* Sepp hoped he would never have those types of thoughts, as it sent a momentary chill down his spine.

The convoy halted in front of the station - it was now 0130 hours, only 30 more minutes before the train departed on its treacherous journey. The soldiers dropped the back ramp of the trucks and assisted the prisoners down, showing a great deal of care and compassion as they did so. Meeting the convoy at the station were Weber's subordinates *Oberleutnant* Roper and *Hauptmann* Fritz as well as four civilian female nurses from the unit. Both officers saluted Weber and Peter Bertram, who then returned the salutes.

Weber then gave the order to Sergeant Strauss to get the prisoners on the train and get them as comfortable as possible. While this was being done, Weber, the Bertrams', Fritz and Roper, moved to the side of the darkened station to talk, out of earshot of the others.

Peter spoke first. "Gentlemen, I cannot thank you enough for what you have accomplished in such short time, it is indeed a miracle. Unfortunately, no medals can ever be given for what we are about to do—I just hope that this will show future generations that in such times, there were a few good Germans still left, who did the right thing. I will not be accompanying you on this journey, I have some accounts to settle in Berlin."

Turning to his brother, Peter said, "Sepp, I have some unfinished business in Berlin. Don't argue, please. This is something that I must do, to clear my conscience and to make amends. If I don't make it out alive, please take care of my family - they are *your family* as well, I hope you realize that. I want to also say that I am so sorry that we have been estranged for so long. You being here has brought me back from the abyss and to the man I once was."

Peter then just said one word, "Himmler."

"What?" Sepp asked.

"Himmler is responsible for the death of our parents; I am sure of it. And Himmler must pay."

"Peter, you can't be serious. Himmler is as heavily guarded as Hitler, if not more."

"Don't worry about me, Sepp. I know my way around *Prinz-Albrecht-Strasse* 8 very well. I will get to him. Trust me." With that, he held out his hand to his brother, who took it, grasping it with both hands.

"God be with you, Peter."

"And you as well, Sepp."

Peter then shook hands with Weber, Roper, and Fritz and again thanked them for their work and wished them luck.

Sepp said his good-byes to Weber, who was also staying behind to face whatever consequences would come his way.

"Good luck, Monsignor, "Weber said, "And God be with you."

Weber then said his good-byes to his subordinates, realizing he would probably never see these two brave young officers again. A final salute and he turned and walked back to his staff car.

"We need to board the train now, Monsignor, if you please," said Fritz, gesturing toward the train. Fritz would be the train commander for the trip.

Prior to their departure, Peter gave Sepp a letter of authorization, signed by himself as HSSPF, in the event they ran into any difficulties with the *Feldgendarme* or other security forces.

At exactly 0200 hours, the train slowly pulled out of Reval station and headed East into the vastness of Russia, as it made its way slowly down the dark tracks and into the darkness that was the night.

12th Partisan Brigade
near Ropscha, Russia
August 15, 1943, 0530 Hours

The 12th Partisan Brigade was led by a Red Army colonel, Vasilii Kozlov, who had been in charge of the unit since late 1942, when he was parachuted into the area to take control of the growing Partisan network in that region. Kozlov, a Jew, had been placed in command of a predominantly Jewish Partisan unit. Many of its members had escaped capture or from ghettos or concentration camps run by the Germans and their collaborators. A few of the Partisans were Red Army soldiers, such as himself, who had been cut off from their units in the early days of the Nazi invasion and had taken to the forests and swamps to carry on the fight against the German invaders. The unit had one of the highest success rates in the field, having killed countless hundreds of enemy soldiers since its formation.

"Comrade Colonel Kozlov," the radio operator called out, "We have a message from Moscow." Handing the deciphered message to his commander, Kozlov took the message and read it carefully, his lips moving silently as he read the text.

Each Partisan brigade had within it an intelligence section, and Kozlov needed to talk with his intelligence chief, Captain Ivan Denisov, concerning the recent message. The brigade was bivouacked in a heavily forested and marshy area a few kilometers from a major road junction and a rail line, from which they would sortie to attack German convoys and troop trains and quickly disappear back into the forests and swamps. The Germans were loath to pursue them once they entered those areas.

Finding his intelligence chief pouring over some area maps, Kozlov called out, "Captain Denisov!"

"Yes, Comrade Colonel," Denisov answered. Kozlov liked the young officer—he was a regular Red Army soldier such as himself, and a Jew as well. Both men had seen a lot of fighting since June 1941 and were lucky to still be alive in 1943.

"Ivan Mikhailovich, I just received this from Moscow. What do you make of it?" he said as he handed the message to Denisov.

The young officer began reading and as he did, Kozlov could see the expression on Denisov's face change and his eyes widened.

"Well, what do you think?" asked the colonel.

"I serve the Soviet Union!" was Denisov's reply, which was a safe answer to give to a senior officer.

"I would expect that response from a cadet at the Frunze Military Academy, Ivan Mikhailovich. Now give me your gut answer. Should we carry out this order?"

While both officers were card-carrying members of the Communist Party of the Soviet Union, they were not big supporters of Stalin, as both had family members who disappeared during the Great Terror of the late 1930s.

"Comrade Colonel, the message states that we are to attack and destroy a train carrying Jews along with their German escort. I don't understand. Aren't the Germans trying to annihilate the Jews here and elsewhere in Europe. The message states that Germans are trying to get these Jews to safety. What do we do?"

"Ivan Mikhailovich, the workings inside the Kremlin are daunting, and I don't profess to understand what makes Comrade Stalin tick. Let me tell you a little story. About two years ago, Comrade Stalin ordered the execution of two very highly respected Polish Jews - Genrikh Erlich and Viktor Alter. Have you ever heard of them?"

"No, Comrade Colonel, I have not."

"Well, both men were members of the Socialist League of Warsaw and were arrested by the NKVD and accused of pro-German activities, including appeals to Soviet troops to stop bloodshed and conclude a peace with Germany. Now, mind you, that these two men are old revolutionaries—Erlich was a representative at the Petrograd Soviet Workers and Soldiers Deputies way back in 1917. You must wonder why a dedicated socialist, revolutionary, and Jew would be accused of being pro-Hitler. It makes no sense whatsoever. I happen to know through some contacts that before their arrest, both he and Alter were trying to create a world association of Jewish figures, such as Albert Einstein and other prominent Jews, to combat Nazism, sort of a Jewish Anti-Hitler Committee. In other words, Ivan Mikhailovich, they were trying to save Jews like us from the likes of Hitler and his henchmen, so that you and I and our children could live in a better world."

The young captain could only nod his head in agreement to what his commander was saying.

"So now, my young friend, we are faced with a bit of a quandary. If we follow orders, we attack the train, no doubt kill some Germans, but also wind up killing the Jews on that train, whom, if it is to be believed, are on their way to freedom from this madness."

Denisov then asked, "Comrade Colonel, what about Commissar Popov?"

"Ah, yes, Comrade Popov, political commissar, here to keep us all on the straight and narrow and making sure we are all good communists," Kozlov answered with a slight chuckle.

Kozlov continued, "Comrade Popov has not seen the message yet as the radioman gave me the message directly after deciphering it. He is not to know of this, Ivan Mikhailovich, is that understood?"

"Yes, Comrade Colonel, it is understood."

"We may not survive this war, you and I, but at least the Jews on that train have a fighting chance at freedom and survival. I am not going to be the one to stop them. We do not attack the train." With that, Kozlov patted his subordinate on the shoulder, turned and walked back to his command post, deep in thought, and half-wishing that he too, was on that train to freedom.

12th Partisan Brigade
near Ropscha, Russia
August 16, 1943, 1100 Hours

As the German *Sondertransport* made its way East, it finally came into view to the Partisan brigade's forward observation/listening post that had been set up near the rail line. The forward observer then contacted Kozlov by radio. "Comrade Colonel, a troop train has been spotted, what are your orders?"

Kozlov knew this had to be the train with the refugees, as he had received further information from Moscow and the Partisan network of the train's number, length of cars, and its timetable, which would place it at his exact location now.

"Hold your fire, I repeat, hold your fire."

"Message received, Comrade Colonel."

With that Kozlov took a deep breath and hoped that by doing nothing to stop the train, the passengers stood a better chance of making their way to freedom. That wasn't to say that another Partisan unit down the line wouldn't attack the train. But Kozlov intended to radio Moscow to inform them that the train had in fact been destroyed and no survivors were reported. The only thing that would stand in his way was the political commissar, Sergei Popov, a ruthless and dedicated Communist. Popov was a humorless individual and not at all well-liked by the men of the brigade. In the Red Army, attack orders had to be co-signed by both the military commander and the commissar, and Kozlov knew that Popov would never agree to allow the troop train to pass uninhibited. For the past few days Popov had been ill, suffering from dysentery and running a high fever, almost delirious at times. He was unaware of the message from Moscow ordering the train's destruction, and that had made Kozlov's decision much easier. However, Popov had been on the mend in the last 12 hours and was up and talking. As Kozlov made his way down the forest path that led to the Partisan headquarters bunker complex, he saw the radio operator leaving the bunker. Kozlov feared that the radioman had told the commissar of the message from Moscow. To his horror, as Kozlov neared the bunker's entrance, he saw Popov, still weak and clinging to the sides of the logs that reinforced the bunker, make his way out.

"Comrade Colonel," Popov yelled, "What is this I hear of orders to attack a Hitlerite troop train? Has it been done? I need details for my report."

Knowing that what he would say next would be considered an act of treason and possibly end with him in front of a firing squad, Kozlov eased into the conversation slowly.

"Comrade Popov, so good to see that you are feeling better. You had us all concerned,"

"Never mind me," he said with the wave of a hand, "What is the status of the train?"

"The train will not be destroyed on my orders. There are 100 Jews on that train hopefully on their way to freedom. Don't ask me how or why the Germans want to save them, but they are, and I am not going to stop them, and neither are you, Comrade."

Popov was incensed at what he heard. "This is treason, I will have your shot!" Automatically reaching for his pistol, Popov realized that his pistol belt was laying on a cot inside the bunker; still weak from the effects of his illness, he had not bothered to strap it on when he left.

Kozlov then drew his own pistol and leveled it at the commissar. "I am very sorry, Comrade Popov, but this is one military action that you do not get to decide on. Keep quiet and move deeper into the woods."

As both men moved further away from the Partisan encampment, Kozlov realized that he would have to kill the commissar in order to save himself and his men, as well as those on the troop train. For his part, Popov realized that this was the end of the line for him—ironically killed by his own side rather than the Germans.[65]

After walking approximately ½ of a mile away from the camp, Kozlov ordered a halt.

"I am sorry, Comrade Popov, I really am. Do you have any last words?"

"You will never get away with this Kozlov, Comrade Stalin will find out and you will be in the Lubyanka at the hands of the NKVD, who don't treat traitors to the Motherland too kindly. So, go ahead and shoot me, there will be more commissars that follow me. Long live Comrade Stalin and the Soviet Union! Death to traitors! Death to Spies!"

With that, Kozlov fired once, striking the commissar in the chest, killing him instantly. He left Popov's body where it fell, under a large fir tree. He then holstered his weapon and slowly made his way back to the camp. In the distance he could hear a train pass. Looking at his watch, it read 11:23, and he knew it was the troop train. He said a silent prayer in Hebrew, asking God to protect the passengers on the train from any harm and to get them to safety.

The train passengers would never know just how close they came to being killed, if not for the courage of one Red Army colonel, who, defying orders and at the risk of his own life, ensured that they would live to see another day.

The Kremlin
Moscow, Russia
August 17, 1943, 1830 Hours

Both General Ponomarenko and Foreign Minister Molotov met with Stalin in the Soviet leader's office.

"Comrade Stalin, we have received confirmation from the 12th Partisan Brigade that the train with the *Zhyds* has been destroyed! Here is the report."

Stalin, puffing on his ever-present Dunhill pipe, took the report from his Partisan general and began to read.

"So, this happened yesterday morning, eh?"

"Yes, Comrade Stalin, near Ropscha. The 12th Partisan Brigade has had great success against the Hitlerite invaders these last couple of years," he said with pride.

"Hmm, yes, I see. I hear nothing but good things about this brigade commander, Kozlov. For a Jew, he is quite the warrior," Stalin said with a chuckle.

"Josef Vissarionovich, now that the train has been stopped, we no longer have to worry about a possible propaganda coup by the Hitlerites or worse yet, the Western Allies. If they had successfully escaped with the help of the Germans and word got out, it would put us on the defensive once again, as it did with the Katyn affair back in April."

Stalin could only nod as he continued to puff on his pipe.

"Vyacheslav Mikhaylovich, let us ensure that nothing like that happens again."

"Yes, Josef Vissarionovich, I can assure you it will not."

Stalin turned to his Partisan chief and said, "Good job, Ponomarenko and pass along my personal thanks to Kozlov and his men."

"Thank you, Comrade Stalin, I know it will be a great honor for them to receive your message."

"Yes, yes, Ponomarenko, now leave us; Comrade Molotov and I have things to discuss."

Thus, with the wave of the *Vozhd's* hand, the chief of Soviet Partisans had been dismissed like a lowly private from Stalin's presence.

Chapter VIII

"The evil that men do lives after them;/The good is oft interred with their bones."
--Shakespeare, *Julius Caesar*

Headquarters
250ᵗʰ Infantry Division
Krasny Bor, Russia
August 18, 1943, 1545 Hours

After three days of travel, the train slowly made its way towards the Leningrad Front; in the process, it passed through a myriad of German units strung out all along the Northern Front. Sepp Bertram had informed the train commander, *Hauptmann* Wilhelm Fritz, that their destination was the lines of the 250ᵗʰ Infantry Division of the German *Wehrmacht*. This was not a German unit at all, but a division made up entirely of Spaniards who had volunteered to fight the Bolsheviks alongside Germany on the Eastern Front. The 250ᵗʰ was in fact the famed Spanish "Blue Division,[66]" which had joined the war effort in the fall of 1941 and had been fighting in the Leningrad sector now for almost two years. The division had distinguished itself in the fight against the Bolsheviks, and its division commander, General Augustin Muñoz Grandes, was one of the few foreign officers serving in the *Wehrmacht* to be awarded the Knight's Cross personally by the *Führer*. But now, with Germany's military fortunes waning, the Spanish dictator, *Generalissimo* Francisco Franco, was beginning to bend under Allied pressure to divest himself from aiding Germany. Franco was also under pressure by his inner circle to open negotiations with the Germans for the withdrawal of the division along with a small aviation unit that had been sent to Russia as well. The Spaniards, being overwhelmingly Roman Catholic, had with them their own military chaplains.[67] One of them, *Padre* Jamie Garcia, was an old friend of Sepp's, and it was he whom Sepp would seek out in the hopes of assistance in getting the prisoners to the Finnish lines. The Spaniards, much like the Finns, had no recent history of anti-Semitism that was then so prevalent in Germany and in Central and Eastern Europe. In some instances, Spanish officers had intervened and given protection to Russian Jews escaping roundups and had refused to hand them over to the SS, causing some tense moments where supposed allies had threatened to open fire upon one another.[68] The German Foreign Ministry had filed diplomatic protests to their counterparts in Madrid, but to no avail. The Spanish Foreign Minister at the time, the pro-Allied Francisco Garcia Jordana

Y Souza had recently replaced the pro-fascist Ramon Serrano Suñer, who also happened to be Franco's brother-in-law (*cuñadisimo* or supreme brother-in-law), so the protests basically fell on deaf ears at the direction of *El Caudillo* himself.[69]

As the train slowly made its way toward the Leningrad sector, Sepp was able to see first-hand the carnage of the past two years of fighting in the East. Rusting tanks and other vehicles lay off in fields where they had been destroyed, marring an otherwise beautiful landscape. Nonetheless, signs began to appear showing that they were nearing their destination. The train halted at the Krasny Bor[70] station which was approximately three kilometers from the Spanish division's main headquarters. The train commander went back to the car where Sepp was seated and told him they were at their destination.

"We are here, Monsignor."

"Yes, thank you *Herr Hauptman*, I can see by the station sign, we have arrived," replied the cleric as he pointed to the station sign which was written in German, Spanish and Cyrillic.

As they both looked out the window, they could see both German and Spanish troops milling about, smoking and joking as all soldiers tended to do. While they did not notice any uniformed SS or Gestapo personnel on the platform, they did notice a couple of uniformed German military policemen, their distinctive silver gorgets around their neck, which gave rise to their popular nickname amongst the troops as *Kettenhunds* ("Chain Dogs").

"They could give us some trouble," the captain said.

Sure enough, no sooner had the captain spoken those words then the two military policemen boarded the train asking to see papers.

The captain hoped the plan they had rehearsed would work. If not, it would be a firing squad for the whole lot of them.

The captain met the two soldiers as they entered the car.

"*Heil* Hitler," they both said in unison.

"*Heil* Hitler," replied the captain.

"I am *Hauptman* Wilhelm Fritz, the train commander. In the train cars behind me are troops and their nurses, along with members of the International Red Cross. Some of the troops have infectious diseases. The cars are quarantined."

When the two military policemen heard 'quarantine' a look of apprehension fell on both their faces."

"What type of diseases do they have, *Herr Hauptman*?" asked the older of the two soldiers. He continued, "I am just curious to know as I was a medical school student until a year ago and was drafted. Instead of a medical unit, they placed me in a military police unit. Just like the army to screw up," he chuckled.

"Well, corporal, you probably heard that at Stalingrad, the Ivan's used biological warfare on our troops. There were reported outbreaks of tularemia[71], which as you know, is carried by rodents, mainly mice and rats."

The corporal nodded in agreement at the captain's comments.

Fritz continued, "Well, there have been other outbreaks here in the East, and the cars behind me are loaded with men who are suffering from it. Their nurses have volunteered to accompany them. Fortunately, the nurses and Red Cross workers were inoculated, so there is no chance in them catching this horrible epidemic.

Both soldiers nodded in unison.

"I have here a list with the soldiers, nurses, and civilian Red Cross personnel that are in the cars behind me. You may check it if you like. You will also see that the letter of authorization is signed by SS *Gruppenführer* Peter Bertram."

"And the priest?" the older soldier nodded in Sepp's direction.

"That priest, corporal, is Monsignor Sepp Bertram, brother of the SS officer whose signature appears on this letter of authorization, and also, I may add, a diplomat of the Holy See who is here on official business with the Reich."

Seeing that he was in way above his head in dealing with diplomats and authorizations signed by a senior SS general, the young corporal returned the authorization letter to *Hauptman* Fritz.

"Thank you, *Herr Hauptman*, we are very sorry to have inconvenienced you."

"You are just doing your duty men; no apologies are necessary. If I may ask a favor, please? As I must stay on the train with the patients, would you be so kind as to escort the good monsignor over to the Spanish headquarters, I understand we are only a few kilometers away from them. The monsignor is trying to find an old friend, a Spanish priest who is now serving as a military chaplain. I am also assuming you have transportation at your disposal?"

The older soldier answered, "Yes, sir, we do, and we will be more than happy to escort the monsignor to the Spaniards." Looking over at Sepp, the trooper said, "Monsignor, if you are ready?"

Sepp got out of his seat and headed toward the train exit. He turned to Fritz and said, "Thank you, *Herr Hauptman*, a job well done," and with it, a wink, showing that they had gotten away with their cover story so far.

As Sepp and the two military policemen climbed down the steps of the train, Fritz let out a sigh of relief. While it wasn't a 'close call,' he could have slipped up if the policemen had conducted a more thorough line of questioning or scrutinized the paperwork more closely. He might not be so lucky the next time around, he thought to himself.

Headquarters
250ᵗʰ Infantry Division
Division Chaplain's Office
Krasny Bor, Russia
August 18, 1943, 1615 Hours

Sepp was escorted to the building housing the 250ᵗʰ Infantry Division chaplains. He bid his two German escorts good-bye and entered the building, which, before the war, had been a two-story wooden schoolhouse. It was still relatively intact and showed little signs of damage despite the heavy fighting that had occurred in the area over the last two years. As he entered the building, a young Spanish NCO seated at a desk by the entrance, jumped up and in Spanish stated, *"Buenos Dias, Padre, necisita ayudar?"*

Sepp, who not only spoke his native German but also English, French and Spanish, replied, *"Sí, yo busco por Padre Garcia."*

"Sí, Padre, uno momento, por favor."

As the NCO left the office to find Chaplain Garcia, Sepp looked around the small office and was amazed at the number of religious artifacts that were exhibited. Crucifixes, small statues of the Virgin Mary and Christ adorned the office. A German military chaplain's office might have a crucifix and nothing more, owing to the unofficial atheistic policy of the Third Reich. He also couldn't help but notice three prominent portraits hanging above him; one of the Holy Father, Pope Pius XII, and hanging on either side of the pontiff's image were portraits of Franco and Hitler. The first thing that came to Sepp's mind about these three images was Christ between two thieves at the crucifixion. He let out a small chuckle at the very thought.

Sepp's concentration was broken when he heard the door behind him open and there stood his old friend, Father Jaime Garcia, now commissioned a Major in the German Army.

"Sepp, you old dog!" Garcia shouted as he embraced Sepp in a bear hug and lifted him off the floor. Garcia was a big man, well over six feet, and almost filled the room.

"It's good to see you *mí amigo*," Garcia said, as he put Sepp down.

"You too, Jaime, it's been a long time. Let's see, the last time we saw each other was in Rome, back in '38, wasn't it?"

"The Monsignor has a good memory. Yes, Easter 1938 to be exact. And now look at you, a monsignor and a *muy importante* member of the Vatican Foreign Office! I've been following your career very closely, Sepp, you should be very proud of your accomplishments. I know I am."

"You haven't done too badly yourself, Jaime. I understand you are very close to *El Caudillo* himself, and was for a while, his personal chaplain.

True?"

"Very true, *amigo*. I had the honor of serving as the *Generalissimo*'s confessor and would say daily Mass in his private chapel at El Pardo Palace. Franco is a remarkable man, Sepp, he smashed Bolshevism in Spain, and hopes to help Germany defeat the Reds right here on their own turf. That's why we *divisionarios* are here."

"Jaime, I have a very delicate issue I would like to discuss with you; is there a place we can speak in private?"

"Of course, *amigo*, let's go upstairs, and we can talk without being disturbed."

As both clergymen climbed the stairs to Chaplain Garcia's second floor office, off in the distance firing could be heard.

"We've had some minor problems with Partisans, Sepp, but nothing too serious. Our boys have given a good account of themselves against the Reds. We even rescued several German units that found themselves surrounded. And to think, no German general wanted us when we first arrived in '41. I guess they are whistling a different tune now, aren't they, Sepp?"

"I heard that your general, Muñoz Grandes even received the Knight's Cross from the *Führer* himself. I guess the OKW[72] and the *Führer* are duly impressed!"[73] he said with a chuckle.

When they reached Garcia's office, a young corporal, who served as the chaplain's administrative assistant, came to attention.

"Sepp, may I present to you my assistant, Corporal Miguel Suarez. He does a very good job of keeping me out of trouble and may I add, he was recently nominated for the Iron Cross, First Class, for bravery under fire."

Sepp extended his hand to the young corporal, who shook it vigorously.

"*Con mucho gusto, Padre*," Suarez said.

"Miguel, Monsignor Bertram and I need to discuss something in private; would you mind giving us some time alone?"

"*Sí, Padre*," and with that Suarez gathered up his helmet and weapon and silently exited the office.

"A heck of a soldier, Sepp. You know, he saved my life, that's why I put him in for the Iron Cross—I wrote up the nomination myself. I hope he gets it."

"I'm sure he will, Jaime."

Settling down into two chairs opposite each other, Garcia asked, "So, what is it that you wanted to talk to me about, Sepp?"

"Jaime, I have a very big favor to ask of you. What I am about to tell you is for me, treasonous and I could be shot." He let that statement sink in for a moment.

"Go on, Sepp, you now have my full and undivided attention."

"The train I arrived on earlier today has 100 Jewish prisoners on it. They are escapees from a concentration camp in Estonia. My brother *Gruppenführer* Peter Bertram and I have facilitated their escape. We are trying to get them to Finland, and once there, on to Sweden and safety."

For a moment, Garcia sat staring at his friend, almost as if he were looking straight through him. He then stammered, "You…you, you have got to be insane, Sepp. If you are found out, you'd be shot by the Gestapo…that collar you are wearing won't mean anything to them. And you say your brother is involved as well?"

"Correct. The Holy Father has entrusted me in saving these peoples' lives. I don't know how I did it, but I finally persuaded my brother that what he was doing was wrong. He seems like a changed man now and is putting his life and that of his family on the line in order to pull this off. What we will need is Spanish military assistance to get us to the Finnish lines. I have contacted the Papal Nuncio in Helsinki and he has spoken directly to Marshal Mannerheim. The Finns will assist, but only once we reach their lines, not sooner."

"You say the Holy Father has charged you with this mission?"

"Yes, through Monsignor Tardini."

"Ah, yes, Tardini. A good man, probably a future pope." Both men nodded in agreement. He continued, "Sepp, I don't know how Esteban-Infantes[74] will take this request. I can meet with him privately, but you should know that the German military liaison, a certain *Oberst* Dietrich, is never too far from him. If word gets out, it will have major political repercussions as well. After all, we are for all intents and purposes, Allies, even though Spain has declared itself as a non-belligerent."

"Jaime, I know this is asking a lot. Would it be possible for you to contact the *Caudillo* directly with this request? I know that he is a friend of the Jews and has given protection to Jews fleeing Nazi occupied Europe. Now that Serrano Suñer is no longer Foreign Minister, Franco may be a bit more inclined to assist the Allied war effort more overtly now that Germany's battlefield fortunes have waned."

"I will tell you what I will do, Sepp. I will talk to Esteban-Infantes. To my knowledge, he is not a racist and has nothing against Jews. He doesn't really buy into all that 'Master Race' Nazi propaganda coming out of Goebbels' office. He is, however, a dedicated soldier, and hates the Bolsheviks."

"Don't we all?" Sepp interjected.

"Yes. We are all fighting to defeat 'godless communism' while in the service of 'godless Nazism.' We've made a pact with the devil and only God knows how this war will end. I've seen what the Reds did during the Spanish Civil War, it wasn't pretty. Women, children, massacred for no apparent reason whatsoever. Some were even killed while attending Sunday Mass. The Reds made it a habit of targeting the clergy. Many of the priests I attended seminary with were gunned down like dogs, Sepp. Nuns murdered and raped, it just goes beyond description. I have heard rumors of what Hitler is doing to the Jews in the East and elsewhere, and God only knows if it is true or not."

"It's true, Jaime, trust me."

"Fine, you say it's true, I believe you. As servants of the Lord, you and I are in the business of saving souls and ministering to the faithful. I will do what I can - I will first talk with Esteban-Infantes - he knows of my connection to Franco and if I hint that I will contact the *Caudillo* directly, he may readily agree."

"Thank you, Jaime, that's all I am asking for."

"You know, Sepp, back in February, hundreds of *divisionarios* witnessed something inexplicable on the battlefield here at Krasny Bor. They reported seeing a large washtub-shaped vehicle of some kind that hovered over the battlefield for a few minutes and then shot up into the sky at tremendous speed, faster than anything they had ever seen."[75]

"Sounds like maybe some new Soviet weapon?" Sepp responded.

"I have no idea, but it frightened the men so that many came to see me afterwards asking if it was some heavenly sign. From their description of this vehicle, it sounds more like something out of an H.G. Wells novel. I like to think that maybe it was a sign from God telling us that we are in the right battling these godless Bolsheviks."

"Maybe you are right," Sepp answered with a chuckle, "I guess we may never know."

"I just had an idea, Sepp. I may be able to stress to Esteban-Infantes the November 1941 instruction from the OKW which directed all commanders in the east to facilitate the missionary activities of Catholic priests in the occupied territories.[76] We could tell him that this is part of a larger overall plan for missionary activity here. What do you think?"

"I think it just may work, Jaime. I am familiar with the protocol that you cited…hopefully the *Wehrmacht* will live up to its word."

"Sepp, what of your brother and his family? Surely, they will face a death sentence when this plan is carried out."

"Peter's family is safe. I arranged travel to Stockholm, and they arrived safely in Sweden last week. As for my brother, I believe he has other plans. I have a sinking feeling that I may never see him again."

Both men were silent for a moment.

"Jaime, can you arrange food and water delivery to the train? The cover story is that the personnel in the cars are under quarantine, that should keep any curiosity seekers away."

"I'll see to it. One hundred people you say?"

"Correct. They were to be human guinea pigs for a new type of gas the Nazis are using in the camps. My brother was to put on a show for Himmler."

"Oh, dear God! Let me talk to the general. I'll arrange for provisions to be brought to the train as well as setting up a quarantine area. We can provide tents and other accoutrements. I will also post a sign saying that the area is quarantined due to infectious disease. That will keep the Germans away. I will meet you back here later."

With that both men stood up, shook hands, and then headed out of the building where an uncertain future awaited them both.

Headquarters
250ᵗʰ Infantry Division
Krasny Bor, Russia
August 18, 1943, 1715 Hours

Chaplain Garcia made his way to the division headquarters to see Esteban-Infantes. Arriving at the general's office, he first stopped at the division adjutant's desk, a certain Major Acosta.

"*Buenos Tardes, Padre*," Acosta said as Garcia approached his desk. "How may I help you?"

"Is *el general* available, I have a very urgent matter to discuss with him."

"It just so happens that *el general* is free for the next fifteen minutes or so. Let me see if he can meet with you."

Acosta rose from his desk, went to the general's door, knocked, and entered without waiting for a response. A minute later he appeared and motioned Garcia to go in.

Garcia marched up to the general's desk and gave a smart salute. "Thank you for taking the time to see me, *mí general*."

"Anything for our division chaplain. Please, take a seat."

Esteban-Infantes, 50 years of age, and a career army officer, had recently assumed command of the division, succeeding his larger-than-life predecessor, General Agustin Muñoz Grandes, who had recently returned to Spain for reassignment. Esteban-Infantes also knew of Chaplain Garcia's special relationship with *Generalissimo* Franco, so he was more than willing to listen to what the priest had to say, lest it get him in hot water somewhere down the road.

"*Mí general*, today I was approached by an old friend, a German priest whom I have known for many years. He has come to me for help with regards to a very delicate matter. The fact is, *mí general*, that he arrived today at Krasny Bor station with a trainload of Jewish escapees. He needs to get them to Finland and then on to Sweden so that they will be safe."

Esteban-Infantes could only stare at Garcia in amazement for what seemed like minutes, but was only seconds. "Are you telling me, *Padre*, that there are Jews here now? How many?" Esteban-Infantes demanded to know.

"One hundred souls, sir. They were to be put to death at a camp in Estonia during an upcoming demonstration for *Reichsführer* Himmler. The Jews are disguised as soldiers and nurses under the care of the Red Cross, only you and I know their true identities, with the exception of course of the Germans that brought them here."

Esteban-Infantes thought for a minute and then spoke. "You know that we could probably be shot by our German friends because of this incident. However, I have nothing personal against *los judios*. As a matter of fact, I have some Sephardic blood in me from my mother's side of the family," he said smiling slightly.

Chaplain Garcia smiled as well, and before he could speak, the general continued.

"I despise Himmler immensely and will do everything in my power to block whatever efforts he is undertaking to kill these people. You know, *Padre*, *los divisionarios* have conducted themselves very well during the last two years, not only on the battlefield, but with the local inhabitants. We may wear German *Feldgrau* uniforms, but the Russian people know that they can trust our men and that we will protect them from harm."

"*Mi general*, do you have any suggestions on how we may get these people to Finland?"

"I am afraid, my dear Garcia, that overland route will be impossible. The Russians are holding at Leningrad, no matter what efforts we, the Germans, and the Finns, are putting into the siege. I do have an idea, though. Perhaps we can use our airmen[77] to fly them to Finland?

"*Mi general*, that is a very good idea! But sir, correct me if I am wrong, the squadron is only armed with fighter aircraft, not transport planes. How would we get them out, shuttle them out one by one in fighters?"

Esteban-Infantes chuckled at Garcia's naivete. No, *padre*, not quite the plan I had in mind. Although you were correct in stating that our boys are only flying fighters. However, a select group underwent training by the Germans and are qualified to fly their Junkers JU-52 transport plane. Perhaps our men could 'borrow' a couple of the aircraft under the guise of a training flight?"

"That's the aircraft the Germans refer to as *Tante Ju* ("Aunt Ju"), is it not, sir?"

"Correct, *Padre*. And there are a number of those aircraft parked on the same airfield as our squadron's fighter planes. Let me get in touch with the squadron commander, *teniente coronel* Rodriguez and talk to him about this situation. If I remember correctly, his wife is a Jewess, or part-Jew, I can't remember which, but I think he might be inclined to assist us. In the interim, get back to your German priest friend and let him know we will try as best as we can to get him and his group to safety. Also see that his 'charges' receive food and water."

"Already done, sir."

"Good. This discussion does not go any further than this office, is that understood, *Padre*?" I know you keep secrets from the confessional, so this shouldn't be too difficult for you," he said with a grin.

"I understand perfectly, *mí general*. Anyway, thank you for at least having the courage to try and help these innocents."

"I have seen a great deal of bloodshed over the years, *Padre*—in North Africa during the Riff rebellion, and of course during our own *guerra civil*, and now here. If I can help spare the lives of noncombatants, I will do so. I will send for you as soon as I hear something, *Padre*."

Both men stood and shook hands. Just then, a knock-on Esteban-Infantes' office door by his adjutant let him know that his appointment was waiting in the anteroom. As Garcia left the commander's office, he could not help but have a smile on his face, knowing that the general was going to do everything in his power to assist Bertram and his people.

"God certainly does work in mysterious ways," he said to himself as he walked out of the division headquarters building and on toward his own office.

Spanish Airfield
Krasny Bor, Russia
August 18, 1943, 1830 Hours

The Spanish airbase lay approximately three kilometers south of the city of Krasny Bor. The Spanish Expeditionary Air Squadron, also known as "Blue Squadron," ("*Escuadrilla Azul*") operated in support of German Army Group North, and its principal mission was the protection of German bombers. The Blue Squadron was assigned to the *Luftwaffe's Jagdgeschwader* 27 (27th Fighter Wing) and was equipped with Focke-Wulf (FW) 190 aircraft. Recently, a select number of the Spanish pilots had undergone training in order to qualify on the JU-52 tri-motor transport, the "workhorse" so to speak, of the German *Luftwaffe*. Ten JU-52 aircraft were currently on the airfield's tarmac, along with a small *Luftwaffe* contingent who were involved in training their Spanish counterparts on the finer points of *Tante Ju*. Included amongst the German cadre were not only pilots, but mechanics and other ground support personnel needed to keep the aircraft operational. *Teniente coronel* Guillermo Rodriguez, was the current squadron commander. Rodriguez had proven himself not only during the Spanish Civil War but had also shot down four Red

Air Force bombers during his stint on the Eastern Front. All he needed was one more "kill" to be given the sobriquet of "Ace," something he hoped would happen soon before he rotated back to Spain. Rodriguez was in his office when a call from Esteban-Infantes' office came through for him. He was ordered to see the division commander *post haste*. Grabbing both his gear and his driver, both men jumped into a German *Kubelwagen* and sped over to division headquarters.

Headquarters
250ᵗʰ Infantry Division
Krasny Bor, Russia
August 18, 1943, 1900 Hours

Teniente coronel Rodriguez reported to his division commander. Both men shook hands and Rodriguez sat down opposite Esteban-Infantes.

"Guillermo, I have asked you here as I have a very delicate matter, I need to discuss with you. It appears that 100 Jewish refugees have landed on our doorstep, so to speak, and we need to get them to safety. I was hoping that your newly trained JU-52 pilots might be up to the task in flying these refugees to Finland."

Rodriguez was dumbfounded after hearing what his commanding general told him. Finally, he cleared his throat and spoke. "*Mí general*, what you are asking is very dangerous. We all know how the Germans have been treating the Jews here and in the rest of occupied Europe, it's no secret. Our men have tried to conduct themselves honorably and I know for a fact, some of them have even taken up with local Jewish women from the surrounding villages. If the Germans find out, there is no telling what they will do to us. We are only one division, and they have hundreds. While we are facing the Red Army, we are also surrounded by the *Wehrmacht*. One word from Hitler and the entire division will become hostages."

Esteban-Infantes looked at his squadron commander intently. "Guillermo, your wife is Jewish, is she not?"

"She has Jewish blood, sir. Her great-grandparents converted about a century ago, and both she and her parents were raised Catholic. But, still, she is proud of her Sephardic heritage."

"As she should be," the general answered with a smile. He then continued. "Guillermo, I would like you and your men to fly these Jews to Finland, from there, it is hoped that they will be able to make it to the safety of neutral Sweden."

"And these are refugees, you say, sir? Refugees from where, if I may ask?"

"Actually, Guillermo, they are escapees from a concentration camp in Estonia. They were to be human guinea pigs for a demonstration to be put on for Himmler by the SS. Some new type of gas to be used to make the killing more 'efficient.'"

A look of absolute disgust came over Rodriguez's face.

"My feelings exactly, Guillermo. Killing an armed opponent in combat is one thing; executing innocent and unarmed civilians, including women and children is another. It's tantamount to cold-blooded murder, pure and simple. I realize the Reds have no qualms about it and certainly neither does Hitler, but I do not want innocents' blood on the hands of this division. We need to help these people. Will you help?"

"Count me in, sir. I will manage somehow to get the Germans out of the way so we can get these people to safety."

"I knew I could count on you, Guillermo! Now, I need you to coordinate with our division chaplain, *Padre* Garcia. It is a friend of his, a civilian German priest, a certain Monsignor Bertram, that has brought these Jews here by train. Surprisingly, several German military personnel are involved in trying to help these people escape. Bertram's brother is an *SS Gruppenführer* who assisted in this mass escape. If you are confused by these events, you are not alone," he said with a chuckle.

"Sir, I will get my pilots together and brief them and get back to you with a plan."

"The sooner, the better, Guillermo. No doubt, the Germans will be hunting these people down and God help them if they are caught."

With that, the general stood up and offered his hand to his subordinate who took it and said, "Sir, by doing this, perhaps we can right a few wrongs that the Germans, in their usual arrogance, have perpetrated."

Esteban-Infantes could only smile and nod in agreement with Rodriguez's line of thinking.

Spanish Airfield
Krasny Bor, Russia
August 18, 1943, 2000 Hours

After returning to the airfield from his meeting with the division commander, Rodriguez gathered all his pilots in a briefing room in one of the hangars. Guards were posted to ensure that no German military personnel were present or could eavesdrop.

"Gentlemen, I have just returned from a meeting with the division commander, and we have a unique opportunity to do something good in this otherwise brutal war. I am looking for volunteers for a flight mission to Finland. We will be flying 100 refugees to our Finnish allies." Rodriguez purposely withheld that fact that the "refugees" were Jews just in case someone talked. The Gestapo and German intelligence had infiltrated almost every facet of life not only for civilians, but for military personnel as well. While he trusted his men emphatically, you never knew who would talk, especially when alcohol was involved.

"The mission will be dangerous," he continued, "as we will be flying over Soviet lines. We will utilize all the JU-52's and whatever fighter support we can muster on our own. Gentlemen, this information is not to be shared with our German friends, is that understood? I know many of you have made friends with the *Luftwaffe* personnel who support us and that is all well and good, but this is a Spanish operation and needs to stay in-house."

There were some murmurs among the assembled pilots, but they soon quieted.

"This is strictly a volunteer operation, so those of you that don't want to participate, you may step out now, there will be no hard feelings and no repercussions--that I can assure you." He let his words sink in for a moment and waited to see if any of his men would back out. To his satisfaction, not one man balked. They were all in it together.

"I will need to work up a plan to present to the division commander. I will need to speak with my primary staff officers (flight operations, personnel, logistics, and intelligence) after this meeting. We will also need to find a way to divert or otherwise occupy our German friends so that there is absolutely no interference on their part." Looking at the men gathered in the hangar, he said, "I want to thank you for your service to the Fatherland and to our *Caudillo*, *Generalissimo* Franco. Sometimes, being a soldier, or in our case, airmen, takes more than killing the enemy. Sometimes it even involves saving innocent human lives."

Headquarters
250ᵗʰ Infantry Division
Krasny Bor, Russia
August 19, 1943, 0930 Hours

Rodriguez reported back to his division commander the next day with what he thought a feasible plan to get the Jews to Finland. It would be risky, but after reviewing their options, the Spaniards decided that the Finnish airfield located at Turku, approximately 155 miles west-northwest of Helsinki, would be their best bet. Laying a large map with an overlay on the division commander's desk, Rodriguez began his brief.

"*Mí general*, my staff worked through the night to come up with what I believe is a solid plan. After viewing several courses of action, it was decided that the joint Finnish/German airfield at Turku, would be our best option. Grid coordinates, 60 28 30N – 22 11 41E."

Esteban-Infantes nodded in agreement and said, "Please continue."

My Brother's Keeper

Continuing his brief, Rodriguez stated, "The airfield is equipped for night landings as well. There are no hangers, although there are a few repair shops and a small administration building. Additionally, there is a seaplane station located along the channel of the Aura River, approximately six kilometers west of the city.[78] This airfield, although joint in nature, is pretty much run by the Finns. There may be a German or two serving as liaison, but as far as we can discern, there are no major *Wehrmacht* or SS units in the area, not even a FLAK[79] unit protecting the airfield. I would recommend sir, that this operation be conducted at night, as the airfield is equipped for night landings. Darkness will probably be our best ally in this matter."

Esteban-Infantes studied the map for a minute then asked, "Tell a bit more about the JU-52. It's range, speed, and capacity."

"*Sí, mí general.* As you are aware, the JU-52, is pretty much the workhorse of the *Luftwaffe.* This model that we have has a range of 540 miles, with a cruise speed of 132 mph, and has a capacity of 18 troops, and has a crew of two. With the amount of personnel, we need to move, six aircraft will suffice."

"Please remind me again of how many JU-52s are at the field at the present time."

"Ten, *mí general,*" Rodriguez answered. "And all aircraft are fully operational, including the fighters. We will also have fighter escort by our own squadron. I have warned my men under the punishment of death, not to breathe a word of this to the Germans."

"All well and good, Guillermo. Now, how do we pull this off under the very noses of the Germans? Have you thought that through?"

"Sir, as you are aware, there are about 20 *Luftwaffe* personnel assigned to the airfield with us, under the command of a new *Oberleutnant.* I think we may be able to draw the whole lot of them away under the guise of a German-Spanish friendship dinner celebrating our mutual fight against the Reds. There is a small establishment a few kilometers away from the airfield which pre-war was a small waystation, combination hostel/tavern. If we supply the food and drink, the proprietor will do the rest."

"Do you think the Germans will fall for it?" Esteban-Infantes queried.

"I think they will sir, especially if it breaks up the monotony for the men. Our hope will be to get them so drunk that they will be incapacitated for at least a day, maybe longer. Our men have the training to secure and operate the airfield without any German supervision. Once the Germans leave the airfield, we can execute the plan."

"This new German *teniente*, is he a committed Nazi? Have you spoken with him?"

"Sir, I get the impression that he isn't a die-hard; he seems like a decent fellow. I've not heard him spouting the usual Nazi propaganda to his men. I could be wrong since he is new, but I get the sense that he, like the rest of us, just wants to survive this place and get back home in one piece."

"Very well. How soon can we move on this?"

"Sir, meteorological reports call for inclement weather mixed with heavy fog conditions over the next six to ten days which will hem us in. My best estimate will be on or about 26-27 August, possibly sooner possibly later, it just depends how the weather cooperates"

"Thank you, Guillermo, I believe we'll be able to pull this off, God willing. Ensure your men keep their mouths shut around our German comrades, I would hate to have them tipped off by some bigmouth."

"*Sí, mí general.*" With that, Rodriguez stood up, saluted his commander, did an about-face and left the general's office. The next six to ten days will be critical if the rescue operation is to succeed.

Headquarters
250th Infantry Division
Krasny Bor, Russia
August 24, 1943, 1045 Hours

Esteban-Infantes was in his office reviewing some upcoming operations plans when he was distracted by a knock on his door.

"Yes, what is it?" the commanding general asked.

His adjutant entered followed by a new company grade officer who had been assigned to the division as a replacement.

"*Mí general,* may I present *Capitano* Jaime Milan del Bosch."

Milan del Bosch came to attention and offered the Falange salute (like the Nazi salute). "*Mí general,* it is an honor."

Esteban-Infantes rose and shook his subordinate's hand vigorously. "I am happy to have you on board, *Capitano.* Please have a seat. I like to get to know my officers personally."

The adjutant had handed the general Milan del Bosch's service record and for a few minutes, both captain and general sat in silence as Esteban-Infantes reviewed his subordinate's record.

"Very impressive record, *Capitano.* I see that you are a veteran of the late *guerra civil* and fought at the Alcazar de Toledo. We need combat veterans such as yourself now more than ever."

"*Gracias, mí general.*"

"I am assigning you to the Second Battalion; your will report to Major Robles and he will get you settled in. I am happy to have you on board." With that, Esteban-Infantes stood up, signaling the interview was over. He shook hands with his new officer and Milan del Bosch left the office. After his subordinate left, Esteban-Infantes remembered some rumors from fellow senior officers that Milan del Bosch was a rabid Falangist and anti-Semite who idolized both Hitler and Franco. The commanding general could only hope that his new captain would not prove to be an obstacle in the upcoming rescue operation.

Spanish Airfield
Krasny Bor, Russia
August 26, 1943, 1420 Hours

The few German troops that were assigned to assist the Spaniards were mainly conscripts, doing their duty with the hopes of surviving the horrors of the Eastern Front. The new German officer in charge, a senior *Oberleutenant,* Hans Koening, appeared outwardly at least, to be a regular guy, well-liked and well-respected by both his troops and the Spaniards as well. The lieutenant even spoke some passable Spanish, which helped, as few of the Spanish spoke German, only the senior-ranking members of the Blue Division spoke German.

On this day, Rodriguez sought out the German OIC and took him aside.

"*Herr Oberleutnant,* a word if you don't mind." He motioned for the German OIC to come into his small office situated in the hanger. The young officer did not seem to terribly mind that he was technically under the command of a Spanish officer. And besides, Rodriguez spoke passable German, so communications were normally good.

"Yes, *Herr Oberstleutnant,* how may I assist you?"

"*Herr Leutnant,* the men are throwing a small get-together tomorrow, just to let off a bit of steam, if you know what I mean, and we would like to invite you and your men to join us. There is an old inn outside of town that will accommodate us, and arrangements are being made as we speak. We will keep a skeleton force here in operations in the event an emergency arises, and since the inn is only a few kilometers from here, we can be back in no time should the need arise. General Esteban-Infantes has already approved it."

In just a couple of sentences, Rodriguez had already answered the young officer's questions before he had a chance to ask them himself. The young German was most happy to hear that the commanding general had given his approval for the get together.

"*Herr Oberstleutnant,* in the spirit of German-Spanish unity and friendship, I am most honored to accept your invitation on behalf of myself and my men."

"Splendid!" Rodriguez answered, "I will inform you of the time for tomorrow's festivities by close of business today."

With that, the German offered a fascist salute, did an about-face, and left the hangar to go back to his men. The plan was now set in motion to have the Germans away from the airfield when the Spaniards took to the skies with their precious cargo on board.

Headquarters
250th Infantry Division
Krasny Bor, Russia
August 26, 1943, 1915 Hours

Sepp, along with Chaplain Garcia were asked to meet with Esteban-Infantes at division headquarters. It would be the first meeting that Sepp had with the Spanish commanding general, and from all indications from Chaplain Garcia, the general was a man who could be trusted and would do all within his power to facilitate the rescue operation.

The adjutant ushered both men into Esteban-Infantes' office where they were greeted warmly.

"Monsignor Bertram, I am very happy to finally meet you," he said while firmly shaking Sepp's hand.

"The pleasure is mine, General."

Esteban-Infantes gestured for both men to sit down and offered some coffee that had been brought in prior to their arrival.

"Monsignor, *Padre* Garcia has briefed me on your operation—I must say it has taken a great deal of courage to pull this off—both you and your brother are heroes, at least in my eyes."

"Thank you, General, for all that you and your troops have done to assist us—from ensuring that food, water and shelter have been provided to these people. The leader of the group, Rabbi Abramovitz, asked me to pass on his personal thanks for providing safety to the group. You are in his prayers."

"Please thank the rabbi for me, his prayers are most appreciated—however, I seriously doubt it includes a prayer for a German victory," he said with a slight chuckle.

Both Sepp and Garcia smiled at the general's comment.

Esteban-Infantes continued, "We plan on flying out your charges in the early hours of August 29-30 as it will be clear flying weather."

Sepp and Garcia were stunned at the revelation.

"That is the best news I have heard in weeks, General. Thank you," Sepp said.

"We are not there yet—we have plans to occupy the Germans so that they are out of the way when we pull this off. Hopefully, they will be so drunk, they won't have an inkling of what's happening."

Both Garcia and Sepp nodded in agreement.

"This will be a night flight, and while the Germans are drinking themselves silly, we will get your charges to the airfield, loaded up and on their way. The destination is a small, rarely used joint German-Finnish airfield in Turku, Finland, northwest of Helsinki. It is within range of the aircraft, and the JU-52's can refuel at the airfield. All of this will be done under the guise of a training/familiarization flight for our pilots on the JU-52."

"Brilliant," said Garcia, "Absolutely brilliant idea. Let's pray it works."

Esteban-Infantes continued, "Once I know that the Germans have left the airfield and are at the inn enjoying themselves, I will send the trucks to pick up your people, Monsignor—probably around 2100 hours, so have them ready. Timing will be everything. Will you be accompanying your charges to Finland, Monsignor?"

"No, General. I am happy to inform you at this time that another part of the plan has been finalized. I had to keep it secret because it involved a neutral nation, Sweden. It appears that King Gustav V of Sweden, with prodding from Count Bernadotte, the Papal Nuncio, and some of the Jewish leaders in Stockholm, has finally given authority for the Swedish Air Force to fly a humanitarian mission to Finland and pick up the Jews and then fly them to Sweden. This of course has been arranged with the Finns and the king has spoken directly with both Marshal Mannerheim and President Risto Ryti."

"That is splendid news, Monsignor. How ironic that you are receiving help from the so-called 'neutrals' in this war, Spain and Sweden."

"General, I will have to convey this information to the nuncio in Stockholm and he in turn, will notify the proper authorities as to the time and place of the pickup at Turku. I will have to use your communications center if I may."

"By all means, Monsignor. Before you send it, you will need to know all the details for your message to the nuncio. I will get *Teniente coronel* Rodriguez here and he can go over the plan in more detail for you. The more the Swedes know, the smoother the operation should run."

Headquarters
250th Infantry Division
Krasny Bor, Russia
August 26, 1943, 2010 Hours

After being briefed by Rodriguez, both Sepp and Chaplain Garcia made their way over to the division's communication center, which was little more than an oversized shack, but vital nonetheless to the division's communication with higher headquarters. Two enlisted signalmen manning the center stood up when Sepp and Garcia entered.

"*Buenos Noches, Padre,*" both men said in unison, immediately recognizing their division chaplain.

"*Buenos Noches,*" Garcia answered. This is Monsignor Bertram, and he needs to send out a message to the papal nuncio in Stockholm. Here is the letter of authorization from the division commander as well as the monsignor's authorization from the Reich Foreign Ministry."

The senior of the two men looked at the paperwork in a cursory manner - he was mainly interested in the authorization letter from his own commander. He then asked Sepp, "Monsignor, please write out on this message pad what you want the message to read and we will get it out. I see from the authorization letter that this is a priority message."

Sepp nodded in the affirmative. He then took the pad and wrote the following message. The message would be veiled in euphemisms so as not to alert the Germans.

Cargo leaving Krasny Bor tomorrow evening destination joint German/Finnish airbase at Turku, grid coordinates 60 28 30N - 22 11 41E. Cargo departs at 2300hours arrival approx 0400 hours.

Sepp showed the message to Garcia, who nodded his approval and said, "Succinct and to the point."

"No need of being verbose, especially if the Germans are intercepting communication messages, even among their own allies," Sepp replied.

Sepp handed the message slip to the signalman who promised the message would be sent out within the hour. Both Sepp and Garcia then left the communications center just as *Capitano* Milan del Bosch was entering. He saluted Chaplain Garcia then entered the building. Both signalmen snapped to attention and were then put 'at ease" by the young officer.

"I have been ordered by the battalion commander to send a signal to the neighboring German unit. What is the procedure?" he asked.

The senior signalman, a corporal by the name of Silva, explained to the captain how the form was to be filled out with all pertinent information on what unit and the intended recipient of the message. Milan del Bosch's message would have to be encoded which would take time. He explained to the young officer that they had just received a priority message to get out and that he would be next.

Leaning against the counter nonchalantly, Milan del Bosch asked matter-of-factly, "Was that priest with our division chaplain from the Vatican?" I heard a rumor to the effect that we had a VIP in our midst," he said half-jokingly.

"*Si, Capitano, es la verdad,*" answered Silva. "He has been here a few days. He arrived with a trainload of troops that had been exposed to some sort of disease and they were quarantined just north of the train station. We have been supplying them food, water, and medicine."

"They are not *divisionarios?*" Milan del Bosch inquired.

"No, *Capitano, las alemanas.*"

"Germans, that's odd. Why wouldn't they be quarantined near a German unit, that doesn't make any sense."

Silva just shrugged his shoulders in an 'I don't know' gesture.

Milan del Bosch was now quite curious as to why a train carrying infected German soldiers would be in their sector of the front and not close to a German unit. It sounded very much out of the ordinary, especially for the 'by-the-book' Germans. He then decided he would make some inquiries on his own as to why they were in the division's sector. And if he could not get a straight answer, perhaps the division's German liaison officer would be able to assist in figuring out this mystery.

The Red Star Tavern
near Krasny Bor, Russia
August 27, 1943, 2100 hours

The Red Star Tavern was located at a small crossroads approximately five kilometers outside Krasny Bor. The elderly couple who owned the tavern had been in business since the turn of the century and their claim to fame was that they had served Czar Nicholas II during the Great War when he and his entourage had passed through their hamlet. When the Bolsheviks came to power in 1917, they changed the name of their establishment from 'The White Eagle' to 'The Red Star' in honor of their new political masters. Their establishment was frequented mainly by Spanish troops, and sometimes, but not often, by German troops as well. The proprietors, Mr. and Mrs. Abushinov, were well into their 70s and had the look of a typical Russian peasant—a look of one who has been beaten down, but not quite out for the count. Both were toothless, arthritic, and hunched over, looking much older than their actual years. Yet, they were happy to host the Spaniards as they were a good lot and treated the native population with respect, unlike their German allies. The Spanish also paid well, so there was no hesitancy to host the gathering.

At approximately 2100 hours, a small convoy consisting of a *Kubelwagen* and four Opel trucks pulled up in front of the tavern. As the senior officer hosting the gathering, *Teniente Coronel* Rodriquez accompanied the group. Riding with him was the German officer, *Oberleutnant* Koening, who was happy to leave the division area and get out into the surrounding area. While the area was relatively secure, Partisans were still active, so all the troops were well armed. Sentries would be posted outside the tavern during the festivities as a precaution. Drunken enemy soldiers would be an inviting target to the Partisans and Rodriguez ensured that the tavern was well-guarded.

As the Spanish and German troops entered the tavern, the proprietors greeted them warmly, with a few *"Buenos Noches," and "Guten Abends"* added for effect.

Approximately 40 men were in attendance, with Spanish and German flags prominently displayed by the head table where Rodriguez and Koening sat along with their senior NCO's.

Rodriguez turned to the German officer and said, "Well, we made it. Time for a little relaxation, so as they say, tonight we eat, drink, and be merry!"

Koening smiled and nodded his approval. He liked the Spanish officer and enjoyed working with the Spaniards. They were fearless in battle, a bit too reckless, but nonetheless had proven to be trustworthy allies. He also liked the Spanish attitude of *mañana,* tomorrow, it could wait until tomorrow. Koening had not seen much action to date - he had flown just a few sorties and reconnaissance missions but that was the extent. Most of the time was spent supervising the Germans attached to the squadron and of course paperwork, *endless* paperwork as far as he was concerned.

Rodriguez then stood up from his chair and in a loud voice said, "Gentlemen, your attention, please."

With that, the talking died down and the tavern was silent except for the sound of glasses being continually filled with beer in the kitchen area and brought out to the tables.

"I would like to propose a toast to our friends and allies in the *Luftwaffe*! Also, a toast to their *Führer*, Adolf Hitler and to our *Caudillo,* Francisco Franco! To Spanish-German friendship! *Viva* Hitler! *Viva* Franco! To victory!"

A resounding "To Victory!" was answered by the troops as they raised their glasses.

With that, Rodriguez sat down, and the noise level rose once again in the tavern as the airmen laughed, joked, and smoked to their hearts' content, letting off a lot of steam in the process. Rodriguez also had another surprise waiting for his German guests. To make sure the Germans would be preoccupied most of the evening after dinner, Rodriguez arranged for some of the local prostitutes to be available. The tavern also had a few rooms and those would be rented out by the hour, courtesy of the Spanish Blue Division.

Koening turned to his Spanish host and said, *Herr Oberstleutnant,* I cannot thank you enough for setting this up, it means a great deal to my men and I."

"Think nothing of it, my dear Koening - you and your men have worked hard - we all have, and we need a break from this godforsaken war."

Both men clinked their glasses and downed the first of many glasses of beer.

"I will have to excuse myself in about an hour, Koening, as I will need to get back to the airfield—I am leaving you in charge of this rabble," he said jokingly.

Koening was a bit taken aback by the Spaniard's announcement. "May I ask you why, *Herr Oberstleutnant?*

"Yes, of course. We had some in-house training scheduled at the last minute, strictly in-house by order of Esteban-Infantes, nothing to concern yourself with."

Rodriguez thought Koening a bit too suspicious and tried to put him at ease.

Koening then asked, "I noted that only a portion of your men are here tonight, what of the others?"

Well of course the others were going to be needed to service the JU-52s taking off in a few hours, the Spaniard thought to himself.

"Again, my dear Koening, those men are part of this last-minute training I told you about. The general said that only a portion of the squadron could attend tonight, and those you see here tonight were recommended by their NCOs as a reward for outstanding performance to date."

The German nodded in understanding, and said, "A pity the rest could not attend." He then signaled for more beer as an attendant came over to him and began to pour.

"Leave the pitcher," Koening ordered, and the attendant did so.

Rodriguez could see that the German officer was on his way to becoming inebriated as were most of the German personnel in the tavern, a good sign as far as Rodriguez was concerned. The more beer the Germans consumed the less chance of their interference as the flight deadline loomed.

Around 2230 hours, Rodriguez stood up and started for the tavern door. Koening had passed out from too much drink and the troops were rowdy and loud, singing both in German and Spanish, quite a sight to behold.

Reaching into his tunic pocket, he pulled out a wad of bills and paid the proprietors, not only for the food and drink, but for the rooms which would be used later in the evening when the 'entertainment' arrived. He then called over his senior NCO, whom he had ordered to stay sober for the evening.

"Juan, I am heading back to the airfield for the mission, try and keep things in order here. Our German friend is out like a light, and if he wakes up, ply him with more beer. Same for the rest of the Germans, they wake or look like they are getting sober, give them more drink."

"Very well, *mí coronel,*" the NCO answered.

With that, Rodriguez left the tavern, passed the sentries posted at the tavern's entrance and climbed into the *Kubelwagen*, his driver having stayed with the vehicle the entire time.

"Back to the airfield, corporal," Rodriguez ordered. His driver then put the vehicle in gear and began the drive back to the airfield. Rodriguez said a silent prayer that they would make it back safe, and that the operation would go off as planned.

Headquarters
250th Infantry Division
Krasny Bor, Russia
August 27, 1943, 2100 hours

Captain Milan del Bosch had been waiting for hours to see the Chief of the German liaison team to the Blue Division, *Oberstleutnant* Wilhelm Knuppel, who had been on an inspection tour of the divisional units. Knuppel, a combat veteran and a former regimental commander, had been selected as the chief liaison to the Blue Division early in 1943. When he finally returned late that evening, he found the Spanish captain waiting for him outside of his office.

"Can I help you, c*apitano?*" he asked in perfect Spanish.

"*Sí, mí coronel,* I wanted to ask if you were aware of the trainload of sick soldiers that arrived a few days ago and are encamped north of the railway station."

"You are new to the division, are you not, *capitano?*"

"My apologies, sir, I forgot to introduce myself, I am *Capitano* Jaime Milan del Bosch, at your service," he said with a slight bow.

Knuppel also made a slight bow and again asked, "So you state that there are a number of ill German soldiers encamped not far from here. This is the first I am hearing of it."

The Spanish division's leadership had been careful not to plan or speak of the operation while the German liaison officers were around. Much of the planning had been done late at night or in the early morning hours.

"Can you take me there, *Capitano?*"

"Sir, I have not yet been there myself. I was informed of this by a few of my men."

"So, it is nothing more than hearsay, correct, *Capitano?*"

"*Sí, Herr Oberstleutnant.* But I have a sneaking suspicion that something is amiss."

"If I were to chase down every rumor coming out of this division, I would not get anything done. It is rumor, *Capitano,* just rumor, and I would advise you to forget it. Now is there anything else?"

Knowing that he was not going to get anywhere arguing with the German, he simply said, "No, sir. Thank you for your time." Milan del Bosch then saluted, did an about face, and walked out of Knuppel's office. If Knuppel wasn't going to help, then perhaps the local *Feldgendarme* might be interested. He adjusted his cap and marched with determination to the motor pool to obtain a vehicle and a driver that would take him to the *Feldgendarme* office located 15 kilometers distant.

Chapter IX

"Once I have settled my other problems, I'll have my reckoning with the Church. I'll have it reeling on the ropes."
--Adolf Hitler

Headquarters
170th Infantry Division/*Feldgendarme* **Office**
Fedorovskoe, Russia
August 27, 1943, 2230 Hours

It had taken over an hour for Milan del Bosch to finally be assigned a vehicle with a driver for the relatively short trip over to the neighboring German division. As they entered the Germans' divisional sector, signs directed them to the *Feldgendarme* office. Milan del Bosch had also taken with him a young Spanish corporal, a soldier by the name of Diaz, who was fluent in German in order to translate for him.

With his driver staying with the vehicle, both Milan del Bosch and Diaz alighted from the vehicle and entered the *Feldgendarme* office, located in a former factory. The duties of the *Feldgendarme* were to ensure discipline among their own troops and to also assist in anti-Partisan actions. In many instances, they assisted the SS in the roundup of Jews and others deemed 'Enemies of the Reich.'

As the Spaniards entered the building, they were amazed at the beehive of activity even at such a late hour, going on in front of them, soldiers and officers moving about with files, escorting prisoners, etc. It was, Milan del Bosch thought to himself, quite impressive to say the least.

Finding a young NCO, he asked, through Diaz, where the officer in charge was located. He was directed down a long hallway to a door with the name, *Major* Hans Rudolph, *Kommandant.*

Straightening his tunic, Milan del Bosch and Diaz entered the office and were met by a German corporal who was surprised to see the Spaniards, who were easily identifiable by the Spanish shield marked *'España'* on their right shoulder sleeves of their uniforms.

Diaz asked if they could speak with the commandant as it was a matter of great importance, at least that's what Milan del Bosch told him to say.

The corporal got up, went into the Major's office and a minute later a German officer emerged from his office, looking every inch the depiction of a Nazi soldier—tall, blond haired and blue-eyed. Major Rudolf also was wearing the Iron Cross 1st Class, a Wound Badge, earned during the early days of the Russian campaign in 1941, as well as two Tank Destruction Badges for single-handedly destroying two Russian T-34 tanks.

Milan del Bosch introduced himself and began to tell Rudolph of what he had heard about an encampment of sick German soldiers that were quarantined north of the railway station in Krasny Bor, and did the good Major know anything about it?

As fate would have it, another German *Feldgendarme* entered the office just as Diaz was telling Major Rudolph of Milan del Bosch's suspicions. This soldier happened to be one of the two *Feldgendarmes* that had boarded the train when it first entered Krasny Bor station days before.

"Excuse me, *Herr Major*, but I could not help but overhear your discussion. Both Corporal Kurtz and I boarded the train the other day when it pulled into the station. There were 100 or so sick troops along with some nurses on board. The OIC[80] showed us a document signed by an SS *Gruppenführer* authorizing the troops to be on the train."

"Do you remember this OIC's name?" Rudolph asked.

"No, sir, I do not. But I do remember the name of the SS officer who signed the authorization list - *Gruppenführer* Peter Bertram. May I add, sir that the SS officer's brother, a priest, was on the train as well. Both Kurtz and I drove him to the Spanish division's chaplain office at the OIC's request." Milan del Bosch then realized he had seen Monsignor Bertram with Chaplain Garcia earlier leaving the communications hut. He asked Diaz to tell that to the Germans.

Rudolph then asked the German *Feldgendarme*, "What type of injuries or sickness were these troops suffering from?"

"Sir, Kurtz and I were told that the soldiers had been exposed to tularemia."

Rudolph nodded as he was aware that German soldiers fighting in Stalingrad earlier in the year had been exposed to the disease.

"Thank you, corporal, that will be all." The soldier clicked his heels, made an about-face and left the office.

"Well, *Capitano*, there you have it. My men are aware of these sick soldiers, and they have been isolated for a reason - tularemia! Quite frankly, I am not going to risk exposing myself or my men to go out there and check on them. They are isolated for a reason and have medical personnel with them. That is good enough for me and it should be for you as well. Now is there anything else I can assist you with?"

Realizing that he was about to be dismissed, Milan del Bosch replied, "No, *Herr Major*, you have answered all of my questions. Thank you very much for your time."

Milan del Bosch and Diaz both snapped to attention, saluted, did an about-face and left the office, heading to the staff car that would take them back to their own unit.

When the two Spaniards left, Rudolph went back to his office and sitting at his desk, went over in his mind the conversation that had just transpired. He thought for a minute and found it rather odd that a senior SS officer would sign a letter of authorization for wounded personnel, particularly since the troops on the train were *Wehrmacht* and not SS. He thought to himself, what was that SS officer's name - Bertram? He wrote it down as he planned to make some discreet inquiries into the *gruppenführer's* background.

Headquarters
170th Infantry Division/*Feldgendarme* Office
Fedorovskoe, Russia
August 28, 1943, 0830 Hours

Major Rudolph had placed a late-night call to his higher headquarters with Army Group North and had fallen asleep at his desk awaiting a call back which did not come until the next morning. An upturn in Partisan activity across the front was making communications more difficult.

The phone rang and Rudolph answered, "*Feldgendarme* office, *Major* Rudolph speaking."

"*Herr Major*, this is *Oberst* Wiedemann, I had a message that you had called last evening. These damn Partisans have been playing havoc with our lines of communication. The Signals boys just repaired some downed wires, so better make it quick, before the lines go dead again."

"*Herr Oberst*, I am calling to inquire about a certain SS officer - a *Gruppenführer* Peter Bertram. Does that name ring any bells?"

"Should it, *Major*? Why are you asking about a senior SS officer? Be very careful where you tread."

"The reason I ask sir, was that his name came up in discussion with a Spanish officer who claims that both Bertram and his brother, who is a Roman cleric, have something to do with a troop train in the Spanish sector full of troops suffering from tularemia."

"*Major*, what has that got to do with us? Has the *gruppenführer* been accused of any crime? If he hasn't, I see no reason to get involved, especially on the word of a Spaniard. Those Latins are always so damn excitable and are prone to exaggeration. Drop it, *Major*, understood."

"*Jawohl, Herr Oberst.*"

With that, the line went dead. Rudolph wasn't sure if Wiedemann had hung up on him or that the line had been cut again by the Partisans. Either way, he was told in no uncertain terms not to pursue the matter and he wouldn't - orders were orders. Besides, he had other more important cases to look into—a policeman's job was never done.

Reichssicherheitshauptamt **(Reich Main Security Office (RSHA))**
***Prinz-Albrecht-Strasse* 8**
Berlin, Germany
August 28, 1943, 1130 Hours

Himmler's personal adjutant, *SS Sturmbannführer* Rudolph Brandt was beside himself. He had just been handed a telex from Klooga Concentration Camp in Reval stating that the SS garrison and 100 special prisoners were missing and that the *Reichsführer SS* was to be informed immediately. The telex had been sent by a visiting SS inspection team sent for his upcoming visit. Brandt knocked on Himmler's massive oak door and waited for him to respond.

"Enter," Himmler shouted and went back to his paperwork.

"*Herr Reichsführer,* I believe you need to see this immediately."

"What is it now, Brandt," he said with a bit of annoyance in his voice.

Himmler began to read the telex and Brandt could see Himmler's eyes begin to widen as he read on.

"This is impossible, Brandt, an SS garrison and their prisoners don't just vanish into thin air! Who oversees that sector of the camp?"

"*Hauptsturmführer* Loss, sir. However, for these special prisoners, *Gruppenführer* Bertram had personally taken charge of the prisoners for your upcoming visit."

"Ah, yes, Brandt, now I remember. Has anyone seen or heard from either Loss or Bertram?"

"No sir. I can order some men from the main camp to go over and check."

"Do it, Brandt, and keep me posted. That will be all." Himmler then returned to his mountain of paperwork, with thoughts of the missing prisoners now beginning to concern him.

Klooga Concentration Camp
Reval, Estonia
Reichskomissariat Ostland
August 28, 1943, 1400 Hours

SS Hauptsturmführer Hans Aumeier, Commandant of Vaivara Concentration Camp, along with a contingent of 15 SS troopers arrived at Klooga. That morning, he had received a telex from the Office of the *Reichsführer SS* ordering him to check on the subcamp at Klooga, and to report back his findings *post haste*. Additionally, Aumeier had dispatched a small contingent to check the villa of the HSSPF, *Gruppenführer* Bertram.

As the small convoy of two vehicles pulled up to the main gate of the camp, they were met with an aerie silence - all that could be heard was the wind. The camp had been abandoned, but where were the garrison and prisoners? Aumeier ordered his driver to proceed to the administration building and quickly alighted from his vehicle, his pistol drawn, not knowing what to expect when he entered the seemingly abandoned offices.

"Search the camp," he ordered to his NCO, who quickly barked orders to his men to fan out and check every building in the camp. A trooper accompanied Aumeier as both entered the camp commandant's office, weapons at the ready. Nothing. No commandant, no secretary, nothing. It is as if the entire camp population had disappeared into thin air.

Minutes later, Aumeier's NCOIC[81] reported to him and informed him that the camp was empty.

"Sir, we did find some empty ration boxes over in the barracks," he told Aumeier.

"Ration boxes! You mean the prisoners were eating rations!"

"It appears that way, sir."

Aumeier slumped into Loss's desk seat and scratched his head. "Where are they? There is no obvious sign of a struggle or a camp revolt - nothing!"

Aumeier began to go through Loss's desk drawers trying to find any tell-tale signs of what might have occurred, but he came up with nothing.

"Sergeant, gather up the men and get them back on the truck, we are heading back to Vaivara."

"*Jawohl, Herr Hauptsturmführer!*" he answered and left the building to gather up the men and load them up into the Opel Blitz truck that they arrived in.

As he was leaving the administration building, Aumeier turned around to investigate the empty offices and began to worry. Just what was he going to tell Himmler? After all, Klooga was a subcamp of Vaivara in which *he was commandant!* He was going to have to draft up a telex in which he put the blame squarely on Loss and Bertram. While assigned to Auschwitz earlier in the year, Aumeier had been found guilty of corrupt practices and theft of gold from the victims of gassing and as a result was transferred on the personal orders of the Commandant, Rudolf Hoss. Needless to say, Aumeier was on very thin ice—his career and possibly his life were now on the line.

As he made his way back to his *Kubelwagen*, he ordered his driver, "Let's go."

The small convoy left the camp, leaving behind a cloud of dust in their wake.

Reichssicherheitsdienstamt (RSHA)
Prinz-Albrecht-Strasse 8
Berlin, Germany
August 28, 1943, 1645 Hours

SS Sturmbannführer Brandt cringed when he read the telex that had arrived from Aumeier--Himmler would explode once he read it. Brandt had seen Himmler lose his temper many times and on occasion had himself been on the receiving end of Himmler's wrath. To his credit, Himmler would normally apologize to Brandt and make it up to him in some small way. Brandt made his way towards Himmler's office and paused in front of the massive oak door before knocking. Adjusting his tunic, he knocked and waited for Himmler's response.

"Enter," Himmler called out.

"*Herr Reichsführer,* per your orders, we have heard back from Klooga camp," and handed Himmler the Telex from Aumeier.

Adjusting his *pince nez* glasses he read:

Upon arriving at Klooga camp earlier today, the camp was found to be entirely empty. A thorough search was conducted of the entire premises, buildings, and outbuildings with negative results. The entire SS contingent as well as the prisoners have vanished. A search of the villa of the Deputy HSSPF, Gruppenführer Bertram was also conducted and found to be empty, neither the gruppenführer nor his family were present at the time of the search. Hauptsturmführer Willi Loss has been commandant of Klooga while Gruppenführer Bertram has for the past month been in overall command of Klooga in preparation for the upcoming visit of the Reichsführer SS. I stand ready for your further orders. Heil Hitler! /s/ Aumeier, SS-Hauptsturmführer.

Putting the telex on his desk, Himmler slowly removed his glasses and massaged the bridge of his nose. "What do you make of this Brandt?"

Brandt was relieved that Himmler did not explode. Perhaps he was suffering from his more frequent bouts of stomach problems. Nonetheless, it was easier talking to a calm Himmler than one who was angry.

"Sir, *Gruppenführer* Bertram is a solid officer—I cannot believe that he would just up and desert his post. Loss, if I recall, had some 'emotional problems' after serving with the *Einsatzgruppen* early on, but seems to have overcome his problems and has performed admirably. Aumeier, of course was transferred from Auschwitz earlier this year due to charges of corruption and theft."

"And he is the one sending me this report? It could be he is trying to cover up his own incompetence and besmirching the names of two good officers. I just visited with Bertram weeks ago and he is the very embodiment of an SS officer. The report said that they checked Bertram's villa in Reval, and there was no sign of him or his family. Make some discreet inquiries with the Foreign Office to see if, God forbid, any of the family members left the country."

"Zu befehl, Herr Reichsführer."

With that, Brandt left Himmler's office for his own, which was right outside Himmler's. Brandt was considered "the gatekeeper" by almost everyone in the SS. You did not see Himmler unless you went through Brandt first (excluding the *Führer,* of course.)

Brandt began making a few calls to the Reich Ministry of Foreign Affairs and made some inquiries as to whether any of the Bertram family had left Reval. An hour later, Brandt received a call back telling him that yes, Lydia, Berthold, and Heidi Bertram had left Reval and had flown to Stockholm the week before. All documentation had been in order. The Foreign Ministry official also noted that there was no return date listed.

"Who signed the authorization for them to travel?" Brandt asked.

"It was signed by the HSSFP for *Reichskomissariat Ostland* Fredrich Jeckeln."

"Thank you, I appreciate your prompt response and please keep this inquiry confidential," Brandt ordered.

"*Heil* Hitler!" came the disembodied voice from the Foreign Ministry. Both men then hung up their respective telephones.

Brandt realized that this did not look good for Bertram. He got up from his desk and once again knocked on Himmler's door.

"Enter," Himmler called out.

"Sir, we have confirmation from the Foreign Ministry that Bertram's wife and two children left for Stockholm last week. They had proper authorization."

"Who signed the travel authorizations?

"HSSPF Jeckeln, sir."

"Well, that makes sense, he is Bertram's superior. Put out an alert for Bertram and the Klooga commandant, Loss. They are somewhere. Get me their files, Brandt."

"Yes, sir."

With that, Brandt left and put in a call to the RSHA personnel office and requested the files on both Bertram and Loss. The files contained the officers' military career and of course emergency contact information, next of kin, etc.

Within the hour, Brandt had the two files and once again entered Himmler's inner sanctum.

"Sir, here are the files. I took the liberty of first looking up their emergency contact information. While Bertram is from Bavaria, Loss is from Berlin. I have the address."

"Send a couple of men to his home; if he is there, bring him to me, I want to ask him a few questions. Also, contact Aumeier and see if he can find Loss's secretary, she may know something."

"*Zu befehl, Herr Reichsführer.*" With that, Brandt left Himmler's office and gave orders to two SS troopers waiting outside of Himmler's office to find Loss at all costs.

Office of the *Reichsführer SS*
Prinz-Albrecht-Strasse 8
Berlin, Germany
August 28, 1943, 1810 Hours

Brandt's two SS troopers found Loss at the home of his parents in the Wedding district of Berlin. He was ordered to report to Himmler immediately and they ensured that he did, escorting the young SS officer to the *Prinz-Albrecht-Strasse*. Loss, quaking in his boots, now stood before Himmler, whom he had only ever seen in movie newsreels.

"*Heil* Hitler!" Loss exclaimed, raising his arm in the Nazi salute.

Himmler weakly returned the salute.

"Loss, why are you not at your post in Klooga at this very moment?" Himmler calmly inquired.

"*Herr Reichsführer,* I and my men were ordered to go on leave by *Gruppenführer* Bertram. He told us we all needed a well-deserved break and that we had all been working hard in preparation for your upcoming visit to Klooga."

Himmler glanced over to Brandt who had been asked to stay for the questioning of the SS officer.

"Brandt, did Bertram request any authorization for leave for either himself or for Loss and his men?"

"None that I know of sir. All requests from senior SS and HSSPF leaders would have come across my desk."

"So, what you are telling me is that Bertram is absent without leave, correct?"

"I am afraid so, sir," Brandt responded.

Turning back to Loss, Himmler asked, "Tell me more about how *Gruppenführer* Bertram arranged for you and your men to have leave."

Swallowing hard, Loss explained to Himmler that Bertram ordered he and his men to go on leave and that Bertram would be responsible for the security of the camp and that another unit, which Bertram did not identify, would take over the guard duty at the camp while Loss and his men were gone. He further told Himmler that Bertram had laid on transportation with the *Reichsbahn* for special transport back to the Fatherland.

Himmler listened intently to Loss's story, his fingers steepled under his nose, looking like a stern schoolmaster that many referred to him behind his back.

When Loss finished, Himmler asked him, "Where are the prisoners?"

"Sir, they were there the evening that my men and I departed. Are they missing?"

Himmler could see that Loss was totally blindsided by his question.

"Yes, Loss, they are missing. All 100 of those Jews gone, vanished into thin air!"

Brandt could see that his boss was becoming more excited by the minute and his face began to flush. Brandt could only feel sympathy for the young SS officer, who by his answers, seemed to have been totally unaware of the events that transpired at the camp after his departure.

"*Herr Reichsführer,*" Brandt interrupted, "Perhaps we need to find the *gruppenführer* first before any accusations are made. I have been reviewing his reports from Klooga - up until now there have never been any discrepancies. And after all, sir, Loss was following orders from a senior officer."

Loss had been standing at attention in front of Himmler's desk the entire time, sweat beginning to pour down his forehead and down his back. He did not know whether he would leave Himmler's office alive.

"Very well, Brandt, you make a good point. Loss, you are to consider yourself under house arrest. My men will be checking on you daily. You are to confine yourself to your parents' home."

"*Zu befehl, Herr Reichsführer,*" Loss answered, relief in his voice.

"You are dismissed, Loss," Himmler said with a wave of his hand.

Loss immediately did an about-face and left Himmler's office, happy to be alive.

"Brandt, close the door," Himmler directed his subordinate.

"Brandt, we have a problem. A senior SS officer is absent from his post and without any authorization orders the commandant of Klooga and his men take leave - on top of that, 100 Jewish prisoners are missing. Connect the dots, Brandt. What does this appear to you? A well-planned escape, perhaps?"

Brandt could only nod his head in the affirmative.

Himmler continued, "This is treason! How can a senior SS officer do this? Bertram has burned all his bridges. Here is a man that I was going to promote to *Obergruppenführer* and give him a combat command! It all makes sense now, Brandt. Bertram sends his family to Sweden for safety and for some insane reason tries to rescue these Jews. It is probably that no-good Jesuit brother of his that brain-washed him and made him do these despicable acts. Send out a message to all Gestapo, *Kripo*, and *Feldgendarme* units. I want both Bertram brothers taken into custody. Circulate any photos we may have of both men. If Bertram did in fact do this, I will have him shot after a summary court-martial."

"*Herr Reichsführer*, do we need to inform the *Führer* of this incident?" Bertram asked quizzically.

Himmler thought for a moment. Normally he would try and alleviate many of Hitler's problems by handling them himself, making him indispensable to the *Führer.*

"Yes, Brandt, inform the *Führer.* Send the telex to Fegelein at *Wolfschanze.*"

"*Zu befehl, Herr Reichsführer,*" Brandt answered and left to carry out Himmler's orders.

Wolfschanze ("The Wolf's Lair")
Rastenburg, East Prussia
August 29, 1943, 1330 Hours

Adolf Hitler, *Führer* of the Greater German Reich was in a foul mood. With the recent failure of Operation *Zitadelle* ("Citadel") in Russia and the Allied invasion of Sicily in the early part of July, along with the overthrow of *Il Duce*, Hitler's mood swings were becoming increasingly prevalent, in part due to the cocktail of drugs his quack physician, Dr. Theo Morrell, was administering to him daily. Hitler had pinned great hopes on the success of *Zitadelle* to carry out offensive operations once again against a Red Army that was growing more powerful and operationally proficient by the day. The Germans had certainly inflicted horrendous casualties against the Bolsheviks, but the *Wehrmacht* too had sustained tremendous losses as well, losses that they could ill afford or replace.

SS *Brigadeführer* Hermann Fegelein, commander of the 8th SS Cavalry Division, *Florian Geyer*, and soon to be Himmler's liaison to Hitler's Headquarters, had received word of Bertram's actions and his complicity in the mass escape of the Jews. It now fell on him to inform the *Führer*, who was still in a foul mood. Fegelein was also engaged to be married to Gretl Braun, sister of Hitler's mistress, Eva Braun. Even with these close ties to the *Führer*, Fegelein was apprehensive about approaching Hitler with the news. Fegelein knew Bertram; he was a solid officer and a good SS man, but he had failed the *Führer* due to the undue influence of his cleric brother, Sepp. There would be hell to pay, no doubt, and Fegelein felt sorry for Peter Bertram and the fate

Hitler had in store for him.

The *Führer* was finishing up his noon-day military conference, and after the last staff officer briefed, the conference began to break up, some officers leaving, and others gathered in small groups, talking in low murmurs. Hitler was on his way out, back to his private quarters, along with Martin Bormann and a small escort, when Fegelein caught up with them.

"*Mein Führer*, if I might have a word, please, it is extremely urgent."

Bormann, known to many as the *Eminence Greis* (Grey Eminence), was totally devoted to Hitler, and had made himself indispensable to the German leader. Bormann had positioned himself so that no one got to see Hitler without Bormann's approval, be they ministers, *gauleiters*,[82] or generals.

Bormann said, "Fegelein, can't it wait, the *Führer* is a bit tired and is going to rest for a while."

"I'm sorry, *Herr Reichsleiter*, but this cannot wait."

Hitler waved Bormann off and said, "What is it Fegelein, more bad news, I suppose?"

Fegelein waited for a moment before he spoke and said, "*Mein Führer*, there has been a mass escape of Jewish prisoners from the Klooga concentration camp outside of Reval in *Ostland*."

Hitler's eyes widened and his cheeks and face became flushed. Before he could utter a word, Fegelein continued.

"*Mein Führer*, the escape was made possible with the assistance of SS *Gruppenführer* Peter Bertram and his cleric brother, Sepp. They facilitated the escape of the Jews and we have information that they are attempting to make their way to Sweden and freedom."

Hitler burst into a rage, his arms waving uncontrollably and cursing Bertram, and ordering his immediate arrest.

"I cannot believe that a senior officer of the SS could betray me in such a manner! It was his Jesuit brother and the Catholic Church that allowed this episode to happen!" Hitler continued to rant as the small group walked towards Hitler's spartan quarters, "I'll go straight into the Vatican. Do you think the Vatican impresses me? I couldn't care less. We'll clear out that gang of swine, then we'll apologize afterward...I couldn't care less!"[83]

When they reached his quarters, Hitler asked Bormann and Fegelein to come in and directed that they be seated. He then undertook one of his many rambling monologues.

> *Once this war is over, we will put a swift end to the Concordat. It will give me the greatest personal pleasure to point out to the Church all those occasions on which it has broken the terms of it. One need only recall the close cooperation between the Church as the murderers of Heydrich.[84] Catholic priests not only allowed them to hide in a church*

*on the outskirts of Prague, but even allowed them to entrench them-
selves in the sanctuary of the altar...the fact that I remain silent in
public over Church affairs is not in the least misunderstood by the sly
foxes of the Catholic Church, and I am quite sure that a man like the
Bishop von Galen[85] knows full well that after the war I shall extract
retribution to the last farthing. And, if he does not succeed in getting
himself transferred in the meanwhile to the Collegium Germanicum of
Rome, he may rest assured that in the balancing of our accounts, no
"T" will remain uncrossed, no "I" undotted![86]*

Hitler then continued, "The Pope is generally a frail old man,[87] thus I
have decided to place Pius XII in 'protective custody' in a nice villa in Bavaria,
where he can sit out the rest of the war in relative comfort and where he can no
longer make trouble for me."[88] He then added with a sinister smile, "Maybe
he'll be shot 'while trying to escape."

Both Bormann and Fegelein looked at each other; a look of surprise
on Fegelein's face, yet one of grim satisfaction on Bormann's, who sought the
church's ultimate destruction.[89]

Hitler continued, "Bormann, get *Obergruppenführer* Wolff here immediately and tell him I want to talk to him. If anyone can handle those duplicitous Italians and that rabble in the Vatican, it is Wolff."

"*Jawohl, Mein Führer!*" With that, Bormann went outside of Hitler's
quarters, grabbed an orderly who was posted outside the door, and ordered him
to bring Wolff, who had arrived earlier in the day, to Hitler's quarters immediately. He then returned to Hitler's side.

Hitler continued, "Fegelein, you will assist *Obergruppenführer* Wolff
with whatever plan he comes up with. As you know, the *Abwehr* is trying to
locate Mussolini so we can release the *Duce* and place him back in charge of
the government. So far, it appears the Italians have been one step ahead of us
in hiding the *Duce,* they appear to be moving him every few days to a different
location. It's like a damn shell game—just when you think you found the pea
under the cup, it is gone!"

"*Zu befehl, Mein Führer,*" Fegelein replied.

A moment later, there was a knock on the door to Hitler's quarters.
"Enter!" Hitler called out.

SS *Obergruppenführer* Karl Wolff, Highest SS and Police Leader for
all of Italy, entered, came to attention, and gave the Nazi salute with a resounding "Heil Hitler!"

Hitler weakly returned the salute, shook Wolff's hand and asked him
to sit down. He then launched into a tirade against the Italians, particularly
against the king and Marshal Badoglio, but he saved his most savage attacks
against the Pope. He then told Wolff,

I have a special mission for you, Wolff. I want you and your troops to occupy Vatican City as soon as possible, secure its files and art treasures, and take the Pope and Curia to the north. I do not want him to fall into the hands of the Allies or to be under their political pressure and influence. The Vatican is already a nest of spies and a center of anti-National Socialist propaganda. How quickly can you prepare this operation?[90]

Wolff, initially taken aback, responded, "*Mein Führer*, SS and police units are currently stretched to their limits, but I will be able to give you a better picture in about a week."

"You have one week, Wolff. It was that Jew-loving Pope who encouraged that "king nutcracker"[91] Victor Emmanuel and some rival Fascist leaders to overthrow the *Duce*. I will make them pay with their lives for their insolence! Fegelein, we will use men from your *Florian Geyer* division[92] as well as the *Hermann Göring* panzer division to carry out the operation. Wolff, you will be in overall command of the operation. Get with Fegelein and *Generalmajor* Conrath[93] and work out the details. I want a briefing in one week. That is all gentlemen, you are dismissed."

With that, all three men, Bormann, Fegelein, and Wolff, jumped to their feet, raised their arms in a Nazi salute, and shouted in unison "*Heil* Hitler!" They then turned and left, leaving Hitler alone with his thoughts and his Alsatian dog, *Blondi*.

Wolfschanze ("The Wolf's Lair")
Rastenburg, East Prussia
August 29, 1943, 1500 Hours

Obergruppenführer Wolff returned to his quarters after his meeting with Hitler, his head spinning. The orders that he had just received from the *Führer*, if carried out, would set in motion a chain of events which would have severe repercussions against the Reich. Wolff, himself a lapsed Protestant, could see that if the Pope and Curia were seized, it would affect many Catholics currently serving in the German armed forces, even within the SS itself, where it was believed that 40 percent of the SS still adhered to the Catholic faith, this despite the best efforts of Himmler to dissuade his army of any organized religious beliefs. Not only would the Allies score a major propaganda coup by such an action, but other predominantly Catholic nations still friendly towards the Reich, such as Salazar's Portugal, Franco's Spain, Pavelic's Independent State of Croatia, and Tiso's Slovakia, would not look too favorably upon the arrest of the Roman Pontiff.

Wolff also worried about a possible mutiny within the ranks of the *Wehrmacht,* particularly from units from Bavaria, which could then possibly lead to open civil war. And then what? As Wolff's mind raced, he believed that this was one order from the *Führer* that he probably should not obey, for the consequences were just too horrific for Germany. Wolff, and many of the senior Nazi leadership still felt that a negotiated peace settlement could still be achieved, particularly if the West could be sold on the dangers of Stalin and Bolshevism. Only months earlier, in April, the German discovery of the mass graves of Polish officers in the Katyn Forest near Smolensk, had raised German hopes that the Western Allies would see the true face of Bolshevism. Even Anglo-American POWs had been brought to the grave site in order to view first-hand the brutality of the Soviet system. Yet, no rupture of the Anglo-American-Soviet alliance occurred, much to the chagrin of Hitler and the rest of the Nazi leadership.[94]

Wolff thought for a moment and realized that he would have to work closely with von Weizsäcker, whom Wolff believed to be a member of the growing anti-Hitler resistance - he just couldn't prove it. He would have to quietly inform the German ambassador of the *Führer's* hare-brained order to kidnap Pius XII, and then have von Weizsäcker pass on the information to the Holy Father. Wolff thought to himself that what he was doing was treason, and that if Himmler or Hitler found out, it would be the firing squad for sure. Nonetheless, with Germany's wartime fortunes waning, it might be good to have the Supreme Pontiff on one's side, especially if the Highest SS and Police Leader for all of Italy were ever to be brought before a war crimes tribunal.

Wolfschanze ("The Wolf's Lair")
Rastenburg, East Prussia
August 29, 1943, 1515 Hours

Before he had a chance to change his uniform, an orderly knocked on Wolff's door requesting his presence at the Officer's *Kasino* to take a telephone call from *Reichsführer SS* Himmler. Wolff's meeting with Himmler was not scheduled for another day as Himmler was still in Berlin, so he was surprised when the request came. Following the orderly, Wolff entered the *kasino* and was escorted over to a small corner table where a telephone had been connected into a corner jack.

"*Wolfchen,*[95] it's good to hear your voice."

"Thank you, *Herr Reichsführer,*" Wolff answered.

Himmler then got right to the point. "*Wolfchen,* I understand that the *Führer* has ordered you to do a feasibility study on 'securing' the Pope and the Roman Curia. I find that most intriguing." Himmler, who was raised Catholic like many of his Nazi brethren, had no love lost for the faith of his youth.

Like Hitler and Goebbels, he too sought the destruction of the Roman Catholic Church.

"*Herr Reichsführer*, as I told the *Führer*, our forces are stretched quite thin right now, and with the collapse of Italy, we are having to do more with less."

"The *Führer* directed you to coordinate with Fegelein and *Generalmajor* Conrath, did he not?"

"Yes, sir, he did." Wolff was becoming suspicious of just how knowledgeable Himmler was on the discussion that had taken place in Hitler's quarters less than an hour previously, even though Himmler himself had not been present for the talks. He now suspected that Himmler had Hitler's living quarters 'bugged' with listening devices.

"*Wolfchen*, you are to follow through with this study and before you brief the *Führer*, I would like to review it, is that clear?" Himmler demanded.

"Quite clear, *Herr Reichsführer*."

"Good, then it's settled! Hopefully, within a month's time, we will be able to clear all of that rabble out of the Vatican once and for all. When you return to Rome, I want you to coordinate with *Obersturmbannführer* Kappler on this mission. Kappler knows every inch of Rome, and I think he's just the man to come up with a reason for German troops to enter the Vatican. Perhaps he could provoke another "Gleiwitz incident"[96] which would do the trick, eh, *Wolfchen*?" Himmler said with a chuckle.

Wolff, a pragmatist and not one to go off half-cocked, thought the idea was mad. First Hitler, and now Himmler, thought they could just march into the Vatican, arrest or even worse, kill the Pope, and the world would not take notice.

"*Zu befehl, Herr Reichsführer*, I will begin the feasibility study immediately!"

"Splendid, *Wolfchen*, splendid! I will see you tomorrow evening in Rastenburg and we shall discuss this further." With that, Himmler rang off.

As he replaced the telephone receiver back in its cradle Wolff could only think of the old saying that 'the inmates are now running the asylum' and that Hitler's erratic behavior was leading Germany more and more down the path to total defeat and ruin.

Finnish Armed Forces Headquarters
Mikkeli, Finland
August 29, 1943, 1645 Hours

General der Infanterie Waldemar Erfurth,[97] German liaison to the Finnish Armed Forces Headquarters, located at Mikkeli,[98] was pouring over maps along with senior Finnish Army officers. Erfurth had been liaison now for two years, and had a good working relationship with Marshal Mannerheim, whom he considered to be an outstanding soldier - "the First Soldier of Finland" as German newsreels trumpeted during Hitler's 1942 visit to Finland in honor of the Marshal's 75th birthday.

Erfurth had received a telex from OKW Chief, Field Marshal Wilhelm Keitel, informing him of the escape of the Jewish prisoners and that they may attempt to transit Finland in order to make their way to neutral Sweden. Erfurth was to use all his powers of persuasion with Marshal Mannerheim to ensure that the Finns would not intervene to assist the escapees. Keitel emphasized that this was a very delicate and sensitive subject, and that he was to be as diplomatic as possible in his arguments. The last thing the Reich wanted to do was lose an erstwhile ally over the 'Jewish Question.'

Erfurth had cursed silently under his breath when he read the telex and knew that this was almost an impossible task to ask of Mannerheim. After all, Finnish soldiers of the Jewish faith were fighting alongside their German allies against the Soviets and the Finns as a whole were not anti-Semitic.[99]

Looking over his map, Erfurth traced the route of the escapees from Estonia across the northern front to just outside the Leningrad sector. He assumed that the Bertram brothers would seek assistance from the Spanish army, which had control over the sector, and who, like the Finns, were not anti-Semitic. If the *Wehrmacht* had acted with force to try and recapture the escapees while they were being harbored by the Spaniards, there would be a rupture of relations between Madrid and Berlin and Franco would no doubt pull the Blue Division out of Russia, at a crucial time where every bit of manpower (German or otherwise) was needed.

Walking over to Mannerheim's office, he asked the Marshal's aide-de-camp if he could speak to the Marshal alone. The aide disappeared for a minute and returned to Erfurth.

"Sir, please go on in, the Marshal will see you."

With that, Erfurth walked into Mannerheim's rather Spartan office. It did not have the trappings of a German field marshal's office, such as historic battle prints, battle flags, or busts of former military leaders. Mannerheim was seated at his desk when Erfurth entered.

"Ah, general, so good of you to stop in," Mannerheim said while rising and extending his hand to his German colleague. "Please, do sit down."

Mannerheim offered Erfurth a cigarette from a case he kept on his desktop, and Erfurth accepted. Mannerheim joined him in a smoke.

"Now, how may I help you?"

Clearing his throat, Erfurth began, "Sir, I received a telex from Field Marshal Keitel earlier today...I should have prefaced this by stating this is a rather delicate matter for the Reich..."

"Go on, I'm listening," Mannerheim said attentively.

Erfurth continued, "The telex contained a very sensitive request from the OKW, to wit, that a number of Jews may attempt to transit Finland in order to reach neutral Sweden. Their escape was facilitated by a rogue SS officer and his cleric brother. We would ask Your Excellency that the Finnish military refrain from attempting to assist them if, perchance, and by luck, they happen to reach the Finnish frontier, and if so, to apprehend them and turn them over to the *Wehrmacht* for repatriation."

Mannerheim continued to puff on his cigarette and was silent for what seemed to Erfurth like minutes.

Crushing out his cigarette in the ashtray on his desk, he stated, "My dear Erfurth, I can understand the position this places you with your superiors and I am not unsympathetic. However, as I told *Reichsführer* Himmler during his visit, Finland does not have a 'Jewish problem' and will treat her Jews as it would any of its other citizens—with dignity and respect. I would have thought this was a non-issue by now. With regards to the escapees that you alluded to—if they are so lucky enough to reach Finnish soil, they will be afforded the full protection of the Finnish military, which will then escort them to Sweden. Under no circumstances, general, is the German 20th Mountain Army to interfere with these Jews if they enter sovereign Finnish territory. May I remind you that the *Wehrmacht* is a guest here in Finland, and I will expect it to conduct itself in an honorable manner and in accordance with the memorandum of agreement drawn up by our two nations in 1941. I will ask, general, that you make this clear to General Dietl[100]. I would hate to see any misunderstandings stand in the way of defeating our common enemy, Mr. Stalin, now would we?"

"No, sir."

"Good, then I think this matter is settled. Is there anything else you wanted to discuss with me at this time?"

"No sir, not at this time."

With that, Mannerheim stood, signaling that the conversation had ended. He extended his hand to Erfurth, who took it.

"General, I consider you an outstanding officer and a friend - I would hate to have anything come between our personal and professional relationships."

Erfurth saluted, did an about face and left the Marshal's office. When he made it to the anteroom, he began to think of what Keitel and the *Führer* would say when he reported back that Mannerheim was not in the least bit interested in the Reich's request—if anything, it appeared to Erfurth that Mannerheim secretly hoped the Jews would make it safely to Finland.

Chapter X

"Not only the history of the past, but also present times afford numberless examples of the very hard-boiled diplomats to be found in the service of the Catholic Church, and of how extremely cautious one must be in dealing with them."
--Adolf Hitler, July 4, 1942

Headquarters
Army Group North
Feldgendarme **Office**
Russia
August 29, 1943, 1230 Hours

Oberst Wiedemann had just returned from a staff meeting with the Army Group commander, *Generalfeldmarschall* Georg von Kuchler. No sooner had he sat down at his desk when a young corporal from the Signals section brought him a telex, which Wiedemann had to sign for. The telex read:

> *All military and civilian police agencies are ordered to arrest on sight SS Gruppenführer Peter Bertram and his brother, Monsignor Josef Bertram, Vatican Foreign Office on suspicion of treason and espionage against the Reich. Both men are considered armed and dangerous and should be approached with utmost caution. Once in custody, the Office of the Reichsführer SS is to be informed immediately so that prisoner transport can be coordinated with RSHA. Heil Hitler!*
> */s/ Brandt*

Wiedemann read the telex and immediately thought to himself that Bertram, whomever he was, must be in a heap of trouble if Himmler's office is sending out this message. He then put the message down and immediately picked it up again, looking at the name 'Bertram.' That was the same name that *Major* Rudolph had queried about just the other day. Now that name shows up on what amounted to a 'Most Wanted' list. Rudolph had also informed him that the SS officer's brother, the priest, Josef Bertram, was with the Spaniards in their sector. Find the priest and you will probably find the missing *gruppenführer.* If he could do that, it would be a nice feather in his cap and a possible promotion, one never knew. He decided to contact *Major* Rudolph over at the 170th Division and let him know that the Bertram brothers were persons of interest and needed to be detained.

Weidemann picked up his telephone receiver and was connected to the Army Group's main communication center. Most calls coming through these days were from either the OKW or from Hitler's *Wolfschanze* Headquarters in East Prussia.

"Connect me with *Major* Rudolph, *Feldgendarme* Office, 170th Division," he ordered.

"I am sorry sir, the lines are down, probably more Partisan activity," the operator reported.

Disgusted, Wiedemann slammed down the receiver on his telephone.

"Damn Partisans," Wiedemann mumbled. The 170th was much too far away to just get in a vehicle and drive over to the division sector. Even if it was relatively close, he would be susceptible to Partisan attacks and that was not a prospect he was looking forward to. He had to think of another way of getting word to Rudolph and soon.

"Damn Partisans," he mumbled as he made his way over to the communications center to find an alternate way of reaching the 170th.

After a five-minute walk, Wiedemann arrived at the communications center, which was a beehive of activity. Wiedemann walked right into the center's commander, a young *Oberstleutnant* by the name of Tuffalo, who jumped to attention when Wiedemann walked in.

"Herr Oberst, how may I be of assistance?"

"I need to get a message to the *Feldgendarme* office at the 170th. The land lines have obviously been cut by the *Banditen* (bandits), so I will need to use the high frequency radio to get this out."

"Sir, we are backlogged with getting messages out—messages for OKW and the *Führerhauptquartier* take precedence. I am sorry, but it will have to wait."

"How long will it take?" Wiedemann asked, visibly annoyed.

"Approximately three hours, give or take."

"Very well. Please give me the form and a pen so I can get this message out. Since time was of the essence, Wiedemann made the message short and to the point:

> *RSHA has ordered immediate arrest of Bertram brothers. Believe that Josef Bertram is currently in your sector or with Spanish division at Krasny Bor. You are ordered to place Bertram under arrest and held for questioning. Contact Army Group Center*

Feldgendarme Office immediately upon securing subject. Heil Hitler! /s/ Wiedemann

Wiedemann looked the message over one last time and then handed it to Tuffalo.

"I will personally see that this gets sent out, *Herr Oberst,*" Tuffalo said.

"Thank you, I will expect nothing less." With that, Wiedemann left the communications center hoping against hope that the radio message would get to Rudolph in time and that Bertram would not slip through their fingers.

Spanish Airfield
Krasny Bor, Russia
August 29/30, 1943, 2300 hours

With the German *Luftwaffe* personnel otherwise engaged at the Red Star Tavern drinking themselves into oblivion, Rodriguez was able to make his way back to the airfield without incident. He quickly took charge of the Spanish airmen already assembled in the hangars awaiting his arrival.

"Men of the *Escuadrilla Azul*, I want to thank you for volunteering for this very unique mission. All of you are heroes—from the mechanics, gunners, armorers and pilots, I salute each and every one of you. You no doubt have been briefed by your section officers—this is a very dangerous mission for all of us. If the Germans find out of what we are about to embark on, we could all very well be shot. The Germans were quite ruthless with their former Italian allies once Mussolini was overthrown, and I dare say, they would be quite brutal with us. Nonetheless, we have the blessing of our division commander, and I believe that we are doing something to help alleviate some of the sufferings that these *judios* have suffered. When the history of this division is written years from now, I hope that our actions today will be one of the highlights of this division's tour in Russia."

As he was finishing up his talk with the squadron personnel, a *Kubelwagen* pulled up outside the hangar and both Sepp and Chaplain Garcia alighted from the vehicle and entered the hangar.

"Ah, here is our division chaplain now," said Rodriguez, "along with the German priest many of you have been hearing about, Monsignor Bertram."

As both men stepped forward, Garcia said, "I would like to give a blessing if I may, *mí coronel.*"

Rodriguez nodded his ascent, and Garcia asked the men to kneel, which they all did in unison.

Heavenly Father, we ask that you protect our brave

airmen as they embark on this very dangerous mission, to help save your Chosen People from certain extermination. Lord, bless our pilots and navigators that they make it through safely and deliver their precious cargo unscathed into the waiting arms of their rescuers. We ask that these Jews be given sanctuary in Sweden and that they may live out the rest of their lives in peace and prosperity. For this we pray. Amen.

A resounding "Amen" was spoken by all the assembled airmen. Garcia then made a lifting motion with his hands to have the airmen stand back up.

'Thank you, *Padre* Garcia," said Rodriguez. "Alright, everyone knows what they need to do this evening. No mistakes, mistakes cost lives. Section leaders, take charge of your men!"

With that order, the hanger became a beehive of activity, with men going in every direction.

Rodriguez then took the Sepp and Chaplain Garcia aside and asked, "What is the status of our 'cargo'?"

Garcia answered, "They are on their way here now - the lorries went down about an hour ago to the temporary shelter area we had set up for them." As he finished talking, they heard the sound of trucks grinding gears as they entered the airfield flight line.

"Sounds like they have arrived," said Garcia, a smile on his face.

Ten Opel trucks then pulled up in front of the open hanger doors. Once the engines turned off, the drivers and assistant drivers got out and opened up the canvas covering the back of the vehicle, in order for fresh air to circulate. The canvas had been pulled down so no one could see the Jews.

Sepp went up to the truck carrying the Rabbi Abramovitz and told him, "We will ask that you stay in the trucks for the time being. We will let you use the latrine facilities before we load the aircraft. You will be given water and rations on the planes. Time is of the essence. We should have you airborne within the hour."

Rabbi Abramovitz closed his eyes in silent prayer. He prayed that God would deliver him from this evil and get he and his people to safety.

As the minutes ticked away the Spanish airmen readied the aircraft, which had been fueled beforehand in order to save time. In the interim, the Jewish prisoners were permitted to use the latrine facilities and stretch their legs. Most just stayed on the trucks and prayed silently that their collective nightmare would soon be over.

By 2345 hours the JU-52's were preparing for take-off, all lined up with their full compliment of crew. Now all that needed to be done was load their passengers. As the Spanish airmen assisted the passengers off the back of the trucks, they were given long hugs and embraces by the grateful Jews. Most had never been on an aircraft before, so added to their fears of being caught was now, for many, the fear of flying. By 0030 hours, the planes were loaded and ready for take-off.

Rabbi Abramovitz was the last to board the last aircraft. Before doing so, with tears in his eyes, he grasped the hands of both Sepp and Garcia. "I cannot find the words to thank you both and all that have done for us. You have delivered us from death's doorstep, while the rest of the world had forgotten us. Monsignor, you and your brother, I will pray for till my last dying breath."

Both Sepp and Garcia choked back tears themselves. "God be with you," said Sepp. "*Vaya con Dios,*" said Garcia.

Abramovitz was assisted into the aircraft, and the door securely closed behind him by the crew chief.

As each aircraft revved up their engines to the maximum RPM's needed for takeoff, Sepp, Garcia, and Rodriguez watched from the hanger area the aircraft assume their position for takeoff. The control tower was manned by a Spaniard and one by one with two minutes between liftoff, the aircraft were airborne, winging their precious cargo to Finland and freedom. Joining the transports were the FW-190's flown by the squadron, which would provide escort for part of the journey.

As the last aircraft disappeared from sight, Rodriguez turned to both clergymen and said, "Well, that is it gentlemen, God-willing, they make it safely to Finland. There shouldn't be any interference from the Reds. Our fighters don't have the range to go all the way to Finland but will escort them part of the way."

He then continued, "So what now, Monsignor? What happens to you? No doubt by now the Germans are aware that both you and your brother are responsible for the escape from Klooga. We can arrange to get you to Spain if you so desire. I know Chaplain Garcia has a direct line to *El Caudillo,*" he said with a smile.

"Sepp, that is something we really never discussed. How do you propose to get back? You and your brother are both wanted men by now. We can get you to Spain if you desire."

"Jaime, I have thought long and hard about this. My place is at the Vatican. I will find a way back."

"I have a thought, gentlemen," Rodriguez said. "It is a longshot but might work. The Italians still have a small air force contingent in Russia, Odessa to be precise. Perhaps they may be able to get you back to the Italian mainland; maybe a crew is rotating back, and you can hitch a ride with them.

It is just a thought."

With the overthrow of the *Duce* in late July, and before the forced disarming of Italian military units still in the field once Italy surrendered to the Allies on September 8, the Italian Air Force still had a small contingent stationed on the Eastern Front in Odessa in the Crimea. The Italians could see the handwriting on the wall and were wary of their German allies. Still, on the surface at least, Italy and Germany continued the war against the Allies.

Sepp nodded in agreement that it was something that he should ponder. The Spaniards had been most helpful, but they could only do so much for him. His main concern now was to get back to Rome and the relative safety of the Vatican.

Rodriguez continued, "There is an Italian air liaison officer by the name of *Coronel* Garcetti, who has paid us a visit on at least two occasions. I can get word to him and see if he can send an aircraft here, perhaps under the guise of a training flight. I cannot promise anything, but it is worth a try."

"That would be wonderful, Rodriguez, thank you," Sepp replied.

Rodriguez then gave both clergymen a mock salute with a smile and headed back to his office at the airfield to attempt to contact Garcetti in Odessa. The vast distances of Russia made it almost impossible for things to get done in just one day, so time was of the essence. Within the hour, he had composed a brief message to be sent out at first light. It was late and Rodriguez was on the brink of exhaustion. He had pulled the wool over the Germans' eyes, but there would probably hell to pay if the Germans found out that the division had been involved in spiriting the escapees to freedom.

Spanish Airfield
Krasny Bor, Russia
August 30, 1943, 0800 Hours

All of the Spanish aircraft, both transports and fighters, had returned safely to base by 0600 hours after an exhausting flight. The fighter aircraft had been the first to return due to their limited range. Fortunately, neither the Red Air Force nor the Germans had challenged the Spanish and it was more of a 'milk run' than anything. The Finns had met the aircraft once they landed, and cared for the escapees, many who literally kissed the ground upon disembarking the aircraft. Luckily, not one German was seen at the joint base and the escapees were cared for by Finnish military personnel. The JU-52's were refueled and as the aircraft were now empty of their human cargo and as there was a good tail wind, they returned to Krasny Bor in record time. The Swedish Air Force had sent ten of their own JU-52's[101] transport aircraft as promised and by 0900 hours, had arrived safely in Stockholm. The escapees were now under the care and protection of the Swedish government and the International

Red Cross.

After all the Spanish transports had returned safely to base, the pilots and other crew members were debriefed by the squadron intelligence officer. It was no small feat that the Spanish were able to accomplish this mission in the limited time available. The senior officer from the transport flight, a *Major* Suarez, asked to speak with Rodriguez as well as Sepp and Chaplain Garcia.

The men met in a small office in the hangar.

"Gentlemen," Suarez said, "I want to let you know that I personally witnessed the personnel loading onto the Swedish aircraft. The transfer went off without a hitch, and they were well cared for by Finnish ground personnel before they loaded up for Sweden. My men and I are grateful to have been part of this humanitarian operation."

"I received word from the nuncio in Stockholm that all the aircraft arrived safely. *Major*, I cannot thank you and your men enough for what you accomplished today. It is nothing shy of a miracle," Sepp said, as he shook Suarez's hand vigorously.

"We are not out of the woods yet, Sepp," Garcia said. "We still have to get you out of the area and soon."

As he finished speaking, an airman knocked on the door, saluted, and said, "*Coronel, Major*, and *Padres*, the commanding general would like to see you in his office immediately, if you please."

"Thank you, we are on our way," replied Rodriguez, as the airman, saluted and then left the office.

"The general probably wants an after-action report from you, Suarez, and I would certainly like to hear more about it." All four men then left the hanger and headed for the division headquarters building by vehicle.

Headquarters
250ᵗʰ Infantry Division
Krasny Bor, Russia
August 30, 1943, 0830 Hours

As the four men made their way to the commanding general's office, they noticed parked in front of the headquarters building a *Kubelwagen* with the markings of the German 170ᵗʰ Infantry Division. This certainly was not unusual as other division representatives often paid a visit to the headquarters for any number of reasons. Today was different, however, as the visitors from the 170ᵗʰ were *Major* Hans Rudolph, *Kommandant* of the *Feldgendarme* as well as two of his troopers, one being Corporal Kurtz, who would be able to identify Sepp.

As the four entered the anteroom to Esteban-Infantes' office, his aide-de-camp took Rodriguez aside and warned him, "Sir, there is a German

Major and two of his troopers in with the general. He is here to arrest the monsignor."

"He has only two men with him you say?"

"Sí, *mí coronel*, only two."

"Ok, do me a favor and get an armed squad together and have them wait outside by the Germans' vehicle. The Germans are not to leave the area with the monsignor, understood?"

"Sí, *mí coronel.*

"Good, now please announce us to the general.'

The aide knocked on Esteban-Infantes door and informed him that Rodriguez and the others were present.

"Show them in," the general ordered.

The three Spanish officers saluted, and Esteban-Infantes returned their salute. He did not offer his guests seats.

"Gentlemen, *Major* Rudolph here is with the 170th Infantry Division *Feldgendarme* office and his has orders to arrest the good monsignor," Esteban-Infantes said while looking directly over at Sepp. "I will let *Major* Rudolph explain."

"*Major*," the general said, nodding in the German's direction. "The floor is all yours."

Clearing his throat, Rudolph said, "Thank you *Herr General.* Monsignor Josef Bertram, I am *Major* Hans Rudolph of the 170th Infantry Division *Feldgendarme* Office and I have orders to place you in custody."

"Who's orders?" Rodriguez sarcastically asked.

"*Reichsführer SS* Himmler's, *Herr Oberstleutnant*," Rudolph answered just as smugly.

Rodriguez then looked to Esteban-Infantes with pleading eyes, asking, "*Mí general*, is there anything we can do?"

Esteban-Infantes, who had read the order and still had it in his hands, looked forlorn. He realized that it was only a matter of time before the Germans would know the full story and Spanish implication in the escape, and Hitler's fury would not be pleasant for all parties concerned.

"I am sorry Guillermo, but the *Major*'s paperwork is in order, and I am sorry, Monsignor, but I am afraid you will have to accompany *Major* Rudolph back to the 170th. I am very, very sorry." The general was sincere in his apologies. He knew the possible consequences in helping the escapees and now it was coming back to haunt him.

A look of despair fell upon all in the room (except of course for the Germans).

Rudolph, pointing directly at Sepp then asked Corporal Kurtz, "Kurtz is this the man you saw on the train and brought to division headquarters?"

"*Jawohl, Herr Major*, it is the same man."

"Good, now we have confirmation. Monsignor, if you please," Rudolph pointed at the door motioning Sepp to exit the office.

"*Herr General*, thank you very much for your cooperation. I will report you and your division's cooperation on this matter to the Group Headquarters." He then made a slight bow, and left the office, his two troopers escorting Sepp out of the building. Sepp seemed resigned to his fate as he was being led out of the building. As they exited however, Sepp and his German escort were met with a fully armed squad of Spanish soldiers, their weapons trained on the Germans.

"What is the meaning of this!" Rudolph exclaimed as he reached for his pistol.

Behind him, Rodriguez very softly said, "I would not do that if I were you, *Herr Major*. My men have very itchy trigger fingers. You and your men drop your weapons, now."

Seeing they were outmanned and outgunned, the Germans did as they were ordered.

"Monsignor, will you please come with me," Rodriguez beckoned to him as Sepp separated himself from his German guards and moved to Rodriguez.

Rodriguez then ordered the noncommissioned officer of the squad to place the Germans in protective custody. "Lock them up but treat them well. Get them some water and feed them until I figure out what to do with them."

"You will never get away with this!" Rudolph protested as he and his men were led away to a building that seconded as a holding cell for division prisoners.

Rodriguez, Garcia and Sepp then went back to Esteban-Infantes' office. The general who had stepped out of his office to talk to his aide, was shocked to see Sepp standing with his operations officer and division chaplain.

"What's going on here? I thought the monsignor was in German custody! Rodriguez, Garcia, explain yourselves! " he demanded.

"*Mi General*," Rodriguez began, "We relieved the Germans of Monsignor Bertram—they are cooling their heels in the holding cell. I take full responsibility for the action, neither Chaplain Garcia nor anyone else in the division is responsible—I and I alone."

Esteban-Infantes was dumbfounded at Rodriguez's admission of guilt.

"OK, fine, you're responsible. Now what happens to us when the Germans don't return to their unit. I am sure they radioed in their location to their higher headquarters when they got here. Once the Germans find out where their men are, I wouldn't be surprised if they don't come charging in with guns blazing."

"*Mi General*, if we can keep the Germans incommunicado for about

48 hours, I believe we can get Monsignor Bertram out of the area safely. There is an Italian air unit in Odessa that is readying to rotate back to Italy soon. I contacted the air liaison officer, *Coronel* Garcetti, whom you have met in the past during one of his visits here. He is willing to assist. Odessa is a long way from here, but we could fly Monsignor Bertram to a halfway point and the Italians will take him to Odessa and hopefully, home."

Esteban-Infantes could only think about the repercussions to such a scheme. He was now more concerned about what the Germans would do, short-term, once they found out that three of their men had been forcibly disarmed and held prisoner by a supposedly allied unit. However, the general also had the highest regards for this priest, who risked his life to save those that were to be sacrificed for Hitler's insane goals for a "Jew-free" Europe.

"Very well, Guillermo, you have 48 hours, and then God only knows what will become of us."

"Thank you, *Mí General*, you won't regret it." Both Sepp and Garcia also added their thanks.

Esteban-Infantes gave them a weak smile and waved them off.

As the three left the general's office, Sepp said, "I think Jaime, that your close association with the *Caudillo* has enabled us to persuade the general into agreeing to go above and beyond with this scheme.

"No doubt, Sepp," said Garcia. "Now we have to get you back to Rome safely, before all hell breaks loose here."

The men drove in silence over to the squadron's operations center where a number of messages awaited Rodriquez. As he and the two chaplains' entered the outer office, the enlisted airmen sprang to attention; Rodriguez waved them to be seated and continued on to his office.

"Gentlemen, please give me a few moments to go over this message traffic and then we will discuss the matter at hand."

Both clergymen made themselves as comfortable as they could in the cheap chairs used to furnish the office. As Rodriguez leafed through the message traffic he came across one that he had hoped to see: a telex from Colonel Garcetti of the Italian Air Force.

"Gentlemen!" he exclaimed, waving the paper above his head, "I think we have the solution to our problem. This message is from the Italian air liaison here in Russia. He has agreed to transport Monsignor Bertram back to Rome! The squadron will be rotating back to Italy by early September, which will give us some time to arrange rendezvous points here in the East for the transfer.

"That's wonderful, Rodriguez!" Sepp exclaimed. "I don't know how you did it, but you did."

Both clergymen had broad smiles on their faces, with Garcia going so far as to hugging Sepp.

"Ok, we now have to move very quickly on this. We still have our German friends 'on ice' and have to decide what to do with them. Monsignor, you will have to keep a very low profile for a few days before you are flown out of here. Perhaps we can put you up in a peasant's hut outside of the base." Rodriguez continued, "I think I know where. The Red Star Tavern! They have rooms and the proprietors and pretty well dispensed towards us, especially after the other night. They made a lot of money off that dinner."

"I am in your hands, Rodriguez," Sepp replied.

As Rodriguez was about to speak, gunshots could be heard off in the distance coming from the direction of the division headquarters..

"Those are close," Rodriguez said.

"Partisan attack maybe?" Garcia chimed in.

"Let me check. Gentlemen, please stay here until we find out what's going on," Rodriguez politely requested of the two clergymen.

As Rodriguez walked out into the hangar area, an airman from the squadron ran up to him and reported. "*Mi coronel*, we just received word that the Germans prisoners tried to escape!! One of the guards were bringing them some food and water and he was jumped from behind. As they made their way out of the cell, they started shooting and our troops returned fire, killing them all."

Rodriguez stared blankly for a moment and then crossed himself. "*Dio Mio,*" was all he could mutter.

"Have the bodies brought here to the hangar," Rodriguez ordered.

"*Sí, mí coronel,*" and the airman drove back toward the division head-quarters area.

Rodriguez then went back to his office and was about to explain to Sepp and Garcia the source of the gunshots when his phone rang.

"Excuse me, gentlemen," he said as he lifted the receiver.

"*Teniente coronel* Rodriguez speaking."

"Guillermo, what happened? What was the source of those shots that were fired?" Esteban-Infantes demanded.

As Rodriguez explained to his commanding general, both Sepp and Garcia overheard what had transpired. As he concluded the call, he stated, "Very well, *mí general*," and hung up the receiver.

"Well, gentlemen, now you know what happened. That makes things a bit easier on us, though. We no longer have to worry about those Germans causing any problems."

He continued, "The bodies are being brought over here. Perhaps you would like to pray over them?"

"Yes, by all means," both priests said in unison.

Minutes later, the sound of a small lorry pulling into the hangar let them know that the bodies of the three German servicemen had arrived. As the truck came to a halt, a crowd of airmen gathered around and watched as the bodies were carefully and respectfully off-loaded from the truck and placed on some pallets. The bodies were covered up with ponchos. Both priests prayed over the bodies, not knowing whether the fallen were of the Catholic faith, but nonetheless, praying for the repose of their souls. Sepp was surprised to see that the airmen too prayed during this very solemn and somber event.

With the prayers for the dead concluded, Rodriguez asked to see the Sepp and Garcia back in his office.

"Gentlemen, thank you for performing the last rites for those fallen. We *divisionarios* never know when it might be one of us that will fall in battle and I would like to think that someone would pray over our remains. Their deaths, however, gives us an opportunity. We can make it appear that they were attacked by Partisans on their way back to their base which will remove any suspicion on what occurred here earlier with our taking them prisoner. What do you think?"

"You won't desecrate the bodies any further, will you?" Sepp asked.

"No, Monsignor. We will shoot up their vehicle and then place the bodies in their vehicle and 'stage' it to make it appear like a Partisan ambush."

Both Garcia and Sepp looked at each other and nodded silently. While Garcia was a uniformed military chaplain, a noncombatant who did not even carry a weapon, his role was to offer spiritual guidance to the men of the division. Both he and Sepp had no stomach for the killing that was, unfortunately, all around them.

"I will have some men undertake the assignment—when the Germans find the remains of their comrades, it will appear as another tragic ambush by the Russians. In the meantime, it will give us time to get Monsignor Bertram home."

The clergymen nodded silently and then left Rodriguez's office, both men lost in their own thoughts and what was to happen in the days ahead.

Headquarters
250th Infantry Division
Krasny Bor, Russia
August 30, 1943, 1115 Hours

Rodriguez had been in the commanding general's office for almost an hour outlining his plan to 'stage' the ambush of the already dead German personnel now lying in the squadron's aircraft hangar.

"*Mi General*, if we place the bodies in a bullet-riddled staff car, once it is discovered the Germans will just assume that they had been ambushed by Partisans, thus removing suspicion from us entirely."

His nerves now frayed to the breaking point, Esteban-Infantes felt he was being pulled deeper into this cover-up and wanted no part of it. *"Basta!*

(Enough!)" he shouted at his subordinate. "This has gone on far too long! I am tired of the deception! I can only do so much and keep the Germans at bay for only so long. Ultimately, they will find out that we were instrumental in flying the Jews to freedom. You need to put an end to all this now, Guillermo, now!"

Rodriguez had never seen his commander so agitated, and he could not blame him. Their lives were in danger if the Germans discovered who was behind the rescue operation. Hitler would have no problem in ordering a general officer to be shot, let alone a lowly lieutenant colonel.

"*Mí General*, I will handle this, I promise."

"I have already received a call from the 170th, inquiring of the where-abouts of our German friends. I told them that *Major* Rudolph had taken ill and was being treated by our medical staff and that they would remain over-night as guests of the division. That seemed to satisfy them. I also told them of increased Partisan activity in the area, so I think that dissuaded them from sending more men this way. They believe Major Rudolph and company are resting comfortably here and will continue back to their own headquarters tomorrow."

"Thank you, *mí General*, that will buy us some time."

"Good, now go and get what needs to be done and report back to me when it is completed."

Rodriguez came to attention, saluted and exited the commanding gen-eral's office. He had been given a reprieve, the general's lie to the 170th Di-vision effectively stopped them from sending out a search party for Rudolph and his two men. Rodriguez hurried back to the hangar and collected a squad of men to put his plan into action. Having gathered ten men, the bodies of the dead Germans were then placed in the back of the truck along with the detail while two men were assigned to drive the German vehicle that Rudolph and his men had originally arrived in. The two-vehicle convoy then left the con-fines of the Spanish cantonment area and headed to a location, pre-selected by Rodriguez, to stage the ambush. It was an area of known Partisan activity, so the Spaniards had to work very quickly, least they too, fall victims to the wily Soviet Partisans.

Rodriguez accompanied the detail, all of which were heavily armed. Rodriguez rode in the cab of the truck guiding the driver to the ambush loca-tion.

"Ok, Miguel, right up here on the left," Rodriguez told the driver. "Stop right here," he then ordered.

Rodriguez then posted his men on either side of the road for security measures, and the rest removed the bodies of the Germans from the back of the truck. Rodriguez then directed the driver of the *Kubelwagen* to drive it into a tree, giving the impression that the vehicle had crashed into it when the occupants were ambushed. This was completed with no injury to the Spanish driver.

After the driver left the vehicle, Rodriguez then gave the order, "Ok, men, open fire!" With that order, the Spaniards commenced firing round after round into the parked vehicle, shooting out its tires, windshield and the entire body of the vehicle. When the order was given to cease fire, the vehicle looked like an overgrown piece of Swiss cheese, due to the many holes in it.

"Ok, now place the bodies in the vehicle, be sure to place the *Major* in the passenger side up front."

Within minutes, the men had completed their grisly task and began loading onto the truck for the drive back to their base. With weapons at the ready in case they ran into Partisans, the vehicle headed back to Krasny Bor, having completed a mission that would never be mentioned in the division's otherwise illustrious history.

Spanish Airfield
Krasny Bor, Russia
September 6, 1943, 0700 Hours

After being hidden in a room above the Red Star Tavern for nearly a week, the day had finally arrived when Sepp was to leave Russia for home. The German troops of the 170th Division ultimately located their dead comrades and chalked it up to a Partisan ambush, thus alleviating any suspicion of Spanish involvement. The search for Sepp within in the 250th Division area was minimal at best—the Germans having more pressing issues than to look for a priest wanted by the Gestapo. The Spaniards themselves had been wonderful hosts and Sepp could never forget the sacrifices made by the *divisionarios* in their aid in getting the Klooga inmates to freedom and for harboring him from the Germans. They would always be in his prayers. Rodriguez had finalized plans with Garcetti of the Italian Air Force. Rodriguez would personally fly Sepp to the rendezvous point, a German airfield at Dno-Griwotschki. Rodriguez would fly Sepp in the rear seat of one of the squadron's two Bf-109 aircraft, the rest being FW-190 fighters. These Bf-109s had been slightly modified with an instructor's cockpit added behind the original cockpit and both were covered by an elongated glazed canopy, making it ideal for this flight. Extra fuel tanks had also been added to cover the longer than normal range flown by this type of aircraft.

From its base in Odessa, Garcetti would personally fly the Italian aircraft, a Fiat G.12 Gondar to the rendezvous site. This transport aircraft had been modified for long-range flights and had a range of 1,420 miles. With a crew of 4, a maximum speed of 242 mph and a flight ceiling of 27,900 feet, the three powerful Fiat air-cooled radial piston engines made this aircraft one of the finest in the *Regia Aeronautica's* inventory. Only three of these transport aircraft existed in the entire *Regina Aeronautica,* and one of them was with the 246th *Squadriglia* of the *Corpo Aereo Spedizonie* in Russia (Expeditionary Air Corps in Russia) now based in Odessa, Crimea.

As Rodriguez's aircraft was being prepared for take-off, Chaplain Garcia and a few of the squadron personnel came to say their good-byes to the German priest. Sepp shook each of their hands and said a few words to each. Finally, he got to his old friend, Chaplain Garcia.

"Jaime, I could not have done this without you - I can't begin to thank you enough for all that you have done, you and your men will forever be in my prayers."

Garcia, with tears in his eyes, gave his friend a warm *abrazo*[102] and whispered, "*Vaya con Dios*, Sepp. I hope to see you again after this crazy war is over."

Rodriguez, decked out in his flying suit, motioned to Sepp that he needed to put one on as well. "You will need to wear the suit, Monsignor, or you will freeze to death without it."

Sepp then went inside the hangar and was suited up with the assistance of two of the squadron's airmen. Ten minutes later he walked out looking like a pilot.

"You look like a top Ace, Monsignor," Rodriguez joked, and that brought about laughter from the assembled group.

"Time to go, Monsignor," Rodriguez said. Both men then walked to the aircraft on the tarmac and were helped into the aircraft by the crew chief and airmen assigned to that specific aircraft. Sepp went in first, behind the pilot and was secured into his seat with a safety harness by the crew chief. With his passenger secured, Rodriguez climbed in into the cockpit and was also assisted by his crew chief in fastening his safety harness. The crew chief then shook Rodriguez's hand and then secured the cockpit canopy.

Rodriguez then started the aircraft engine and once maximum RPM's were reached, he gave a 'thumbs up' signal and began to slow roll out towards the main runway. Upon receiving clearance from the tower, Rodriguez took off, with the runway quickly disappearing from under him as he climbed into the clouds, slipped the bonds of earth, and then vanished from sight. Once airborne, Sepp withdrew his rosary from his flight suit and began to pray— pray for a safe and successful journey and for those who had assisted him. But most of all, he prayed for his brother Peter, whom he had not seen or heard from since the night they departed Klooga. It was this fear, this primal fear of the unknown that all men have that kept Sepp awake nights. However, now he felt tired, more tired than he had ever been in his life or so it seemed, and as the aircraft leveled out, Sepp could hear the air rushing past the canopy and for some reason the sound comforted him, and he quickly fell asleep.

Dno-Griwotschki Airfield
Dno, Russia
September 6, 1943, 1400 Hours

The first leg of journey was about to end. Sepp was startled awake as the aircraft touched down at the Dno-Griwotschki airfield in northwest Russia. The airfield, occupied by the Germans since July 1941, was located some 94 kilometers east of Pskov, Russia.[103]

As the aircraft touched down a vehicle with a "follow me" sign on the back drove out and Rodriguez followed it to a hangar area. As he rolled toward the hangar, he could see various buildings that housed workshops, barracks, and administrative buildings. The vehicle and plane finally came to a halt at a huge hangar. Awaiting them was a small group of personnel, one of them a *Luftwaffe* Major. Before they existed the aircraft, Rodriguez turned to Sepp and said, "Monsignor, let me do all the talking, ok?"

"I am in your good hands, Rodriguez."

Two *Luftwaffe* personnel climbed up onto the aircraft wing and began to pull the canopy back and assisted both men out of the aircraft.

After Rodriguez climbed down, the German Major saw Rodriguez wore the rank of *Oberstleutnant,* and that he was outranked. The Major quickly saluted, and Rodriguez returned the salute with a flourish. He then stuck out his hand and introduced himself and Sepp.

"*Herr Major*, I am *teniente coronel* Guillermo Rodriguez, and this is Monsignor Josef Bertram."

The Major shook both his visitors hands and offered a slight bow.

"A pleasure to meet you both. I am *Major* Frederick de Coppens. You are Spanish, *Herr Oberstleutnant,* correct? And you, Monsignor, we don't get too many flying priests here," he said with a chuckle. "As a matter of fact, you are the first! Let me welcome you both to Dno airfield. May I ask the purpose of your visit?"

Here is where Rodriguez's cunning took over. "*Herr Major*, I don't know if you are aware of the OKW order of November 8, 1941, that instructed all commanders-in-chiefs of the German armies in the East to facilitate the missionary activities of the Catholic priests in the Occupied territories."

De Coppens stared blankly at Rodriguez before he answered.

"No, sir, I am unaware of such an order. However, if you say it exists, then I am more than happy to facilitate your stay here."

"I am actually dropping off Monsignor Bertram who is scheduled to be picked up by an Italian Air Force transport sometime later today. We had coordinated with the *Regia Aeronautica* and the aircraft should arrive around 1700 hours today. I must return to Krasny Bor, so I hope that you will make the Monsignor comfortable and extend to him every courtesy possible until the

Italians arrive."

"By all means, *Herr Oberstleutnant.* Monsignor, if you will follow me, we can get you fed and get you a bunk for a few hours until the aircraft arrives."

"Thank you, *Herr Major*, that is very kind of you, I will take you up on the offer."

Before he followed the Major over to the mess hall for something to eat, Sepp said his goodbyes to Rodriguez.

"You must be exhausted from the flight bringing me here; can you wait awhile longer before flying back to Krasny Bor?"

Rodriguez reached into his flight suit and pulled out a small packet of white pills. "No need to worry, *Padre*, these little babies will keep me awake. They give them out to all *Luftwaffe* pilots. It's called Pervitin."[104]

Sepp shook his head in amazement and then said, "Well, if you say so. I cannot thank you enough for what you and your men have done. I always knew the Spanish were a hearty lot, and very devoted. May God continue to bless and keep you and bring you home safely to Spain."

The two men shook hands, with Rodriguez saying, "*Gracias, padre y vaya con Dios.* Till we meet again, *adiós.*"

Ground crews were busy refueling Rodriguez's plane for a quick turn-around flight back to Krasny Bor. Rodriguez was offered a bratwurst sandwich and a small thermos of coffee and after a quick latrine stop, climbed back into his aircraft to begin the long flight back. From the mess hall, Sepp and Major de Coppens watched as Rodriguez's aircraft rolled down the runaway and was airborne disappeared quickly behind the clouds.

"Monsignor, I must say this is highly irregular for an unannounced flight to just pop out of nowhere with obviously a very important person on board."

Sepp, sensing the major was probing for answers, told the German officer a bit of a white lie.

"You see, *Herr Major*, I am trying to facilitate the letter of the OKW directive, and adding to that, to also offer spiritual comfort to our troops. Like you, I am German, and although I am not a military chaplain, there is a shortage of Catholic chaplains within the armed forces. I know that the *Luftwaffe* does not have its own chaplaincy, so while I am here, I will be happy to hear confessions and give a blessing to anyone who so desires. I cannot offer communion, as unfortunately, I do not have any consecrated Hosts with me."

De Coppens seemed a bit embarrassed at Sepp's recognition of the fact that indeed there were no chaplains within the *Luftwaffe*, it being the most fanatical National Socialist branch of all the German armed forces.

"Monsignor, I will make an announcement that any airmen who wishes confession to meet you in the mess hall within the hour, how does that sound? It will give you a chance to eat and freshen up."

"That sounds fine, *Herr Major*, thank you."

"I myself am a lapsed Evangelical, Monsignor, but I still think it important that the men have some spiritual outlet, no matter what *Herr* Goring[105] directs," de Coppens said with a slight chuckle. "So, for now, Monsignor, let's get you fed and rested up until our Italian friends arrive." De Coppens then signaled for an orderly who brought them both a hot meal of bratwurst, black bread and some piping hot coffee.

Dno-Griwotschki Airfield
Dno, Russia
September 6, 1943, 1715 Hours

The Italian aircraft was sighted by aircraft spotters at approximately 1710 hours and the massive aircraft began its approach to the airfield. Many of the *Luftwaffe* personnel had not seen this type of aircraft before, although in fact the *Luftwaffe* did have a few in its inventory. The aircraft taxied to the end of the runway and then slowly turned around and began its approach to a string of hangars. A ground guide appeared near the hangars and directed them to a parking area. The pilot then turned off all the engines, and for a few moments, there was no movement in the aircraft. An assembled group of *Luftwaffe* personnel stood ready to greet their visitors and were getting impatient until the door of the aircraft opened. An Italian Air Force officer, *Colonnello* (Colonel) Nicolo Garcetti, emerged from the aircraft. A veteran pilot, Garcetti was tall, with slightly greying hair and mustache, and he looked the part of an aviator—with a crushed cap riding at a jaunty angle atop his head and wearing a fleece-lined bomber jacket, he could have been mistaken for a pilot serving with the US Army Air Forces.

The *Luftwaffe* reception crew consisted of Major de Coppens, and three subordinate officers.

"Welcome to Dno airfield, *Herr Oberst*, I am *Major* de Coppens," he said saluting and then offering his hand to the Italian pilot.

"Thank you, *Major*, it is good to be on *terra firma* once again," Garcetti joked. "It has been a long flight from Odessa to say the least."

De Coppens introduced his officers and Garcetti reciprocated as the rest of his crew emerged from the aircraft.

"I believe, *Herr Oberst*, that this Fiat G. 12 Gondar is the first of its kind to land here at Dno. Would you mind terribly if my officers and I inspect it—I for one have never seen one."

Garcetti replied, "By all means. I will have Senior Sergeant Barone, my crew chief, give you a tour of the aircraft, he is familiar with every inch of it."

Nodding to his crew chief, Garcetti said, "Barone, if you don't mind giving our hosts a tour, please?"

"*Si, Colonnello,*" the crew chief replied, as the *Luftwaffe* personnel excitedly climbed on board and were given a briefing on all the performance capabilities on the aircraft—cruising speed, service ceiling, range, armament, etc. The Germans came away duly impressed.

After the tour of the aircraft, Garcetti asked de Coppens, "*Herr Major*, can you direct me to the priest, Monsignor Bertram as we have yet to meet."

"Of course, sir. I believe Monsignor Bertram is in his bunk resting - I will send someone for him, and you can meet in my office - I will make myself scarce so you two can have some privacy."

"That is very kind of you, *Herr Major*, I don't want to put you out."

"No trouble at all, sir," de Coppens said. "Let's head over to my office, it's over in one of the hangars. Not much to look at, but at least you will have some privacy." De Coppens led Garcetti to one of the hangars where a number of aircraft were being worked on by *Luftwaffe* mechanics.

"Here we are, sir. I will see that your men are billeted and get some food in them." While he was still talking to Garcetti, there was a knock on the office door; "Enter," de Coppens yelled out as it was hard to hear at times over the mechanics drills in the hangar.

"Sir, I have Monsignor Bertram," the airman reported.

"Please show him in," de Coppens responded.

Sepp entered the relatively small office and Garcetti immediately introduced himself, "Monsignor, it is so very good to finally meet you."

"Thank you, *Colonnello* Garcetti, the pleasure is all mine." Before Sepp could say more, de Coppens excused himself and said, "Gentlemen, take as much time as you need, my office is entirely at your disposal." With that, he left, closing the door behind him leaving Sepp alone with the Italian officer.

"I want to thank you for agreeing to this mission, *Colonnello*, I know it is dangerous and clearly out of the norm for the Italian air force to fly such a mission."

"I must say, Monsignor, that Rodriguez was a very good salesman when it came to selling me on flying this mission. I have to say, my interest was piqued."

"How much did Rodriguez explain to you, *Colonnello*?"

"Enough to know, Monsignor, that your life is in danger if you continue to stick around in Russia much longer. You are aware of course, of Mussolini's overthrow in late July. The government of Marshal Badoglio has promised Hitler that the war will continue, and that Germany and Italy will remain allies - however I do not believe a word of it. We flew in from a base in Odessa on the Crimea - we are one of the last Italian units on the Eastern Front and I can tell you the Germans do not trust us one iota. The last orders we received from

Rome were that we were to rotate back to Italy no later than 7 September. As a matter of fact, the rest of the squadron aircraft have already departed for Italy - we have the dubious distinction of being the last Italian aircraft on the Eastern Front. So here we are."

"*Colonnello,* I cannot thank you enough for sacrificing your chance to return home early in order to get me."

"You should know, Monsignor, that my co-pilot and the four other crewmembers all volunteered for this mission. They had a ticket home and yet they too understood the importance of getting you back."

"How much do they know?"

"Let's just say enough that they want to ensure you make it back safely to Rome. Another thing, Monsignor - it will probably be a different Italy that we go back to. Rumor has it that the Germans were looking to rescue Mussolini and install him once again as *Duce*. No one, but a few in the Badoglio government, knows where he is. I pray to God that he stays hidden from the Germans."

"I agree with you, *Colonnello,* having Mussolini back in charge of Italy once again would plunge Italy into one large battleground. Italy was not prepared for war in 1940, and it is in worse shape now than at the beginning of the war. No good can come out of Mussolini being in power once again."

"I think *Herr* Hitler would disagree with you, Monsignor," Garcetti said, a bit of sarcasm in his voice.

Changing the subject, Sepp asked, "What time do you plan on leaving here tomorrow, *Colonnello?*

"I want to ensure we get enough crew rest time, Monsignor. I am aiming for a departure time of 0630 hours. Our hosts will billet and feed us tonight and tomorrow morning for breakfast."

"I look forward to meeting your crew, *Colonnello.*"

"And they look forward to meeting you as well, Monsignor. They are aware of your exploits and are duly impressed."

Sepp smiled and nodded in acknowledgement of the compliment.

"Then, *Colonnello,* may I suggest we head to the mess hall for some food and get to know each other better as I believe it is going to be a long flight."

"A very good idea, Monsignor, I could go for some hot coffee and some food."

Both men left de Coppen's office and made their way to the mess hall where Sepp was introduced to Garcetti's crewmembers. After the meal, Sepp as well as the Italian airmen retired for the evening. The next day would be long with an over 800-mile flight to Bratislava, Slovakia, and then on to the Eternal City, Rome.

Dno-Griwotschki Airfield
Dno, Russia
September 7, 1943, 0630 Hours

After a good night's sleep and a hearty breakfast provided by their German hosts, Sepp and the Italians were ready to depart for their long flight back to the Italian mainland. The Italians had been in Odessa for almost a year and were itching to return home. Italian-German relations had sunk to a new low after the *Duce's* overthrow, and both sides were wary of each other, so the Italians were more than anxious to return home.

Before boarding the aircraft, Sepp gave a blessing to the crew and also to the *Luftwaffe* personnel assembled - they were after all, his own countrymen, and he wished them no harm, even if they were serving a criminal regime.

Both Garcetti and Sepp extended their thanks to de Coppens and his men for their hospitality.

"Safe travels, *Herr Oberst*," de Coppens said, and pointing to Sepp joked, "You should have no problems with the flight as it appears God is your co-pilot."

The assembled group chuckled at de Coppens humorous quip and then it was time for the Italians to depart.

Once inside the aircraft and secure, Garcetti fired up the three engines and began the safety checks with his co-pilot and crew - after what seemed an eternity for Sepp, the plane began to move to its take-off position. Revving to its maximum RPM's, Garcetti received permission to take-off from the small operations center at the airfield. Releasing the aircraft's brakes, the plane made its way down the runway and was soon airborne, Dno airfield quickly disappearing from sight.

Over the intercom, Garcetti announced that they would be flying at maximum altitude of 29,000 feet, and to get comfortable as it was going to be a long flight.

"Next stop, God-willing, Bratislava, Slovakia," Garcetti announced. With that, the intercom went silent, and Sepp, along with the four enlisted crewmembers, made themselves comfortable in the cabin of the aircraft. The Germans had given them sandwiches and coffee, along with some German chocolates, so they were going to make themselves as comfortable as possible. As the plane reached its maximum altitude and cruising speed, Sepp found the droning of the aircraft's engines soothing and was quickly lulled to a deep, sound sleep.

John R. Dabrowski

Pressburg Airfield
Bratislava, Slovakia
September 7, 1943, 1515 Hours

The Italian aircraft landed at Pressburg airfield[106], a Slovakian Air Force base located approximately 8 kilometers northeast of the capital city of Bratislava. A small German *Luftwaffe* training mission was assigned to the base.[107] Since 1939, when the Czechoslovakian state ceased to exist and was finally dismembered by Nazi Germany, Slovakia was made an independent (read Nazi puppet) state with a Roman Catholic cleric, Monsignor Josef Tiso, as its president. Slovakia had been an ally of Germany since the start of the Second World War, even sending troops into Poland to assist the *Wehrmacht* in its attack on that nation. Tiso also sent forces into Russia in 1941 to assist Hitler in the conquest of the Soviet colossus. The Slovak army's performance in Russia had been so dismal that it was sent to the rear echelon as support troops. Nonetheless, much like Japan, Italy, Germany, and other countries, Tiso had signed the Anti-Comintern Pact[108] in 1941, thus formally throwing in his lot with the Nazis.

As the aircraft taxied towards a set of hangars, Sepp could see that the airfield was not very large—some hangars, workshops and administrative buildings made up the entire base. Off in the distance he saw what appeared to be a couple of German-made fighters with Slovak national markings on it. These markings were similar to the German *Balken Kreuz*, but instead of black, they were blue in color with a white border and a red disk in the center. In addition, the airfield also held a few Czech-made Avia B-534 training aircraft.

The aircraft finally came to a full stop, its brakes squeaking loudly. When the crew chief opened the side door he was met by a welcoming committee consisting of three Slovak Air Force officers, one captain and two lieutenants.

Garcetti was the first to leave the aircraft, his co-pilot and the rest of the crew followed. Sepp was asked to stay on board until Garecetti could get a good reading as to whether his hosts were hostile or not. As Italy was still technically an ally, there probably would be no problem arising from their visit—he just wanted to be assured of that fact.

"Good day, colonel, and welcome to Pressburg airfield, I am Captain Zeljko, Slovak Air Force," he said, saluting and then offering his hand to Garcetti. Zeljko then introduced the two junior officers and Garcetti reciprocated in kind by introducing his co-pilot and his crew.

"I do not believe we have ever had the pleasure of an Italian aircraft having landed here at Pressburg, so I believe you are the first," Zeljko said.

"Well, captain, I will take that as a great honor," Garcetti replied. He then continued, "Captain, we have another individual on board, a priest by the name of Monsignor Bertram. He is a civilian cleric, assigned to the Vatican, and we are assisting him in returning to Rome. I hope you extend every courtesy to him."

"By all means! You are aware, colonel, that our own president is a priest. Please, have him join us."

Garcetti motioned to one of his men, who went into the aircraft and returned with Sepp in tow.

Garcetti made the introductions and the Slovak officers seemed doubly pleased to have a cleric in the midst.

Garcetti continued, "Captain, we still have a long way to Rome, and I would request refueling and a once-over by your mechanics on our aircraft. We would also like to remain overnight if that is permissible."

"By all means, colonel. Our base is entirely at your disposal. We will get you fed and then some billeting - it is not the Ritz I am sorry to say, but you should be comfortable for tonight," Zeljko joked.

Garcetti smiled and then added, "I noticed a couple of German BF-109's at the end of the runway. Are there German personnel here?" Garcetti was fully aware of Sepp's situation, and the more he could avoid the Germans, the better.

"Yes, we have a small *Luftwaffe* training mission here; they seem like good lads and really haven't given us any trouble. They pretty much stick to themselves when the training day is over. Most of them are probably in town right now drinking it up and looking for loose women." Zeljko then realized there was a priest present, was visibly embarrassed, and then said, "Sorry, Monsignor, no offense intended."

Sepp could only smile, and answered, "None taken, captain."

With that, Sepp, his Italian aircrew, and the Slovak officers made their way to a small mess hall while Slovak air force mechanics, who seemingly appeared out of nowhere, began to work on the plane and ready it for its flight early the next morning.

Pressburg Airfield
Bratislava, Slovakia
September 7, 1943, 1930 Hours

After a filling meal, Sepp retired for the evening into his small billet. The room was spartan - a cot, a small table with one chair, a wardrobe with a mirror, and a small sink. A communal latrine was located at the other end of the barrack.

Sepp took out some stationery embossed with the Papal coat of arms and began to write a letter to President Tiso, whom he had met years before in Rome. Tiso was not highly regarded by Pius XII, and the feeling was probably mutual. Yet, Sepp was going to take a chance and send the cleric-president a letter requesting that Peter be given asylum in Slovakia. He had received no word from Peter in weeks and realizing he was probably grasping at straws he composed his letter:

My Dear President Tiso-
I hope that you remember me from our days in Rome prior to the war. I am writing this letter to you from Pressburg airfield outside of your capital city. Time does not permit me to attempt to seek an audience with you, so I will ask in this letter. My brother, SS Gruppenführer Peter Bertram has committed a crime against the Reich and no doubt faces the death penalty if tried and convicted. I do not know of his whereabouts at this time. Peter is guilty of the crime of saving the lives of Jewish prisoners about to be put to death. I know for a fact, that your Excellency had ordered a cessation of deportations in Slovakia in this last year. As a man of God, you know in your heart that what Hitler is doing is against the law of God and man. Peter has taken action and 100 Jews have been spared from certain death. I implore as an old friend and fellow cleric, to please consider giving Peter sanctuary in your country. I was Peter's accomplice in assisting the Jews to escape, having been sent to Russia at the behest of the Holy Father. We succeeded in our mission. With God's grace I should be back in Rome within the next 48 hours. From the Vatican I should be able to find out Peter's fate and hopefully be in communication with him. May God bless you and the Slovak people. I hope to see you again in more happier times. Yours in Christ,

Josef Bertram

When he finished, he re-read the letter, checking for spelling and punctuation errors. As a Vatican diplomat, he was used to writing clear, concise missives rather quickly and getting them out to their intended recipient. After reading it one last time, he sealed it in an envelope. He intended to give the letter to Captain Zeljko prior to his departure. From their present location, the airfield was less than 10 miles from the presidential palace, so it would probably not be too much of an effort for a courier to deliver the letter to Tiso. As he lay down to sleep, he prayed that the next 48 hours would see him arrive safely back to his beloved Rome.

Pressburg Airfield
Bratislava, Slovakia
September 8, 1943, 0720 Hours

After breakfast in the mess hall, Sepp and the Italian air crew said their good-byes to their Slovak hosts. Sepp had slept well the night before, probably the best sleep he had had in weeks. He was nearing exhaustion and was running now on pure adrenaline.

Sepp took Captain Zeljko aside. "Captain, I want to thank you for your kindness and hospitality towards me and my Italian friends, it is most appreciated and will not be forgotten. I do have one favor to ask."

"Anything, Monsignor, just name it."

Sepp hesitated for a moment and then produced the letter from inside his cassock. "Can you deliver this letter to President Tiso for me. He is an old friend from before the war," he said while handing the letter to the startled Slovak officer.

"President Tiso?" Zeljko asked incredulously.

Sepp nodded his head affirmatively.

"I will see what can be done although I cannot promise you anything, monsignor, but I will try."

"That's all I ask, captain."

Shaking Zeljko's hand for the last time, Sepp turned and walked to the aircraft and was assisted up the steps by one of the crew. As the crew chief secured the door, Garcetti started the engines on the tri-motor aircraft, and it soon began a slow roll towards the runway. When the aircraft reached its maximum RPMs, Garcetti pushed the throttle forward and the plane began lumbering down the runway and was soon airborne. As Garcetti gained control of the aircraft he told his co-pilot to set course towards Rome. Unbeknownst to Sepp and the Italians, the Badoglio government of Italy was about to conclude an armistice with the Allies, thus throwing Italy into turmoil and civil war, along with a massive influx of German troops into Italy itself. Italy was about to face a nightmare of massive proportions.

Chapter XI

"The Catholic Church as but one desire, and that is to see us destroyed."
--Adolf Hitler, August 11, 1942

Office of the Slovakian President
Bratislava, Slovakia
September 8, 1943, 1230 Hours

Monsignor Josef Tiso, a Roman Catholic cleric, and since 1939, president of the independent state of Slovakia, had just finished reading the letter from Sepp that had arrived via military courier from the airfield at Pressburg. The two clerics were old acquaintances, having met in Rome in the mid-1930s. Tiso, a staunch Slovak People's Party nationalist, had allied his nation with Hitler, in the hopes of protecting his small nation from being gobbled up once again by Hungary or some other Central European power. For a man of God, Tiso had shamelessly permitted the deportation of Slovakian Jews for 'resettlement' to the East - however, upon learning that 'resettlement' meant Auschwitz, he ordered a cessation to all deportations. The Greek Catholic Bishop of Presov, Monsignor Pavol Gojdic, beseeched the Pope in 1942 to induce Tiso, in the interests of the Church, to resign, and have a secular statesman take over his function and thus avert an impending worse evil.[109] That, coupled with an admonishment by Pius XII, kept Tiso in check for the time being. Tiso had troubled relations with Pius XII, with the Pope having chastised Tiso for the injustices carried out during his rule, telling the cleric-president to "act like a priest rather than a politician."[110] The Pope also criticized Tiso's regime by stating that "The injustice wrought by his government is harmful to the prestige of his country and enemies will exploit it to discredit clergy and the Church the world over."[111]

Upon reading Sepp's letter requesting assistance to grant Peter refuge, Tiso was in a quandary. The thought of having to answer to an irate Hitler once he found out that one of his SS officers, now a traitor, was safely tucked away somewhere in Slovakia, sent shivers down his spine. Tiso's cousin and current president of the Supreme Court of the Slovak Republic, Stefan Tiso, was present for his weekly lunch with the Slovak leader. Monsignor Tiso sought his cousin's counsel.

"Stefan, I am in a bit of a dilemma. I just received a letter from an old acquaintance of mine, a Monsignor Bertram, who has requested that his brother be given refuge here. The brother is a senior SS officer who seems to have had a change of heart when it came to implementing the 'Final Solution'.

As a matter of fact, he helped lead the escape of some 100 Jews from a camp in Estonia."

"Yes, Josef, I remember hearing about the incident via our ambassador in Stockholm. Very brazen, indeed, and this Bertram now has the gall to ask you to give his brother sanctuary here in Slovakia? He must be mad! You know as well as I, we are walking a precarious tightrope with Berlin, and they would use any pretext to send in their forces. No, cousin, I would counsel against permitting this SS traitor any sanctuary. Anyway, he's as good as dead. Besides, how well do you know this cleric, Bertram?"

"We were acquaintances in Rome before the war. He appeared to be a decent chap, for a German, and worked closely with the Holy Father. He claims in his letter that the Pope had actually sent him on this mission to save the Jews. He then somehow converted his brother's way of thinking and the both of them helped the Jews escape to Sweden. I have to applaud the audacity of his actions."

"Yes, no doubt Hollywood will make a movie of it after the war, and have that swashbuckler, Errol Flynn, play the role of your friend Bertram."

Both men laughed at Stefan's joke.

"Very well, Stefan, thank you for your input on this. I will inform Monsignor Bertram of my 'deepest regrets' in denying *Gruppenführer* Bertram a safe haven here. As you stated, he's as good as dead. Also, I think I will inform Berlin about this letter, just to let them know what the brothers Bertram are up to."

President Tiso placed Bertram's letter aside on his desk, and both cousins then adjourned to a small dining room off the president's office for their weekly luncheon to discuss the conduct of the war and the affairs of state.

Chapter XII

"The banner is at last unfurled: Chief Rabbi of the Christian World."[112]

Radio Stockholm
Karlavagen, Stockholm
Sweden
September 8, 1943, 1130 hours

Radio Stockholm news announcer Lars Hendrikson showed up early for his noon broadcast. On his desk in the small announcer's booth, he used to broadcast the twice daily news events, he found, laying on the top of the stack of news items he was scheduled to read, a government news bulletin. Lighting a cigarette, he sat back in his chair and began to read the announcement. As he read on, he slowly sat up, his eyes widening and his mouth agape to the point his cigarette fell out of his mouth. He quickly picked up the burning cigarette and stubbed it out in his ashtray. "This is unbelievable!" he said aloud to no one in particular.

He called to his secretary, "Ingrid, Ingrid, listen to this…" He then read aloud the government news bulletin:

> *His Majesty's government has announced that on 29/30 August the Royal Swedish Air Force, in coordination with the Finnish Armed Forces, rescued 100 former Jewish inmates of the Klooga Concentration Camp in German-occupied Estonia, who were scheduled to be put to death on 30 August. They were aided in their dramatic escape by anti-Nazi elements within the German Armed Forces as well as from members of the Spanish division currently fighting alongside Germany on the Eastern Front. The former prisoners have been offered permanent residency by His Majesty's government and most have agreed to remain in Sweden after the war. A spokesman for the rescued prisoners have extended thanks to their rescuers, who must remain nameless, so as to protect them from retribution by the German government. The fact that the inmates were rescued by German military personnel and Spaniards fighting under the Nazi banner should be cause of concern for the Hitler regime. Perhaps*

*chinks are beginning to appear in Hitler's armor and
the men carrying out his plans for Lebensraum are
now having second thoughts. Can this be the beginning of the end?*

Hendrikson put the bulletin back on his desk and asked his secretary,
"What do you think of that, Ingrid? According to this account, it appears the
Germans are having a change of heart in their dealings with the Jews, or at
least certain members of the German *Wehrmacht*. That must be sending Hitler
into fits of rage."

"I suppose so," said Ingrid, who showed no real interest in this breaking news, and went back to her typing.

At noon, Hendrikson conducted his news broadcast with the lead item
of course being the government announcement of the rescue. From here, it
would be picked up by the BBC and other western news outlets, UPI, AP, and
others. When he finished his broadcast at 12:30, he went back to his desk
to re-work some of the bulletins in time for his 6PM broadcast. Hendrikson
needed more information than the government bulletin had given. He wanted
the names of those brave individuals who had risked their lives to save the
Klooga prisoners, and he wanted the identity of the units involved in the rescue. He considered himself a good reporter and rule number one was to get
all the facts. This by far was the story of the year, more so, in his eyes, than
the invasion of Sicily, the overthrow of Mussolini, or the failure of the German offensive at Kursk. Here was a story of the Germans saving the lives of
their sworn ideological/racial enemies. And while it was a minority within the
Wehrmacht that had pulled this off, could it just be the tip of the iceberg with
possibly more members secretly saving Jews? This was something he needed
to find out. His first stop would be at the Foreign Office, where he had a number of contacts, who might be able to help.

"Ingrid, I am heading over to the Foreign Ministry to see if I can follow up on this story, I will be back later this afternoon."

Ingrid just nodded her head and kept on typing. Hendrikson often
wondered why the station had hired her—she had zero personality, but it probably helped her that she was related to the station manager. Hendrikson then
left for the Foreign Ministry with hopes of finding more about this historic
news event.

Swedish Ministry of Foreign Affairs
Stockholm, Sweden
September 8, 1943, 1430 Hours

Hendrikson made his way over to the foreign ministry where he had a contact within the office of the Swedish Foreign Minister, Christian Gunther. Gunther had been foreign minister since late 1939, and it was on his shoulders that rested Sweden's defense of its declared neutrality during the current conflict. To date, he had succeeded. Hendrikson's contact within the Ministry was Arvid Dahlerus, an old friend from their university days. Over the years, Dahlerus had given his old college friend inside information which Hendrikson then always cited as 'an anonymous source within the Foreign Ministry.' Dahlerus, although still a minor ministry official, was quickly moving up the ministry's ranks. He had accompanied Foreign Minister Gunther to Berlin on at least two occasions and had made some important contacts within Ribbentrop's Foreign Ministry.

Knocking on Dahlerus' office door, Hendrikson entered without waiting for a response.

"Hello Arvid, how are you?"

"Lars, old man, how are you?" as Dahlerus rose from his desk to shake his old friend's hand. What brings you here?"

Dahlerus motioned his friend to sit on one of the comfortable chairs in his office. Hendrikson had noticed that over the years, Dahlerus' office accommodations within the Ministry had improved greatly—a sign of his growing importance, no doubt.

"Arvid, I have a favor to ask. I just read a news bulletin from the Ministry during my noontime broadcast, the one on the rescue of the Jews from the Klooga camp. It's a fascinating story. How long have we known about it?"

Dahlerus hesitated in answering his old friend. "Lars, we have known for a week, and that, my friend is all I can say. If we give out any specifics, such as names, units, and the like, we could be endangering those very individuals that assisted in the escape. I am sorry, Lars, but I simply can't. I could very well lose my job if I did. I hope you understand. Perhaps, someday, after this crazy war is over, the full story can then be told. I can tell you this much—aside from the usual government ministries involved, we had a number of prominent Swedish civilians play a behind-the-scenes role, if you will. Count Bernadotte and the Wallenberg brothers were instrumental in persuading the king into permitting the escapees to come to Sweden. Additionally, the papal nuncio was also involved."

"The papal nuncio? That means the Vatican had some hand in this?"

Dahlerus could only smile and say "Lars, I have said enough. If you want to try and get more information out of the individuals I mentioned, go right ahead. I doubt they will talk, and do not mention my name. If you do, I will deny it. Sorry, old boy."

Resigning himself to the fact that he could not get his friend to talk, Hendrikson got up from the chair and offered his hand to Dahlerus. "It was worth a try Arvid. Hope to see you soon, maybe at the club Friday evening, eh?"

"I can't promise anything, Lars, they have me working late most evenings these days, but we will get together soon, I promise. And if I do receive any further information that is deemed releasable to the public, you will be the first to know."

Hendrikson let himself out of Dahlerus' office and slowly made his way to the elevator. One of the great humanitarian stories of the war lay within his grasp, but for now, no one was talking.

Wolfschanze ("The Wolf's Lair")
Rastenburg, East Prussia
September 8, 1943, 1500 Hours

Adolf Hitler was sitting in the small officer's *kasino* at his Eastern Front headquarters launching into one of his infamous monologues that had many spellbound and others bored to tears. Seated around the *Führer* were a few of his secretaries, the ever-present Martin Bormann, Foreign Minister von Ribbentrop, and Hermann Fegelein. As Hitler droned on, a foreign ministry official quietly entered the *kasino*, and spying Ribbentrop, quietly walked up to him and asked to talk with him in private. Ribbentrop discreetly moved away from the circle around Hitler and left with the official.

"What is it, Werner, can't it wait?" Ribbentrop asked coldly.

"*Herr Minister*, I thought you should be the first to see this. This was just picked up from a Radio Stockholm news broadcast earlier today. No doubt the BBC and other enemy stations will be broadcasting it as well in addition to carrying the story in their newspapers."

Ribbentrop read the bulletin and could only mutter, "*Mein Gott*, I will now have to inform the *Führer* of this. He will be livid. If what the Swedes are saying is true, the armed forces can no longer be trusted. This will be a propaganda coup for the Allies, and they will no doubt use it to weaken our troops' morale."

The official could only look at Ribbentrop with a certain amount of sympathy, knowing full well that Hitler would probably lash out at his Foreign Minister and would bear the brunt of Hitler's fury.

"Thank you, Werner, I will take it from here," Ribbentrop said with a weak smile.

"I stand by for your further orders, sir."

With that, Ribbentrop re-entered the *kasino* to see Hitler still haranguing his captive audience.

Ribbentrop thought best to wait until Hitler had completed his storytelling to inform the *Führer* of the news. Fortunately, he did not have to wait long, as Hitler finally finished and then with a wave of his hand announced, "Alright, everyone back to work!"

The *Führer* seemed to be in relatively good spirits, a change from the depression that had plagued him ever since Stalingrad. Perhaps it was the news that German intelligence had a possible lead as to Mussolini's whereabouts that had the *Führer* a bit giddy - one never knew. Ribbentrop was hesitant to approach Hitler and steeling himself, finally cornered the German leader.

"*Mein Führer*, a word, if you please."

"Yes, yes, Ribbentrop, what is it?"

"This news bulletin was intercepted from a broadcast made from Radio Stockholm earlier today. I think you need to read it."

Hitler took the bulletin and began to read it. As Ribbentrop looked on, he could see Hitler's face begin to flush and eyes widen. Then it came - the explosion.

"How dare those Swedes broadcast such lies! I could crush them like a bug if I wanted to! How dare they publish such slander against the Reich! I will march right into Stockholm and arrest the king and all those other aristocratic buffoons!"

Bormann who was close by, was handed the bulletin. "Read this, Bormann," Hitler ordered.

Bormann, who saw a conspiracy under every rock and who undermined others within Hitler's inner circle in order to appear indispensable to the leader then remarked, "*Mein Führer*, it is just as you had discussed previously - the *Wehrmacht* is full of traitors, particularly within the OKW. They are doing everything to undermine your orders."

Hitler, however, was more aggravated at the Swedes. Sweden was important to the German war machine as Germany purchased much needed iron ore from the Scandinavian nation. To date, the Swedes had been very careful on what they said or printed about their powerful neighbor to the south, especially since German troops occupied neighboring Norway, Denmark and were active in Finland. Additionally, recent reports coming out of Sweden from pro-German Swedish officials as well as German spies indicated that the Allies were attempting to bring Sweden into the war. This enraged Hitler who ordered more troops to Scandinavia.[113]

Hitler then started raging about the Spanish. "And look here!" he said, pointing at the bulletin, "It says the Spaniards were involved as well! I will bet that wily Franco had a hand in it as well! I should have marched into Spain in

1940 after Franco refused to enter the war and join us in an attack on Gibraltar. We should have never scrapped Felix!"[114] Hitler continued, "And here I had such high hopes for the Spaniards. Muñoz-Grandes was an outstanding leader - this fellow Esteban-Infantes can't hold a candle to him."

Pausing, Hitler then turned to Bormann and said, "I am ordering that the Spanish division be disarmed and interned - that ought to dissuade any of our other so-called allies from going behind our backs."

Ribbentrop interjected, "*Mein Führer*, while I know this news is unsettling, disarming the Spaniards in such a critical area of the front would be catastrophic for us. The Spaniards have held firm against the Soviet 55th Army and have withstood repeated attacks. Also, what sort of message would it send to our enemies - that we are weak and that we can't even control our own allies. Certainly, the entire Spanish division is not responsible for the escape of the Jews - I would recommend an investigation to find out who the ring leaders were and punish them accordingly."

Hitler, now a bit calmer, said, "Perhaps you are right, Ribbentrop, the Spaniards overall have conducted themselves like true warriors, much more so than those Italians. Very well, I rescind my orders on their being disarmed, but I want to know who those individuals were who helped facilitate the Jews escape."

"Very well, *Mein Führer*," Ribbentrop answered.

Bormann and Hitler then moved off towards Hitler's private bunker to discuss Party matters, leaving Ribbentrop to his own devices. He was now left with having to calm Germany's other allies, who by this period of the war, were having second thoughts about their alliance with the Reich. Most had begun to put out 'peace feelers' to the Western Allies, with the hopes of extracting themselves from Hitler's clutches and being overrun by the advancing Red Army. Later that day, however, the Badoglio government of Italy would surrender to the Allies sending Hitler into a rage that would result in his ordering a massive influx of German troops through the Brenner Pass and into Italy.

El Pardo Palace
Madrid, Spain
September 8, 1943, 1630 Hours

Spanish Foreign Minister Francisco Garcia Jordana y Souza entered *Generalissimo* Francisco Franco's opulent office in El Pardo Palace.[115] "*Excelencia,*" he addressed the Spanish Head of State, "We have a demarche from the German Foreign Ministry delivered earlier today by Ambassador von Strohrer.[116] It concerns the *divisionarios* involvement with the escape of the Jewish concentration camp prisoners to Sweden. It was announced on Swedish radio earlier today. Hitler and von Ribbentrop are furious to say the least. Von

Strohrer told me in confidence that the only reason that Hitler did not order that the division be disarmed by force was that he needed our men in Krasny Bor because of their excellent combat record."[117]

The diminutive Franco[118] who was sitting behind his desk, asked in his high-pitched, rather sing-song voice, "Well, what do the Germans expect us to do? It is a *fait accompli*. What do they want us to do, fly back to Sweden and bring the Jews back so they can kill them?" he asked sarcastically.

Jordana let that bit of sarcasm slip by. Jordana, who was pro-Allied, saw this as an opportunity to try and sway Franco into pulling the Spaniards out of Russia once and for all. Spain was under intense pressure by the Allies to end its support of Nazi Germany. Franco, who owed his position as *Caudillo* of Spain to both Germany and Italy during the Spanish Civil War, looked upon the Blue Division as the 'blood debt' that he owed the Nazi leader. The British had hinted that if Franco did not withdraw its support of Germany, it could risk having its territory of the Canary Islands and colonial holdings in Africa occupied by the Allies. It would be a bitter pill to swallow if Spain's territories were taken from her.

"*Excelencia*, have you given any possible consideration to withdrawing the division back home? This incident with the Jews has raised the ire of the Germans; I think they now view us with suspicion. I don't think that is a very good mix amongst allies, do you?"

Franco thought for a moment. "Jordana, I have been thinking for a while of ordering the division home. They have given a good account of themselves against the Bolsheviks. Muñoz Grandes and Esteban-Infantes are both held in high esteem by the Germans, particularly Muñoz Grandes. We are still recovering from the late *guerra civil,* and our economy is still weak. I don't want to risk an embargo or economic sanctions by the British or the Americans. The winds of war have shifted, Jordana, Germany has lost the initiative in the East, and I fear she will not regain it. Italy is for all intents and purposes lost, with Mussolini still missing in action. I want you to start negotiations with the Germans on disengaging the division from Russia and bringing it home to Spain. Those are my orders."[119]

"Yes, *Excelencia.*"

With that, the Spanish Foreign Minister withdrew, leaving Franco to his thoughts. The Spanish Chief of State had such high hopes at the beginning of the war. He had met Hitler at the French-Spanish frontier town of Hendaye in October 1940 to discuss possible Spanish entry into the war on the side of the Axis. For nine hours Hitler had harangued him about declaring war on England and entering the fray on the side of the Axis. Franco proved too wily, even for Hitler, telling the German leader that he would only enter the war when certain conditions had been met. These conditions were impossible to meet, even for the Germans. Hitler, exasperated by the talks, would later complain to Mussolini, that "rather than going through talks again with Franco, he would rather have three or four teeth pulled out."[120]

As Franco resumed his paperwork, his attention was drawn to the three portraits on the wall behind his massive desk: those of Hitler, Pope Pius XII, and Mussolini.

The Kremlin
Moscow, Russia
September 8, 1943, 2000 Hours

Soviet Foreign Minister Molotov nervously entered Stalin's office, for the news he was about to give the Soviet leader was not good.

"Josef Vissarionovich, I have a cable from our ambassador in Stockholm—I am sorry to say, not good news."

Stalin took the cable and read it and then exploded.

"Those *Zhyds* are now in Sweden? How did they get there if their train was destroyed by our Partisans weeks ago?" Stalin was enraged that his orders had been disobeyed. "Where is Ponomarenko, why isn't he here?"

"Josef Vissarionovich, Ponomarenko is at a meeting with the General Staff. I can have him sent for if you want."

"No, that will take too long. This cable makes the Germans look like a bunch of knights in shining armor riding to the rescue. This is not the image we want of the Hitlerite invaders - we have to keep them in the most unfavorable light. The Spanish must pay as well. I will see that the 55th Army attacks them without respite - I want them annihilated! What bothers me the most was that we were lied to - that *Zhyd* commander of the 12th Partisan Brigade sent us a message that the train was destroyed, and all occupants eliminated. Well, it is the 12th Partisan Brigade that will be destroyed instead."

Molotov was taken aback by Stalin's threats on destroying one of the more successful Partisan units within the Red Army's order of battle. There was little Molotov could do - his area was foreign affairs, and besides, once Stalin made up his mind, there was no changing it.

Stalin continued, "I will have Beria send in an NKVD unit to wipe them out. That will teach them not to disobey my orders."

With that, the die was cast. Stalin telephoned his secret police chief, Lavrentiy Beria, a fellow Georgian, and just as ruthless as his master. Beria was ordered to gather enough forces for an airborne attack on the 12th Partisan Brigade's position. It was to be swift so that the Partisans would have no idea what hit them. These were tried and true tactics that both Stalin and Beria had perfected over many years - put your intended victims at ease and then hit them when they least expected - it was guaranteed to be a success.

Chapter XIII

"I will not move from Rome. Here I was placed by the will of God and therefore, by my own will or with my consent I shall not leave my seat. They would have to tie me up and carry me out, because I intend to remain here!"[121]
--Pius XII on learning of the German plan to kidnap him

Horst-Wessel Platz 14, Apartment 3
Horst-Wessel Stadt
Berlin, Germany
August 30, 1943, 1030 Hours

After leaving Sepp and the others at the Reval station, Peter made his way back to Berlin. With his family now safe in Sweden, he was about to carry out what in all probability would be a suicide mission - to kill Himmler. Peter was able to use the identity papers of a deceased SS officer who had died in Russia several months earlier. Both the deceased and Peter had similar physical features and when he first saw the identity papers, he thought they may come in handy someday. Well, that someday was now. He assumed the identity of Reinhard Bauer and was able to travel without hindrance back to Berlin. Arriving at the Anhalter *Bahnhof,* Peter immediately set off for the rather seedy, rundown, working class district of Berlin, *Horst-Wessel Stadt,* which up until 1933, was known as the district of *Friedrichshain.* That all changed when the Nazis assumed power and renamed the district *Horst-Wessel Stadt,* after the fallen Nazi Storm Trooper and pimp of the same name, who was murdered by the Communists in 1930 and who had been given almost instantaneous martyr status for the Nazi cause. The Party's anthem, 'The Flag Held High,' (better known as the *Horst Wessel Lied*), whose lyrics Wessel had written, was still performed at party rallies and functions, particularly by the *Alter Kampfer* (the Old Fighters) who had marched with Hitler in the attempted Munich Beer Hall Putsch of 1923.

Peter had found the address of former *SS Rottenführer* (Corporal) Willi Prost from the *Reichssicherheitshauptamt* (Reich Main Security Office or RHSA) Personnel Office located at *Prinz-Albrecht-Strasse 8.* Prost had been drummed out of the SS for taking liberties with a young boy and for child pornography, which automatically warranted a long prison term under Paragraph 175 of the German Criminal Code.[122] However, Prost avoided a prison term through the direct intervention of a high-ranking officer close to Himmler, who suggested that Prost instead be posted to a "poacher unit" in the East, the dreaded *SS Sonderkommando Dirlewanger*, commanded by Dr. Oskar Dirlewanger,[123] in order to redeem himself. Fate once again intervened on Prost's behalf as he was soon found to be suffering from syphilis and was therefore declared unfit for frontline service. The SS, however, was still able to utilize his limited talents by using him as a *V-Mann*,[124] or informer, to report on suspicious activities by his neighbors. For his troubles, Prost was given a few *Reichsmarks* each month so that he could survive, but just barely.

Peter stood outside of Prost's first floor apartment, No. 3, and put his ear to the door. He could hear movement inside the apartment, and there was music playing, probably from a phonograph or a radio. Peter took a deep breath and knocked on the door. He heard shuffling, and the music was turned off. Again, another knock on the door.

"*Herr Prost*, this is *Gruppenführer* Bertram, I order you to open the door at once!"

Peter could hear footsteps coming closer to the door and heard the bolt and chain being pulled back. The door opened.

"Ah, *Gruppenführer* Bertram, it has been a long time. Please do come in."

Peter entered the apartment, which was little more than a hovel. An unmade bed in the corner, a chester drawer set, a sink with a wash basin, a small hotplate, and a flimsy straight back chair with a small table made up the furnishings. The room was lit by a single bulb hanging from the ceiling. To use the toilet, Prost had to use the community bathroom located down the hallway.

Peter looked around the apartment wrinkling his nose, making it obvious to Prost that he was rather disgusted with the surroundings. It smelled like stale beer and rotting garbage.

"I'm terribly sorry, *Gruppenführer*, but today is the maid's day off and I really wasn't expecting any company," he sarcastically told Peter.

"You live like a pig, Prost. I've seen better accommodations in Jewish *Shtetls*[125] in the East."

Prost gave a grunt and then asked, "How may I help the *Gruppenführer*? This certainly isn't a social call now, is it?"

"Prost, I never did like you, and how you got into the SS in the first place, I will never know. You were a disgrace to the uniform when you served. That said, I want to know about my parents' death back in '40. They were killed in an auto accident; however, I don't think it was an accident. Do you know anything about it?"

Prost lit a cigarette, took a long drag and blew the smoke upward towards the ceiling. "Nineteen-forty, you say? Hmm, I really can't remember back that far, although a few *Reichsmarks* might help jar my memory," he said with a smirk.

Peter, without a word, lunged at Prost, delivering a punch to his jaw that knocked the former SS man down flat on his back. Peter then stood over him and drew out his Walther service pistol, aiming it at Prost's head. "Start talking, Prost, or I will blow your brains out right here and now."

Prost rubbed his jaw, wiped his mouth, and then spit out some blood onto the floor.

"You pack a pretty good punch, Bertram," dropping all formality and no longer addressing Peter by his SS rank.

"On your feet, Prost," Peter ordered.

Prost got up slowly, still rubbing his jaw. "What do you want to know?"

"My parents were killed three years ago in an auto accident, although I don't think it was an accident. Something Himmler said makes me believe that someone tampered with their vehicle. You wouldn't happen to know anything about that, would you, Prost?"

Lighting another cigarette, Prost moved over to the straight back chair and sat down.

"Yes, I know something about the accident—it was a set-up planned by your friend Himmler and the late 'Hangman of Prague,' himself, Reinhard Heydrich."

Peter was taken aback by this revelation - that two of the highest-ranking SS officers were responsible for the death of his parents.

"Why, Prost? Why did they want my parents dead?"

"Because, *Herr Gruppenführer*, they were becoming an embarrassment to the SS, especially your father, who didn't know when to keep his mouth shut. You would have thought that he would be proud to have a son who was a rising star within the SS; but alas, that wasn't the case, was it?" he said with a smirk.

"Go on," Peter ordered, his pistol still aimed at Prost.

"One day, I was summoned to Heydrich's office - I was literally quaking in my shoes - I thought it was because of my earlier indiscretions..."

"You mean your penchant for young boys," Peter interrupted.

Prost looked at him annoyed. "As I was saying, when Heydrich summoned me, I thought it was because of the earlier incident, but it wasn't. He sat me down, offered me a cognac, and then offered me a job. He said by taking the job, it would be a way of rehabilitating myself for my past transgressions against the Reich."

"And maybe against nature as well. What type of job did he offer you?"

Prost took a long drag on his cigarette and then looked squarely at Peter. "Why, to kill your parents, of course."

Peter felt his knees buckle and had to hold on the frame of the doorway where he stood.

"How did you do it?"

"The brake line - I cut the brake line to your parents' auto - it was really quite easy. I had followed them for about a week, watching their every move, learning their daily routine. I finally got the chance to cut the brake line late one evening, as I had learned they were planning on taking a short trip the next day. With petrol rationing, not many people were driving. I'm assuming your position in the SS facilitated their obtaining ration coupons for petrol?"

Peter lowered his head and shook it slowly. Prost was correct; Peter's position in the SS had enabled his parents to obtain petrol coupons - Lydia had talked him into ensuring that his parents could at least still drive even with wartime rationing in place. It was the only thing he relented on when it came to his parents. He had not forgotten the humiliation they had caused him, and he could still feel the sting of his father's slap across his face those many years before.

"I must have hit a nerve, Bertram, you don't look so well," Prost said with a chuckle.

Peter could now feel his seething rage begin to swell and it was getting more difficult to retain his composure. Still, he needed to know more.

"So, you killed my parents on orders from Heydrich, correct?"

"Correct, Bertram. And Heydrich was ordered to do it by Himmler."

"Was the *Führer* involved?" Peter asked, not knowing what the answer might be.

"To my knowledge, no. I don't think the *Führer* would waste his time plotting to kill a couple of old pensioners, as he was probably much too busy planning the invasion of Russia," Prost mused.

"How much?" Peter asked.

Prost gave him a quizzical look, then asked, "How much, what?"

"How much were you paid to kill my parents?"

"Oh, that! Well, you'll be happy to know that I did it for a song. Plus, I was assured that I would not be prosecuted if and when this ever came to light. I was assured that as long as both Himmler and Heydrich were alive, I would be protected."

"Heydrich is dead, and that only leaves Himmler standing in the way," said Peter.

"So, Bertram, now you know the whole story, so go ahead and shoot - you will be doing me a favor." Looking around his room, Prost said, "After forty years of life, this is all I have to show for it." He then turned and looked at Peter. "Go ahead and shoot."

Peter raised his pistol and aimed it at Prost's head. "You disgust me, Prost. I'm not going to kill you, but I'll make sure you never harm a youngster again." With that, he lowered his weapon, and aimed instead at Prost's groin, firing one shot. Prost fell back in his chair, screaming and writhing in agony, with blood splattered everywhere.

Peter then pocketed his pistol and left Prost's apartment. The shot had alerted some of the neighbors who peered out of their apartments.

"Mind your business, all of you - this is a matter of state security."

With that pronouncement, all the apartment doors slammed almost in unison, as none of the occupants wanted to get involved with the Gestapo or any other members of the Reich's multi-faceted security apparatus.

As Peter quickly walked away from Prost's apartment, he tried to comprehend what the former SS man had told him - that both Himmler and Heydrich were responsible for the death of his parents. Heydrich was now dead, and that left Himmler to answer his questions. One just couldn't barge into the office of the second most powerful man in the Reich after Hitler and demand answers. It would be suicide to say the least. Yet, the death of his parents haunted him after all these years - outwardly their loss appeared not to bother him—but in those quiet moments, late at night, it gnawed at his very being. He decided then and there that he would confront Himmler and get the answers he sought, even if it meant interrogating the *Reichsführer SS* at the point of gun. And once he had those answers, he would then kill Himmler.

Office of the *Reichsführer SS*
***Prinz-Albrecht-Strasse* 8**
Berlin, Germany
August 30, 1943, 1520 Hours

All the evidence that Peter had collected pointed to the fact that Himmler himself had ordered the death of his parents back in 1940. Now Himmler was going to pay with his life. Bertram knew that he would not get out of this alive - once he shot Himmler, SS security forces would gun him down where he stood - he would have little chance of escape. All that transpired this last month of Sepp's visit, made Bertram realize that his participation in the Final Solution to the Jewish Question, was criminal. It went against both the laws of God and man. How could he have been so blind all these years? His parents had been correct in predicting that Hitler was the devil incarnate and that he would lead Germany into ruin. The military setbacks on the battlefields, the increased bombing of the homeland, all pointed to the fact that his parents were correct in their assessment of the 'Bohemian Corporal.' Bertram had been surprised to learn that his father had been involved in the infant resistance movement against Hitler in 1940. His father had belonged to the Catholic Center Party, which of course had been outlawed, but members met secretly and carried out small acts of resistance against the regime, such as issuing pamphlets and secretly putting up posters condemning the Nazis.

In one of his previous visits to *Prinz-Albrecht-Strasse*, Bertram had been shown a secret entrance/exit into the building, a door disguised as a large air vent, in the event Himmler and other ranking SS officers needed to escape the building in a hurry. It had no guard in order to make it appear as inconspicuous as possible from the outside. Walking near the hidden entrance, he carefully ran his hand across the vent's surface until he felt the outline of a door which was spring released. Finding the release, Bertram pressed it and the door slowly opened. Bertram quickly slipped inside and closed the door behind him with a large handle that was attached on the inside. The passageway led to the building's generator room, and as he walked closer, he could hear the hum of the huge generators which provided electricity and other facilities to the headquarters. For all intents and purposes, the building was self-contained and self-sufficient. Bertram had been previously shown a set of staircases that if followed, would take him directly to Himmler's office. The stairs would lead to a false wall in Himmler's office, behind a bookcase. He could then push another spring-loaded button and the bookcase would open, leading right into the SS chief's lair.

As he neared the top of the steps, Bertram tensed and began to perspire heavily; his shirt was drenched under his armpits as well as his back. With pistol in hand, he made his way up to the end of the stairs and was face-to-face with the back of the false wall. He put his ear to the wall and listened carefully as there was no telling if Himmler was alone or not. Bertram distinctly heard the telephone receiver being replaced in its cradle. He then heard Himmler's chair push back and footsteps coming closer to the bookcase. Bertram began perspiring even more; he then heard the door to Himmler's private washroom close and the toilet seat being dropped. Knowing Himmler suffered from severe stomach cramps on occasion, Bertram bet that the SS chief would be indisposed for a while, thus giving him time to make his way into the office and surprising Himmler when he least expected it.

Once out from behind the bookshelf, he slowly pushed it back into place. He also quickly checked to see if the massive oak door to Himmler's office was locked, which it was not. He then quietly locked it. He heard the toilet flush, and the sound of a faucet running as the germophobe Himmler carefully washed his hands.

Himmler strode out of the washroom and once again was seated at his desk, a pile of paperwork awaiting his attention.

As Himmler returned to his paperwork, he caught a movement out of the corner of his right eye.

"*Guten Tag, Herr Reichsführer,*" Bertram said rather menacingly.

Startled, Himmler jumped in his seat.

"Bertram, how did you get into my office?" Himmler demanded.

"Down the chimney like Santa Claus," Bertram answered smugly.

Himmler was incensed that a subordinate would take such a tone with him. "How dare you, *Gruppenführer*, address me in such a manner! You have the gall to show your face in my headquarters after you and your brother helped those Jews escape! Well, you being here only makes things easier for me." Himmler then reached for the intercom on his desk to summon his aide.

"I wouldn't do that if I were you, *Reichsführer.* Please keep your hands where I can see them. I also know you have a Walther in your top middle drawer, so take that out barrel first and be so kind as to throw it to the side. I locked your office door while you were in the toilet. If you make a sound or scream for help, I will kill you right here and now before I get the answers I came for." Himmler, realizing Bertram had the drop on him, did as he was told.

"Very well, *Gruppenführer,* I am now unarmed, and at your mercy. So now what? Are you going to kill me in cold blood? You will never make it out of this building alive, you know that. Give me your gun, and I will put you on medical leave; there is a nice sanitarium at Hohenlychen,[126] about 100 kilometers north of Berlin, where you can get the help you need. We can forget about the incident at Klooga, and no disciplinary action will be taken against you or your family, I assure you."

"Your assurances, *Reichsführer*, are worthless to me. I came here planning to kill you and I will. I know it is suicide, but it is worth it. I believe you are familiar with the quote by the Englishman Edmund Burke, who stated 'that all that is necessary for the triumph of evil is for good men to do nothing.' Well, I've sat around and have done nothing for far too long and now I intend to rectify my mistakes. But first you are going to answer some questions for me."

A few moments passed before he cleared his throat and spoke.

"*Reichsführer*, this little visit concerns the death of my parents in 1940."

Himmler was taken aback, and then spoke. "It was a tragic accident, so what of it?"

"It wasn't an accident. I have learned their automobile was deliberately tampered with and the brake line cut to make it look like an accident."

Himmler began to squirm uncomfortably in his seat, as though he knew what Bertram would be saying next. Still, he remained quiet.

"After reviewing the police report of the accident, and doing some further investigation on my own, I discovered that the culprit was a former SS man, who had been dismissed from the service because of his fondness for young boys. Still, the SS kept him on as an informer, and after some persuasive questioning, he told me something very disturbing. Would you like to know what that was, *Herr Reichsführer*?"

"Go on, Bertram, I'm listening," Himmler stated, his fingers steepled and held in front of his mouth and elbows resting upon the top of his desk. Bertram now had Himmler's full and undivided attention.

"My informant told me that *Obergruppenführer* Heydrich was the man behind my parents' death. He ordered that my parents be eliminated, because they proved to be an embarrassment to the party, particularly due to my father's outspokenness. It bothered the higher echelons of the party that the father of a rising officer in the SS just couldn't keep his mouth shut, so Heydrich shut it for him permanently."

"This is all news to me, my dear Bertram," Himmler smiled. "As you recall, Heydrich is no longer with us, having been murdered by those Czech *schwein* in the pay of the British. There is very little I can do. I'm sorry that some renegade SS man and a sexual deviate was involved. I can have this deviate arrested and thrown in a concentration camp for violating Paragraph 175 if that will make you feel any better about this whole affair. After all, he's probably the one that cut the brake line on your parents' car in the first place. Give me his name, and I'll have him picked up immediately."

"No need for that, he's probably dead by now. I shot him in the groin after he gave me the information I needed. He has probably bled out by now. What has also bothered me for a long time was something that you said to me when you arrived at the airfield in Reval during your visit last month."

Himmler gave him a quizzical look. "Just what *did* I say, *Gruppenführer*? Refresh my memory if you please," Himmler said smugly.

"It's what you didn't say, *Reichsführer*. When we were talking about my parents' death, you almost slipped up and said that my parents were *eliminated*. You caught yourself, but the damage had been done. You knew that my parents were murdered, didn't you?"

Himmler stared blankly and swallowed hard.

"My brother was right, both you and the *Führer* are nothing but madman. I pray to God that when I meet Him, he will forgive me for my sins, much as he did the good thief at Calvary the day He was crucified. May God forgive me for what I'm about to do."

As Bertram raised his pistol to fire, air raid warnings sounded as Berlin once again came under attack by Allied bombers, as German FLAK units in the government district began to open fire. Almost immediately Brandt tried to open the door to get his boss to the air raid shelter below, but found the door locked.

"*Herr Reichsführer*, are you alright? Please open the door, we are under attack, and we need to get to the air raid shelters below. *Herr Reichsführer* can you hear me?" Brandt began pounding on the massive thick oak door.

"You see *Gruppenführer*, you're trapped; that door is the only way out. Brandt will have a half dozen guards here in a minute and if need be, they will fire through the door to get to me. Don't be a fool, give yourself up."

"Not quite, *Reichsführer,* you forget how I got into your office in the first place, through your secret passage," Bertram said, nodding in the direction of the bookcase. "It just dawned on me, *Reichsfuhrer,* that today is August 30. Today you were scheduled to come to Klooga to watch 100 Jewish prisoners die as a result of a new type of gas; instead, it is you that will die."

Before Bertram could shoot, the first bombs struck the government district, shattering windows and hitting close to their location. Himmler was now petrified, not so much now by Bertram's threat, but that a direct hit would kill him while this lunatic had a gun trained on him. Just then, a direct hit outside of the building exploded knocking both Himmler and Bertram to the floor, and in the process, the pistol fell out of Bertram's hand. Bertram was dazed, and surprisingly, Himmler was agile enough to get up and rush to the door, unlock it and let the security detail in.

"Arrest this traitor," he ordered, while the bombs were still falling outside. "He was going to kill me; the only thing that saved me was the air raid. I guess I have Providence to thank for that. Get up you *schwein*," Himmler ordered.

"No," Bertram answered back. "You want to kill me, do it now."

Himmler's adjutant and the security detail looked at Himmler for guidance.

"*Herr Reichsführer*, what are your orders?" Brandt asked.

"Shoot the *schwein* now. I order you to shoot him!"

The SS men opened up with machine pistols and riddled Bertram's body full of bullets, killing him instantly.

When the firing stopped, Himmler went over to the body and spit on it. "You filthy *schwein!* I'm going to ensure your bloodline ends now. Brandt, get in touch with the Gestapo chief in Rome, *Obersturmbannführer* Kappler.[127] I want his Jesuit brother taken care of as well. His brother's name is Monsignor Josef Bertram. He is to be shot immediately if captured, understood?

"*Jawohl, Herr Reichsführer*", Brandt replied.

Pointing to Bertram's corpse, Himmler ordered "Get his body out of here now, I don't even want to look at this traitor." With that, the SS detail picked up Bertram's lifeless body and carried it out of Himmler's office. With the air raid sirens now sounding an "all clear" signal, Himmler sat down behind his desk and stared blankly at the shattered windows and broken glass that littered his once pristine office. He then began to shake uncontrollably at the thought of just how close he had come to being murdered by one of his own men. Unfortunately, Himmler could not dwell on this incident too long as he was due in Rasternberg that evening and had to make his way to the airfield and the flight to Hitler's headquarters.

Chapter XIV

"One had only to watch the changing of the guard to see that the Italian soldier had no enthusiasm for his profession."
--Field Marshal Albert Kesselring, C-in-C South

"Half of Italy is German, half is English, and there is no longer and Italian Italy."[128]
--Italian Partisan Emmanuele Artom

Pratica di Mare Airfield
Rome, Italy
September 8, 1943, 1445 Hours

The Italian aircraft bearing Sepp and the plane's crew arrived in Rome to the cheers of all onboard. It had been a long, exhausting flight for all, but now they were finally home. As the aircraft taxied to a hangar following a ground guide vehicle, the co-pilot made mention that there appeared to be a large number of German vehicles at the airfield. Garcetti, busy keeping his focus on the ground guide, had paid little attention to what his co-pilot had said. The aircraft halted at the far end of the airfield and the engines were turned off.

"Gentlemen, welcome back to Italy!" Garcetti said, as the crew and Sepp cheered once again.

The crew chief opened up the cargo door and noticed two German *Kubelwagens* racing down the tarmac towards them followed by an Opel truck full of troops.

"*Colonnello*, you better come take a look at this. It appears we have company, *Tedesci!*"[129]

"What are you talking about, Sergeant?" Garcetti asked.

The German vehicles skidded to a halt on both sides of the aircraft. A young *Wehrmacht Leutnant*, pistol in hand was the first to alight from the vehicles. Pointing his pistol upward towards the cockpit window, he ordered the crew, in perfect Italian, to exit the plane with their hands up. In the interim, the troops from the lorry, disembarked and surrounded the aircraft.

Sepp, from his location in the cabin of the aircraft could see clearly what had transpired. What he and the aircraft's crew were totally unaware of was that earlier in the day while they had been in mid-flight, it was announced that Italy had surrendered to the Allies. Italy and Germany were now enemies.

"Out of the aircraft I said, now!" the young officer barked.

"We better do as he says, the aircraft is surrounded and we are not going anywhere," Garcetti said.

Garecetti was the first to leave the aircraft followed by his co-pilot, the four crewmembers and then Sepp. None of the Italians were armed, having left their weapons on the plane.

"Check the aircraft and make sure no one else is on board," the officer ordered one of his NCO's.

"All clear, *Herr Leutnant*, just some weapons stacked in the corner," the sergeant reported as he exited the aircraft.

"You may lower your hands, gentlemen. My name is *Leutnant* Alois Rauter and you are now under arrest."

Garcetti then stepped forward and said, "What is the meaning of this, under arrest, we are allies!"

"You mean you haven't heard, *Colonnello*, Italy has surrendered to the Allies. We are no longer allies but enemies," he said sarcastically.

The German officer could see by Garcetti's and the rest of the crews' facial expressions that they were totally unaware that Italy had surrendered.

"What do you plan on doing with us?" Garcetti asked.

"You are to be interned until the *Führer* makes a final decision on your status."

One of the crew members, a young airman named Caprietto, a giant of man, lunged at the officer, but he was set upon by three German troopers who pummeled him to the ground with their rifle butts, rendering him unconscious.

"Anyone else care to try something stupid like your friend here?" Rauter asked.

The remainder of the crew could only cast their eyes downward, a sign of dejection.

"And what about you priest," he asked Sepp. "Why are you here?"

Sepp answered in German and told Rauter that he was a German national and assigned to the Vatican Foreign Office. As proof, he pulled out his original travel orders and handed them to Rauter.

Rauter was taken aback that Sepp was a German and that he was a diplomat for the Vatican. The orders were signed by Ambassador von Weizsäcker. Seeing that Sepp obviously was a VIP of sorts, Rauter handed Sepp back his travel orders, clicked his heels and bowed slightly.

"I am very sorry to have inconvenienced you, Monsignor Bertram, you are free to go. We will be more than happy to give you a ride to the operations center here at the airfield. But I am afraid you will have to provide your own transportation from there on."

Sepp silently said a prayer of thanks. "Before I go, *Herr Leutnant*, may I say good-bye to the crew. We have flown all the way from Russia together and I have become very attached to them."

Rauter nodded his ascent and Sepp made his way to each of the crew, shaking each of their hands along with words of thanks and encouragement and ended with him giving a blessing over the still unconscious Caprietto.

"Load the crew onto the truck," Rauter ordered. Silently, the Italians walked over to the parked Opel and climbed up the lowered tailgate. Caprietto was carried over by two German soldiers and hoisted up, helped on board by his crewmembers already on the truck. As the truck pulled away, Sepp said a silent prayer that the men would fare well and survive their ordeal.

"So, Monsignor, it appears you were caught totally unaware of this historic day - those duplicitous Italians switching sides and surrendering to the Allies. To be honest, they were more a hinderance than help. We could do without them, along with the Romanians and Hungarians to boot!" Rauter said with a laugh.

Sepp could only force a weak smile at Rauter's joke.

"Hop on in, monsignor, we will give you a ride to base operations."

"My kit bag, it is still on the aircraft, may I get it?" Sepp asked.

"I will send my driver in for it. What does it look like?"

"A small black leather overnight bag, nothing fancy."

Rauter ordered his driver to go back to the aircraft and retrieve Sepp's bag.

While Sepp and Rauter were alone in the vehicle, the German officer pondered aloud, "Where have I heard your name before, monsignor? Bertram...Bertram...Do you have a relative serving in the *Wehrmacht,* a high-ranking officer perhaps?"

"No, I do not, *Herr Leutnant.*"

"I never forget a name. It will come to me."

The driver returned with Sepp's bag and handed it to him. With that task done, Rauter ordered his driver on to the base operations building located about ¾ mile away. As they slowly drove down the tarmac, Rauter continued to ramble on about the treachery of the Italians and how worthless they were as allies.

Within minutes, they had arrived at base operations and the vehicle had come to a halt.

"Here you go, Monsignor, base operations. I am sure someone here will allow you to use a phone to arrange a ride. Good luck." Rauter held out his hand and Sepp shook it with a word of thanks for the short lift. Sepp then entered the base operations building which was now being run by *Luftwaffe* personnel rather than men of the *Regia Aeronautica.*

Rauter ordered his driver to turn off the vehicle engine for a moment, and the vehicle sat silently in front of the base operations building.

"You know, Hans," Rauter said to his driver, "I just can't put my finger on it, but the name 'Bertram' seems awfully familiar, where have I heard it?"

"Perhaps, *Herr Leutnant*, the priest is a wanted criminal," the driver joked.

Rauter was about to give his driver a sharp rebuke when he realized that his driver was right - Bertram was wanted by the Gestapo for questioning.

"Hans, you are right! The priest is wanted by state security. Now it is all coming back to me. His brother was a senior SS officer, and both were implicated in facilitating in a mass escape of prisoners."

Hans' eyes widened with disbelief. "You mean, *Herr Leutnant*…" as he struggled to finish the sentence.

"Exactly, Hans," Rauter said. "I am going in to get our priest friend. Wait here and if you see a Gestapo or *Feldgendarme* unit, flag them down and tell them what is going on."

"*Jawohl, Herr Leutnant*," said Hans.

With that, Rauter exited his vehicle, unholstered his sidearm and walked into the base operations building. He could see Bertram at the main counter talking to a young *Luftwaffe* airman who seemed eager to help the cleric.

Walking slowly and sauntering up next to Bertram, Rauter told the young airman that Sepp would no longer be needing the phone. When Sepp looked at the German officer, he saw that Rauter had his pistol aimed at him. "It appears, Monsignor, that you are wanted by the Gestapo for questioning. You will come with me, please." Rauter motioned with his pistol for Sepp to move towards the entrance of the building. Just then a *Luftwaffe* Major who had been alerted by the airman at the counter, intercepted Rauter.

"What the hell is going on here, *Leutnant?* Why in God's name are you holding this priest at gunpoint?"

"*Herr Major*, this man is wanted by the Gestapo, and I intend to bring him in; I suggest you stay out of my way."

Livid at being spoken to in such a manner by a junior officer, the *Luftwaffe* Major, a stickler for military protocol, exploded with anger. "This is now a *Luftwaffe* facility, and I will not allow some young upstart to come in here, with weapon drawn without so much of an acknowledgement to his military superiors. What do you have to say for yourself, *Leutnant?*"

Rauter began to stammer an answer that the Major found unacceptable. The Major then signaled to two *Fallschirmjager* (paratroopers) of the 2nd *Fallschirmjager* Division[130] on guard duty within the facility, to come over to him.

"Place this officer under arrest immediately," the Major ordered. "Your pistol, if you please, *Herr Leutnant*," he demanded. Rauter meekly handed over his weapon to the *Luftwaffe* officer and was then led off by the two paratroopers who confined him into a locked office in the rear of the facility until a decision was made on what to do with him.

The Major then turned to Sepp and said, "I am sorry, Father, I apologize for the actions of this arrogant young officer. Let me be clear that he is a *Wehrmacht* officer and not a member of the *Luftwaffe*. You are free to go."

Sepp nodded his thanks and walked out the entrance of the facility his mind racing and, in his haste, totally missed seeing Rauter's vehicle, along with his driver still parked in front of the facility.

Hans watched in shock as Sepp strolled out of the building, kit bag in hand, and began walking out toward the main entrance of the airfield. The young driver wondered where his officer was. He had gone in, but never came out of base operations. As Sepp moved further away from the base operations building, Hans felt helpless. As fate would have it, a vehicle was making its way slowly toward his location. It then came to a halt in front of his vehicle and both passengers got out of the car and began walking into the base operations. The men were dressed in black leather trench coats, fedoras and just had a look about them that spelled - Gestapo.

Mustering his courage, Hans walked up to the two men before they could enter the building. "Excuse me, gentlemen, would either of you happen to be with state security?"

"What gave us away, sonny, the trench coats or our bubbling personalities?" the one agent joked. Seeing Hans was serious, the other agent answered, "Yes we are with the Gestapo," and at the same time pulling out his warrant disk identifying him as a member of the secret state police.

Hans then explained the situation and pointed to the distant figure rapidly disappearing from view as Sepp got closer to leaving through the main entrance of the airfield.

"That is Monsignor Bertram and I believe he is wanted by the Gestapo," Hans blurted out.

"Bertram!" both agents explained in unison. They both looked at each other, muttered a word of thanks to the young soldier and got back in their car, made a U-turn and sped towards the airfield entrance.

Sepp kept up his gait, not trying to look overly suspicious, but nonetheless desperately trying to get off the airfield as quickly as possible before the Germans realized their mistake and placed him under arrest. As he unconsciously quickened his pace, he heard the sound of an automobile engine that was drawing closer. Just then an auto shot past him and then jumped the small sidewalk curb, blocking Sepp's further movement. Both men jumped out and with weapons drawn, placed Sepp under arrest.

"You are Monsignor Bertram, yes?" asked one agent.

Sepp thought about denying it, but he realized then and there that his luck had finally run out. It was a good run, but fate had other plans for him.

The agents took his small bag, handcuffed him and placed him in the back of their vehicle for a ride to the nearest Gestapo precinct, which was only two kilometers away.

Gestapo sub-station 5
Rome, Italy
September 8, 1943, 1625 Hours

The main Gestapo prison was located at *Via Tasso145*[131]; however, due to the size of the city, the Gestapo had set up various sub-stations throughout the city in order to best expand their reach. It was at one of these precincts, closest to the airfield, that Monsignor Sepp Bertram was being held in custody. He had been apprehended outside the geographic boundaries of the Vatican City, thus the Germans ensured that there was no breach in violating the neutrality of the Holy See. While he was not mistreated, his Gestapo guards showed him nothing but contempt.

"Well Monsignor, it appears that both you and your brother have raised the ire of the *Reichsführer SS*," the Gestapo captain said with an added bit of sarcasm. He then added, "Oh, and by the way, I have a bit of news about your brother…the traitor is dead! He attempted to kill the *Reichsführer* but failed miserably and was gunned down like a dog by the *Reichsführer's* security detail."

Sepp felt as if he was punched in the stomach when he learned of his brother's death; no, it was murder. He sat down on the cot in his cell and put his face in his hands and wept uncontrollably. However, he was satisfied in knowing that Lydia and the children were safe in Sweden and that his brother had atoned for his sins for serving the Nazi regime.

"I have another surprise for you, Monsignor," the guard quipped. "You are to be shot at dawn. Would you like me to get you a priest to hear your confession?" The two Gestapo guards laughed out loud at that little bit of gallows humor and then went outside for a smoke, leaving Bertram alone with his thoughts.

"I'll be dead at dawn," he said to himself. "Well, I'm ready to meet my Savior."

When the guards returned from their smoke break, Bertram asked the senior officer, "*Herr Hauptsturmführer*, I'd like to take you up on your offer for a priest to hear my confession, if you don't mind."

The Gestapo officer thought for a moment and said, "Fine, Monsignor, you will have a clergyman to confess your sins to. Make sure you add treason to your multitude of sins against the Reich. Any priest in particular that you wish to confess to?"

"Yes, *Padre* Giuseppe Scavone, is the pastor at San Antonio di Padua right up the street here. He is an old friend. If you wouldn't mind asking him,

I would be most obliged."

"Consider it done, Monsignor. Dolf, run up and get *Padre* Scavone up at San Antonio and bring him here," he ordered his subordinate.

Within twenty minutes the Gestapo officer returned with a very frightened *Padre* Scavone in tow.

The senior Gestapo man then pointed to the back room stating, "Monsignor Bertram wishes you to hear his *last* confession. Go on back," he ordered.

Padre Scavone had a perplexed look on his face, as he knew nothing until just then of Bertram's arrest and incarceration. He went back to the holding cell and saw his friend sitting on his cot, looking forlorn and hopeless.

"Monsignor, what has happened? Why has the Gestapo arrested you?" Bertram then related to his Italian friend what had transpired over the last month. He then added, "Giuseppe, I wish you to hear my confession."

"*Sí*, Monsignor," *Padre* Scavone answered, and heard his friend's confession.

When all was said and done, Bertram thanked his friend and apologized for alarming him, stating that "I'm sure you were quite concerned when the Gestapo man showed up at the rectory doorstep." Before Scavone had a chance to answer, the Gestapo captain came back to the holding area and announced that a firing squad had been selected for the execution.

"Instead of using German troops for the firing squad tomorrow morning, we are going to use our erstwhile Italian allies to do the job for us. It should also prove to us their loyalty to the Axis partnership. That ought to add insult to injury, eh, *Padre*?" he asked sarcastically.

He continued, "A black shirt unit here that has remained loyal to the *Duce* will be doing the honors. A *squadristi* under *Capitano* Ricci will be here at sunrise tomorrow; the execution will take place in the courtyard out back." With that, the Gestapo officer turned and walked back to the front office to join his comrade.

"Giuseppe, you better go now. Thank you for coming and hearing my confession. When you see Cardinal Tardini again, please tell him what has transpired."

"I will, Monsignor. God bless you always." With that, *Padre* Scavone turned and left the holding area and walked back to the rectory of San Antonio di Padua, all the while fingering his rosary on the long walk back.

Via Flaminia
Rome, Italy
September 8/9, 1943, 0500 Hours

With news of the Italian surrender earlier on September 8th, Hitler's reaction was swift and brutal. German military units in and around Rome, in accordance with contingency plan *Unternehmen Achse* (Operation Axis), and with Teutonic efficiency, moved against their former Axis partner in a series of lightning engagements that caught the hapless Italians completely off-guard. The German 3rd *Panzergrenadier* Division, engaged Italian troops along the *Via Falminia* on the northern outskirts of Rome. There the Germans encountered stiff resistance from Italian troops attempting a delaying action in order to bolster defenses inside the city. Elsewhere, elements of the 2nd *Fallschirmjaeger* Division were dropped over targets and quickly neutralized Italian units attempting to make a stand.[132] Within 24 hours, the Germans had achieved complete military superiority and controlled Rome and its environs. Thousands of Italian soldiers were taken into captivity and sent to POW camps while thousands more were made slave laborers in Germany and throughout occupied Europe. A number of Italian soldiers were able to shed their uniforms and hide out in Rome, blending in with the civilian population; while others were able to join the Partisans and continue the fight against the hated Germans. The Germans publicly vowed to respect the territorial integrity and neutrality of the Vatican, thus temporarily alleviating fears that Hitler would march in, arrest Pius XII along with the Curia. Thus, the Vatican remained an island oasis of freedom surrounded by a city gripped by terror and oppression.

Gestapo sub-station 5
Rome, Italy
September 9, 1943, 0600 Hours

Dawn broke early that day, and *Capitano* Ricci and his ten-man Fascist militia squad had arrived about a half hour prior to sunrise. Scattered fighting was still going on in parts of the city as the Germans attempted to wrest Rome from its Italian defenders. The Gestapo captain was duly impressed that the execution squad had arrived well ahead of time. He would make sure he put that little tidbit of information in his report to the *Via Tasso*. Ricci was a die-hard fascist, a veteran of the Spanish Civil War and the campaigns in Ethiopia and Greece and was still supporting the *Duce* even though he had been overthrown almost two months earlier. Still, Ricci had trouble executing a priest. But orders were orders, and if they weren't carried out, the Germans could cause a lot of trouble in the form of reprisals. Best to get the execution over with and then back to the barracks for a hearty breakfast and maybe a visit to the new brothel that opened on *Via Teresa*. Still, his conscience continued to bother him.

"*Capitano Ricci*, I'm *Hauptsturmführer* Eichorn, thank you for coming on time. I will make sure I mention you favorably in my report to the *Via Tasso*."

"*Grazi, Herr Hauptsturmführer*. I'd like to get this over with quickly if you don't mind. The men are none too happy about executing a priest. I had to really give them a pep talk to tell them that the clergy were really the enemy of the fascist state and as good fascists, we needed to rid not only Italy but the world of this Jesuit influence."

"And did your talk succeed, *Capitano* Ricci?"

"I guess we will know in a few minutes, won't we, *Hauptsturm-führer?*"

Eichorn was none too pleased with Ricci's flippant response. *A typical Italian, much like those damn Spaniards, a que sera attitude on getting things accomplished,* he thought to himself.

"*Capitano*, if you don't mind, have your men take the monsignor out back and tie him to the post. Ask him if he wants a blindfold and a cigarette, you know the usual procedure."

Ricci then ordered two of his men to get Bertram and take him out back for the execution. As they marched into the courtyard, Bertram was surprised to see his friend *Padre* Scavone with his missal and deep in prayer. Next to Scavone was the sergeant of the guard, Sergeant Giovanni Scavone, the *padre*'s cousin. It would be Sergeant Scavone who would be commanding the firing squad. This of course was unbeknownst to Bertram, and to Eichorn.

As the rest of the squad assembled, Ricci and Eichorn entered the courtyard to watch the proceedings. Eichorn read the execution order signed by Himmler and then stepped back to let the Italians carry it out.

Bertram had refused the customary blindfold and cigarette. He stood there defiant and to both Eichorn's and Ricci's surprise, he was not tied to a post, which allowed his hands to be free to pray the rosary.

Ricci gave the order that brought the squad to attention.

"Ready – aim - fire!" ordered Ricci.

Nothing happened.

Eichorn went up to Ricci and yelled, "What the hell is going on here Ricci? Order them to fire again!"

Ricci again gave the order to fire, and again nothing. Sergeant Scavone then ordered his men to turn their guns on Ricci and Eichorn.

"Drop your weapons gentlemen. We're not about to carry out this insane order."

Ricci did as he was told, whereas the arrogant Eichorn went for his pistol and was cut down by a hail of gunfire. Two other Gestapo officers who came out to witness the execution also went to return fire but were immediately shot and killed by the firing squad.

Two of the members of the firing squad kept their weapons trained on Ricci, who was trembling and had soiled himself in the process, a large wet stain forming on the front of his trousers. The two militiamen had a good laugh at their commanding officer's plight.

The rest of the squad, headed by Sergeant Scavone, knelt in front of Bertram, and asked for absolution. The sergeant spoke on behalf of all his men and said, "Monsignor, please forgive us for putting you through this."

Bertram could see that the sergeant was sincere—most of the militiamen were of peasant stock and had been conscripted. Most would have preferred being back with their families or on their farms in Calabria.

"Sergeant, please get up. Yes, you are forgiven, and I thank you from the bottom of my heart for saving my life. You all will not be forgotten."

Turning to his friend *Padre* Scavone, he said, "Giuseppe, I owe you my life."

Padre Scavone was a man of few words, and simply nodded and then said, "Monsignor, you must get back to the Vatican City immediately. I'm sure my dear cousin and his men will provide you a military escort."

Bertram smiled and said "Fine, that would be most satisfactory. But what about *Capitano* Ricci here. What will become of him?"

Ricci was now crying uncontrollably and pleading for his life.

"Please *padres*, please do not let them kill me, please, I beg of you! I never meant to harm anyone. I hate the *Duce*, hate him, I say," spitting at the ground and trying to show his contempt for the former Italian leader.

"Giuseppe don't kill him. Can you turn him over to the Partisans? Now don't lie, I know you have contacts with them."

Padre Scavone broke into a broad smile. "*Sí*, monsignor. I will have the men take *il Capitano* to the Partisans and they can take care of him. I will ask them to spare his life, as you requested. The men here will probably go over to the Partisans themselves or desert after they leave here. I will have Giovanni personally escort you to the Vatican."

Padre Scavone then spoke with his cousin; "I will send word to Monsignor O'Flaherty in the Vatican. Whatever you do, do not let Monsignor Bertram fall into Kappler's hands."

"Understood, Giuseppe," Sergeant Scavone replied to his cousin.

"Kappler along with Koch[133] have made it quite clear of what they will do to O'Flaherty if he is caught - I can imagine what they have in store for Monsignor Bertram," *Padre* Scavone said, his voice trailing off.

Sergeant Scavone approached Sepp and said, "Monsignor, we need to leave here immediately; it will only be a matter of time before some of the other Germans return to the station house from their normal rounds. In the meantime, we need to get you a disguise so you can make it back to the Vatican undetected."

Looking at some of his men, he saw that Private Micella appeared to be roughly Sepp's height and weight and said to him, "Micella, take off your uniform and give it to the Monsignor, quickly!" With that, the young soldier happily stripped off his uniform down to his skivvies and traded them with

Sepp.

"Here you go, private, at least take my pants to wear," Sepp said with a chuckle. The men exchanged clothes, with Micella opting not to wear the Roman collar, but took the black jacket and wore it over his undershirt.

"You look good, *Padre*, like a real soldier," said Sergeant Scavone. "Now we must move towards the Vatican boundary and somehow get you over the line[134] and to safety. May I suggest we wait until nightfall. We've observed that the Germans pull some of their men off the line at night and it may be easier to slip past them then."

"I'm in your hands, Sergeant," Sepp said.

Gestapo sub-station 5
Rome, Italy
September 9, 1943, 0650 Hours

Two Gestapo officers that had returned to their station were met with a grisly sight - three of their colleagues had been shot to death. Immediately drawing their pistols, they carefully searched the area, but the culprits were long gone. On close examination, the bodies of the three slain officers were riddled with multiple gunshot wounds.

"Must have been that damn militia unit that was here to carry out that priest's execution this morning. There is no sign of them or the priest's body for that matter. They probably had a change of heart and helped him escape."

"What shall we do?" asked the junior of the two officers.

"Kappler needs to be informed of this immediately, and a dragnet be ordered across the city for those culprits. I'll call him now."

With that, he went to the phone and placed his call directly to Gestapo headquarters. "This is *Hauptsturmführer* Shults, please connect me with *Obersturmbannführer* Kappler, this is very urgent."

As he waited for the switchboard at Kappler's headquarters on the *Via Tasso* to patch him through, Shults lit a cigarette and waited until Kappler's distinctive voice came on the line.

"Kappler here, what is it?"

Almost instinctively, Shults dropped his cigarette and came to attention, even though Kappler could in no way see him. "*Herr Obersturmbannführer* this is *Hauptsturmführer* Shults from Sub-station 5, I wish to report the murders of three of our officers here at the precinct."

For a moment there was dead silence on the line, then slowly and deliberately, Kappler asked "Who were they, Shults? Do you have any suspects?"

"Yes, sir. They were officers Eichorn, Verhine and Becker. We found them shot in the courtyard behind the precinct. All three were killed by multiple gunshot wounds. Sir, there was an execution scheduled to be carried out earlier this morning on a priest, a Monsignor Bertram, by an Italian Fascist unit. It appears they turned their guns on our men rather than the priest."

"Bertram," Kappler hissed over the phone. "I want that man alive so I can personally put a bullet in him. Shults, I want you to secure the area, and I am sending reinforcements to your location immediately. You will be the on-scene commander. I would suspect that they are going to make their way to the Vatican, and no doubt that Irish Jesuit O'Flaherty is somehow involved. I'll make them both pay if they are captured. I will be at your location shortly Shults." With that, Kappler hung up the receiver.

Shults then turned to his young partner, "Werner, it appears that all hell is going to break loose as soon as Kappler gets here with reinforcements. You better look sharp."

Within twenty minutes, the area outside the precinct was a beehive of activity as SS and Gestapo men in trucks, armored cars and light tanks cordoned off the area for a ten-block radius and began a house-to-house search for Bertram, but to no avail. Local residents were questioned but reported that they had neither seen nor heard anything, even though most were up and about and beginning their workday.

"These damn Italians, they are a worthless people!" Kappler exclaimed in utter frustration and contempt. "Of course, no one has seen or heard a thing, they are all covering up for their families and friends in the resistance. I have nothing to show for but three dead officers on my hands and now must inform the *Reichsführer SS* of this setback."

"What are your orders, *Herr Obersturmbannführer*?" asked Shults.

"I want an all-points bulletin on Bertram. The man who brings him in will receive a three-day pass. Also, double the guard on the Vatican-Rome boundary. Bertram is more than likely not wearing his clerical garb, so he could be dressed as anyone. Bottom line, Shults, I want him found!"

"*Jawohl, Herr Obersturmbannführer*!" exclaimed Shults.

With that, Kappler climbed into his staff car and took off, his driver gunning the engine and speeding off down the narrow jarring cobbled-stone streets of Rome.

Chapter XV

"Now the Pope is nearer to Himmler than to *Himmel*"[135]
--Quip from an unknown German officer upon the painting of a white line marking the boundary of Rome and the Vatican City

Office of the Head Notary
Vatican City
September 9, 1943, 1330 Hours

The sounds of battle entered into the Vatican office of Monsignor Hugh O'Flaherty, a gregarious Irish-born Roman Catholic cleric, when a messenger, who had dodged numerous firefights still raging within the city, stopped by and deposited a small envelope on O'Flaherty's desk without saying a word. Working as the *Primo Notario,*[136] it was an open secret within the Vatican that O'Flaherty was assisting the Allies by aiding escaped POWs and Jews on the run from the Nazis and Italian Fascists. In fact, O'Flaherty was acting on direct orders of the Pope. O'Flaherty had to date, frustrated all German attempts to kidnap him from within the confines of the Vatican City, which had declared strict neutrality during the conflict, or to assassinate him outright. O'Flaherty was given the moniker 'The Scarlet Pimpernel of the Vatican,' and received the grudging admiration of both friend and foe alike. At age 45 and standing a very formidable 6'2", O'Flaherty was an accomplished golfer and boxer, not your usual run-of-the-mill Roman cleric. O'Flaherty had been assigned to Rome since the 1920s, so he knew the city intimately. He also knew he had a 30,000 Lire price placed on his head by the Gestapo, and that his nemesis, SS *Obersturmbannführer* Herbert Kappler as well as the Koch Gang, would stop at nothing to kill or capture him. If captured, O'Flaherty knew he would be tortured. O'Flaherty could only guess the contents of the envelope that had been just delivered to him—that someone else needed to be saved from the clutches of the Nazis.

Opening the envelope, O'Flaherty read with astonishment that the individual needing his assistance was none other than Sepp Bertram. O'Flaherty put the letter down for a minute as he absorbed the shocking news. He and Sepp had worked together on many occasions and O'Flaherty was very fond of his fellow clergyman. He also knew the writer of the letter, *Padre* Scavone and read that Bertram was being escorted by Scavone's cousin, Giovanni. O'Flaherty smiled knowing that Bertram was now in good hands; yet time was of the essence and Bertram needed to be brought back safely into the confines of the Vatican City before every German in Rome would be looking for Bertram - if they weren't already.

Pontifical Institute of Oriental Studies
Piazza Santa Maria Maggiore
Rome, Italy
September 9, 1943, 1745 Hours

Within the city of Rome itself, the Vatican owned property, which was considered extraterritorial, meaning that while it was located outside the boundaries of the Vatican City, it was still considered part of the Vatican, and would enjoy certain immunities, such as those accorded to foreign embassies. Surprisingly, the Germans and Italian Fascists adhered to this status and a "hands-off" policy on the extraterritorial properties was for the most part, strictly enforced.[137] The Vatican's extraterritorial properties were extensive, consisting of churches, convents, monasteries and Pontifical Colleges. Probably the best known of all the extraterritorial properties is Castel Gandolfo, the Pope's summer palace located approximately fifteen miles southeast of Rome.

Sergeant Scavone had disbanded his squad after they left the Gestapo precinct and ordered the men to take to the hills and join the Partisans if they so desired. Their duty to the Fascist state was now over. It was up to Scavone to get Sepp safely to the Vatican City. *Padre* Scavone had sent a message ahead to Monsignor O'Flaherty and it was hoped that at a prearranged time, Sepp could be handed off and then whisked safely back to the Vatican. For the time being, both Sergeant Scavone and Sepp were safe, having sought refuge in one of the Vatican's extraterritorial properties, this one being the Pontifical Institute of Oriental Studies located on the historic Piazza Santa Maria Maggiore. It was here that they would await word from Monsignor O'Flaherty to make their move to cross into the Vatican City.

Sepp was still dressed as an Italian militiaman, and while he wanted to change into a clerical garb, it was decided that he should remain in mufti for the time being. In the meantime, the priests at the Pontifical Institute fed both men and made their stay as comfortable as possible. No questions were asked by the clergy at the Institute, and both Scavone and Sepp believed that they probably were neither the first 'fugitives' to be harbored there nor would they be the last.[138]

"Monsignor Bertram, I will head over to the Vatican City and see if I can contact Monsignor O'Flaherty. I would suspect that the Germans will probably increase the guard force around the Vatican perimeter to ensure you don't make it over the line."

"Do you think they will be looking for you as well, sergeant?"

"I don't think so. The squad has been disbanded, they've taken *Capitano* Ricci with them, so there really is no one to identify who made up the original squad in the first place. I should be just another pretty face in the crowd," Giovanni joked. "Don't worry about me, Monsignor, I will be fine." With that, he turned and left the Institute, making his way toward the Rome-Vatican City boundary line.

Office of the Commander of the Papal Swiss Guard
Vatican City
September 9, 1943, 1100 Hours

The barracks of the Papal Swiss Guard were located near the papal apartments so that the guard could react quickly to any immediate threats to the Pope. *Oberst* (Colonel) Heinrich Pfyffer von Altishofen, commander of the Papal Swiss Guard since 1942, watched with alarm as German armored cars and troops began to assemble along the Rome-Vatican City boundary line. Von Altishofen came from a long line of family members dating back to 1652, who had distinguished themselves as having served as commander of the Papal Swiss Guard, and judging from the activity outside, it appeared that that distinguished lineage was about to end. Von Altishofen was aware of rumors that the Germans wanted to kidnap the Pope as well as the Roman Curia and place them in protective custody, and quite frankly there was really nothing much to stand in the Germans' way if they chose to do so. Von Altishofen commanded 110 men, nothing more than a reinforced company-sized element, and most armed with ceremonial swords and Halberds.[139] His men were armed with some modern weapons as well, mainly the Schmeisser Dreyse Model 1907 pistol and the SIG MKPO Hungarian-made submachine gun, but they were no match for the weaponry now arrayed against them. While any armed attack on the Vatican would be met with spirited resistance by his men, it would ultimately be futile against such a well-trained and well-equipped force. [140] Viewing the troop buildup through his field glasses, von Altishofen noted the presence of *SS Obersturmbannführer* Kappler, excitedly giving orders and directing his men. Kappler was well known to just about everyone in the Holy See, and for that matter, Rome. Both he and Kappler had the opportunity to meet in 1942 when von Altishofen first assumed command of the Swiss Guard. At the time, Kappler had sent him a congratulatory telegram and invited him for a celebratory drink at a local restaurant. Von Altishofen accepted the invitation and found Kappler to be quite cultured, fluent in the native language (as Altishofen was Swiss, both men alternated speaking German and Italian), and a connoisseur of fine wine, beautiful women, and all things Italian. During their initial meeting, Kappler had told Altishofen that he hoped and prayed that Germany would never have to violate the Vatican's sovereignty, and that he as SS leader in Rome, would respect the Vatican's neutrality. *However*, Kappler had warned him, *if* the *Führer* deemed it necessary for Germany to violate the Vatican's sovereignty for geo-political purposes, it would be with a heavy heart that he, Kappler, would lead his men into the Vatican proper and then of course, all bets were off.

Fearing that a German attack was imminent, Altishofen picked up the phone and called his second in command, *Oberstleutnant* (Lieutenant Colonel) Peter Weiss. "Peter, *Oberst* von Altishofen here - put the men on alert, I believe we have a situation with our friend Kappler. Come up to my office immediately, I'd like you here when I contact Monsignor Montini." He then hung up the phone and, standing by his window overlooking St. Peter's Square, continued to peer through his field glasses at German forces now arrayed along the boundary line.

Office of the Commander of the Papal Swiss Guard
Vatican City
September 9, 1943, 1120 Hours

Oberstleutnant Weiss had hurriedly made his way to Altishofen's office. Without saying a word, von Altishofen handed his field glasses to his deputy and pointed towards the boundary line.

"What do you make of it, Peter?" asked von Altishofen.

"Could be just a simple show-of-force, sir, nothing more, although I don't recall ever seeing that many troops or armored cars before. Perhaps a fugitive they are trying to capture before he makes his way here?"

"Perhaps, although it's that damn Kappler that has me worried, Peter. He doesn't make it over this way unless there is really something big brewing. I know he has his sights set on Monsignor O'Flaherty, but this seems a bit overboard, don't you think?"

"Do you think, Colonel, that the Germans will cross the line?"

"I don't know, Peter, and I don't just want to sit here and find out. I'm going to contact Monsignor Montini and get some direction." With that, von Altishofen picked up the phone receiver and dialed Montini's direct line. After a few rings, the Vatican's Assistant Secretary of State answered his own telephone.

"Montini here."

"Excellency, this is *Oberst* von Altishofen. Is Your Excellency aware of the buildup on the boundary line by German forces?"

"No, *Oberst*, I am not. I have been in the Papal library for hours and am only now getting back to my office. Where is the buildup?

"All along the boundary, Excellency, all 109 acres."

"Do you believe a German attack is imminent? Is the Holy Father in danger?" Montini asked excitedly

"I don't know, Excellency. I have ordered the Swiss Guard force on full alert. What are your orders?"

"Have your men stand fast, *Oberst*, you know the rules of engagement. The Holy Father's protection is first and foremost. I will contact the German ambassador immediately to see what his people are planning. No doubt this is Kappler's doing."

"It is, Excellency. He is standing on the boundary line as we speak."

"Thank you, *Oberst*. Keep me apprised of the situation." With that, Montini hung up the phone and then let out a long sigh. "God help us," he muttered to himself as he hurried off to the Papal apartments in order to warn Cardinal Maglione and the Holy Father that their worst fears were about to come true.

Papal Apartments
Vatican City
September 9, 1943, 1145 Hours

Monsignor Montini entered the Pope's private ten-room suite to find the pontiff and Cardinal Secretary of State Maglione reviewing some documents.

"Your Holiness, and Your Eminence, I am sorry to interrupt you both, however a situation has arisen that I feel you need to be informed about."

"What is it, Montini?" asked the pontiff.

"Along with the Germans occupying Rome, troops under the command of Kappler are now gathering along the boundary line - I think this time they may actually cross."

A look of shock appeared across Pius XII's thin face. Crossing himself and without saying a word, he rose from his desk and disappeared into an anteroom. Within minutes, he returned with an envelope that he gave to Cardinal Maglione.

"In the event that the Germans come for me, this is my letter of resignation, and you are to see to it that it is published in *L'Osservatore Romano* and is announced on Vatican Radio. I have been preparing for this for a long time. If Hitler wishes to arrest me, then he shall arrest Eugenio Pacelli, a simple parish priest, *and not* Pius XII."[141]

St. Peter's Square
Vatican City
September 9, 1943, 1210 Hours

A detachment of Swiss Guard armed with modern weapons was sent to the boundary line facing the German troops centered around Kappler. Von

Altishofen soon made an appearance, and both he and Kappler came face-to-face on the boundary line.

"*Herr Oberst*, so good to see you again," Kappler stated sarcastically.

"*Herr Obersturmbannführer*, may I ask the reason for this show-of-force along our boundary?"

"Quite a simple explanation, von Altishofen, we are pursuing a fugitive priest who is responsible for the murder of three of my men, and I want him!"

"I don't know what you are talking about, Kappler. What priest would out-and-out murder German soldiers?" Von Altishofen knew that priests throughout occupied Europe had indeed at times taken up arms against the Nazi occupiers, and served with Resistance units, so there was precedence.

"His name is Monsignor Bertram, and we know he is assigned to the Vatican Foreign Office. He was last spotted in the city of Rome and it is my job to see that he does not make it back to the Vatican. Don't worry, von Altishofen, your precious neutrality will not be violated - we will stay on our side of the line, unless ordered to do otherwise."

With that, Kappler turned and faced his men telling them, "You are to observe to the letter, the neutrality of the Holy See. Any man caught in violation will be severely punished, that I can assure you. However, force will be met with force if the Swiss Guard makes a move across the boundary line. You have your orders."

With that, Kappler turned the group over to young *SS Hauptsturmführer*, entered his staff car, and was driven back to his headquarters on the *Via Tasso*.

As both sides squared off along the boundary line, von Altishofen said a silent prayer that cooler heads would prevail, and that neither side would provoke an incident that they would later come to regret.

Office of the German Ambassador to the Holy See
Villa Napoleon Mission
Rome, Italy
September 9, 1943, 1305 Hours

Ambassador von Weizsäcker was having a rough day. Aside from the fallout of the German occupation of Rome itself, a cable from Reich Foreign Affairs Minister Joachim von Ribbentrop had arrived ordering him to place pressure on the Pope to curtail the anti-German activity that was freely taking place within the confines of the Vatican. The Germans knew that not only were fugitive Jews, resistance fighters and escaped Allied POWs being sheltered within the Vatican and its extraterritorial properties, but that certain clerics, such as Monsignor O'Flaherty and now Monsignor Bertram, were actively trying to undermine the authority of the Reich. Von Ribbentrop closed his message with the sentence 'The *Führer* is losing patience with the Holy See and would not be responsible for his actions if Vatican clerics continued undermining the authority of the Reich. If this continued, the Reich would have no choice but to re-evaluate its relationship with the Holy See and the protocols signed in the Concordat of 1933.'

"*Mein Gott in Himmel!*" he exclaimed. "Have those madmen in Berlin taken leave of their senses?" he asked himself. Von Weizsäcker had nothing but contempt for his boss, von Ribbentrop, whom he and others referred to as 'that former champagne salesman,' which in fact von Ribbentrop was. Many within the Reich Ministry of Foreign Affairs directly blamed von Ribbentrop for miscalculating the British and French reactions with the German declaration of war on Poland in 1939. When it was announced that both Britain and France had declared war on Germany on September 3, 1939, Hitler had turned to his foreign minister and contemptuously asked him, "Now what?" Now, four years into a war that Germany could no longer win, the Reich was steadily losing territory. The military situation reports were grim—German forces were being forced back on all fronts. The overthrow of Mussolini in late July had only added to Germany's woes, with more troops needed and more hostile territory to occupy. As he was mulling over a response to the cable, his telephone rang.

"Von Weizsäcker."

"*Herr* Minister," his aide spoke, "Monsignor Montini is on the line for you. He states that it is extremely urgent."

Von Weizsäcker got along well with both Montini and Tardini, their relations being cordial and correct in a diplomatic sort of way. Montini was not one to constantly call and make demands of the German ambassador. On occasion, both men had reciprocated with luncheon invitations held in their respective gardens—the settings a sea of tranquility in an otherwise topsy-turvy world.

"Monsignor, so good to hear from you. How may I be of assistance?"

"*Herr* Minister, are you aware of the buildup of German troops on the boundary line?"

Von Weizsäcker was taken aback at Montini's revelation. "No, Monsignor, I am not aware of this."

Montini then stated the obvious, "It appears to be the doing of *Obersturmbannführer* Kappler. I was under the impression that any military moves involving the Holy See were to be coordinated through your office."

Von Weizsäcker's blood began to boil when he heard that Kappler was behind this move. He thought to himself that while he, von Weizsäcker bent over backwards to ensure that relations between the Reich and the Holy See were 'correct,' it was men such as Kappler who always managed to derail his plans.

"Monsignor Montini, I assure you that I was unaware of this move by Kappler and will get to the bottom of it immediately. I will call you back within the hour."

Hanging up the telephone, he called in his deputy, the Embassy Secretary, Sigismund von Braun, a career foreign ministry official, who was quietly working against the Nazi regime.[142] "Sigismund, please get *Generalmajor* Stahel on the line."

"Something wrong, *Herr* Minister?"

"That idiot Kappler is causing us trouble once again - there is a build-up of our forces on the boundary as we speak."

Von Braun was taken aback by the news and quickly ran to his desk in the anteroom and picked up the phone. "Connect me with the Military Governor's office at once," he barked into the receiver.

After a minute, a voice on the other end answered, "Military Governor's office, this is *Oberst* Hochhuth speaking."

"*Herr Oberst,* this is *Herr* von Braun in Ambassador von Weiszäcker's office, the Minister would like to speak with *Generalmajor* Stahel immediately, it is urgent."

"One minute, *Herr* von Braun," Hockhuth stated as he put down the receiver and walked to Stahel's office, while both von Braun and von Weizsäcker waited on their respective telephones for Stahel.

It wasn't long before the *Luftwaffe* general's voice was heard.

"*Generalmajor* Stahel here; how may I assist you, *Herr* Minister?"

Both von Weizsäcker and Stahel knew each other professionally and socially and while not close intimates, had assisted each other in the past. Although a dedicated Nazi, *Generalmajor* Rainer Stahel realized maintaining cordial relations with the Vatican would also ensure a measure of stability in Rome itself, and he did not want any problems during his tenure as Rome's Military Governor.

"Rainer, we have a problem with Kappler," von Weizsäcker stated. "He has sent more troops to the boundary line, and I am afraid some fool with an itchy finger is going to start shooting and that of course will be perfect fodder for Allied propaganda. I can just see the headlines now, 'SS troops open fire on St. Peter's Square.'"

Stahel was shocked at the news - Kappler had evidently taken it upon himself to move the troops into place and had not coordinated the move with the Military Governor of Rome.

"*Herr* Minister, I will have the troops immediately returned to their barracks."

"I have your assurance on that, Rainer? I have to let Monsignor Montini know that we will handle this problem immediately."

"You have my word, *Herr* Minister."

"Thank you, Rainer, I knew I could count on a professional soldier such as yourself to handle this and not some SS thug." With that the ambassador hung up the telephone and then let out a sigh of relief.

"Sigismund, I am going to see Monsignor Montini and let him know that the situation is under control." With that, von Weizsäcker left his office and set out for St. Peter's Square where he was then able to see first-hand the German troops aligned along the boundary line. He walked hurriedly across the vast square until he reached the office of the Vatican Secretary of State.

Office of the Vatican Secretary of State
Vatican City
September 9, 1943, 1410 Hours

"Ambassador, Monsignor Montini will be with you in a moment, he is currently with the Holy Father," said a young Irish priest, whom von Weizsäcker had not seen before. "Please have a seat, and I will let you know when he returns, which should be shortly."

With that, the German ambassador sat down in a plush chair while the young cleric went back to the paperwork, piled high upon his desk, barely looking up as he worked.

Approximately ten minutes had passed when Montini finally arrived back at his own office. The young cleric rose and informed Montini that the German ambassador was waiting. Montini came out to the anteroom and greeted von Weizsäcker and cordially shook the German diplomat's hand.

"Ambassador, it is very good to see you, thank you for coming over. I trust the incident we discussed is under control?"

"Yes, Monsignor. After we spoke, I called the Military Governor directly and he assured me that he would handle the situation immediately. If you would like, we can walk over to the boundary line and see for ourselves."

"Why not, it will be good to get out for some fresh air," Montini answered, and both men made their way out of the Secretary of State's office and onto St. Peter's Square and began walking toward the boundary line. On any given day before the troop buildup, the Germans normally kept two sentries on the border at St. Peter's Square, in order to prevent German soldiers from entering Vatican territory in uniform. Civilians could freely cross the line as there were no barricades or barbed wire. The other parts of the Vatican with their high walls, were not accessible. Today, of course, was different, as there must have been 50 soldiers on or behind the boundary line along with two armored cars parked nearby in a show-of-force.

As both men neared the boundary line, von Weizsäcker noticed a staff car pull up along the demarcation line, the military governor's pennant fluttering from the front of the vehicle. The German troops suddenly came to attention and when the vehicle rolled to a halt, out stepped *Generalmajor* Stahel.

"Well, it appears my phone call worked, Monsignor, the military governor himself is taking matters into his own hands and ordering the troops back to their barracks." Both men had smiles on their faces, but those smiles soon faded. As they approached, they saw Stahel mingling with the troops and talking with them - a far cry from demanding them to pack up and leave. Stahel noticed both the ambassador and Montini making their way to the boundary line from St. Peter's Square and went over to meet them.

"Ambassador, Monsignor Montini, very good to see you both," Stahel said cordially while making a half-bow. Stahel may have been a die-hard Nazi, but he was very correct in his dealings with diplomats, be they German or otherwise.

"I'm afraid I have some bad news for you both - after I spoke with you, ambassador, the phone rang, and it was a call from *Reichsführer SS* Himmler." He let that sink in before continuing.

"It appears our friend Kappler put in a call personally to Himmler and explained the situation, that he was attempting to capture your Monsignor Bertram in connection with the murder of the three Gestapo officers in Rome. I have orders from the *Führer* himself, conveyed to me by Himmler, not to interfere in this matter. I am very sorry, but my hands are tied," he said, holding out both wrists together as if bound by an invisible rope.

"Reiner, you cannot be serious?" an exasperated von Weizsäcker asked.

"Very serious, I'm afraid, *Herr* Ambassador. You know as well as I, that the SS are a law unto themselves. Who am I to question the *Führer's* judgment? Again, I am very sorry, but the troops will have to stay until ordered to be withdrawn." With that, Stahel made another half-bow, turned on his heel, and entered his staff car, which then slowly drove away.

Beads of sweat began to form on von Weizsäcker's brow, and he dabbed it with his handkerchief. "I'm very sorry Monsignor Montini, I did what I could."

Montini, visibly annoyed, stated, "Are you aware that the Holy Father has a letter of resignation already written and signed? In the event *Herr* Hitler decided to march in and seize the Holy Father, he will be taken into custody, not Pius XII, but a simple priest by the name of Eugenio Pacelli."

"The Holy Father would actually resign?" the ambassador asked in amazement.

"You see, Ambassador, Hitler may order the arrest of the Holy Father, the Roman Curia, myself, it makes no difference. The Church will survive, I can assure you, as it has for the last 2,000 years. It has survived persecution from the Romans and others, and it will certainly survive the Nazis." With that, Montini turned and walked slowly back to the Secretary of State's office, leaving von Weizsäcker alone to grudgingly admire the churchman's faith and determination and to question his own wavering faith in the *Führer*.

Pontifical Institute of Oriental Studies
Piazza Santa Maria Maggiore
Rome, Italy
September 9, 1943, 1930 Hours

Sergeant Scavone returned to the Pontifical Institute later in the day after observing the actions at the boundary line for almost a full day. He made mental notes of the comings and goings of soldiers, when relief shifts were implemented, the number of men involved, and the weapons and equipment being used. With fighting still raging in parts of the capital, the situation could change from day-to-day. Perhaps more men would be sent to the boundary once the Germans were in complete control of the city - until then, it was anyone's guess.

Sepp welcomed the Italian sergeant upon his return. "Sergeant Scavone, I was beginning to worry about you. What were you able to find out?"

"Monsignor, unfortunately I was not able to contact Monsignor O'Flaherty, as there is a large German buildup along the boundary line. I think our best bet will be to get you across the boundary line at night. I have an idea, which may or may not work. They're looking for a priest, but I don't think they will challenge one of their own officers, do you?"

"What are you getting at, Sergeant?"

"We could steal an SS or *Wehrmacht* officer's uniform for you, and you walk close enough to the line unchallenged by the Germans. After all, you *are* German, so there won't be any difficulty with the language," he chuckled. Scavone continued, "At the first opportunity, you make a dash across the demarcation line."

"Now where do you propose to get a uniform, Sergeant?" Sepp asked.

"Leave that to me, Monsignor. If all goes according to plan, I can probably have one for you this evening. Please trust me."

"No one is to get killed in the process, Sergeant, is that understood?"

"I promise you, Monsignor, no one will be killed. Now, let me get some food in my belly and then I'll be off."

Both men walked down the corridor to the Institute's dining room where they had a spare meal of pasta, bread, and wine while Scavone laid out his plan to Sepp.

Via Teresa **34**
Rome, Italy
September 9, 1943, 2200 Hours

Sergeant Scavone stood across the street of one of Rome's newest brothels, as he watched from the shadows as the clientele entered and left the establishment. With the influx of more German troops to the city, the brothel could expect a booming business for the foreseeable future. Being an NCO, Scavone had heard rumors that the establishment was visited by high-ranking Fascist officers as well as *Wehrmacht* and SS officers during its first weeks of operation. The women were for the most part, young, healthy, and attractive—three criteria that most senior officers looked for when they sought out female companionship. On this particular night, Scavone saw a German staff car pull up to the curb outside of the establishment and squinting as hard as he could, he was able to make out the figure of what appeared to be a German officer, alight from the automobile, his distinct red piping on his trousers identifying him as a member of the general staff. The officer then said something unintelligible to his driver, who then pulled away from the curb and sped away. The officer then lit a cigarette, adjusted his tunic and bounded up the steps leading in. Prior to the war, Scavone had worked as a tailor, and could guess a man's height and weight just by looking at him. Scavone thought that the German's uniform would fit Sepp like a glove. He decided that a brothel would be the easiest place to secure a uniform, especially when the owner was otherwise engaged and not wearing it.

After cautiously looking up and down the street, Scavone emerged from the shadows and slowly approached the brothel. He was still in uniform, so he could always tell anyone that challenged him that he was waiting for his boss, who happened to be inside getting his ashes overhauled. No such challenge took place, however, and Scavone climbed the steps to the brothel. He hesitated for a moment before he turned the doorknob to let himself in. He entered a foyer that led into a sitting room that was gaudily decorated. In the background he heard music playing on a Victrola along with women's voices and some giggling and laughter.

Scavone was looking for a certain prostitute that he knew from his hometown, Maria Delgado, whom he had run into at the marketplace weeks before. She had been out shopping for food for the brothel's kitchen and she was taken aback when Scavone approached her. When he inquired at what she was doing in Rome, she hesitated and from the look of embarrassment on her face, Scavone was able to deduce that she had resorted to prostitution in order to survive. Scavone gave her money, which at first, she refused to accept, but he insisted. And when she offered herself to him, he refused, stating that he just wanted to help an old friend, and besides, he was married and was faithful to his wife of five years. Maria told him that if he ever needed anything - a place to stay, food, or female company, he could stop by and ask for her.

As Scavone quietly entered the parlor, a female voice challenged him. "May I help you, Sergeant?"

As he turned around, he saw a middle-aged, matronly woman, wearing too much rouge, standing there with her hands on her hips. Obviously, this was the establishment's madam.

"Pardon me, *Signora*, but I am looking for a young lady, Maria Delgado. Is she working tonight?" He felt odd about using the word 'working,' in describing Maria's profession, but he guessed that they were called 'working girls' for a reason.

"Maria is currently with a customer, but you can have your pick of the others, if you want. It will cost you 50 Lira, payable in advance." With that she held out her hand demanding the money.

"Is her customer per chance, a German officer that just arrived?' he asked

"Not that it is any of your business, but yes, the officer just arrived."

"What room is she in," he demanded.

"I told you Sergeant; she is with a customer. You can either wait, pick someone else, or get the hell out."

Scavone narrowed his eyes and moved closer to the madam, who now had a look of fear on her face. "Please, Sergeant, don't hurt me. I didn't mean to yell at you. You can have Maria, free if you want. She is on the house!"

Scavone grabbed the woman by the shoulders and shook her violently. "You and your kind disgust me, using these women like chattel and giving them up to the highest bidder. Now, I ask you again, *Signora*, what room is Maria in with her customer?"

"Room 4," she replied.

"Thank you. Now I need to keep you secure for about ten minutes and then I'll be on my way." Looking around, he found a door that led to the basement of the house. Motioning to the door, he said, "Let's go," as he forcefully guided her towards the basement.

"Please don't hurt me or rape me," she pleaded with him.

"Don't worry *Signora*, you're much too old and are not really my type," he said with a chuckle. The madam frowned at the insult and under her breath mumbled, "*Bastardo*."

When Scavone and the madam arrived in the basement, he guided her to a straight-back wicker chair that was off to the side. Finding some rope hanging on a hook by the stairwell, he then commenced to tie her up. "Now *Signora*, I am going to go to Room 4 to do what I came here to do. You are not to make a sound, understand?"

The madam mumbled "Yes," and scowled at Scavone.

Scavone quietly climbed the basement steps, turned out the light and then locked the door from the outside, leaving the key in the lock. He drew his service revolver and quietly climbed the steps to the second floor where all the bedrooms were located. Arriving outside Room 4, he carefully placed his ear to the door to listen. He could make out two people talking in a low voice and then he heard a slap and a woman cry out in pain.

Turning the doorknob slowly, he found that the room was not locked. Taking a deep breath, he then rushed into the room, gun drawn. He found Maria on the floor with the German officer standing over her with a whip in his hand. The officer spun around at the sight of this intrusion.

"Who the hell are you and what do you want?" he demanded.

The officer was standing there in his skivvies, his uniform tunic and more importantly his pistol belt draped over a chair in the corner closest to Scavone. There was no way the officer could have made it to his gun alive.

"Drop the whip and put your hands up, *Tedesci*, now!" he ordered. He then motioned Maria to come over to him. She still held her hand to her left cheek where the German had slapped her hard. He was a masochist and had brought along his own whip. When Maria refused to agree to his sado-masochistic plans, he began roughing her up. Scavone had arrived just in time before the German could do any real harm.

"So, what are you going to do with me, Sergeant, shoot me?" the officer asked.

"I would like nothing better, *Herr Oberst*, but I don't want to disturb the other clientele," he said with a grin.

"Maria, does that closet have a lock on it," he asked motioning to a door across the room.

"Yes, it does," she replied.

"Good. Now, *Oberst*, if you would be so kind as to remove your undergarments and move to that closet."

The German was indignant at Scavone's order. "I most certainly *will not*. I am an officer of the German *Wehrmacht*, and I will not be treated in such a manner."

"Do as you're told, *Oberst*, or I will blow off that poor excuse of 'Teutonic manhood'" he said, pointing at the colonel's groin. "So much for the Germans being the 'Master Race,'" Scavone quipped. He looked over at Maria and saw a slight smile come across her face.

"Maria, do you have anything to tie him up with? Rope, belts, scarves, anything like that?"

"Yes, I do, here in a box under my bed." Maria reached under her bed and pulled out a small cardboard box, which looked to Scavone as if it held all of Maria's worldly possessions. See reached in and pulled out three scarves and two belts. "Will this work?" she asked, holding them up high.

"Perfect," Scavone said. He then motioned the German over to the closet.

"Maria, come here and tie his hands behind his back nice and tight," Scavone directed.

"With pleasure," said Maria. She stood behind the German and tied his hands tight until he winced from the pain. "That ought to hold him," she said.

She then stood in front of the bound officer and slapped his face. "That's for earlier, *Colonnello*. You are lucky I don't ask my friend here to kill you - I'm sure he would be happy to comply."

The German officer began to shake at the thought of his dying in a brothel and his body being found there. No doubt, it would have brought disgrace to his family.

Pushing the officer in the closet, Scavone ordered him to sit on the floor. He then bound his legs tight with a belt and a scarf. For good measure, he then stuffed one of Maria's panties into the officer's mouth in order to gag him.

"I wonder what your superiors would say, *Herr Oberst*, if they knew that you like to beat young women. I'm sure they will know soon enough," Scavone chuckled. With that, Scavone shut the closet door, locked it, and pocketed the key.

"Maria, get some clothes together, you can't stay here. Once they find our friend here in the closet, they will come looking for you."

"But where will I go?" she asked nervously.

"You'll come with me; I know where you will be safe. But you must hurry."

Throwing on some old clothes, Maria packed a few days' change of clothing.

While Maria was packing, Scavone gathered up the German officer's uniform, along with his boots, pistol belt and weapon, and stuffed them into a laundry bag that Maria had used for her own clothing.

"This is really what I came for," holding up the laundry bag and patting it as they left her room.

"Where is Madam Togliatti?" she asked Scavone as they descended the steps.

"Oh, is that the old witch's name? I have her tied up downstairs in the basement. I'm sure they will find her when they come searching for our friend upstairs."

"Wait!" she said, as she hurried over to a photo of Mussolini hanging on the wall in the parlor. She quickly removed the frame from the wall, and turning it around, removed the backing. Scavone watched in surprise as Maria removed some Lire notes that she had hidden behind *Il Duce's* portrait.

"I hid my earnings in a place they would probably never look," she chuckled. "I'm glad it's still here. I've been saving this for a 'rainy day.'"

"Let's get out of here, before someone sees us," Scavone said.

"Let's not look suspicious," Maria said, and once outside the brothel, she took his arm and they slowly walked down the *Via Teresa*, as if they were two lovers on an evening stroll on a warm, quiet and moonlit Roman night.

Pontifical Institute of Oriental Studies
Piazza Santa Maria Maggiore
Rome, Italy
September 9, 1943, 2145 Hours

Sergeant Scavone and Maria Delgado strolled along the darkened Roman streets as if they had not a care in the world. Since Scavone was in the uniform of a Fascist militiaman, military patrols did not challenge him, but gave him a wink and a nod when they saw a pretty girl on his arm.

"Probably getting his ashes overhauled," he heard one militiaman say, as the other laughed.

Scavone had wanted to punch him, but that would only cause trouble, and he needed to make it back to Sepp as soon as possible.

The pair made it to the Pontifical Institute of Oriental Studies without incident. The cleric in charge of permitting entry was taken aback when he saw Maria with Scavone, and for a minute, was unsure of what to do. Women were not permitted within the confines of the Institute, and this woman, obviously a prostitute, certainly would not be welcome.

"Sergeant," the priest said, "I am sorry, but your companion cannot enter."

Scavone was about to argue when Sepp showed up at the door.

"Scavone, I'm glad you made it back safe and sound. And who is this young lady?"

"Monsignor, may I present *Signorina* Maria Delgado, an old friend of mine from my village."

Sepp took the woman's hand and shook it. "How do you do, Maria, I am Monsignor Bertram. Please come in."

As the pair attempted to enter with Sepp, the priest attempted to bar Maria's entrance.

"Monsignor Bertram, may I remind you that this is holy ground, and that *this* woman is an affront to the Lord. I am sorry, but I cannot permit her entry. She is not welcome here."

Taking the priest aside, Sepp said, "*Padre* Blanco, I appreciate your concern and in following the directives of the Holy See - however, this woman's life is obviously in danger, as is mine. Sergeant Scavone has been on a very dangerous mission to assist me, and may I remind you that I am on a personal mission for the Holy Father. No doubt, *Signorina* Delgado has assisted Sergeant Scavone, and has come here at a great personal risk."

"But she is *una prostituta!*" *Padre* Blanco exclaimed.

"So was Mary Magdalene, *Padre.* Or have you forgotten your scriptures? I'm afraid I am going to have to insist that she enter, and now," Sepp said forcefully.

"Very well, Monsignor," Blanco said with an air of resignation. "Just please try and keep her out of sight of the others."

The pair followed Sepp up to his room where he offered Maria and Scavone something to drink. "I can probably get you both something from the kitchen if you are hungry," Sepp said.

"Yes, please," both Maria and Scavone said in unison.

"Before you go, Monsignor, I have brought you a gift." Emptying the contents of the laundry bag onto Sepp's bed, out fell boots, a tunic, trousers, an officer's cap, and a pistol belt, along with a pistol and ammunition.

"Not bad for a night's work," Scavone said with a laugh. "I could not have done it without Maria's help, Monsignor. I wanted you to know that. Her life is now in danger, because the officer I 'borrowed' the uniform from was one of Maria's 'gentlemen callers' to put it mildly. Once they find him, they'll put out an all-points bulletin on Maria and me, and then we're doomed."

"You're both safe here for the time being. The Germans have yet to enter one of the Vatican's extraterritorial properties, so I don't think they'll start now. The Germans want to stay in the good graces of the Vatican, at least for the time being," Sepp said.

"The uniform should fit you well, Monsignor, the German was about your size," Scavone said.

"Thank you both, I don't know how I will ever be able to repay you for what you have done for me—risking your lives like this."

"Just make it to the Vatican City, Monsignor, that's all the thanks I will need. Also, I would ask that you take Maria with you."

Sepp was a bit taken aback at Scavone's request but seeing that she would be arrested if the Germans found her, he certainly could not refuse the request.

"I will do what I can to get her to the Vatican. Perhaps we can find a nun's habit for Maria to wear, and she could just cross the boundary line without raising suspicion." The thought of dressing a prostitute as a nun was certainly an act of desperation. But then again, these were desperate times, and called for desperate measures.

"I will talk to *Padre* Blanco to see if he can obtain a nun's habit. In the meantime, however, let's get you both fed and rested. I have a feeling that tomorrow is going to be a very busy day for all of us."

Chapter XVI

"As soon as I touched upon the question of the Jews and Judaism, the serenity of the meeting ended at once. Hitler turned his back to me, went to the window and started drumming his fingers on the pane… Still, I went on, voicing our complaints. Hitler suddenly turned around, went to a small table from which he took a water glass and furiously smashed it to the floor. In the face of such diplomatic behavior, I had to consider my mission terminated."[143]

--Monsignor Cesare Orsenigo, Papal Nuncio in Berlin, describing a meeting he had with Hitler in early 1943

Pontifical Institute of Oriental Studies
Piazza Santa Maria Maggiore
Rome, Italy
September 10, 1943, 1645 Hours

Beginning the evening of September 9 and lasting into the next day, the battle for Rome took place, with elements of the Italian Army putting up a heroic defense of the Eternal City. The King and Marshal Badoglio had fled south to Allied held areas without leaving explicit instructions to the *Commando Supremo*. Italian army units were at a loss of what to do once the Germans converged on the city *en masse*. Many Italian units were disarmed without firing a shot, while others, such as the *Ariete, Piave* and *Granatieri di Sardegna* Divisions fought heroically against overwhelming odds, in many instances offering stiff resistance to the invaders. By the end of the day, however, Rome was firmly in German hands.

Because of the day's earlier fighting and confusion that reined within the city, it took the better part of the day for *Padre* Blanco to obtain a nun's habit for Maria, but finally by late afternoon he had all the accouterments to outfit Maria as a religious nun.

"We should probably attempt to make the crossing around 2300 hours tonight. From what I observed the other night, that apparently is when the guard force will be lightest," Scavone said.

"We are in your hands, Sergeant," Sepp replied. He continued, "Maria, why don't you change into the nun's habit now and we'll 'inspect you' so to speak, to ensure you're wearing the habit correctly. Some sharp-eye guard just might notice something out of place."

"Yes, Monsignor, I'll go change now," Maria replied.

Maria left the two men and headed for a small storage room that had been converted to a small bedroom to accommodate her during her stay.

"What I think we should do, Monsignor, is this. At around 2300, we send Maria across and then you can follow about fifteen minutes later. Perhaps we can send word to Monsignor O'Flaherty, that you will be making the crossing," Scavone said.

"I don't know about contacting O'Flaherty—he is a wanted man by the Germans and if Kappler happens to get his hands on him, he will surely kill him."

"We will need a cover story for you in case you are questioned by the guards on why you are entering Vatican City at such a late hour. Any suggestions, Monsignor?"

"I could tell the guards that I am to meet with the commander of the Swiss Guard in order to deconflict any incidents that may result in either side opening fire on the other. I think they would probably believe that, don't you?"

"Very well, Monsignor. We'll plan on attempting a crossing at 2300 hours tonight. May God be with us."

"Yes, sergeant, may He be with us indeed."

Vatican City-Rome Boundary
September 10, 1943, 2240 Hours

At 2230 hours, a bit earlier than planned, Maria crossed the Vatican City-Rome boundary with no difficulty whatsoever. Sergeant Scavone and Bertram had watched her cross from the shadows of a porch about 50 yards away, which gave them an unobstructed view of the boundary line. The German troops waved her through with no problem, one of them even wishing her a pleasant evening. Maria had been instructed to find the nearest Swiss Guardsman and to inform them of Monsignor Bertram's impending crossing and that he was in danger of being detained by the Germans.

Scavone looked at his watch, it was now 2245 hours, only fifteen more minutes before Bertram would make his attempt to cross the boundary. Scanning the boundary line, there was no activity on the other side. Both men had hoped that some of the Swiss Guard would make their way to the boundary line in a show-of-force. However, this had not occurred. Both men wondered aloud if Maria had been able to find help. With the minutes ticking away, they decided to go ahead with the plan, Swiss Guard or no Swiss Guard. Scavone then gave Bertram a last minute 'once-over' of his uniform, ensuring that his appearance was that of a German Army staff officer. "You can almost pass for the real thing, Monsignor," he said with a chuckle and then gave Bertram a mock 'Heil Hitler' salute.

"Well, let's hope it is enough to fool the guards. I only need a few minutes. I hope I can pull it off."

"Alright, Monsignor, only five more minutes until you cross. Remember, just stroll up to the guards as nonchalantly as you can, ask them how things are going and then ask for a light. Ease yourself as close to the boundary line as possible, and when you get the chance make a run for it. I doubt very much they would shoot into the direction of the Vatican."

At 2300 hours Scavone said, "Show time, Monsignor."

The two men shook hands. "I can't thank you enough, Sergeant Scavone. You saved my life, and I am forever in your debt. Perhaps when this war is over, we can meet up again."

"That would be nice, Monsignor, I will certainly look forward to that day. God be with you."

With that, Bertram stepped from the shadows and began a slow steady walk toward the boundary line and hopefully freedom. Unbeknownst to Bertram, the guards had recently been given a wanted poster with an artist sketch and general description of the wanted priest. The Germans had not taken his photo when he was first apprehended, thinking he would be immediately executed. When he escaped from the Gestapo, he managed to collect his personal effects, to include his passport, which he still had in his possession.

The two German guards were chatting with each other when one noticed Bertram's approach.

"Look sharp, Joachim, looks like an officer approaching," said the one guard named Albert.

"I wonder what the hell he wants at this hour of the night?"

Both soldiers snapped to attention when Bertram approached.

"Guten abend, Herr Oberst" both men chimed simultaneously.

"Guten abend," replied Bertram. "I trust all is quiet."

Jawohl, Herr Oberst, the guard named Joachim replied. "It has been very quiet, just a few crossings this evening, the last one about fifteen minutes ago, a nun."

"That's good to hear, men. Pulling out a cigarette, Bertram asked, "May I trouble either of you for a light?"

Joachim replied, "Sorry, sir, but neither one of us smokes."

Bertram was taken aback by the soldier's response. Just his luck that he was talking to probably the only two soldiers in the entire German Army stationed in Rome who did not smoke.

Joachim then said, "Sir, let me run down to the other guard post, I know that the two men on duty there are smokers."

"No need for that, private, I can wait until I get back to my room."

"No, trouble at all, sir," and Joachim took off at a trot for the other guard post approximately 100 feet away."

"Your friend seems very eager to please," Bertram said.

In the few minutes that he had been there, Albert had been staring intently at Bertram, and the cleric began to get nervous.

"Sir, may I see your *Soldatbuch*, please. Just a routine check." The *Soldatbuch* was issued to every service member in the *Wehrmacht* and contained all the soldier's pertinent information such as rank, pay, etc. Had this been a real German officer, he more than likely would have been infuriated at this request and given the young soldier a harsh reprimand on the spot. Instead, Bertram was blindsided by the request and for a moment, could not answer.

"Herr Oberst, your Soldatbuch, please." This time the request was firmer, with a tone of anger thrown in for good measure.

Looking off to his left, Bertram saw Joachim returning from the other guard post, no doubt happy that he scored some matches for a senior officer. Now panicking, Bertram turned and ran toward the boundary line which was only 10 feet away. He began to run, but the guard was young, agile and healthy, (probably because he didn't smoke) and tackled Bertram before he could make it to the boundary line.

Seeing the commotion ahead, Joachim ran to his post to find Albert standing above Bertram with his weapon drawn. "Albert, what are you doing! Have you gone insane! This is a *Wehrmacht Oberst*! They will have you court-martialed, or worse!"

"I think we have an imposter here, Joachim. Look at this poster." He handed the wanted poster to his fellow guard and Joachim scrutinized it.

"I think you have the fugitive priest here, Albert, good job!"

The commotion brought other guards to the post and soon a staff car with the officer of the guard making his usual rounds, pulled up. A German captain came over to the guard post to see what was transpiring.

"What's going on here?"

"Herr Hauptmann, I believe we have a man wanted by the Gestapo here. He is a priest and was in the uniform of one of our officers."

The captain was shown the wanted poster and then compared it to the man standing before him.

"Are you the priest Bertram?" he asked.

"I am," Bertram replied.

The captain then read the wanted poster further. "It says here to contact *Obersturmbannführer* Kappler if apprehended."

There was silence for a few seconds when the name "Kappler" was mentioned, for his brutal reputation struck fear even amongst the Germans themselves.

The captain, who was a decent man, helped Bertram up off the ground. "I am sorry, Father, but I have to take you in. Orders are orders. Do you have any other clothing aside from what you are wearing?"

"Yes, *Herr Hauptmann*, I do. I have my cleric garb underneath the uniform, just so I wouldn't be shot as a spy if captured."

"A smart decision on your part, Father. Let's go." With that, the captain escorted Bertram to his staff car and ordered the driver to the *Via Tasso,* the notorious prison and headquarters of the German *Sicherheitdienst Polizei* (Security Police) and the lair of *Obersturmbannführer* Herbert Kappler himself.

As Sepp was being led away, a squad of Swiss Guard arrived at the demarcation line—too late to rescue him. They could only watch in horror as Sepp was taken into German custody. Sepp gave them a forlorn look of utter despair as the vehicle sped away.

Watching the entire event from a safe distance was Sergeant Scavone, who stood helpless in the shadows watching Bertram being arrested. Scavone carried only a pistol, he was no match for the German guards who carried submachine guns. He could only watch and pray that the man he had come to know and admire these past few days would somehow be spared. Scavone would let his cousin, *Padre* Scavone, know what had transpired. Perhaps his cousin could get word to the Vatican and just maybe, *maybe*, the pontiff could intercede on Bertram's behalf. Once Bertram was loaded into the staff car, Scavone quietly slipped away and headed back to San Antonio di Padua church on the other side of the city to see his cousin.

Headquarters *Sicherheitsdienst* (SD)-Rome
Via Tasso 145
Rome, Italy
September 10, 1943, 2345 Hours

Bertram was marched up the steps to the second floor of the prison and placed in a segregation cell. Surprisingly, his captors had been rather lenient with him, the captain going so far as telling him that he himself was a Catholic and within the same breath offering Bertram a cigarette, which he politely declined.

Bertram was very frightened, more so than the first time he was in Gestapo custody and ready to face a firing squad. This time there would be no disgruntled Italian soldiers ready to save him. He was now in the belly of the beast, and he believed his time on earth was now quickly drawing to a close. He pulled out his rosary beads which the Germans had permitted him to keep and began to pray.

While Bertram was deep in prayer, he heard footsteps outside his cell door, then the rattling of keys, and finally the cell door opening. Behind the guard emerged *Obersturmbannführer* Herbert Kappler, whose official title was

Oberbefehlshaber des Sicherheitspolizei und SD (head of the German police and security services) for occupied Rome.

"Well, Monsignor Bertram, I finally get the pleasure of meeting you. I must congratulate you on being such a noble adversary and being able to allude such a massive manhunt for so long. I think you were a bit foolish in trying to cross the boundary - did you think we would not circulate your description to our guards?"

"No, *Herr Obersturmbannführer*, I never underestimated you for one second. Your reputation for being 'efficient' precedes you."

"Thank you, Monsignor, I will take that as a personal compliment. As much as I would like to stay and chat, I have a previous engagement tonight with my superior, *Standartenführer* Dollmann[144], perhaps you have heard of him? I know that he will be delighted to hear that we have you. Get a good night's sleep, monsignor, because tomorrow, you and I are getting to get better acquainted, that I can assure you."

With that, Kappler turned and left, and the SS guard then shut the cell door, leaving Bertram once again alone with his thoughts and prayers and what the coming days ahead would bring.

Villa Wolkonsky
Via Umberto Biancamno
Rome, Italy
September 11, 1943, 0030 Hours

The Villa Wolkonsky was one of two German embassies set up in Rome. Since 1920, the Villa Wolkonsky had housed the German diplomatic mission to Italy, while the Villa Napoleon, once the residence of Napoleon's favorite sister, Paolina, housed the diplomatic mission to the Holy See.

Kappler had been invited for a late-night visit to the embassy by *Standartenführer* Eugen Dollmann for drinks and to discuss better ways of combating the growing Italian resistance movements within Rome itself. Dollmann, at age 43, first came to Italy in the late 1920s as a student of Italian art history. In the ensuing years he came to love Italy and became quite fluent in the language. He was in every sense, a Renaissance man, and detested the cruelty conducted by many of his colleagues in the SS. During the interwar period, Dollmann became acquainted with many of the leading Italian notables of the period. In 1938 he was called upon to be Hitler's translator during the Munich Conference in which Mussolini was in attendance and again in the Ukraine in 1941, during Mussolini's visit to the Eastern Front.

"Kappler, very good to see you, I apologize for the late hour," Dollmann said, shaking his visitor's hand.

"Good to see you too, sir. I have some very good news to share with you."

Dollmann motioned for Kappler to sit in one of the plush chairs in one of the embassy anterooms. Drinks poured, both men settled into their chairs.

"So, Kappler, what is this good news you have for me?"

"We got him, sir. We got the priest Bertram hours ago while he was trying to slip across the boundary line. He was dressed in a *Wehrmacht* officer's uniform. One of our guards was sharp enough to notice him and took him into custody. He is currently a guest of the Reich at the *Via Tasso*."

"Kappler, that is wonderful news! Both men then leaned out of their chairs in order to clink their schnapps glasses. "Prost!" they said in unison. Dollmann continued, "I will send a report later today to the *Reichsführer SS*, whom I know will be delighted to hear the good news, especially in light of the treasonous events perpetrated by *Gruppenführer* Bertram in Reval. No doubt you will receive a promotion out of this Kappler."

Kappler smiled at the thought of promotion to colonel. Over the years he had applied for, but was consistently turned down by higher headquarters, for transfer to a combat unit. His talents had now paid off handsomely.

"Kappler, what do you propose to do with the priest?"

"Sir, I intend to get as much information out of him concerning the mass escape from the camp in Reval and see if he can shed some light on the resistance groups in Rome. And I intend to use whatever means possible. That Roman collar will not stand in my way when I interrogate him

"I am just thinking out loud, Kappler, but I think maybe you could hold off in your interrogation of the priest. We, and you, have been wanting to get your hands-on Monsignor O'Flaherty for quite some time. I think we may now have found a way."

"How so, sir?" asked Kappler, now intrigued.

"I was thinking, Kappler, that we arrange for an exchange, Monsignor Bertram for O'Flaherty. I understand that Bertram has the confidence of the Pope, and O'Flaherty does not. Let's offer them a trade, then. We give them Bertram and they give us O'Flaherty. An even exchange, don't you think, Kappler?"

As Dollmann spoke, he could see his subordinate's eyes begin to widen. He had struck a nerve at the mention of O'Flaherty, who had been Kappler's nemesis since he arrived in Rome. Kappler had special plans for O'Flaherty if he ever fell into his hands. Now it all seemed quite possible.

"Sir, while Bertram has caused us some headaches, we really need to put a stop to O'Flaherty's activities immediately. He has literally aided *thousands* of Jews and escaped prisoners of war, while Bertram is responsible for the escape of what, 100 or so Jews? A drop in the bucket, I say. Bertram certainly is the lesser of two evils."

"I agree wholeheartedly, Kappler. So, this is what we will do. Bertram is to remain in the *Via Tasso* until such time arrangements can be made for an exchange. I will speak with Ambassador von Weizsäcker and see what he has to say. In the meantime, Kappler, you are to handle Bertram with 'kid gloves' as the Americans like to say. I know that you are chomping at the bit, but a bigger prize awaits you, that I can assure you of. You will just have to wait a bit longer."

"*Zu befehl, Herr Standartenführer,*" Kappler replied. "I will await your further orders."

Villa Wolkonsky
Via Umberto Biancamno
Rome, Italy
September 11, 1943, 0115 Hours

Upon Kappler's departure Dollmann immediately picked up the phone and contacted Ambassador von Weizsäcker, whom Dollmann knew to be a late 'night-owl'. Both men disliked Kappler to the core, and Dollmann intended to sabotage Kappler's plans with regards to swapping Bertram for Monsignor O'Flaherty.

"*Herr* Ambassador, Dollmann here; my apologies for the late hour phone call," he said as the ambassador answered his phone.

"Good to hear from you Eugen; no need for apologies, I was wide awake and reading."

"You no doubt have heard that Bertram is in custody, he was caught by one of Kappler's men last night trying to cross the line into the Vatican City, wearing a *Wehrmacht* uniform no less!"

"Yes, Eugen, I was informed about an hour ago. The Holy Father will not take too kindly to it and the Vatican Secretary of State will no doubt lodge a protest."

"*Herr* von Weizsäcker, I have come up with a plan that may be suitable to all parties concerned. Can we meet someplace, certainly not here and certainly not your office or residence. Perhaps at the zoo. I always like going there from time to time, especially the ape house just to see how little we have progressed in millions of years," he said with a chuckle.

The ambassador had to laugh at himself. Dollmann was known throughout Rome as a great raconteur and storyteller and a sharp wit. The war hadn't dulled him one bit.

Rome Zoological Garden
Rome, Italy
September 12, 1943, 1000 Hours

The Rome zoological garden was located on a 42-acre plot located on part of the original Villa Borghese estate in Rome. Both Dollmann and

Weizsäcker met in front of the ape house at the appointed time, Dollmann having arrived first. When Weizsäcker finally arrived, he found Dollmann leaning over the railing with a small bag of popcorn in his hand, popping kernels into his mouth just like a kid. Von Weizsäcker had to chuckle at the sight. The ambassador was accompanied by a two-man security detail, and he waved them off, telling them to take a bench just far enough away that they could keep him in sight but also out of earshot. What he was about to discuss with Dollmann was treason and both men could wind up in a concentration camp, or worse.

The zoo was practically empty, as many of the exhibits had closed due to wartime restrictions and food was becoming more difficult to obtain for the animals. Many of the lions and other carnivores that required a great deal of meat could no longer be cared for and had to be euthanized. When the Italians had their African empire at the beginning of the war it was easy to obtain wild animals from the continent, but by 1943, Italy had lost all its African colonies and could no longer import such exotic beasts.

"Good morning, *Herr* Ambassador," Dollmann said cheerfully, "a beautiful Roman day, isn't it?"

"Good morning, Eugen, yes, a lovely day to take in the sights, sounds and *smells* of the zoo," he said jokingly. Both men laughed.

"You know, I have been watching these apes for a while prior to your arrival and I really believe that not much separates us humans from the Great Apes. Look at these gorillas, massive creatures, can rip a man to pieces if they wanted to."

"Yes, Eugen, you are right, but remember, man is the only creature that kills for sport and not for survival. If we are to believe all the rubbish coming out of Goebbels' ministry, Germany has initiated a policy of Social Darwinism, the survival of the fittest. It is an open secret of what we are doing to the Jews and other so-called *Untermensch* in the East, and I am afraid that when this war ends, we will be on the losing side. I do not think the Allies will be too merciful when it comes to putting us on trial."

"Gives me chills just thinking about it. If you don't mind, Ambassador, can we please discuss the matter at hand, to wit: what are we to do with Bertram and O'Flaherty?"

"Kappler is a very dangerous man, he has Himmler's ear, and by extension, the *Führer's,* therefore we must be very, very careful. Let's look first at O'Flaherty. He's Irish, and Ireland is neutral, as a matter of fact the Irish Embassy in Rome is the only English-speaking embassy left. If we move against O'Flaherty, we risk alienating the Irish, and need I remind you, the Reich needs all the friends it can get."

"Agreed," said Dollmann.

"Now, in the case of Bertram, who of course is German, but has been assigned to the Vatican for many years, do we want to risk the chance of alienating the Holy See by executing one of their own. The Pope has been silent up until now, but killing a priest assigned to the Vatican just may make Pius do something foolish, such as speaking out against the Reich. I don't think we want that scenario either. However, that may just be the impetus we need to get Bertram released."

"How so, Sir?"

"I will go to Montini and inform him that Bertram is being held at the *Via Tasso*, which I am sure will not sit well with the Pope once he is informed. I will then send a cable to Berlin informing them that the Vatican has threatened to voice its concern over Vatican Radio concerning the arrest of a priest assigned to the Holy See. This no doubt will be brought to the attention of Himmler and pressure will be placed on him by the *Führer* to release Bertram."

"As I understand it, Ambassador, the *Führer* was livid when he heard that the Bertram brothers led the escape from the camp at Reval, and that a senior SS officer, Bertram's brother, Peter, was one of the ringleaders. It certainly is an egg on the face of the *Reichsführer SS*."

"Ambassador, this is now becoming a major *cause celebre* and I think will also widen the gap between Himmler and Ribbentrop who personally loathe each other."

"Exactly, Eugen. I have no faith in either that chicken farmer or champagne salesman. All I know is that as ambassador to the Holy See, it is my job to keep the Vatican neutral during this conflict, and I plan to do just that. Kappler's stunt the other day in massing troops along the demarcation line almost resulted in a shooting war, and that, my dear Dollmann, we cannot risk. Your job, Eugen, as a member of the SS, will be to persuade Himmler to order Bertram's release so as not to upset the Holy See. Tell him that you are hearing rumors that the Pope is about to make an announcement condemning the Reich. Also remind our friend Kappler that *nothing* happens to Bertram while he is a guest in the *Via Tasso*, *nothing*. Is that understood?"

"Yes, sir, perfectly."

"Alright, I need to get back. I don't want to be absent too long from the office, people begin to wonder. Plus, I have the distinct feeling that my security detail will no doubt report our meeting to the Gestapo which means Kappler will know of it."

"A very innocent meeting between high-ranking officials of the Reich, sir, nothing more," Dollmann dead-panned.

Von Weizsäcker took his leave, shaking Dollmann's hand and wishing him luck.

Dollmann lingered a bit longer before heading back to his office. Before he left, he took one more look at the gorillas and sighed, saying, "I guess some of us humans should be on display in the zoo while you throw peanuts and bananas at us." With that, he nonchalantly made his way towards the zoo exit, his mind racing on the events in the coming days. This plan would either succeed or he and Weizsäcker would be facing a firing squad before too long.

Vatican Secretary of State's Office
Vatican City
September 12, 1943, 1130 Hours

Ambassador von Weizsäcker was able to make an appointment with Monsignor Montini, telling Montini's scheduling secretary that it was 'urgent' that he see the assistant secretary of state at his earliest convenience. He also told the secretary that the meeting concerned Monsignor Bertram. Von Weizsäcker was told that Montini would see him immediately and within the hour both men sat face-to-face in Montini's office.

"Monsignor, I appreciate you seeing me on such short notice. I wanted to inform you that Monsignor Bertram has been apprehended and is currently being held at the *Via Tasso.*"

"May I ask why he is being held?"

"He is wanted in connection with the murder of three Gestapo members here in Rome and of course his alleged connection with the mass escape of prisoners from a prison in Reval, Estonia."

"You mean, *concentration camp,* do you not, Ambassador?"

Von Weizsäcker, embarrassed, corrected himself, "Yes, concentration camp, I am sorry. Monsignor Bertram is being treated well, I had one of my representatives visit him earlier today and he has not been harmed."

"Ambassador, it may not surprise you, but we know that Monsignor Bertram was arrested the other night, I mean, it was right here at the demarcation line, how could we not notice? We also know that he is being held at the *Via Tasso* in cell 4 to be exact."

"I see that the Vatican's intelligence sources are impeccable as usual," von Weizsäcker said with grudging admiration in his voice. "Monsignor, my job as an ambassador is to ensure cordial relations exist between the Holy See and the Reich, and I will do everything in my power to ensure that Monsignor Bertram is released as soon as possible, you have my word."

"What do you intend to tell von Ribbentrop back in Berlin, if I may ask?"

Von Weizsäcker waited a few seconds before answering. "I intend to send a cable telling the foreign minister that if Bertram is not released then the Holy Father may be forced to denounce the Reich publicly."

Montini smiled at the prospect, but knowing the Vatican's strict neutrality, realized that such an act would probably never take place. He then said, "No doubt this will put both the foreign ministry and the SS at odds, will it not?"

"Yes, it will."

"Divide and conquer, I like that, Ambassador," Montini said with a smile. "It is quite Italian, and may I go so far as to say it is almost worthy of the Borgias."

"I hope to have Monsignor Bertram released within the next few days. In the interim, I will have a representative of my office visit with him and Kappler has been told by his senior officer here, *Standartenführer* Dollmann, that Bertram is not to be harmed."

"Thank you, Ambassador, I appreciate that. The Holy Father is very fond of Monsignor Bertram, he is one of the rising stars in the Holy See's diplomatic corps, and if he is harmed in any way, I don't know if the Holy Father will be able to remain silent."

Montini let his words sink in and then continued. "In 1940, *Herr* von Ribbentrop met with the Holy Father for what I believe was a cordial discussion. However, Cardinal Maglione was not so cordial or diplomatic in his talks with von Ribbentrop. He did not mince any words with your foreign minister; as one who was present, I can tell you that by the time Cardinal Maglione was through talking, von Ribbentrop was squirming in his seat and could not wait to get out of there fast enough!"

Von Weizsäcker could only smile at the thought of his boss uncomfortable as the veteran Vatican diplomat berated him.

"Monsignor, I will do everything in my power to put this incident behind us."

"Ambassador, you are a decent man, and in my past meetings with you, I think I have gotten to know you pretty well. You are not a Nazi, and if I were a betting man, I would have to say that you are doing everything in your power to subvert the Nazis here in Rome."

With that, Montini stood up, offered his hand to the German ambassador and said, "Thank you for coming by, I will of course inform the Holy Father of what you have told me. I will also keep you in my prayers, Ambassador, as you above all people, are going to need God's guidance."

Hotel Campo Imperatore
Gran Sasso Plateau
near Assergi, Italy
September 12, 1943, 1400 Hours

Benito Mussolini, the former *Duce* of Italy for 21 years, was miserable. At 62, he was an old man, suffering from ulcers and depression. The once hale and hearty *Duce* was now a shell of his former self. Only days earlier,

Mussolini had been brought to this former ski lodge, accessible only by cable car, some 3,000 meters above sea level, 'the highest prison in the world' as he would later state. Prior to his arrival, Mussolini had been moved around by the Badoglio government to ensure that he was not rescued by his German ally. Hitler had been infuriated by the *Duce's* removal in late July and swore to rescue his friend and fellow dictator. For well over a month, the Germans followed every miniscule lead on where Mussolini might be, but none came to fruition. The Italians were always a few steps ahead of their German pursuers. In early September, however, the Germans received a break—intercepted Italian communications stating that 'security preparations around the Gran Sasso complete,'[145] pointed to the fact that Mussolini had been moved once again, this time to the Gran Sasso plateau, high in the Apennine Mountains of eastern Italy. German airborne forces and a small group of SS men under the command of Hitler's 'Commando Extraordinaire,' *SS Hauptsturmführer* Otto Skorzeny landed on the Gran Sasso in a daring glider attack, capturing the imagination of friend and foe alike. Mussolini was rescued from his second story quarters without a shot being fired - the 200 *Carabinieri* soldiers guarding the *Duce* having been taking completely by surprise at the swiftness and boldness of the German attack. Within minutes, Mussolini was liberated from his captors.

"*Duce*, the *Führer* has sent me to rescue you!" exclaimed Skorzeny as he burst into Mussolini's room.

"I knew my friend Adolf Hitler would not leave me in the lurch!" answered *Il Duce*.

A photograph taken in front of the *Campo Imperatore* Hotel in the immediate aftermath of the rescue shows a tired but smiling Mussolini, dressed in a black slouch hat and black overcoat, surrounded by his German rescuers as well as the Italian guards, who surprisingly had not even been disarmed by the Germans!

Getting Mussolini off the mountaintop proved to be a bit of a problem, as the only way to and from the hotel was by cable car. Fearing that if they took the Italian dictator down the mountain and travelled overland, they would be subject to possible Partisan attack, an alternative plan was put forth by the Germans - Mussolini would be flown off the mountaintop in a small short-take-off and landing aircraft known as the Fi-156 Fiesler-Storch (Stork). The aircraft was used quite extensively by the Germans, mainly for battlefield reconnaissance and courier service. A Storch was called in and landed at the top of the plateau.

Surprisingly, both German and Italian soldiers worked hand-in-hand to clear the boulders and large rocks strewn across a narrow, improvised landing strip so that the aircraft could land and then take off once Mussolini was safely on board. The arrival of the aircraft on the mountain plateau, piloted by a very capable *Luftwaffe* officer, *Hauptmann* Heinrich Gerlach, brought a great sense of relief to the rescue party.

"*Duce*, it is pleasure to meet you," Gerlach said as he introduced himself to the dictator after disembarking from the aircraft.

Mussolini, who spoke passable German, answered, "Thank you *Herr Hauptmann*, I am looking forward to getting away from this prison."

"Shall we go then," Gerlach stated as he began to move toward the parked aircraft, with Mussolini and most of the German rescuers in tow.

Mussolini, however, was not to be his only passenger. Skorzeny, who had been entrusted by his *Führer* to bring back Mussolini, demanded that he accompany both Gerlach and the *Duce* on the flight. Gerlach protested vehemently, telling the SS officer that the plane would be dangerously overloaded and besides, could only hold two people. At 6'4" and well over 200 lbs., Skorzeny's extra girth would endanger the aircraft's takeoff.

Skorzeny could be very persuasive in his arguments, and finally Gerlach relented, telling the SS officer, "If anything goes wrong during takeoff, *Herr Hauptsturmführer*, it is your responsibility, not mine."

"Very well, Gerlach, I assume full responsibility if anything goes wrong. The *Führer* has ordered me to bring back the *Duce* safely and I intend to carry out those orders. Suppose, *Herr Hauptmann*, that the takeoff does result in a catastrophe? My supreme consolation will then be only to blow my brains out. How could I ever face the *Führer* and announce to him that my mission had succeeded but that Mussolini had died shortly after being freed?"[146]

Gerlach could only look at Skorzeny with amazement and was for a moment speechless.

"Alright, for God's sake, climb in," Gerlach said as the three men moved toward the aircraft, with Mussolini sitting in the copilot seat and Skorzeny's bulk squeezed in behind the luggage rack. Mussolini himself was a licensed pilot and seeing the predicament he was now in, was none too pleased at the risk Skorzeny now posed.

With all the passengers on board, the pilot ordered a few soldiers to hold the aircraft back until the plane reached its maximum RPMs and then signaled for them to release the aircraft. As the rescuers looked on, Gerlach rolled the plane down the improvised strip, the plane bouncing over half-buried rocks that had been too large to move. The pilot pushed the throttle and the aircraft gained speed and altitude. At the edge of the plateau, a huge precipice loomed and as the aircraft left the plateau, it plunged into the precipice. The troops on the ground looked on in horror as the aircraft simply disappeared, and they feared the worse - that the aircraft had crashed. What seemed like eternity passed until the troops heard the drone of an aircraft engine and saw the Storch gain altitude and wing its way towards Rome. A cheer went up from the assembled troops, both German and Italian, that Gerlach's expert piloting skills had saved the day.

From the Gran Sasso, Mussolini and Skorzeny were flown to *Practica di Mare* airfield outside of Rome where they transferred to a *Luftwaffe* He-111 bomber which then carried them to Vienna. In Vienna, Mussolini was reunited with his wife, Rachele, and their two youngest children. The next day, September 13, Mussolini was flown to a long-anticipated reunion with Hitler at the Wolf's Lair. Those that witnessed the dictator's warm handshake as he welcomed the *Duce* to freedom claim that they saw tears in Hitler's eyes.

The rescue captured the Allies completely off-guard, boosted German morale after a string of battlefield defeats in the early part of 1943, and ensured that Mussolini would once again be *Duce*, albeit to a much smaller geographic area and under direct German control.

Chapter XVII

"Am I my brother's keeper?"
--Genesis 4:9

Gate of Sant' Anna
Vatican City
September 12, 1943, 2400 Hours

The Gate of Sant' Anna was located on the Eastern portion of Vatican City not far from the Swiss Guard barracks and served as an entrance into the city-state from the *Via di Porta Angelica*. It had been agreed that the swap for both clerics would take place at midnight and that Kappler would come with only two men and no more. Kappler had suspected some sort of ruse but agreed to the terms put forth by the Vatican because of his desperation to finally capture the elusive Monsignor O'Flaherty. The plan was that Kappler, and his men would meet the Swiss Guard commander, *Oberst* von Altishofen and two of his men, who would then turn over O'Flaherty to the Germans. Vatican however, had no intention whatsoever to turn over O'Flaherty to what would be tantamount to a death sentence at the hands of the Gestapo. Instead, von Altishofen hid ten of his men within the dark shadows of the entrance gate, hiding them in doorways and behind some pillars. At his signal, once Bertram was safely in Vatican custody, the Germans would be faced with a *fait accompli,* as 10 heavily armed Swiss Guardsmen would appear out of the shadows. Outmanned and outgunned, Kappler and his men could only slink away with their tails between their legs. At least, that was the plan. No telling how the Germans would react even in the face of being overwhelmed.

Teutonic efficiency dictated that the Germans arrive early and knowing this, von Altishofen deployed his men earlier, ensuring that they were hidden in the shadows, His men were armed with submachine guns which made them more than a match for the small German force.

At 11:55, Kappler and his men, along with Bertram, who had been in position since 11:45, heard footsteps echoing off the cobblestone road of the approaching Vatican representatives. He could see only shadows approaching until a streetlight on the *Via di Porta Angelica* near the entrance allowed him to see the features of four men: O'Flaherty, von Altishofen and two accompanying Swiss Guardsmen. When von Altishofen finally halted he was face-to-face with Kappler, mere inches apart.

"*Guten nacht, Herr Oberst,*" Kappler stated. "I see that you are right on time, midnight on the dot," he said with a chuckle.

Von Altishofen, ignoring Kappler, and noticing Bertram's dishevled appearance and some dried blood under his nose, spoke directly to Bertram. "Are you alright Monsignor?"

"I am fine, *Oberst,* thank you."

Kappler then spoke up, "Enough with the niceties, von Altishofen, you two can catch up once he is back on Vatican soil. Oh, and by the way, the blood under the *padre's* nose is from where he 'tripped and fell,'" the SS officer said with a snicker.

Von Altishofen, now angry, ordered Kappler to hand over the priest.

Bertram, who was handcuffed, was released by one of the accompanying SS guards. As he was about to step foot onto Vatican territory, Kappler grabbed him by the arm and in a menacing whisper said, "You are a very lucky man, *padre.* You escaped my clutches this time; next time you may not be so lucky." He then released his grasp of Bertram's arm and the German cleric was now a free man, having stepped onto Vatican territory. He was then escorted into the Vatican proper by a Swiss Guard and soon disappeared from sight.

"Alright, von Altishofen, I kept my side of the agreement, now send over O'Flaherty."

O'Flaherty had been standing approximately five feet behind von Altishofen during the initial swap. He now moved closer, but still far enough away from the Germans that they couldn't just reach across and pull him onto the *Via di Porta Angelica.*

"I am afraid, my dear Kappler," said von Altishofen, "that Monsignor O'Flaherty will be staying with us for the foreseeable future." With those words von Altishofen gave the command and ten heavily armed Swiss Guard emerged from the shadows, their weapons trained on the three Germans.

"Drop your weapons now, Kappler, you don't stand a chance." Kappler was armed with the standard German Luger pistol, while his two men were armed with the MP-40 submachine gun. Both SS men dropped their weapons to the pavement and put their hands up.

Kappler's face distorted into one of rage, while his hand moved toward his holster.

"Don't be a fool, Kappler, you will be dead before you hit the ground. Now, ever so slowly, with just the tips of your fingers, take out your weapon and throw it on the ground."

Not taking his eyes off the Swiss Guard commander, Kappler reluctantly did what he was ordered. All the Germans were finally disarmed.

What happened next, not even von Altishofen expected. O'Flaherty walked up to Kappler and without saying a word punched him right in the jaw, knocking him out. In his younger days the priest had been an amateur boxer and at more than 40 years old, could still pack a punch, as demonstrated by the unconscious SS officer on the pavement before him. The priest then turned and walked back into the portage soon disappearing, leaving behind the bewildered SS troopers and Swiss Guardsmen alike.

"Pick him up and get him out of here, von Altishofen ordered the two SS men. I am sure his jaw is going to be sore for the next few days," he said with a chuckle.

Seeing that Kappler was unconscious, one of the SS men, a trooper by the name of Kaprovich yelled, "*Herr Oberst,* I wish to defect!" Von Altishofen was taken aback by the request.

"Why do you want to defect*?*"

"I am Ukrainian and was forced into serving in the SS. I am tired of this war and these butchers that I have been forced to fight for. Please help me."

Looking over at one of his men, von Altishofen could see that he had sympathy for the SS man's plight, and slightly nodded his head as if to say, 'give the guy a chance.' Von Altishofen then turned to the SS trooper and simply said "Welcome to the Vatican City, *Herr Oberschütze.*"[147]

With that, the SS man jumped onto Vatican soil, leaving behind his bewildered comrade and a still unconscious Herbert Kappler.

Gate of Sant' Anna
Vatican City
September 13, 1943, 0015 Hours

The SS trooper left with Kappler, whose name was Kaiser, was able to flag down a passing German patrol in their *Kubelwagen* vehicle. Both soldiers in the vehicle got out to assist in lifting Kappler into the back seat of their vehicle. "Do you want us to take you to a hospital?" the driver asked Kaiser. "No," the SS man replied, "Take us to the *Via Tasso,* it will be safer there."

The German vehicle sped off and within twenty minutes pulled up in front of the *Sicherheitdienst* (SD)[148] headquarters in occupied Rome. "Give me a hand with him," Kaiser asked the two soldiers, and the three men carried Kappler into the building.

The duty officer, a certain *Hauptsturmführer* Erich Priebke[149], seeing them carrying in Kappler asked, "What in God's name happened here?"

Kaiser explained the situation to Priebke, explaining that the tradeoff went badly, that Kappler was knocked out by a priest, and that one of their own had deserted over to the Vatican.

"Bring *Obersturmbannführer* Kappler into my office here and lay him on this couch," Priebke ordered. Kaiser, get the doctor and have him report to me." The duty officer then dismissed the two soldiers, thanking them for their assistance and sending them on their way. He also ordered them not to make mention as to what had happened. After all, he thought to himself, this was an

SD matter and should be kept 'in-house.'

Kappler began to stir, and the duty officer quickly got him a glass of schnapps, helping him into a sitting position. *"Herr Obersturmbannführer,* are you alright?" Priebke asked, clear concern in his voice.

Rubbing his jaw and not fully awake, an angry Kappler said, "Ah, Priebke, what a night I have had. Those miserable scoundrels in the Vatican have double-crossed me! I will make them pay for their insolence, trust me!"

Priebke then offered his commander a glass of schnapps. "Here, sir, drink this, it will make you feel better."

"Danke Schön, Priebke," and Kappler downed the drink in one swallow.

A knock on Priebke's door saw Kaiser and the SS doctor, Dr. Ludwig, awaiting permission to enter the office.

"Come," said Priebke, motioning them both in.

Dr. Ludwig looked over Kappler. "What happened, sir," he asked.

For a moment, Kappler did not answer, realizing that if word got out that he was knocked out by a priest, he would be the laughingstock in all of Rome, perhaps within all the Reich itself.

Looking over at Kaiser as if to silently say "not a word of this to anyone," Kappler told the doctor and Priebke, "Those filthy cowards attacked me from behind and pushed me to the ground. When I hit the pavement, I landed face first, hitting my jaw. The assailants then took my weapon and were about to shoot when both Kaiser and Kaprovich came on the scene. They both saved my life, and I am eternally grateful. By the way, where is Kaprovich?" he inquired.

Kaiser and Priebke both knew Kappler was lying through his teeth in order to save face. Dr. Ludwig swallowed the story whole and began to treat Kappler, ordering that he rest and put an ice pack on his now obviously very swollen jaw.

"Thank you, doctor, that will be all," Kappler said in dismissing the physician. "Please close the door on the way out."

With the doctor gone, Kappler rose from the couch. "Gentlemen, you know what I told the doctor is not the truth. However, that is what will be placed in the report that I am sending to the *Reichsführer SS* and *Obergruppenführer* Wolff. Neither of you are to breathe a word on how events really occurred tonight, is that clear?"

In unison, both Priebke and Kaiser answered, *"Jawohl, Herr Obersturmbannführer!"*

"Kaiser, where is Kaprovich?" Kappler again inquired.

The SS trooper looked very sheepish and did not answer quick enough.

"I asked you a question, man! Where is *Oberschütze* Kaprovich?" Kappler asked angrily.

"Sir, while you were knocked out, er, I mean unconscious, Kaprovich deserted over into the Vatican."

Kappler, now seething with anger upon hearing the news yelled, "What! And you didn't try to stop him? Why didn't you shoot that dirty Russian?"

"Sir, there was nothing I could do. We had all been disarmed as you remember, and there was at least a half dozen or more Swiss Guard with their weapons trained on us. There was nothing I could do."

Kappler realized that there was really nothing the young soldier could have done to prevent the desertion, but nevertheless remained angry. "You are dismissed, Kaiser, and remember, not a word to anyone."

"*Zu befehl, Herr Obersturmbannführer,*" said Kaiser, at the same time giving the Hitler salute. He executed an about-face and left the office, closing the door behind him.

"Priebke, we have a problem. If getting punched in the jaw by a priest isn't embarrassing enough, we now must contend with trying to get a deserter back from the Vatican. I will have to enlist the aid of *Standartenführer* Dollmann and Ambassador Weizsäcker for this delicate matter. Your thoughts on this, Priebke?"

Priebke was no fool and had been in the SD long enough to see the political in-fighting within that organization that had been going on for years. He also knew that he had to be as diplomatic as possible when dealing with the mercurial Kappler.

"Sir, I think it is a very good idea to enlist the aid of the ambassador and *Standartenführer* Dollmann. It makes sense as they have a direct line to the Vatican leadership. Whether they will give up our man is another story. We know for a fact that the Vatican is hiding thousands of escaped Allied POWs, downed airmen and Jews and even some of our own deserters in properties in and around Rome that are Vatican owned. Since the Pope has taken a strict neutral stance in this war and tries not to take sides, I seriously doubt he will order that our man be turned back over to the Reich, particularly if it means an automatic death sentence."

"This desertion is an embarrassment to the SS and to me personally as it happened on my watch. Hell, I was there when it happened!"

"But sir, you were unconscious when it happened."

"All the more reason to get back at that nest of vipers in the Vatican! There have been rumors abounding that the *Führer* wants to move into the Vatican, arrest the Pope and the Curia and deal with that rabble once and for all. I will personally present this case to the *Reichsführer SS* and to the *Führer* himself if given the chance."

Priebke could only listen to Kappler's ravings with faked interest. A lapsed Catholic himself, Priebke realized that even if the Germans marched into the Vatican tomorrow and arrested Pius XII and the Roman Curia, the Roman church would survive as it had for the past 2,000 years.

"And lastly, Priebke, once we capture O'Flaherty, and we will capture him, rest assured, I will personally deal with him. And it won't be pleasant."

With that, Kappler turned and left Priebke's office and headed up the steps to his own office on the second floor, holding an ice pack on his still swollen jaw.

Papal Apartments
Vatican City
September 13, 1943, 1000 Hours

Later in the morning after his safe return to the Vatican, Sepp Bertram was escorted to the Office of the State Secretary in order to brief Cardinal Maglione. Maglione was overjoyed when Sepp stepped into his office. The normally stoic Italian prelate jumped from his desk and hugged Sepp for what seemed like an eternity.

"Thanks be to God that you are safe, you had us all worried Sepp," Maglione said

"Excellency, you were not the only one who was worried. There were a few moments when I thought I'd never see the inside of the Vatican again."

"I must inform His Holiness that you have returned safely to us. Please sit down and I will return shortly."

Maglione left the room to see if the Pope could meet with Sepp. As Sepp looked around the room, he could see all the ecclesiastical trappings of Maglione's office. Sepp often wondered what it would be like to be the Vatican Secretary of State, an office that he aspired to someday. However, historically, the office has been held by an Italian, as had the papacy, and with the current wartime situation, it would be a proverbial 'cold day in Hell' before a German cleric held the position anytime soon.[150]

Sepp's thoughts were interrupted by Maglione's return. "The Holy Father would like to see you now, Sepp. Please follow me."

Both clerics walked down the long hallway to the Pope's private apartments. Knocking lightly, the cardinal entered the apartment first.

"Your Holiness, Monsignor Bertram is here as you requested."

With that, Sepp entered and approached Pius XII, knelt and kissed the Pope's ring. The thin, ascetic-looking pontiff, wearing a cream-colored cassock, zucchetto and gold cross, was happy to see him.

"Please rise, Sepp. It is so good to have you back. I feel as if my own son has returned from a terrible ordeal. God has answered my prayers and has delivered you safely back to us. You have also performed nothing short of a miracle in rescuing the Jews from the jaws of death." Sepp hardly knew what to say and was overwhelmed with emotion.

"Sepp, please have a seat. Cardinal Maglione, I'd like to speak to Sepp alone, if you don't mind."

Maglione bowed slightly and backed out of the apartment, shutting the door behind him.

The Pope sat down opposite Sepp and looked straight at him and then spoke. "There are two crosses now side by side in Rome...the cross of Christianity and the cross of neo-paganism (meaning the swastika).[151] With Mussolini's overthrow and the Allied landings here in Italy, it's only a matter of time before Rome itself is a battleground. We have heard rumor of Mussolini's rescue just yesterday by German paratroops, it has yet to be confirmed."

Sepp listened attentively as the Pope spoke.

"Sepp, I am very sorry to learn of your brother's death. I have been praying for him since I learned of it. You were instrumental in bringing him back to the faith, and I, for one, look upon his death as a martyr to our faith. He disregarded his own safety and that of his family to assist you in rescuing those Jews. You should be proud of him that he was finally able to escape the grip of Nazism. I understand that your sister-in-law and her children are safe in Sweden."

"Yes, Your Holiness, they made it safely to Stockholm - my brother ensured that they were out of Germany before we did the rescue. He knew what Hitler's response would be once he was identified as being part of the plot."

"Yes, the principle of *Sippenhaft*," I know it well, said the Pope. "Families sharing the responsibility of a crime by one of its members. Absolutely brutal and archaic, it dates to the Medieval Ages, and I know that Hitler as well as Stalin have used this principle to strike back at their enemies, real or imagined."

"Your Holiness, I feel totally responsible for my brother's death, and this is something that will stay with me for the rest of my life. I realize Peter's path took him away, for a while at least, from the faith he was brought up in. His years in the SS were marked by rapid promotions and assignments of greater responsibility. I know for a fact that he was at the sites of mass executions of Jews in Poland and Russia, but he told me that he, personally, had never executed anyone, Jew or Gentile. He told me that Himmler himself chided him for not carrying out an execution in person, and that Himmler was pushing his field commanders to become more aggressive and involved, 'getting their hands dirty,' as he referred to it."

"Sepp, your brother is with the Lord now, trust me, I am sure Our Savior has forgiven Peter his past sins and transgression, and that he is with your parents now, enjoying eternal life. You were not your brother's keeper, Sepp, make no mistake about that; Peter was an adult, able to think and act for himself. He joined the SS against the wishes of your parents, but after all the years of Nazi indoctrination, he finally came back to his faith. You are responsible for having rescued him from the abyss. Just imagine if he had carried out the execution of those Jews, then what? He would have been branded a war criminal by the Allies, and if he survived the war, would have been a hunted man until he was brought to justice. I can assure you, when the Allies win, and they *will* win, there will be a reckoning with Germany—Hitler, along with his henchmen will have to answer for their crimes. You, Sepp, have done a great service to the Church, and for that I will always be grateful. Now that you are back, you can assume your usual duties with the Secretary of State's Office."

"Thank you, Your Holiness, I am looking forward to resuming my duties here."

With that, the Pope ended the conversation, and Sepp left the papal apartments for his own office. Over two months had passed since he last sat at his office desk, and he thought of the mountains of paperwork that probably awaited his attention. As he crossed St. Peter's Square to his office, he smiled and looking at the beautiful basilica, said softly to himself, "It's good to be home again."

Rome Zoological Garden
Rome, Italy
September 13, 1943, 1500 Hours

Both Dollmann and von Weizsäcker met once again in front of the apes' cages to discuss the events of the previous day, to wit, the desertion of a German soldier to the Vatican and the assault on Kappler by Monsignor O'Flaherty, and the unconfirmed reports of Mussolini's rescue from the Gran Sasso.

"Did O'Flaherty really knock Kappler out cold?" von Weizsäcker asked incredulously.

"He sure did, with just one punch, so I was told. Kappler fell like a sack of potatoes," Dollmann replied with a chuckle. "Oh, to have been a fly on the wall to witness that."

The ambassador could only chuckle at Dollmann's irreverence.

"Eugen, because of this incident, Kappler is going to cause us some trouble. I have it on good authority that he plans to appeal directly to Hitler via Himmler to invade the Vatican and arrest the Pope."

"God, not again. I thought we finally put all this marching into the Vatican talk to rest."

"Obviously not, Eugen. Can you imagine if it did happen? We would be condemned the world over as if we are not vilified as it is. Once Hitler gets his mind set, there is no dissuading him. Eugen, I am going to ask you to work your magic with Kappler and use all your powers of persuasion not to have him contact Himmler. Best you inform *Obergruppenführer* Wolff of these recent events, if he hasn't already been informed."

"Right now, Ambassador, Kappler's pride is wounded; he is embarrassed for himself and the good name of the SS. I heard he told a couple of his subordinates that he sustained his injuries as he was attacked from behind and knocked to the ground and his weapon stolen. Quite a yarn if you ask me. I will have Kappler over for drinks tonight and see if I can talk some sense to him. Perhaps I can persuade him not to contact Berlin."

"Or Wolff can order him not to do it," von Weizsäcker added.

"That too, sir, yes; *Obergruppenführer* Wolff can also give him a direct order not to go directly to Himmler, but instead transmit anything going to Berlin be sent via Wolff as the HSSPF for Italy. Once Wolff receives it he can conveniently 'lose it,' and that sir, would be the end of it. I believe *Obergruppenführer* Wolff is enough of a realist that the years of victory and conquest for the Reich are behind it and gobbling up more territory, even a mere 109 acres that the Vatican makes up would not be worth the political fallout. The *Duce's* rescue has bolstered morale and has raised Himmler's stature in the eyes of the *Führer* and others, even though there were only a handful of SS men participating in the raid. The rest were *Fallschirmjaeger* under General Student's command."

"Yes, Himmler is gloating over this achievement, no doubt. Nonetheless, do talk with Kappler as we discussed and give it your best shot, Eugen; we'll talk again soon."

With that both men shook hands and went their separate ways, von Weizsäcker's security detail following closely behind him once he signaled them that he was ready to leave.

Villa Wolkonsky
Via Umberto Biancomno
Rome, Italy
September 13, 1943, 1900 Hours

Kappler arrived at Dollmann's embassy apartment at precisely 1900 hours as requested, having been admitted by Dollmann's valet.

"Kappler, so good of you to come," Dollmann said as he shook Kappler's hand. "Please come into the sitting room. Would you care for a brandy, or schnapps perhaps?"

"Schnapps would be fine, *Herr Standartenführer.*"

Dollmann poured two glasses, and then raised a toast, "To final victory!" Dollmann then gestured for his subordinate to have a seat.

"So, Kappler, I hear you met with some unfortunate business at the hands of some Partisans the other night, you are certainly lucky you were not killed. That is a nasty bruise you have on the side of your jaw."

Kappler stared back at Dollmann for a second before answering. "Yes, *Herr Standartenführer* and right outside one of the gates leading into the Vatican City. I was hit from behind and my weapon taken from me. It happened all so quickly. The bandits were probably lurking in the shadows waiting for me to pass."

Dollmann knew of course that Kappler was lying through his teeth but decided not to call the man on it and to pretend to believe every word he said.

"I do plan, *Herr Standartenführer*, to send a full report to *Reichsführer* Himmler as I know that there has been some talk among the Reich leadership to finally march into the Vatican and clear out those troublemakers, starting with the Pope himself. I have no doubt that the Vatican was somehow behind the attack, and not to mention as well, that one of the men accompanying me on the rounds defected while I was unconscious and was given sanctuary in the Vatican City."

"Yes, my dear Kappler, about that report you intend to send to the *Reichsführer SS*; I would recommend to you that you first send it through *Obergruppenführer* Wolff, in order to receive his endorsement, and his office will forward it up through the chain of command. Now I know you have a 'direct pipeline' so to speak with Himmler, but you must remember he is a very busy man, and quite frankly, who knows if your report will ever reach him. By first sending it through Wolff, I can guarantee it will be seen by Himmler."

Dollmann could tell by the expression on Kappler's face that he did not like his suggestion of not contacting Himmler directly. "*Herr Standartenführer*, are you *ordering* me not to send the report directly to the *Reichsführer*?"

"Ordering is too strong a word, don't you think Kappler? Let's just say I am highly suggesting that you take my advice. No doubt your honor and the honor of the SS has been besmirched, and we'd all like to get the culprits responsible, but these are difficult times for the Reich and its leaders, and this would only give them one more thing to worry about. Relations between the Reich and the Vatican are key; we have been very lucky that the Pope has so far remained neutral; that of course could change overnight. All he has to do is go on Radio Vatican and condemn the *Führer* and well, that would be it, we would be finished. Do you see my point?"

Keeping his anger in check, Kappler downed his drink and suddenly stood up. "I thank you, *Herr Standartenführer* for the drink and enlightening conversation, I shall take it to heart. I bid you goodnight." With that, Kappler gave the Hitler salute, turned on his heels and walked out. Very calmly, Dollmann nursed his drink and while doing so scanned the sitting room of the fine etchings of Rome that hung on the walls. Dollmann loved Rome and Italy and in the back of his mind he now began to realize that all of this, his love affair with Italy and everything Italian, and his tenure in the Eternal City would soon be coming to an end.

Headquarters, *Sicherheitsdienst* (SD)-Rome
***Via Tasso* 145**
Rome, Italy
September 13, 1943, 2230 Hours

Kappler was in a foul mood when he arrived back at his office on the *Via Tasso*. Speaking to himself he said, "How dare that *Stiefmutterchen*[152] tell me what I can and cannot do! I will show the great *Standartenführer* Dollmann just what it takes to be an SS man. I will go into the Vatican myself and get both Bertram and O'Flaherty and then we will see who has the last laugh."

With news of Mussolini's rescue having reached him earlier in the day, an idea slowly began to formulate in his head. He, Kappler, could just don clerical garb and walk straight into the Vatican without so much as a second look. Rome was filled with priests, monks and other religious, so he would blend right in. At the *Via Tasso,* the Gestapo kept the clerical garb of former priests who had died during interrogation, so finding one that fit him would not be a problem. Additionally, the SD had disguise kits for operatives that were used in undercover operations. False beards, mustaches and even wigs as well as flesh-toned makeup were available to undercover agents, and now were to be used by Kappler. A sinister smile slowly crept across his face. He would finally deal with the two priests that had given him so many problems since his arrival in Rome. Then and only then would he report to Himmler *directly* that these two priests were no longer a problem. Just then he remembered the famous quote attributed to King Henry II of England which led to the death of the Archbishop of Canterbury, Thomas Becket in 1170; "Will no one rid me of this troublesome priest?" He smiled and quietly said to himself, "I will rid us of two troublesome priests and maybe throw in the Pope for good measure." With that, he got up from his desk and headed downstairs to the evidence room to look for clerical garb that might fit him. He noted that it was ironic that clerical garb was black as were the uniforms of the SS, who had been given the moniker "the Black Order" at its inception in the 1920s. *Only fitting*, he thought to himself, as he made his way down into the bowels of the *Via Tasso*. "Besides," he said to himself, "Why should Skorzeny get all the credit for rescuing the *Duce*? I will show the world what just *one* SS man can accomplish when he puts his mind to it, and I won't need a company of paratroops to help me succeed."

Chapter XVIII

"There he is - Monsignor Hugh O'Flaherty, a mad Irish priest, but dangerous, too dangerous to live. He has given us more trouble than any other man in Rome and it must stop. He knows he will be arrested if we catch him outside of Vatican territory and we have so far failed to lure him across that line, or spot him when he has slipped away into the city...Seize him and hustle him across the line. I don't want to see him alive again and we certainly don't want any formal trials. He will have been 'shot while escaping. Understood?"[153]
--SS *Obersturmbannführer* Herbert Kappler's order to Gestapo agents in Rome to kidnap Monsignor Hugh O'Flaherty, The Scarlet Pimpernel of the Vatican, 1943

St. Peter's Square
Vatican City
September 14, 1943, 0900 Hours

Kappler had found clerical garb that fit him like a glove. The dead priest's name was still embroidered in the lining of the jacket, so he just assumed the name of the late *Padre* Giovanni Contarino, whom Kappler personally tortured only a month prior. He remembered the priest now, an average-height, middle-aged man, who was accused of hiding Jews and helping the Partisans. Kappler had grudgingly admired the man as he did not talk after nearly four days of interrogation and torture. Finally, Kappler had ordered him to be shot. In preparing his disguise, Kappler had donned a false goatee along with a mustache and a pair of blackrimmed eyeglasses with plastic lenses. He did his best to cover up the bruise on his jawline with makeup that made the bruising all but disappear. Rather than a wig, he parted his hair down the middle, which to his amazement, greatly changed his image. Looking in the mirror he saw a totally different man—which was what he intended.

As Kappler walked closer to the Rome-Vatican boundary line, he became a bit nervous. Certainly, there was the off chance that he might be recognized, but those chances were slim, he thought to himself. Nonetheless, he kept his right hand on the small 9mm pistol he kept in his pocket, more for courage than anything else.

Crossing the boundary line was simple, the German sentries not even bothering to give him a second look. Today would be a day for simple reconnaissance, to familiarize himself with the city if his plan backfired. He would find a vantage point somewhere in the city, probably where the most pedestrian traffic was taking place; priests and nuns scurrying about in the daily routines, running from one building to another. Kappler thought to himself that Bertram and O'Flaherty had to come out into the open sometime, and when they did, he would be ready. Kappler realized that his best bet would most likely be to stake-out the *Palazzo del Governatorato,* which housed the Pontifical Commission for the Vatican City State. All the services essential to the day-to-day running of the Vatican were administered there. Kappler reasoned that sooner or later both clerics would have to make their way to the *Governatorato* for any number of reasons. A large garden with numerous trees across from the main entrance of the building would be able to give him a bit of concealment as he observed the comings and goings of the building. Kappler gave himself one week to complete his self-appointed mission of killing both priests. Failure was not an option. Happy with himself in finding what he considered the perfect observation point, he decided to leave and head back to the *Via Tasso.* On his way out, he purchased a copy of the Vatican daily *L'Osservatore Romano,* which included the pontiff's daily schedule and other happenings within the Vatican City. An article on the front page of the newspaper caught his eye and gave him an idea on how he might finally land his quarry.

Headquarters, *Sicherheitsdienst* (SD)-Rome
***Via Tasso* 145**
Rome, Italy
September 14, 1943, 1055 Hours

Back in his office in the *Via Tasso,* Kappler read the *L'Osservatore Romano* news article with interest. The article read:

In 1939, workmen were digging a grave and chapel for the recently deceased Pope Pius XI, whose dying wish was to be buried in the Vatican grottoes and to make space more accessible to pilgrims. Less than a foot below the floor of the grottoes, they hit the upper corner of an ancient mausoleum. This unexpected discovery prompted Pope Pius XII to launch an excavation of the site. On June 28, 1939, the vigil of the feast of Saints Peter and Paul, the Holy Father ordered a series of excavations under the Vatican grottoes. Eventually, in 1942, bones were discovered very close to where tradition had always held Saint Peter was buried. Once wrapped in a purple and gold cloth, signifying the person was held in great esteem, the bones were found in a marble-lined niche within the wall, which was inscribed with the words in Greek *Petros eni-* "Peter is here." The bones from the feet were absent - compatible with someone who was crucified upside down and cut down from the cross. While these excavations had originally been carried out in secret, it was known by most who worked inside the Vatican City and were readily accessible to clergy, who routinely stopped by to see how the *Scavi*[154] were progressing. The Holy Father has long been interested in archeology as well as the great potential of enlisting science in the service of faith. Tomorrow, at 1300 hours, the Holy Father plans to visit the excavation site and invites all clergy to join him in this visit to pay homage to St. Peter. The Holy Father has also decreed that the excavation workers are to be given a holiday with pay in honor of the occasion.[155]

After reading the article, Kappler now knew how he could get to both men - they would all be together at the excavation site tomorrow at 1300 hours. "There really is a God," he said to himself and smiled. "This could not have been better if it were gift-wrapped and laid at my doorstep." Kappler would be able to blend in very easily with the hundreds of clerics who would be in attendance. Knowing this, Kappler donned his clerical garb once again and headed back to the Vatican, this time to find the excavation site and perform a little reconnaissance of the area. The article had read that clergy would often stop by the site to view the excavation's progress, so his being there would not arouse suspicion.

St. Peter's Square
Vatican City
September 14, 1943, 1420 Hours

Having entered Vatican City once again and in full disguise, Kappler headed to the excavation site near St. Peter's Basilica. As with his first visit, Kappler was armed with his pistol hidden in his pocket. As Kappler entered the Basilica he could not help but notice the beauty of this structure, which in its present form had undergone construction between 1506-1626. *One could not help but be in awe at the Medieval craftsmanship*, he thought to himself. Kappler saw a construction worker exiting the Basilica and asked him if he was working at the excavation site. He was in fact one of the workers and pointed the way to the site for Kappler. When he arrived at the site, Kappler saw several clerics standing at the top of a spiral staircase railing and all were looking down at the excavation site. Kappler then eased his way in, nodding and smiling at the clerics and he joined them in observing the excavations. Kappler realized that at tomorrow's ceremonies, the attendees would be standing where he was now, at the top of the stairwell and not in the crypt as there was no possible way hundreds of men would be able to fit in the crypt at one time. He would arrive early tomorrow and try to stay within the shadows and keep a watch for Bertram and O'Flaherty. He would then have to isolate them somehow from the rest of the group and wait until the ceremony was complete and the rest of the attendees had gone. Perhaps he could even take the men down to the crypt area and kill them as the workers were to be given the day off on orders of the Pope, so there would be no witnesses. Kappler then moved slowly away from the railing and began to look for a possible escape route should the need arise. If need be, he would shoot his way out and try and make it back to Rome. Most of the Swiss Guard would be armed with their ceremonial weapons, but one never knew if a plainclothes guard might be in the crowd armed with a very modern handgun. That was the chance he would take. He could only hope that both Bertram and O'Flaherty would be present at tomorrow's ceremony.

St. Peter's Basilica
Vatican City
September 15, 1943, 1200 Hours

Disguised as a priest once again, Kappler arrived early and made his way to the excavation site. A few clerics were already there, milling around and talking. Kappler was shocked to see how little in the way of security had been accorded for the ceremony. If this had been the *Führer* making a public appearance, the SS, Gestapo, SD, and every other security formation within the Reich would have been out in force. The Italians, much like the Spanish, always seemed to take a *Que Sera* attitude with life, and that seems to have spilled over into the Vatican. But unlike Hitler, no one seemed to be gunning for the Pope, hence the lackluster security measures in place.

Kappler found a large column approximately 10 feet back from the stairwell where he could observe the attendees as they entered the area. Both Bertram's and O'Flaherty's images were deeply seared into his memory. He had long imagined torturing both men if they had ever fallen into his hands. Unfortunately, there would be no time for torture today, just a quick bullet into each man; not what he had originally planned, but it would have to suffice.

As it moved closer to 1300 hours, more and more clerics began to arrive, and the rather confined area began to fill up. An area was set aside near the top of the stairwell for the Pope as he would address the crowd and lead in devotional prayers.

At approximately ten minutes to one o'clock, Kappler caught a glimpse of O'Flaherty, walking in with another priest, whom Kappler did not know, or care to know. O'Flaherty was the target. Five minutes later, Pope Pius XII entered, and all knelt. Accompanying the Pope was Bertram who halted just near the stairwell while the Pope continued to his reserved spot by the stairwell. The Pope motioned that all should rise, and then began to talk to the crowd about the history of the excavation and its importance along with the possible use of forensics to determine that the bones found in the crypt were that of St. Peter.

While the Pope was speaking, Kappler slowly began to maneuver his way toward the back of the crowd to get as close as he could to O'Flaherty. While Bertram was a nuisance, the Irish priest was the bigger prize, and due to Bertram's proximity in the front near the Pope, it would be difficult to get to him. More than likely the Pope would leave first after the ceremony and Bertram with him, thus giving Kappler only a clear shot at one target.

As the ceremony continued, Kappler had managed to move to a point about 10 feet behind the unsuspecting O'Flaherty, who was focused on the Pontiff. Kappler carefully felt for his pistol, patting it lightly, just to reassure himself that he was ready.

As the Pope concluded his comments, he thanked the assembled clergy for attending, gave a final papal blessing and began to leave the Basilica. Surprisingly, Bertram stayed behind, and the Pope was escorted out by some members of the Curia and Swiss Guardsmen. As the Pope passed, Kappler now saw his chance. He managed to ease his way behind O'Flaherty, and with the small pistol well concealed in his hand placed the barrel in the small of O'Flaherty's back.

"Just act normal, Monsignor, and make your way up to the stairwell towards Bertram," Kappler whispered.

O'Flaherty slowly turned around and saw his nemesis. "So, Kappler, we meet again. A bit early for Halloween, isn't it, dressing up like a priest and all that. I must applaud you on your choice of disguise, you fit right in. You have a lot of guts coming into the heart of the Vatican just to kill me. All right, get it over with then, I am ready to meet my Maker."

"It won't be that easy, Monsignor. Now, very carefully move up to where Bertram is standing."

O'Flaherty very slowly made his way up toward the stairwell, moving opposite the human traffic that was heading out of the Basilica. Bertram saw the big Irish priest approach him, smiled and went to shake his hand when he then saw a bearded cleric peer from behind the priest's shoulder.

"Hello, Bertram, remember me?" Kappler said with a sinister grin.

Bertram was shocked to see the SS officer *in mufti* and in their midst and for a moment was speechless.

"He's got a gun in my back, Sepp, better do what he asks."

"Both of you move towards the railing and we will wait until everyone clears out. Then we are all going to take a nice little trip down to the crypt to see the bones of St. Peter. When I get done with you both, pilgrims will be able to see the bones of two troublesome priests as well! Martyrs for the cause, maybe?"

"You will never get away with this Kappler, you know that. Kill us and the Pope goes on the radio and condemns Germany, Hitler and your cause is lost. Don't be a fool," Bertram said.

Kappler could only smile. "Just a few minutes more gentlemen before the place empties out. Look as though you are interested in the crypt; you might as well be as it will be your final resting place."

After what seemed an eternity, the last priest left the area and only Kappler and his two hostages remained. "Ok, now very carefully, open the gate and head down the steps. It's nice the Pope gave the workmen off today, it makes my job that much easier," he said with a laugh.

With Kappler trailing behind them, gun in hand, both priests led the way down the spiral staircase into the crypt area. Once they reached the bottom, they moved further down the excavation tunnel, which was lit by electric lights strung at the top of the tunnel.

"That's far enough, stop right there," Kappler ordered. He then struck O'Flaherty in the back of the head with the butt of his pistol, knocking the priest to the ground and rendering him temporarily unconscious.

"That's for sucker punching me the last time," Kappler spit out.

"Now, for you Bertram, you Jew-lover. You and your brother have besmirched the good name of the SS by helping those Jews escape. Now you are going to pay for your insolence. And you call yourself a loyal German! You are a disgrace to the Fatherland, you *schwein*! Now you will join your brother."

As Kappler raised his pistol, O'Flaherty began to stir and moan, distracting Kappler for a moment as he turned to look at the Irish priest. A workman's shovel left propped up against the wall was the closest weapon available - Bertram grabbed it and swung it with all his might, hitting Kappler in his hand holding the gun, and breaking his hand in the process. Writhing in pain, Kappler dropped the gun and held his now profusely bleeding hand to try and stem the bleeding.

"What have you done to me, priest!" yelled Kappler.

Bertram in the interim, had picked up the gun and tossed it behind him, far out of Kappler's immediate reach. Kappler then felt a strong hand on his right shoulder - it was O'Flaherty who was now fully conscious and in a foul mood. He spun the SS officer around and with a right hook to the jaw, sent him to the ground. With only one good hand, Kappler could not effectively defend himself. O'Flaherty walked over to him and picked him up by the front of his cassock, once again punched him in the face, and continued until the SS man collapsed to the ground, badly beaten and bloody.

"Sepp, are you alright?" asked O'Flaherty.

"Yes, Hugh, I am fine. That was some performance. You were like another Max Schmeling,[156]" Sepp chuckled.

"Let's contact the Swiss Guard and get him out of here. There is some rope over behind you, tie his hands good and tight while I go get help."

Bertram tied the still unconscious Kappler's hands and retrieved the pistol while O'Flaherty went for help. Within 20 minutes, a detachment of Swiss Guard, armed with automatic weapons and led by their commander, *Oberst* von Altishofen, arrived on the scene.

"Monsignor Bertram, are you alright?" asked the Swiss Guard commander.

"I am fine, *Herr Oberst,* Monsignor O'Flaherty has once again taken care of our friend here," said Bertram pointing to the still unconscious Kappler.

Von Altishofen could only laugh at the SS officer's plight, the second time in as many weeks he was knocked out by O'Flaherty.

"You are becoming a one-man army, Monsignor O'Flaherty," von Altishofen joked. "We could use you in the Swiss Guard if you ever give up the priesthood."

Just then Kappler started to come to and realized he was once again at the mercy of the Swiss Guard. "Wake up, sleepy head," von Altishofen joked. "You are becoming quite a nuisance, Kappler, and this time it won't be so pleasant. You have violated Vatican neutrality and attempted to kill two of our diplomats. I don't think Ambassador von Weizsäcker will take too kindly to your actions. And look at this - your beard is about to fall off." Von Altishofen then roughly yanked Kappler's false disguise off, leaving the SS officer looking ridiculous with bits of white spirit gum still attached to his face.

Addressing the guardsmen that were with him, von Altishofen ordered Kappler removed and brought to the Swiss Guard barracks. "Get him cleaned up and see if he needs any medical attention, then lock him in a cell until we know what to do with him."

As Kappler was led away, O'Flaherty called out, "So much for your idea of a Master Race, Kappler; you can't even take a punch from an overaged Irishman!" The assembled guardsmen could only laugh at O'Flaherty's comment as they led the hapless SS officer away.

Swiss Guard Barracks
Vatican City
September 15, 1943, 1422 Hours

The Swiss Guard had brought Kappler back to their barracks where he was cleaned up and his broken hand tended to by a doctor. The once arrogant Kappler had the wind taken out of his sails, and anyone looking at him could see it. Battered, disheveled and dejected, he looked nothing like the 'spit and polish' SS officer he prided himself to be. Once treated, he was placed in a cell and given some hot tea. He was informed that the German ambassador would be paying him a visit in a short while and to probably expect the worse.

Kappler was not a man that was easily frightened; however, he soon realized that he was now the center of an international incident, one which could have lasting repercussions for the Reich. Kappler soon heard voices out in the hallway leading to the cells and recognized the voice of Ambassador von Weizsäcker. As the footsteps of the guard and ambassador drew nearer to his cell, Kappler stood up, his one good hand grasping one of the bars on the cell door.

"You idiot!" von Weizsäcker shouted. "Do you have any idea of the trouble you have caused the Reich? This stunt of yours could cost us the war! The Pope is furious that the neutrality of the Vatican City has been violated by Germany and *you*, Kappler, are to blame for this mess. I have informed the *Reichsführer SS* and *Obergruppenführer* Wolff on this matter, and I am sure that Himmler will inform the *Führer.* I certainly hope you have some warm clothing, as I think your next posting will be to the Russian Front! You are a disgrace, Kappler, and not fit to wear the uniform of an SS officer!" With that, von Weizsäcker turned and walked out, meeting up with the guard who had escorted him in. When Kappler heard the outer door close, he sunk into his cot in a deep depression. He knew that Wolff and he had their differences in the past and that Wolff would probably recommend to Himmler to have him removed from Rome and sent to Russia. This was not the manner in which he had hoped to get a combat assignment. Now all Kappler could do was hope and pray that the *Reichsführer SS* would see things a bit differently and spare him the humiliation of removing him from his post.

Office of the *Reichsführer SS*
***Prinz-Albrecht-Strasse* 8**
Berlin, Germany
September 15, 1943, 1700 Hours

SS Sturmbannführer Rudolph Brandt, adjutant to the *Reichsführer SS,* was given a telex from the officer in charge of the communications center for the RSHA. After quickly reading it, he realized that it needed to be brought to Himmler's attention immediately. Straightening his tunic, Brandt knocked on the massive oak door leading into Himmler's office.

"Enter," Himmler responded.

Brandt entered, stood exactly three feet in front of Himmler's desk and rendered the Hitler salute. "Heil Hitler!"

Himmler weakly returned the salute. "Yes, Brandt, what is it?"

"*Herr Reichsführer,* this cable just in from Italy, from Ambassador Weizsäcker concerning *Obersturmbannführer* Kappler."

Himmler held out his right hand and Brandt placed the cable into his hand and then stepped back, awaiting further orders.

Himmler read the cable, his lips quietly moving as he thoroughly reviewed the message.

When he was done, he placed the cable on his desk, removed his *pince nez* glasses and rubbed the bridge of his nose, a sign to Brandt that a stress headache was coming on.

"I cannot believe, Brandt, that von Weizsäcker would have the audacity to heap such scorn against a member of the SS. I have full faith in Kappler, he is doing an outstanding job in weeding out members of the resistance in Rome and other anti-German elements, even in the Vatican. When this war is over, the *Führer* has promised to move into the Vatican and arrest Pius and his minions! Let's see them complain then."

Himmler thought for a minute and then told Brandt, "Send a cable back to the ambassador and inform him that we are in receipt of his message and that no further action will be taken against Kappler. He stays put. Tell the ambassador that the *Führer* has been duly informed and is in concurrence. That will be all." With that, Brandt executed an about face and left Himmler's office in order to draft up the *Reichsführer's* response. Hitler of course, would never learn of the cable, as Himmler shielded his *Führer* from many of the problems faced with conducting the war.

Chapter XIX

"Quo Vadis?"

Papal Apartments
Vatican City
September 16, 1943, 1000 Hours

Vatican Secretary of State Maglione arrived for his daily morning briefing for the Pope, bringing with him the daily edition of *L'Osservatore Romano* for Pius XII to read.

"Your Holiness, take a look at the headlines in today's daily, it is now official - Mussolini has been rescued by the Germans! It is all over the news, to include the BBC and Radio Berlin!"

Pius took the newspaper and read the account of the rescue. After he was done, he placed the newspaper on his desk, sighing as he did so.

"Maglione, this will not bode well for Italy, I am afraid. Civil war will break out, no doubt. The Allies are still in the south of the country, the Germans in the central and northern part, and according to the article, Mussolini is planning on setting up a rump state in the north, the Italian Socialist Republic, near Saló. There is, very little that we can do, Maglione, except pray that the Allies get to Rome quickly."

"Your Holiness is aware, I am sure, that the Partisans in the north are mainly communists, and if, God forbid, they are able to gain the upper hand on the battlefield, Italy could have a communist post-war government."

"That is the reoccurring nightmare I have, Maglione. If Italy has a post-war communist government, it will leave us as an island surrounded by hostile territory under their control. I don't know if the church would be able to survive. We would be replacing one dictatorship with another, and I don't think a communist-run government in Italy would allow us to exist. It would probably abrogate the Lateran Treaty[157] and then march in and take over."

"Your Holiness, at least Hitler has allowed the churches to stay open, while Stalin confiscated the Orthodox and Catholic churches and monasteries and turned them into stables and prisons and otherwise have desecrated them. Priests and religious have been arrested, executed and sent to prison camps."

"You are right, Cardinal, of course. Hitler appears to be the lesser of two evils. Godless communism must not be allowed to gain a foothold in Italy or Western Europe for that matter. Our missionaries in Russia had all but been liquidated by 1940 and much of the church properties were given to the Orthodox Church. While the war is on, Stalin is putting on a public relations campaign, mainly for the benefit of Roosevelt and Churchill, showing them that religious freedom has returned to the Soviet Union and the West has bought into it hook, line and sinker. I think Churchill has a better understanding of Stalin's post-war plans than does Roosevelt."

After sipping a glass of water, the Pope continued, "Both the British and the Americans are also beginning to funnel more aid to the communist Partisans here in Italy and elsewhere. American OSS[158] and British SOE[159] operatives have parachuted into Yugoslavia to help Tito, because, quite frankly, Tito's Partisans are doing an effective job against the Axis in Yugoslavia. Communism is on the march, Maglione, and while I loathe Hitler and his minions, I have seen first-hand what communism represents - I pray the Anglo-Americans wake up to that fact and aren't fooled by Stalin's current 'charm offensive' aimed at the West."

"Perhaps, Your Holiness, Monsignor Bertram can be of help once again. In the past he has dealt with Ustashã thugs in Croatia, Fascists here in Italy, and Nazis in Russia - I cannot think of a better qualified individual to tackle the growing communist threat here in Italy."

Offering a weak smile, the Pope answered, "Perhaps later Maglione - Sepp has been through a great deal these past months, and he is also dealing with the loss of his brother. Yes, God has spared his life so he can serve the church further. Sepp has had enough adventures these past months to last five lifetimes. However, he is still a wanted man and the Germans, especially our friend Kappler, will stop at nothing. That was recently proven with Kappler's violation of our territory. But you raise a good point - we know for a fact that there are clerics fighting alongside some of the Red brigades in the north, perhaps Sepp can act as an intermediary to those clergy fighting with the communists Partisans. Just recently, two former army chaplains, a *Don* Ascanio De Luca and *Don* Redento Bello, organized a resistance group called the *Osoppo Brigade*, made up of Catholics in the northern Friuli Region.[160] They have been coordinating their efforts with the communist-led Garibaldi Brigades, so there is hope."

Pausing for a moment to gather his thoughts, the Pope continued, "You know, Maglione, the attitude of our clergy is especially important in the rural areas of the country, where a priest can influence whether or not the village should support the communists. I believe that the real control of the Italian Catholic masses remains with the clergy.[161] This we will have to seize upon and exploit if we want to defeat the communists. This is where our Monsignor Bertram may be of assistance."

Maglione could only smile and nod his approval at the Pontiff's musings.

Pius XII continued, "I believe you know Father Pankratius Pfeiffer, Superior General of the Salvatorian Order here in Rome - I have used him periodically as my liaison with the German High Command in Rome. He has become friendly with a certain *Luftwaffe* officer, Kurt Mälzer - both of them are from Bavaria and Mälzer is Catholic as well. Mälzer, I might add, is on the staff of Field Marshal Kesselring.[162]"

"What will you have Father Pfeiffer do, Your Holiness?"

"Mälzer has Kesselring's ear, and the field marshal may be able to bring some pressure to bear on Kappler and order him to 'back off,' so to speak."

"But Your Holiness, Kappler is an SS officer and as I understand it, is answerable only to Wolff, Himmler, and Hitler."

"Yes, Maglione, but Wolff also answers to Kesselring, and I think an order from the Field Marshal will carry some weight. At least it is worth a try."

Maglione smiled and nodded his head in agreement at the Pope's plan. All they could do now was pray and hope that Kesselring, being far more diplomatic than many of his underlings, would order Kappler to 'stand down' and leave Sepp and O'Flaherty in peace. It all rested on Father Pfeiffer's influence with Kurt Mälzer and all of his powers of persuasion to get the Germans to agree with the Pope's request.

"Cardinal, I have asked Father Pfeiffer to pay a visit to Kesselring's headquarters with the hopes that his friend Mälzer might intervene on our behalf, and he is scheduled to do so later today. If and when he hears from the Germans, I would like to have both you and Sepp present when he reports back to me."

"As Your Holiness wishes," Maglione said with a slight bow of his head.

With that, the Pope signaled that the meeting was over and asked to be alone for private prayer and meditation. Italy had just entered a new phase of the war, one that would have direct impact on the Holy See and that would bring more and more German troops to the very gates of the Vatican itself.

Hauptquartier, Oberbefehlshaber Sued (Headquarters, Commander-in-Chief (C-in-C) South or *OB Sued*)
Frascati, Italy
September 16, 1943, 1345 Hours

Located some ten miles southeast of Rome on the northern slopes of the Alban Hills, the small, picturesque town of Frascati was the location of Field Marshal Albert Kesselring's OB South headquarters where Father Pfeiffer travelled to visit his friend, *Generalmajor* Kurt Mälzer[163] a *Luftwaffe* officer assigned to Kesselring's staff. Mälzer, a no-nonsense type of officer, had previously been assigned as a Department Head in the German Ministry of Aviation in Berlin as well as the commander of *Flugbereitschaft* 17 (Executive Transport Wing 17) in Vienna, prior to his posting to Rome. He had met his fellow Bavarian, Father Pfeiffer upon his arrival in Rome, and for some unknown reason, took an immediate liking to the 71-year old priest. Mälzer, a Catholic, had assisted Pfeiffer with some small favors, such as using his influence in having prisoners released from either the *Via Tasso* or the *Regina di Coeli* prison. On this day, upon Pfeiffer's arrival at the German Headquarters, he was escorted to Mälzer's office, where an aide announced him to the general and then beckoned him to enter the office.

"*Guten tag, Herr Generalmajor,*" Pfeiffer said, extending his hand to Mälzer.

"Father Pfeiffer, so good to see you," Mälzer said as he rose from behind his desk to greet the cleric. "Please do have a seat. Would you care for some real coffee?" Mälzer asked somewhat jokingly, as coffee could now only be acquired by the average Roman on the black market.

"Yes, please that would be nice."

Mälzer picked up the phone and asked his aide to bring in some coffee and some sweets for his visitor. Once that was done and the two men were alone, Pfeiffer spoke first.

"You have been helpful to the Holy See in the past, and the Holy Father is most appreciative as am I. He has asked me to convey to you his blessings for your continued good health and safety."

Mälzer smiled and nodded his thanks.

Pfeiffer continued, "The Holy Father has also asked me for your assistance in handling a rather delicate matter, to wit, the protection of two of our priests assigned to the diplomatic office - Monsignors Josef Bertram and Hugh O'Flaherty. I am sure you are familiar with both names by now."

Mälzer almost choked on his coffee when the names were mentioned - he knew only too well that both priests were high on the Gestapo wanted list in Rome. Word had also gotten out of Kappler's antics at the Vatican, which brought a smile to the German general's face.

"Father, I know of the two men that you speak of - as a matter of fact, the entire headquarters is familiar with them. I can sympathize with you - quite frankly, I am not too happy with Kappler's antics and would be happy to see him sent to the Russian front as a lowly private. Unfortunately, that decision is not mine to make."

"Can you, *Herr General,* perhaps take up the issue with Field Marshal Kesselring? It would be a request coming directly from the Holy Father and if agreed to by your superior, I am sure that the Holy Father will use his influence with the Allies and also with the Resistance to ensure that the good offices of the Vatican can be used as an intermediary between the Allies and yourselves if so desired. Let me be frank, *Herr General*, the war has decidedly turned against Germany, and with the Allies now in control of Sicily and in southern

Italy proper, it is only a matter of time before they fight their way up to Rome. It may take months, maybe years, but they will come. And when they do, wouldn't it be nice to have the Vicar of Christ in your court?"

The priest was blunt, but he was also correct in his assessment.

"Very well, Father, you make a good case. I will take it up with Field Marshal Kesselring this afternoon. I believe he will see things as you do. I can see that the Pope is a practitioner of *realpolitik*. I will contact you as soon as I have an answer."

Standing up, Pfeiffer held out his hand to Mälzer and thanked him for his time.

"God be with you, *Herr General*," and he left Mälzer's office much more optimistic than when he had entered.

Papal Apartments
Vatican City
September 18, 1943, 1600 Hours

It had taken all of two days for the Germans to reply back to Father Pfeiffer's request. Upon learning of their reply, Pfeiffer immediately contacted the Pope's personal secretary to set up an audience, which was quickly granted. Pfeiffer arrived promptly for his meeting with Pius XII. He entered the Pope's living quarters, knelt and kissed the papal ring then stood up, taking a seat at the Pope's direction. It was only then that Pfeiffer realized that both Maglione and Sepp were seated behind him.

"You know both the Cardinal Secretary of State and Monsignor Bertram, do you not?" asked the Pope gesturing with his hand in their direction.

Pfeiffer nodded to both clerics in recognition, smiling slightly.

"Now, what news do you bring me from the Germans, Father?" the pontiff asked.

Clearing his throat, Pfeiffer reported that "After hearing back from Field Marshal Kesselring's headquarters concerning Monsignors O'Flaherty and Bertram, I believe we have come to some sort of unofficial understanding concerning the Germans interests in both men. According to *Generalmajor* Mälzer, Kesselring agreed that Kappler's antics of late have been an embarrassment and have given the Reich a 'black eye' in its public relations campaign to win over the hearts and minds of the Italian population. The Italians are weary of war, tired of Mussolini, and only want to be left alone. That said, Mälzer informed me that Kesselring had gone straight to *SS Obergruppenführer* Wolff and spoke with him to put pressure on Kappler to back off."

"Wolff takes his orders directly from Himmler, does he not, Father?" interjected Sepp.

"Yes, Monsignor Bertram, he does. But Kesselring is the senior military commander on the ground and Wolff, as far as I am concerned, is nothing more than a glorified policeman with the rank of Lieutenant General, while Kesselring outranks him. Wolff still needs to toe the line. So, I hope and pray that enough pressure is brought on Kappler that he will back away from intimidating or attempting to kidnap our clergy."

"The Pope smiled and said, "Thank you, Father Pfeiffer, for using your contacts with the German High Command, I pray they stick to their agreement."

"Your Holiness, I believe both Mälzer and Kesselring are honorable men, even if they are German," Pfeiffer joked, knowing that both he and Bertram were German nationals.

"Even if the Germans do back off, there is still the Koch Gang to contend with as well as the other gang in Florence, headed by Carità,[164]" said Bertram.

"They are minor irritants, Sepp, although we still must remain vigilant," said the Pope.

The Pope continued, "Gentlemen, thank you for coming to this meeting, it has been most enlightening. Sepp, if I may see you alone, please after the others leave."

Both Maglione and Pfeiffer took their cue to exit the papal apartments, leaving Sepp alone with the Pope.

"Sit here Sepp," the Pope said patting a chair closest to him.

Sepp sat down facing the pontiff, who then spoke.

"Sepp, you have been through a great ordeal these past months and went above and beyond what was asked of you, and I am most appreciative. As you are aware, Mussolini has been rescued by the Germans and plans to set up his regime in the northern part of the country. I want you to go up there and be my eyes and ears on how the Fascist regime conducts itself against the Church and also the Jews in the area. No doubt, under German influence, the new regime will be harsher against the Jews and against us than when the regime was centered in Rome. I would like you to go to Milano as its new auxiliary bishop—you have certainly earned my trust and I know the Curia will agree with me when I put forth your name. What do you say to that, Sepp?"

Sepp was dumbfounded at the Pope's offer, for a few moments he could not even speak, until finally he found his voice.

"Your Holiness, I am deeply honored and humbled by your words and by the offer to be the auxiliary bishop of Milano - I humbly accept your offer and I only pray that I will live up to your expectations to carry out the church's mission in these most difficult times."

The Pope, normally a very serious individual, had a large smile on his face - he was very fond of Sepp and saw in him a future prince of the church, a cardinal, if all went according to plan. "I am very happy to hear that, Sepp. I will notify Cardinal Schuster[165] in Milano and let him know of your decision. This will also get you out of Rome and away from Kappler. This new posting will be a difficult one, Sepp, as you will have to only deal with the die-hard Fascists bolstering Mussolini, but the Germans as well, who will be calling the shots. Mussolini will be nothing more than Hitler's puppet. This is not the *Duce* of old - he is a sick, broken old man - no more bombastic orations from him on his balcony at the *Palazzo Venezia*. I can tell you now that the Holy See does not plan to recognize Mussolini's new government, this so-called Italian Socialist Republic, either in a *de facto* or *de jure* manner."

Sepp could only nod in agreement of what the pontiff was saying. Mussolini would be nothing without German military backing, nothing more than a stooge of the Nazis, and Hitler was going to make sure that his old Axis partner still contributed to the war effort.

"One other thing, Sepp. Northern Italy is a hotbed of communist activity, and it must not gain a foothold in post-war Italy. A number of our clergy are currently fighting alongside the Partisans and have made temporary alliances with the communist-led Garibaldi brigades. They have some influence and can hopefully sway some of the Partisans to come back to their Catholic roots and abandon communist ideology. No doubt, so-called commissars are filling their heads with Marxist/Leninist poppycock. You may have to venture out from the cathedral on occasion and make your way to Partisan-held territory - I am counting on you, Sepp."

"When would you like me to leave for Milano, Your Holiness?"

"Would two weeks' time be agreeable, Sepp? I want you well-rested before you begin your new posting. Also, I will have Father Pfeiffer arrange to have a good conduct pass for you signed by Kesselring himself which should enable you to travel to Milano unhindered."

"Thank you, Your Holiness. Again, I am humbled to accept this new posting and will strive to the best of my ability to fulfill the church's mission."

"One last thing, Sepp, and I know this will make you happy. We received word from *Padre* Scavone that his cousin, the Army sergeant that helped you escape, has deserted to the Partisans and is well. He wanted you to know that. Also, the young woman whom you sent into the Vatican disguised as a nun is also well. Unfortunately, she has returned to her old profession."

"Thank you, Your Holiness, I have wondered what happened to Sergeant Scavone. He's a good soldier and will come through this war unscathed, I am sure of it. I will keep both he and Maria in my prayers."

"God be with you, my son. I will see you before you depart for Milano in two weeks." The Pope then invoked a blessing on Sepp and then the audience was over.

Sepp left the papal apartments and headed toward St. Peter's Basilica to pray. Even as war surrounded the Vatican City, with enemy troops literally at its gates, the Vatican still emitted a feeling of tranquility and peace. As he entered the huge basilica, he found a pew and knelt. He remembered just days before of Kappler's attempt to kill both he and Monsignor O'Flaherty in this very place. He remembered back to his time in Russia, where against all odds, he accomplished the impossible, saving 100 Jews from the jaws of death and helping them to freedom. He had outwitted the Gestapo on his return to Rome and had beat them at their own game. He had cheated death and was a survivor.

He had survived, but Peter had not. Sepp could take some consolation that Lydia and the children were safe in Sweden, able to sit out the rest of the war in relative comfort. It would probably be some time before he saw them again. He could also take consolation that Peter had died honorably - all he knew was that he had been shot and did not know the specifics surrounding his death. Peter had realized the path he was taking as an SS officer implementing Hitler's Final Solution in the East went against every law of God and man. This had been a journey of sorts - one of redemption and forgiveness, courage in the face of adversity, with good triumphing over evil. Now the Holy Father had another mission for him, and he wondered if he was up to the task. In memory of his brother and for all that had fallen in their battles against the Nazis, the Fascists, and the Communists, he would do what was humanly possible for good to finally triumph. Before leaving he said a prayer to the Virgin Mary, one that he had prayed since the war began for Italy back in 1940:

O Most Blessed Virgin Mother of Mercy, at this most crucial time, we entrust Italy to your loving care. Most Holy Mother, we beg you to reclaim this land for the glory of your Son. Overwhelmed with the burden of the sins of our nation, we cry to you from the depths of our hearts and seek refuge in your motherly protection. Look down with mercy upon us and touch the hearts of our people. All for the glory of God. Amen.

Sepp then left the basilica and walking across St. Peter's Square, stopped to look back at the imposing structure which had stood since the year 1626. A smile came across his face as he remembered years before of visiting a small chapel near the ancient *Porta Capena* in Rome. The chapel, he remembered, bore a weathered ancient Latin inscription *Quo Vadis, Domine?* (Where are you going, Lord?)[166] For Sepp, the answer to that ancient inscription was now in the hands of God that would, in time, be revealed to him.

Chapter XX

"The only difference Mr. Stalin and Mr. Hitler is the size of their respective mustaches."
--*The Wall Street Journal*, 1941

The Aftermath

In the aftermath of the rescue of the prisoners from Klooga, both
Hitler and Stalin sought revenge in their respective countries on all who had
assisted with the escape. Both dictators practiced the policy of *Sippenhaft,*
whereby the family of an accused individual shared responsibility for a crime,
thus justifying some sort of collective punishment. For Hitler, the escape of
prisoners from Klooga Concentration Camp was unforgiveable and was seen
as a betrayal by the SS. While Peter had been killed in Himmler's office, his
family was safe in Stockholm and Sepp safe within the confines of the Vatican
walls. However, the Bertram brothers had received assistance from serving officers within the German *Wehrmacht,* and those men paid with their lives. The
Gestapo, after a brief investigation, arrested, and ultimately executed *Oberst*
Weber, along with his Jewish wife, as well as *Hauptmann* Fritz, and *Oberleutnant* Roper for their roles in the escape from Klooga. *SS Hauptsturmführer*
Willi Loss was returned to duty at Klooga after he was found to have been
obeying a direct order of a senior officer and that he had no prior knowledge of
the planned escape.

The Spanish officers of the 250th Infantry Division fared much better
than their German counterparts. Not wishing to alienate Franco further, as Hitler still needed wolfram from Spain for his war machine and Spanish harbors
as safe havens for German U-boats, no action was taken against the officers of
the Blue Division. By the end of 1943, most of the division was withdrawn
from Russia after negotiations with Berlin, while a number of die-hard an-
ti-communists Spaniards opted to continue to fight the Soviets till the end of
the war.[167]

Herbert Kappler remained at his post at the *Via Tasso*, with Himmler's
backing and basically ignoring Field Marshal Kesselring's orders to 'cease
and desist' harassing the Vatican clergy, particularly Monsignor O'Flaherty,
who still retained a price on his head. Kappler would remain at his post until
just prior to Rome's liberation in June, 1944, leaving with the retreating *Wehrmacht.*

Stalin's justice was also swift and brutal. Anyone who had failed him
was ordered eliminated. Upon learning that the Jews on the train had not been

attacked by the 12th Partisan Brigade as he had ordered, Stalin ordered an elite NKVD unit to eliminate the brigade in its entirety. The NKVD unit was air-dropped almost on top of the 12th Partisan Brigade and a two-day battle ensued between both Soviet forces. Added to the fray, Red Air Force aircraft attacked the known Partisan positions, eliminating the last vestiges of resistance, leaving no survivors.

The Partisan agents in Reval who had kept tabs on the Bertram brothers were also dealt with. Stalin specifically ordered that the young female agent, Tatiana, who had infiltrated the Bertram household, be executed as she failed to provide more information than was given. Knowing that she was the paramour of the agent "Walter" Kuzin, Kuzin was ordered to execute his lover under threat of his own death if he did not carry it out. He did, and having shot Tatiana, turned the gun on himself.

Thus, both Hitler's and Stalin's revenge were now complete.

Postscript

The novel you have just read is of course, a work of fiction, while some of the characters in the story are historical figures of the period. Below are the post-war fates of some of the historical characters portrayed in this novel.

Hans Aumeier. In June 1945, Aumeier was arrested and extradited to Poland to face trial as a war criminal for his service at Auschwitz. He was found guilty by a Polish court and sentenced to death. He was hanged on January 28, 1948 in Krakow, Poland.

Count Folke Bernadotte. In February 1945, Bernadotte negotiated with *Reichsführer* Himmler for the release of Scandinavian concentration camp inmates, which was successful. In 1948, as the United Nations mediator in Palestine, he was assassinated by a militant Jewish terrorist group.

Rudolf Brandt. At war's end Brandt was captured by British forces. He was later indicted by the US Military Tribunal and charged with a variety of crimes. He was found guilty of being responsible for the administration and coordination of the experiments at the Nazi concentration camps. He was hanged on June 2, 1948, his 39th birthday.

Sigismund von Braun. During post-war denazification, von Braun was classified as "discharged" despite his party membership, as he had assisted in hiding personnel from deportation. In 1954, he once again entered diplomatic service, this time for the Federal Republic of Germany, culminating with his appointment as German ambassador to France from 1972-1976. He died in 1998
.

Eugen Dollmann. At war's end, Dollmann was protected from criminal prosecution of his involvement in war crimes by the Archbishop of Milan, with whom he had discussed the possibility for a separate peace between Nazi Germany and the Western Allies in Operation Sunrise. The archbishop hid Dollmann in a mental institution in Laveno-Mombello. In 1946, after returning to Rome, he was briefly arrested but later released after intervention by the OSS. He lived out the rest of his life in Germany where he worked as a translator. He died in 1985.

Vittorio Emmanuel III. In 1946, the diminutive king abdicated his throne in favor of his son, Umberto II hoping to strengthen support for the monarchy against an ultimately successful referendum to abolish it. He then went into exile to Alexandria, Egypt. He died in 1947.

Emilio Esteban-Infantes. When the Blue Division was withdrawn from Russia by Franco in late 1943, Esteban-Infantes returned to Spain a hero, having been awarded the Knight's Cross personally by Hitler. After the war, Esteban-Infantes served as the president of the Supreme Council of Military Justice, commander of Spain's VII Military Region and head of Franco's military household before finishing his career as Chief of the Central General Staff. In 1958, he published his memoirs, *Blue Division: Spanish Volunteers in the Eastern Front.* He died in 1962, aged 70.

Francisco Franco. Franco outlived his fellow European dictators and ruled Spain with an iron fist until his death on November 20, 1975 at the age of 82. Franco did achieve some legitimacy to his regime after the war by both ecclesiastical and secular powers - in August 1953, Spain signed a Concordat with the Vatican, and a month later, September 1953, signed a bilateral defense agreement, the Pact of Madrid, with the United States.

Heinrich Himmler. On May 21, 1945, Himmler, disguised as a German soldier, was captured by British forces who were initially unaware of the important prisoner they held. Two days later, for reasons unknown, Himmler voluntarily identified himself to his captors and as he was being searched, bit into a cyanide capsule he had hidden in his mouth. Efforts to revive him failed. British forces buried Himmler in an unmarked grave in some nearby woods outside of Luneburg, Germany.

Adolf Hitler. The German leader committed suicide on April 30, 1945 in his Berlin Führerbunker shortly after marrying his longtime mistress, Eva Braun. Both the body of Hitler and Braun were then taken to the Chancellery Garden area and burned. Their alleged remains were found by the Red Army after the fall of Berlin. To date, rumors still abound that Hitler and many of his loyal followers made good their escape from Berlin as the Red Army tightened its noose around the German capital.

Herbert Kappler. Captured at war's end he was tried by an Italian court and sentenced to life in prison, Kappler was held responsible for the Ardeatine Cave massacre in 1944, whereby 335 Italians were executed as a reprisal in an attack that killed 35 German soldiers in Rome. While a prisoner, one of the few visitors to visit Kappler was his old nemesis, Monsignor Hugh O'Flaherty. The men became friends. In 1976, and suffering from terminal cancer, Kappler was smuggled out of an Italian prison allegedly in a suitcase by his wife and died shortly thereafter in Germany, a free man.

Wilhelm Knuppel. Following his stint as Chief of the German Liaison with the Spanish Blue Division, Knuppel went on to serve as the Chief of the General Staff of the XXXVIII Army Corps and finished up the war as the Chief of the General Staff of the 4th Panzer Army. Promoted to the rank of *General-major* on May 1, 1945, he was captured at war's end and released in 1948. He died in 1968.

Kurt Mälzer. Mälzer survived the war and was sentenced to death for war crimes for his role in the Ardeatine Cave massacre of March 1944. While this war crime is beyond the scope of this book as it occurred a year later than the storyline coverage, it is important to note that Mälzer's sentence was commuted to life imprisonment. He died in 1952.

Carl Gustav Mannerheim. In 1944, Mannerheim was elected president of Finland and he led the country out of the war with the Soviets, signing a separate peace treaty with Moscow in September 1944. As part of that treaty, the Finns drove the German forces out of northern Finland in the 1944-45 War of Lapland. He resigned from public life in 1946 and died in Switzerland in 1951, a hero to the Finns.

Jaime Milan del Bosch. Milan del Bosch would survive the war and rise to the rank of Captain-General of the Valencia military region in Spain. On February 23, 1981, he participated in the attempted military coup against the government of King Juan Carlos and was later arrested and dismissed from the army after the failure of the coup. He died in 1997.

Vyacheslav Molotov. The Soviet Foreign Minister nicknamed "old iron arse" by his contemporaries, would outlive most of his Communist cronies, dying in his own bed in 1986, aged 96. After Stalin's death in 1953, Molotov's influence in the Soviet government began to wane, especially after Khrushchev's denunciation of Stalin in 1956. He would be expelled from the Politburo in 1957 but would later be rehabilitated. At the time of his death, he was the last surviving major participant of the Bolshevik Revolution in 1917. Upon news of his death, American Columnist/Commentator George Will wrote of Molotov, "Stalin's henchman Molotov, 96, died old and in bed, a privilege he helped to deny millions."

Giovanni Montini. Ultimately elevated to Vatican Secretary of State, Montini was elected Pope in 1963 after the death of Pope John XXIII. Montini would take the name Pope Paul VI and his pontificate would last until his death in 1978.

Benito Mussolini. After his overthrow on July 25, 1943, he was imprisoned by the Italian government at various sites until the Italians finally settled on the Hotel Campo Imperatore on the Gran Sasso in the Apennine Mountains. The hotel, some 7,000 feet above sea level was "the highest prison in the world," according to *Il Duce*. On September 12, 1943, German forces rescued Mussolini in a daring glider raid that caught the Italian guards completely by surprise and rescued the former dictator. Mussolini would ultimately be placed in charge of the Italian Socialist Republic or the Saló Republic as it was known, a rump state in northern Italy and a puppet of the Germans. Mussolini was captured and shot by Italian Communist Partisans on April 28, 1945 at Dongo, Italy, near the Swiss border.

Hugh O'Flaherty. The Irish priest survived the war and was recognized with numerous awards for his heroic rescue efforts during the war. O'Flaherty regularly visited Herbert Kappler in prison, sometimes being the former SS man's only visitor. In 1959, he baptized Kappler as the SS man converted to Catholicism. In 1960, O'Flaherty suffered a series of strokes and returned to his native Ireland where he died in 1963, age 65.

Pankraitius Pfeiffer. During the German occupation of Rome, Father Pfeiffer regularly visited the *Regina Coeli* prison and Gestapo headquarters at the *Via Tasso* and on many occasions, was able to secure the release of a prisoner held in either of those two facilities. Often referred to as the "Angel of Rome," Fr. Pfeiffer was killed in a street accident in May 1945, weeks after VE Day.

Pope Pius XII. After the war, Pius XII was criticized over his actions for not speaking out more forcefully on the Holocaust. Pius XII's pontificate would end with his death in 1958. In 1963, a play by German playwright Rolf Hochhuth, *Der Stellvertreter* ("The Deputy") portrayed Pius XII as having failed to act or speak out against the Holocaust. To date, Pius XII actions are still controversial. As of this writing, Pius XII is currently undergoing the process of sainthood in the Roman Catholic Church. As of 2009, he was declared Venerable as the process to sainthood continues.

Panteleimon Ponomarenko. After the war, Ponomarenko continued to serve the Soviet Union as a member of the Presidium; he also served as First Secretary of the Communist Party for the Kazakh SSR in 1954, before becoming Soviet Ambassador to Poland (1955-57); Ambassador to India (1957-59), and finally to the Netherlands (1959-62). He died in 1984, aged 81.

Erich Priebke. A wanted war criminal for his role in the Ardeatine Cave massacre of 1944, he fled to Argentina after escaping from a British POW camp in 1946. Priebke lived quietly in San Carlos e Bariloche, Argentina, until 1994 when interviewed by American newsman Sam Donaldson of ABC News, Priebke freely admitted that he was a wanted war criminal. In 1995, he was extradited to Italy to stand trial for his major role in Italy's worst wartime massacre. The first trial sentenced Priebke to 15 years in prison - this rather light sentence caused so much public outrage in Italy that he was given a second trial in 1996 which resulted in a life sentence. Priebke died in prison in 2013, aged 100.

Angelo Roncalli. Roncalli stayed at his post in the Balkans until 1944 when he was made nuncio to newly-liberated France. Post-war, Roncalli rose rapidly through the ranks of the Roman Catholic hierarchy culminating with his election as Pope in 1958 after the death of Pius XII. Roncalli took the name of John XXIII, becoming one of the most beloved pontiff's of the 20th Century. It was during his pontificate that the Second Vatican Council was initiated. John XXIII died before the council could complete its work. Often referred to as the "Good Pope," he was canonized a saint in 2014.

Otto Skorzeny. After his successful operation in rescuing Mussolini, Skorzeny was feted as a hero of the Third Reich and Nazi propaganda went into overtime praising his exploits. In 1944, he successfully kidnapped the son of the Hungarian Regent, Admiral Miklos Horthy, in order to keep Hungary in the war on Germany's side. During the Battle of Bulge in December 1944, he commanded a group of English-speaking German soldiers disguised as Americans that played havoc behind Allied lines. It was during this period that he was given the moniker 'The Most Dangerous Man in Europe," by the Allies. Captured at the end of the war, he was put on trial for war crimes but was acquitted. While being held over in prison awaiting a decision of a denazification court, he escaped with the help of three former SS officers dressed in American military uniforms. He then ultimately made his way to Spain and was given protection under the Franco regime. He lived as a free man in Spain and Ireland until his death from cancer in 1975.

Reiner Stahel. After his stint as military commander of the city of Rome, in July 1944 he was transferred to Vilnus, Lithuania where he became the garrison commander of that city. Having participated in putting down the Warsaw Uprising by the Polish Home Army, he was dispatched to Bucharest, Romania in August 1944, whereupon he was captured by the Soviet NKVD and imprisoned in the USSR, dying in 1955 at the Voikovo officer prison.

Josef Stalin. The Soviet dictator emerged as one of the great victors of WWII even though he was, along with Hitler, responsible for its start in 1939. The liberated nations of Eastern Europe came under Soviet dominance post-1945 and they too would be ruled with an iron fist until Stalin's death on March 5, 1953.

Jozef Tiso. In August 1944, the Slovak National Uprising against the Tiso regime took place and German troops were sent to Slovakia to help quell the uprising. He remained in office during the German occupation, but merely in a puppet status. He lost power when the Red Army rolled into Slovakia in April 1945. Having fled to Bavaria, he was ultimately arrested by US Army personnel and extradited back to the newly reconstituted Czechoslovakia to stand trial in October 1945. Found guilty of treason he was executed in Bratislava on April 18, 1947.

Stefan Tiso. He would ultimately hold the positions of Slovak minister of justice, foreign minister, and prime minister before the end of the war. In 1944, he pressed for death sentences against leaders of the pro-Allied Slovak National Council. He also emphasized his desire to see a Final Solution in Slovakia, considering Jews to be "enemies of the state." In a post-war trial, he was given a life sentence and died in prison in 1959.

Ernst von Weizsäcker. Arrested and placed on trial as a war criminal by the Allies, he was sentenced to five years imprisonment by an American military tribunal at Nuremberg in 1949. He was released eighteen months later under a general amnesty. He died in 1951, shortly after his release from prison.

Karl Wolff. At war's end, Wolff assisted with the surrender of German forces in Italy (Operation Sunrise), going behind Hitler's back in negotiations with Allen Dulles, the Chief of the Office of Strategic Services (OSS) in Bern, Switzerland. For his service, he was not tried at Nuremberg, but instead appeared as a witness for the prosecution. In 1946, he was sentenced to four years of hard labor by a German court but served only one week before being released. He later became a highly successful advertising agent in Cologne. He died in 1984.

Wehrmacht and *Waffen-SS* Officer Ranks

Wehrmacht	*Waffen-SS*	US Equivalent
General	*SS-Gruppenführer*	Lieutenant General
Generalleutnant	*SS-Brigadeführer*	Major General
Generalmajor	*SS-Oberführer*	Brigadier General
Oberst	*SS-Standartenführer*	Colonel
Oberstleutnant	*SS-Obersturmbannführer*	Lieutenant Colonel
Major	*SS-Sturmbannführer*	Major
Hauptmann	*SS-Hauptsturmführer*	Captain
Oberleutnant	*SS-Obersturmführer*	First Lieutenant
Leutnant	*SS-Untersturmführer*	Second Lieutenant

Bibliography

Alibek, Kenneth. *Biohazard.* New York: Random House, 1999.

Andrew, Christopher and Oleg Gordievsky. *KGB: The Inside Story.* New York: Harper-Collins Publishers, 1990.

Annussek, Greg. *Hitler's Raid to Save Mussolini.* Cambridge, Massachusetts, 2005.

Bartulin, Nevenko. *"The Ideology of Nation and Race: The Croatian Ustashă Regime and Its Policies Toward Minorities in the Independent State of Croatia, 1941-1945."* Doctoral Dissertation, University of New South Wales, Australia, November, 2006.

Ben-Ghiat, Ruth. *Strongmen: Mussolini to the Present.* New York: W. W. Norton and Company, Inc., 2020.

Berezhkov, Valentin M. *At Stalin's Side.* New York: Birch Lane Press, 1994.

Bettina, Elizabeth. *It Happened in Italy.* Nashville, Tennessee: Thomas Nelson Publishers, 2009.

Botsch, Gideon, et al., *The Wannsee Conference and the Genocide of the European Jews: Catalogue of the Permanent Exhibition.* Berlin: Bonifatius GmbH, Druck-Buch-Verlag, 2009.

Blet, Pierre. *Pius XII and the Second World War According to the Archives of the Vatican.* New York: Paulist Press, 1997.

Blood, Philip W. *Hitler's Bandit Hunters: The SS and the Nazi Occupation of Europe.* Washington, D.C.: Potomac Books, Inc., 2006.

Boyar, Jane & Burt. *Hitler Stopped by Franco.* New York: Marabella House, 2001.

Bowan, Wayne. *"A Great Moral Victory: Spanish Protection of Jews on the Eastern Front, 1941-1944,"* in *Resisting the Holocaust,* Ruby Rohrlich (Ed.). New York: Berg Publishers, 2000.

Burns, James MacGregor. *Roosevelt: The Soldier of Freedom, 1940-1945.* New York: Harcourt, Brace, Jovanovich, Inc., 1970.

Carroll, James. *Constantine's' Sword: The Church and the Jews.* New York: Houghton Mifflin Company, 2001.

Ciszek, Walter J. *With God in Russia.* New York: McGraw-Hill Book Company, 1964.

Cornwell, John. *Hitler's Pope.* New York: Viking Press, 1999.

Coppa, Frank J. *The Papacy, the Jews, and the Holocaust.* Washington, DC: The Catholic University of America Press, 2006.

Dabrowski, John R. *The United States, NATO and the Spanish Bases, 1949-1989.* Ph.D. Dissertation. Kent State University, 1996.

de Blassio Wilhelm, Maria. *The Other Italy: The Italian Resistance in World War II.* New York: W.W. Norton & Company, 1988.

Deschner, Karlheinz. *God and the Fascists.* Amherst, New York: Prometheus Books, 2013.

de Zeng, Henry L. IV. *Luftwaffe Airfields 1935-45 (Czechoslovakia).* Available from http://www.ww2.dk/Airfields%20-%20Czechoslovakia.pdf.;Internet; accessed on September 25, 2020.

de Zeng, Henry L. IV. *Luftwaffe Airfields 1935-45 (Finland).* Available from http://www.ww2.dk/Airfields%20-%20Finland.pdf.; Internet; accessed on September 22, 2017.

de Zeng, Henry L. IV. *Luftwaffe Airfields, 1935-45 (Russia).* Available from http://www.ww2.dk/Airfields%20-%20Russia%20and%20Ukraine.pdf; Internet; accessed on September 23, 2020.

Dollmann, Eugen. *With Hitler and Mussolini: Memoirs of a Nazi Interpreter.* New York: Skyhorse Printing, 2017.

Eisner, Peter. *The Pope's Last Crusade.* New York: Harper Collins Publishers, 2013.

Erfurth, Waldemar. *Warfare in the Far North* (DA PAM 20-292). Washington, DC: US Government Printing Office, 1951.

Evans, Richard J. *The Third Reich at War*. New York: The Penguin Press, 2009.

Failmezger, Victor. *Rome City in Terror: The Nazi Occupation, 1943-44*. New York: Osprey Press, 2020.

Fermi, Laura. *Mussolini*. Chicago, Illinois: University of Chicago Press, 1961.

Friedlander, Saul. *Kurt Gerstein: The Ambiguity of Good*. New York: Knopf Publishers, 1969.

Friedlander, Saul. *"Pius XII and the Third Reich," Look,* Vol. 30, No. 10, 17 May 1966, pp. 36-50.

Glantz, David. *The Battle for Leningrad, 1941-44*. Lawrence, Kansas: University Press of Kansas, 2002.

Gallagher, J.P. *The Scarlet and the Black*. San Francisco, California: Ignatius Press, 2009.

Godman, Peter. *Hitler and the Vatican: Inside the Secret Archives that Reveal the New Story of the Nazis and the Church*. New York: The Free Press, 2004.

Goni, Uki. *The Real Odessa*. New York: Granta Books, 2002.

Graham, Robert. *The Vatican and Communism in World War II*. San Francisco, California: Ignatius Press, 1996.

Hatch, Alden. *A Man Called John: The Life of Pope John XXIII*. New York: Hawthorne Books, 1963.

Hayden, Mark. *German Military Chaplains in World War II*. Atglen, Pennsylvania: Schiffer Military History, 2005.

Joseph, Frank. *Military Encounters with Extraterrestrials: The Real War of the Worlds*. Rochester, Vermont: Bear & Company Press, 2018.

Katz, Robert. *The Battle for Rome: the Germans, the Allies, the Partisans, and the Pope*. New York: Simon & Schuster Publishers, 2003.

Klee, Ernst, Willi Dressen, and Volker Riess (Eds). *The Good Old Days: The Holocaust as Seen by Its Perpetrators and Bystanders.* New York: Free Press, 1988.

Kleinfeld, Gerald R. and Lewis A. Tambs. *Hitler's Spanish Legion: The Blue Division in Russia.* Carbondale, Illinois: Southern University Illinois Press, 1979.

Kranzler, David. *Thy Brother's Blood: The Orthodox Jewish Response During the Holocaust.* New York: Mesorah Publications, Ltd., 1987.

Kross, Jaan. *The Conspiracy & Other Stories.* London: The Harvill Press, 1995.

Kurzman, Dan. *A Special Mission: Hitler's Secret Plot to Seize the Vatican and Kidnap Pope Pius XII.* Cambridge, Massachusetts: Da Capo Press, 2007.

Lester, Elenore. *Wallenberg: The Man in the Iron Web.* Englewood, New Jersey: Prentice-Hall Publishers, 1982.

Lunde, Henrik O. *Finland's War of Choice: The Troubled German-Finnish Coalition in WWII.* Philadelphia, Pennsylvania: Casemate Publishers, 2011.

MacLean, French L. *The Cruel Hunters: SS-Sonderkommando Dirlewanger, Hitler's Most Notorious Anti-Partisan Unit.* Atglen, Pennsylvania: Schiffer Publishers, 1998.

MacLean, French L. *2000 Quotes from Hitler's 1000-Year Reich.* Atglen, Pennsylvania: Schiffer Military History, 2006.

McKale, Donald M. *Nazis After Hitler.* New York: Rowman and Littlefield Publishers, Inc. 2012.

Megargee, Geoffrey P. (Editor). *Encyclopedia of Camps and Ghettos, 1933-1945, Volume I.* Bloomington, Indiana: Indiana University Press, 2009.

Moorhouse, Roger. *Berlin at War.* New York: Basic Books, 2010.

Morris, Charles R. *American Catholic.* New York: Times Books, 1997.

Ohler, Norman. *Blitzed: Drugs in the Third Reich.* Boston: Houghton Mifflin Hartcourt Publishers, 2017.

Padfield, Peter. *Himmler.* New York: Harry Holt & Company, 1990.

Parisella, Antonio (ed.) *The Museum Narrates: The Liberation of Rome from the Nazi Occupation.* Rome, Italy: Gangemi Editore International, 2000.

Petrosillo, Orazio. *Vatican City.* Rome, Italy: Edizioni Musei Vaticani, 1997.

Preston, Paul. *Franco.* New York: Basic Books, 1994.

Ready, J. Lee. *The Forgotten Axis: Germany's Partners and Foreign Volunteers in World War II.* Jefferson, North Carolina: McFarland & Company, Inc., 1987.

Rees, Laurence. *Auschwitz, A New History.* New York: MJF Books, 2005.

Reid, Anna. *Leningrad: The Epic Siege of World War II, 1941-1944.* New York: Walker & Company, 2011.

Riebling, Mark. *Church of Spies: The Pope's Secret War Against Hitler.* New York: Basic Books, 2015.

Rigg, Bryan Mark. *Hitler's Jewish Soldiers: The Untold Story of Nazi Racial Laws and Men of Jewish Descent in the German Military.* Lawrence, Kansas: University of Kansas Press, 2002.

Rigg, Bryan Mark. *The Rabbi Saved by Hitler's Soldiers.* Lawrence, Kansas: University of Kansas Press, 2016.

Rubenstein, Joshua. *The Last Days of Stalin.* New Haven, Connecticut: Yale University Press, 2016.

Rychlak, Ronald J. *Hitler, the War, and the Pope.* Huntington, Indiana: Our Sunday Visitor, 2000.

Salisbury, Harrison E. *The 900 Days: The Siege of Leningrad.* New York: Harper & Row, Publishers, 1969.

Scurr, John. *Germany's Spanish Volunteers 1941-45.* London: Osprey Publishing, 1980.

Trevor-Roper, Hugh (editor). *Hitler's Table Talk, 1941-44*. New York: Enigma Books, 2000.

Vaksberg, Arkady. *Stalin Against the Jews*. New York: Alfred A. Knopf, 1994.

Waller, John H. *The Devil's Doctor: Felix Kerstin and the Secret Plot to Turn Himmler Against Hitler*. New York: John Wiley & Sons, 2002.

Ward, James Mace. *Priest, Politician, Collaborator: Josef Tiso and the Making of Fascist Slovakia*. New York: Cornell University Press, 2013.

Weinberg, Gerhard L. *Visions of Victory: The Hopes of Eight World War II Leaders*. New York: Cambridge University Press, 2005.

Wistrich, Robert. *Who's Who in Nazi Germany*. New York: Macmillan Publishing Company, 1982.

Wolf, Hubert. *Pope and Devil*. Cambridge, Massachusetts: The Belknap Press of Harvard University Press, 2010.

Yahil, Leni. *The Holocaust: The Fate of European Jewry*. New York: Oxford University Press, 1990.

About the Author

John R. Dabrowski is the retired Chief Historian for the Department of Defense's Missile Defense Agency, Redstone Arsenal, in Huntsville, Alabama. He is also a retired US Army Reserve Colonel with 33 years' service. He holds both undergraduate and graduate degrees in History from East Stroudsburg University, East Stroudsburg, Pennsylvania, and a doctorate in History from Kent State University, Kent, Ohio. He is a graduate of both the US Army and US Air War Colleges and additionally holds a Master of Strategic Studies degree awarded by the US Army War College, Carlisle Barracks, Pennsylvania. He is a former adjunct instructor of American History at Northwest Florida State College as well as a current 4th Degree Knight of Columbus and member of the American Legion. He and his wife Mary are the proud parents of Keith and Christina, and they make their home in Navarre, Florida. His previous novel, *To Sup with the Devil* was published in 2011 by Word Association Press. This is his second novel.

Look for more books from Winged Hussar Publishing, LLC – E-books, paperbacks and Limited-Edition hardcovers. The best in history, science fiction and fantasy at:

https://www. wingedhussarpublishing.com

https://www.whpsupplyroom.com

or follow us on Facebook at:

Winged Hussar Publishing LLC

Or on twitter at:

WingHusPubLLC

For information and upcoming publications

Endnotes

[1] Tardini, since 1937 had filled the post of Secretary of the Congregation for Extraordinary Ecclesiastical Affairs and the first section of the Secretariat of State. Tardini also had links with several departments within the Holy See to include the Commission for Russia. See Peter Godman, *Hitler and the Vatican: Inside the Secret Archives that Reveal the New Story of the Nazis and the Church* (NY: The Free Press, 2004), p. 95. Monsignor Giovanni Battista Montini, the future Pope Paul VI (1963-78), oversaw the second section of the Secretariat of State. It was announced in June 2014 that Paul VI was to be beatified on October 19, 2014, thus taking him a step closer to sainthood in the Roman Catholic Church. See Edward Pentin, "Pope Paul VI to be Beatified October 19," *National Catholic Register*, June 1-14, 2014, p. 5.

[2] The Vatican Secretary of State was Cardinal Luigi Maglione until his death in 1944.

[3] *Norodny Komissariat Vnutrennikh Del*, or People's Commissariat for Internal Affairs.

[4] The Concordat of 1933 between the Holy See and the Third Reich ensured that Catholic Chaplains would be represented within the German armed forces. Article 27 of the Concordat gave the Nazis influence over the nomination of the Catholic army bishops and the Catholic military clergy. See Karlheinz Deschner, *God and the Fascists* (Amherst, NY: Prometheus Books, 2013), p. 99. The first report the Vatican received of the genocide of Jews came from Monsignor Giuseppe Burzio, the Charge d' affairs in Slovakia, who alerted the Pope on October 27, 1941. Drawing upon the information supplied by Catholic chaplains attached to the Slovakian army units supporting the Germans on the Eastern Front, Burzio described the horrors of the first stage of the Holocaust. Additionally, the military chaplain stationed with Italian troops in the East, Father Pirro Scavizzi, personally informed the Pope that the elimination of Jews through mass murder was almost total. See Cappo, *The Papacy, the Jews, and the Holocaust,* pp. 193, 200.

[5] On March 19, 1936, Pope Pius XI condemned "atheistic communism" in his encyclical entitled *Dilectissima nobis.* See Godman, *Hitler and the Vatican*, p. 96.

[6] Two of the more famous were the *Spartacists* leaders Karl Liebknecht and Rosa Luxembourg, who upon capture, were shot and then thrown into the Berlin's Landwehr Canal.

[7] The Independent State of Croatia was a Nazi puppet state formed in 1941 after the defeat of Yugoslavia. The head of state was Ante Pavelic, known as the *Poglavnik* (Leader). Under his leadership, Croatia and the *Ustashă*, committed unspeakable crimes until the end of the war. Pavelic escaped justice by fleeing to South America in 1945 and later to Spain where he died in 1958 under the full protection of the Franco regime.

[8] For more on the *Ustashă* regime and Jasenovac see Nevenko Bartulin, "The Ideology of Nation and Race: the Croatian *Ustashă* Regime and Its Policies Toward Minorities in the Independent State of Croatia, 1941-1945," Doctoral Dissertation, University of New South Wales, Australia, November 2006.

[9] One such visitor, *SS Brigadeführer und Generalmajor der Waffen SS* Ernst Fick, Inspector for Ideological Education, wrote in 1944 to his superiors in Berlin that the *Ustashă* had killed between 600,000 to 700,000 concentration camp inmates "the Balkan way," implying they were killed by extreme brutality and cruelty. See Andrew Borowiec, "Croatian-run Death Site Remains Dark Secret," *The Washington Times*, July 5, 1994, p. A10. See also Deschner, *Gods*

and Fascists, pp. 198-199.

[10] The Finn's referred to the period of hostilities with the USSR from 1941-44 as the "Continuation War." In a bizarre twist of fate, some Finnish soldiers of the Jewish faith were fighting alongside their German allies against the Soviets. Additionally, within the German armed forces, a number of partial Jews served within the *Wehrmacht* and were given what was known in the Berlin vernacular as a "Persil certificate," Persil being Germany's leading laundry detergent at the time, which would then "cleanse" them of their Jewishness. For a thorough investigation into Jews serving in the *Wehrmacht* see Bryan Mark Rigg, *Hitler's Jewish Soldiers* (Lawrence, KS: The University Press of Kansas, 2002). Rigg came across documents from the *Wehrmacht's* personnel office dated 1944 that referred to 77 high-ranking officers of mixed Jewish race or married to a Jew. Rigg's research suggested that the number of Jews serving in the *Wehrmacht* had been previously underestimated.

[11] Later Pope John XXIII (1958-63).

[12]This is the actual response Roncalli gave to von Papen. See Alden Hatch, *A Man Called John: The Life of Pope John XXIII* (NY: Hawthorn Books, Inc., 1963), p. 116.

[13]Years after the war, during the beatification process for Pope John XXIII, it was learned that the money Roncalli, then nuncio to Turkey, used to purchase freedom for Jewish refugees, had come from Von Papen himself. See James Carroll, *Constantine's Sword: The Church and the Jews* (NY: Houghton Mifflin Company, 2001), pp. 685, fn. 24.

[14] The attack occurred on February 24, 1942 in Ankara, Turkey. The assassination attempt was carried out by a young Macedonian in the employ of the Soviet NKVD. The attacker shot at von Papen and his wife, and missed, and then the bomb he was preparing to throw prematurely detonated, killing the attacker instantly.

[15] James MacGregor Burns, *Roosevelt: The Soldier of Freedom, 1940-1945* (NY: Harcourt Brace Jovanovich, Inc., 1970), p. 152; Pierre Blet, S.J., *Pius XII and the Second World War: According to the Archives of the Vatican* (NY: Paulist Press, 1999), p. 124.

[16]Blet, *Pius XII and the Second World War*, p. 134.

[17] In response to FDR's assurances that the churches were open in the USSR, the Vatican released a list of papal representatives who were in Soviet prisons or who had disappeared in Russia. A follow-up US request that the Soviets release jailed clergy was ignored. See Charles R. Morris, *American Catholic* (NY: Times Books, 1997), p. 240.

[18] *Ibid*, p. 126.

[19] German word for "Baron."

[20] Von Weizsäcker, a Catholic, was an old acquaintance of Pius XII. Upon his accreditation to the Vatican in 1943, the papal limousine that took him to his audience with the Pope flew both the papal flag and the swastika side-by-side. Morris, *American Catholic,* p. 240.

[21] This was known as "Operation Pontiff" and was first drawn up by Martin Bormann in 1940 but was shelved until a more suitable time. See Dan Kurzman, *A Special Mission: Hitler's Secret Plan to Seize the Vatican and Kidnap Pope Pius XII* (Cambridge, MA: DaCapo Press, 2007), pp. 59, 70, 74. In 1943, the original plan was updated and renamed "Operation Rabat-Fohr." The basic nature of the plan was to have men of the 8th SS Division Florian Geyer, disguised as Italians, to enter the Vatican and seize the Pope after killing all the members of the Curia. Then,

troops from the Hermann Goring panzer division would surge into the Vatican to "rescue" the pontiff and kill the disguised SS men, thinking they were Italian assassins rather than SS compatriots. Thus, no witnesses. If the Pope tried to escape, he too would be shot. The motive for this operation seems to have been the concerns in the Nazi leadership about the Pope's perceived pro-Allied stance and also his lack of antagonism towards the Jews. See Ibid. pp. 116-117.

[22] Von Weizsacker's other son, Richard von Weizsäcker, would survive the war and later served as the President of the Federal Republic of Germany, 1984-1994. He died on 31 January 2015, aged 94.

[23] Von Weizsäcker had been made an honorary colonel in the SS in April 1938 at the insistence of his boss, German Foreign Minister von Ribbentrop, even though he felt no loyalty to the SS whatsoever. See John Weitz, *Hitler's Diplomat: The Life and Times of Joachim von Ribbentrop* (NY: Ticknor & Fields Publishers, 1992), p. 194.

[24] Sweden's national currency.

[25] Related to the Swedish royal family and descendant of one of Napoleon's Marshals who worked with the Holy See to save Jewish people in Europe.

[26] Hans Lehmann was a successful Swedish merchant who was a strong supporter and spokesman for the Orthodox Jews living in Sweden. During the war, he was instrumental in arranging safe haven in Sweden for Jews fleeing Nazi-occupied Europe. See David Kranzler, *Thy Brother's Blood: The Orthodox Jewish Response During the Holocaust* (NY: Mesorah Publications, Ltd., 1987), pp. 220-221.

[27] Dr. Felix Kersten was a Finnish citizen of Baltic German origin, and who, during the war, was Himmler's attending masseuse and physical therapist, the only man who could ease Himmler's debilitating stomach pain. Toward the war's end, Kersten had gained a great deal of influence with the *Reichsführer SS* and manipulated him into negotiating the release of Scandinavian Jews held in concentration camps to the Swedish Red Cross in the closing days of the war. Himmler also used Kersten as an aide who proved useful as a go-between with representatives of the Western Allies via neutral Sweden. Kersten has been hailed by many as one of the unsung heroes of the Second World War. See John H. Waller, *The Devil's Doctor: Felix Kersten and the Secret Plot to Turn Himmler Against Hitler* (NY: John Wiley & Sons, Inc., 2002).

[28] Abram Hewitt was assigned to the Office of Strategic Services (OSS) in Stockholm, Sweden, under the cover as a representative of the US Commercial Company and had met Jacob Wallenberg in 1932 while in Stockholm representing a trustee in the bankruptcy of the International Match Corporation. While reorganizing the company, the Wallenberg's had assumed control of the Swedish Match Corporation and its international subsidiaries. See Waller, *The Devil's Doctor*, pp. 141-144.

[29] This is a true account of what had transpired on August 20, 1942, when Gerstein shared a train compartment with von Otter on a trip from Warsaw to Berlin and related to him the mass executions, he had witnessed only days earlier at Belzec concentration camp in Poland. He asked von Otter, as a neutral, to transmit this information to the Swedish Foreign Office, which it was, but it went no further, and was not passed on to the Allies. Gerstein survived the war and surrendered to French authorities in May 1945. While incarcerated, he wrote what came to be known as the "Gerstein Report," in which he recounted his experience at Belzec and his conversation with von Otter on the train. Gerstein "named names" of some of the perpetrators to such an extent that his report was used as evidence by Allied prosecutors at Nuremberg. Gerstein committed suicide on 25 July 1945, probably as a result of overwhelming remorse

and guilt. For the full "Gerstein Report" see http://www.deathcamps.org/belzec/gerstein.html. See also Saul Friedlander, *Kurt Gerstein: The Ambiguity of Good* (NY: Knopf, 1969); see also Elenore Lester, *Wallenberg: The Man in the Iron Web* (New Jersey: Prentice-Hall Publishers, 1982), pp. 51-52. Another account of the Nazi systematic annihilation of European Jewry came from a Swedish colony in German-occupied Warsaw. One of the Swedes living in this colony, Sven Norrman, secretly shot a film of atrocities taking place and the film was smuggled out to Sweden. See Lester, *Wallenberg*, p. 51.

[30] In October 1943, Sweden gave asylum to nearly 8,000 Danish Jews in one of the most dramatic rescue operations of Jews during the Holocaust.

[31] Speech by Heinrich Himmler to SS Leaders in Posen, Poland, October 4, 1943. See https://www.facinghistory.org/holocaust-human-Himmler-speech-Posen-1943.

[32] Ibid.

[33] For Fuhrer and Victory!

[34] The SS officer training school in southern Germany.

[35] SS *Brigadeführer* Erich von dem Bach-Zelewski was Himmler's chief of anti-Partisan warfare on the Eastern Front. He would be given overall responsibility for quelling the Warsaw Uprising of 1944.

[36] Bach-Zelewski became psychologically ill as a result of the *Einsatzgruppen* actions on the Eastern Front; he experienced "visions" of the killings in which he had participated. See Laurence Rees, *Auschwitz, A New History* (NY: MJF Books, 2005), p. 52. Himmler sent an SS physician by the name of Ernst Grawitz to tend to Bach-Zelewski. In a report written in March 1942, Grawitz stated that Bach-Zelewski suffered especially from "reliving the shooting of Jews that he himself had conducted and other difficult experiences in the East." See Donald M. McKale, *Nazis After Hitler* (NY: Rowan and Littlefield Publishers, Inc., 2012), p. 27. See also Philip W. Blood, *Hitler's Bandit Hunters: The SS and the Nazi Occupation of Europe* (Washington, D.C: Potomac Books, Inc., 2006), pp. 68-70. Himmler himself suffered from severe stomach cramps which only increased in frequency as the war progressed and German military reversals mounted. His cramps were only soothed by his personal Finnish masseuse, Dr. Felix Kerstin. See John H. Waller, *The Devil's Doctor: Felix Kerstin and the Secret Plot to Turn Himmler Against Hitler* (NY: John Wiley & Sons, 2002). Many members of the *Einsatzgruppen* themselves succumbed to nervous breakdowns during their murderous killing sprees in the East. One example was SS *Standartenfuhrer* Paul Blobel, who would go on to command *Kommando 1005*. Blobel suffered a nervous breakdown in the Summer of 1941 according to a SS man who served with Blobel in *Sonderkommando 4a*. According to the testimony of *SS-Obersturmfuhrer* August Hafner, Blobel "Had completely lost his mind. He was threatening to shoot *Wehrmacht* officers with his pistol. It was clear to me that he had cracked up..." Blobel was taken to a hospital in Lublin which was known as a 'loony bin" by the troops in order to recuperate. See Ernest Klee, Willi Dressen, and Volker Riess (Eds.) *The Good Old Days: The Holocaust as Seen by Its Perpetrators and Bystanders* (NY: The Free Press, 1988), pp 111-112.

[37] Unlike Hitler, Mussolini had a working knowledge of the English language. There exists newsreel footage of Mussolini, filmed by Fox Movietonews news in the late 1920s, of *Il Duce* addressing his English-speaking viewers; while his English is heavily accented it is quite understandable.

[38] Italian Expeditionary Corps in Russia or CSIR.

[39] In the immediate aftermath of Mussolini's overthrow, the new government of Marshal Pietro Badoglio outwardly professed friendship with Germany and that it would continue to fight alongside its German allies announcing on Italian radio that '*la guerra continua.*' However, secretly, Badoglio dispatched emissaries to open talks with the Allies with regards to a separate Italian surrender. For the immediate future, Italian military units still functioned independently in the Balkans, the Dodecanese Islands, and other areas, to include a small contingent of Italian airmen in Odessa, Russia. These units ultimately would be forcibly disarmed by the Germans once Hitler found out about the Italian duplicity taken behind his back. In some instances, the Italian units resisted their one-time allies. *Unternehmen Achse* (Operation Axis) was launched by the Germans from September 8-19, 1943, to disarm Italian military units (approximately 60 divisions) still in the field. On the Greek island of Cephalonia, the Italian 33rd Division ("Acqui") put up stiff resistance until they were overwhelmed and surrendered. Most of their officers were then executed by the Germans, while the enlisted men were sent to labor camps in Germany. The fate of the Italian garrison on Cephalonia was the subject of the novel, *Captain Corelli's Mandolin* (1994) written by Louis de Bernieres and later made into a movie of the same name starring actor Nicholas Cage in 2001.

Upon his dismissal as Prime Minister, Mussolini was shunted around to various locations by the Badoglio government until he was ultimately secured at the Hotel Campo Imperatore on the Gran Sasso high in the Apennine Mountains. The Germans ultimately located Mussolini and in a daring raid that stunned the Allies, Mussolini was rescued in a glider-borne attack carried out by elements of the German *Fallschirmjager* and SS on September 12, 1943, in 'Operation Oak.' Mussolini was then installed in Saló, northern Italy to rule the Italian Socialist Republic for the next 20 months (1943-45), as nothing more than a German puppet.

[40] Laura Fermi, *Mussolini* (Chicago: University of Chicago Press, 1961), p. 431. The exchange quoted between Mussolini and the king is according to Marshal Badoglio, though not present, was informed of the exchange by the king himself.

[41] Elite paramilitary gendarme unit used in Italy to the present day.

[42] Cited in Ruth Ben-Ghiat, *Strongmen: Mussolini to the Present* (NY: W.W. Norton and Company, Inc., 2020), p. 225.

[43] One such known spy was Estonian Alexander Kurtna, a former seminarian, who after quitting his studies in Rome, took a position with the Vatican Archives as a researcher. See Victor Failmezger, *Rome, City in Terror: The Nazi Occupation 1943-44* (NY: Osprey Publishing, 2020), p. 151.

[44] According to at least one historian, the paranoid Stalin was obsessed with plots against him orchestrated by the Vatican. See Christopher Andrew and Oleg Gordievsky, *KGB: The Inside Story* (NY: Harper-Collins Publishers, 1990), p. 339.

[45]In February 1926, Pope Pius XI had summoned Jesuit bishop Michel d' Herbigny to establish a clandestine church hierarchy in Moscow. Subsequently, in June 1926, he created a new Vatican Commission for Russia to deal with Soviet affairs and was headed by d' Herbigny. See Coppa, *The Papacy, the Jews and the Holocaust*, p. 168. Relations between the Vatican and the USSR had been broken since 1929. In 1930, Pope Pius XI had sponsored a "Crusade of prayer" against the "Russian persecutors of religion." The Soviet government-sponsored newspaper, *Izvestia*, responded in a February 18, 1930 article that "the Pope assumes the role of leader in the struggle against the Soviet Union assigned to him by world capitalism." See Godman, *Hitler and the Vatican*, p. 99.

[46] This statement made by Stalin has had many claimed origins—some sources say he asked the

question of Winston Churchill in October 1944; other sources have Stalin asking the question to Eisenhower in 1945. For one such source, see Valentin M. Berezhkov, *At Stalin's Side* (NY: Birch Lane Press, 1994), p. 310. It is ironic to note that years later, on February 21, 1953, the American Bishop, Fulton J. Sheen, predicted Stalin's death during a broadcast of his very popular television program, *Life is Worth Living.* During the program, Sheen wove an elaborate comparison using the words of Shakespeare's *Julius Caesar* to condemn the leaders of the Soviet Union. Sheen delivered Marc Antony's famous speech replacing the Romans with those of high Soviet officials. In place of Caesar, Sheen named Stalin. At the climax of the soliloquy, Sheen stated, "Stalin must one day meet his judgement." Within two weeks of the broadcast, Stalin was dead after suffering a massive stroke. It appeared to all that had watched the broadcast in February that Sheen had all but called down the wrath of God on the Soviet dictator. At Stalin's death, the Vatican called upon Catholics to pray for Stalin's soul. "He has arrived at the end of his life and must account to the Almighty for his actions." See Joshua Rubenstein, *The Last Days of Stalin*, (New Haven, Conn: Yale University Press, 2016), p. 122.

[47] Father Walter Ciszek (1904-1984) was born in Shenandoah, Pennsylvania to Polish immigrant parents and joined the Jesuits in 1928. In response to Pope Pius XI's appeal for missionaries to Russia, he was assigned to Poland. In 1941, he entered Russia using false papers and was later arrested by the NKVD in June 1941 and accused of being a spy. He spent five years in Lubyanka prison and later sentenced to 15 years in the Gulag. He later returned to the United States in a prisoner exchange negotiated in 1963. See Walter J. Ciszek, *With God in Russia* (NY: McGraw-Hill Book Company, 1964) and "Catholic Man of the Month: Father Walter Ciszek," *Columbia* (Vol 92, No. 12), December 2012, p. 5; Graham, *The Vatican and Communism*, p. 133. In 1924, the year of Lenin's death, there were 200 Catholic priests in the USSR; by 1938, there were only two. See Coppa, *The Papacy, the Jews, and the Holocaust*, p. 177. According to German author Karlheinz Deschner, a special seminar in Rome called the *Collegium Russicum* was set up to teach clergy Russian, Ukrainian, and other Slavic languages in order to prepare them for missionary activities inside the USSR. In 1940, Jesuit graduates from the *Collegium Russicum* crossed into the Soviet Union in disguise and using false names in order to, according to Deschner, "to spy for the Vatican." These clergy were especially active in the Ukraine. See Deschner, *God and the Fascists*, p. 177.

[48]Ciszek, *With God in Russia*, p. 74.

[49] Archbishop Jan Cieplak was the highest-ranking Catholic clergyman in the Soviet Union when that nation was formed in 1917. He was harassed by the Communist authorities for resisting the nationalization of church properties. In a 1923 show trial, he was sentenced to death for creating a "counter-revolutionary organization." Pressure from the West eventually forced the Soviets to commute the sentence to a ten-year prison term. After just one year in prison, he was abruptly released and sent to Poland where he received a hero's welcome. He later left for a tour of America and died in 1926 in New Jersey. See "Catholic Man of the Month: Archbishop Jan Cieplak, *Columbia* (Vol. 94, No. 2), February 2014, p. 5.

50 One of the most notable successes of infiltrating a Partisan disguised as a maid occurred in September 1943, when a female Soviet Partisan, Elena Mazanik, successfully carried out the assassination of the *Generalkommissar* of White Russia (Belarus), Wilhelm Kube in an operation code-named 'Blow-up.' Mazanik was employed as a maid at Kube's house in Minsk and hid a time bomb in his mattress. The bomb exploded killing both Kube and his wife. Mazanik survived the war and was awarded the USSR's highest military award, Hero of the Soviet Union.

[51] Ethnic Germans or people claiming German origin living outside of Germany proper. *Volks-*

deutsche were found in Poland, Hungary, Romania, the Baltic States and Russia.

[52] *Kriminalpolizei* or *Kripo* for short.

[53] In German, literally "By your orders."

[54] Initials for the *Nazionalsocialist Deutsches Arbeit Partie*, National Socialist German Workers Party or Nazis for short.

[55] A *Schnellboot* is a German version of a US Navy PT boat.

[56] Terijoki was the first town to be captured by the Red Army in 1939 during the Winter War with Finland. It would be the seat of the short-lived and communist Finnish Democratic Republic. It was merged in 1940 with the Karelin SSR to form a Soviet Republic after Finland had ceded the area to the USSR in the Moscow Peace Treaty of March 1940. The town would be recaptured by the Finns during the Continuation War with the Soviet Union from 1941-44.

[57] Most of these individuals were considered "*Mischling*" (half-caste) and were either half-Jews or quarter-Jews as prescribed by the Nurenberg Laws of 1935. Many *Mischlings* sought to obtain legal waivers or *Genehmingungs*, granted by the Nazi leadership, which was a toleration of their status because of their service to the Reich. The most sought-after legal solution to *Mischling* disqualification was for a legal review and determination of pure blood, racially untainted with Jewish blood, the so-called *Deutschblutigkietserkarung*. Hitler reviewed each one of these requests personally, and if approved, the formerly classified *Mischlings* were cleared of any Jewish taint. See Bryan Mark Rigg, *Hitler's Jewish Soldiers: The Untold Story of Nazi Racial Laws and Men of Jewish Descent in the German Military* (Lawrence, KS: University of Kansas Press, 2002).

[58] Pius XII was fluent in German, having served as the Papal Nuncio to Germany from 1917-1930.

[59] One of Stalin's greatest fears was that the Western Allies would arrive at a separate peace with Germany which would then allow Germany to focus its attention solely on the Eastern Front, perhaps with assistance from the West. According to historian Gerhard Weinberg, Stalin was prepared to consider renewed negotiations with the Germans at various points during the war, from late 1941 to the summer of 1944. One rumor abounded that on May 17, 1943, Ribbentrop and Molotov met behind the German lines at Kirovograd to discuss peace negotiations, but to no avail. See Gerhard L. Weinberg, *Visions of Victory: The Hopes of Eight World War II Leaders* (NY: Cambridge University Press, 2005), p. 108 and Vojtech Mastny, "Stalin and the Prospects of a Separate Peace in World War II" *American Historical Review*, 77 (1972), pp. 365-88.

[60] In Russian, "To your health."

[61] Derogatory Russian term for Jew ('Yid').

[62] This would ultimately be the Russian Liberation Army (ROA) which was formed in early 1945, too late to have any major impact in the war in the East. Vlaslov would later be executed for treason by the USSR. For more on this subject see Jurgen Thorwald, *The Illusion: Soviet Soldiers in Hitler's Armies* (NY: Harcourt Brace Jovanovich, 1975).

[63] An Orthodox Jewish college or seminary. Prior to the Second World War, Eastern Europe and the Baltic States were homes to some of the great centers of Jewish learning. Most were lost during the war.

[64] The *Wehrmacht* security divisions were set up at the beginning of 1941 were intended to perform policing, security and counter-insurgency duties in the rear of the main German field armies. There were approximately seven of these divisions in action, mainly in the East. Most were made up of overaged personnel and not as effective as frontline divisions.

[65] On June 6, 1941, just weeks prior to the invasion of the USSR in Operation Barbarossa, Hitler issued the notorious *Kommissarbefehl* (Commissar Order) by which Soviet commissars that were captured by the Germans were to be summarily executed as a purported enforcer of the "Judeo-Bolshevik" ideology in the Soviet armed forces..

[66] The Blue Division or *"Division Azul"* in Spanish, received its name from the blue tunics many of the Spanish Falangists wore as part of their uniform. Once in German service, they were given *Wehrmacht* field gray uniforms and wore an arm shield marked "España" to denote they were from Spain. For an in-depth history of the Blue Division see John Scurr, *Germany's Spanish Volunteers, 1941-45* (London: Osprey Publishers, 1980) and Gerald R. Kleinfeld and Lewis A. Tambs, *Hitler's Spanish Legion: The Blue Division in Russia* (Carbondale, Ill: Southern Illinois University Press, 1979).

[67] Twenty-four members of the Spanish Army's Ecclesiastical Corps volunteered for the Blue Division in 1941. Afterwards, there were many Catholic chaplains assigned to the division. See Mark Hayden, *German Military Chaplains in World War II* (Atglen, PA: Schiffer Military History, 2005), p. 123.

[68] These tensions were not just limited to Germany's allies but also existed between the SS and *Wehrmacht* as well. One little-known recorded incident took place on July 26, 1942, in Przemysl, Poland, when a SS commando unit attempting to enter the Jewish ghetto in order to carry out a liquidation action, found itself blocked by a German Army unit commanded by Lieutenant Albert Battel who threatened to open fire on the SS if they did not withdraw, which they did. Battel had the backing of his immediate superior, Major Max Liedtke. Later in the day, some 100 of the ghetto occupants were evacuated by the army and given protection at the local army barracks. This incident reached *Reichsführer SS* Himmler, who vowed to have Battel expelled from the Nazi party and arrested immediately after the war was over. This threat was never carried out and Battel survived the war and died in 1952. In 1981, Israel recognized Battel as the "Righteous Among the Nations." See Wikipedia entry, "Albert Battel," http://en.wikipedia.org/wiki/Albet_Battel, accessed on 12 June 2013; Dr. Gideon Botsch, et. al., *The Wannsee Conference and the Genocide of the European Jews: Catalogue of the Permanent Exhibition* (Berlin: Bonifatius GmbH, Druck-Buch-Verlag, 2009), pp. 126, 131; Wayne Bowan, "A Great Moral Victory: Spanish Protection of Jews on the Eastern Front, 1941-1944," in *Resisting the Holocaust*, Ruby Rohrlich (Ed.), (NY: Berg Publishers, 2000), pp. 195-211.

[69] In the latter stages of the war, Spanish envoys, particularly in Budapest, Hungary, saved a number of Jews by issuing to them Spanish passports, thus saving them from deportation and almost certain death at the hands of the Nazis. In 1978, three years after Franco's death, *The American Sephardi*, the Journal of Sephardic Studies of the Yeshiva University, wrote that "However general history may judge him, in Jewish history he [Franco] shall certainly occupy a special place...Putting to one side any other considerations, Jews should honor and bless the memory of this great benefactor of the Jewish people who neither sought nor reaped any profit in what he did." Cited in Jane & Burt Boyar, *Hitler Stopped by Franco* (NY: Marabella House, 2001), pp. 314-317. In 2010, it came to light that Franco had in fact drawn up a list of some 6,000 Jews then living in Spain in order to turn them over to the Germans if the occasion had arisen. The order was signed by Franco's head of security, Jose Finat Escriva de Romani, Count of Mayalde. He personally handed over the list to Heinrich Himmler when he was ap-

pointed Spanish ambassador to Germany. This revelation runs contrary to popular opinion that Franco protected Jews from the Holocaust, showing that he was prepared to send them to Nazi Germany for extermination. See Edward Owen, "Franco Drew Up List of 6,000 Jews in Spain for Hitler," *The Daily Telegraph*, 21 June 2010, http://www.telegraph.co.uk/history/world-war-two/7841759/Franco-drew-up-list-of-6000. Accessed on 24 November 2014.

[70] The scene of very heavy fighting from February 10-13, 1943 between the Spaniards and the Red Army. The Blue Division's tenacious defense thwarted the Soviet 55th Army's plans to break the blockade of Leningrad. The Spaniards suffered approximately a 75% casualty rate (some 3600 men) during this battle, while inflicting well over 10,000 casualties on the Soviets.

[71] One author, Dr. Kenneth Alibek, claims that the Red Army used tularemia as a biological weapon during the battle of Stalingrad (1942-43) that caused a widespread epidemic that killed thousands on both sides. See Kenneth Alibek, *Biohazard* (NY: Random House, 1999).

[72] *Oberkommando der Wehrmacht*, or High Command of the German Armed Forces.

[73] Hitler praised the Blue Division, referring to it as "equal to the best German ones," and that ". . .the Spaniards have never yielded an inch of ground. One can't imagine more fearless fellows. They scarcely take cover. They flout death. I know, in any case that our men are always glad to have Spaniards as neighbors in their sector." Quoted in *Hitler's Table Talk*, pp. 179-180; additionally, Hitler praised the Spaniards stating that "the Spanish soldiers stood next to our Finnish allies on the first rank of all our allies on the Eastern Front..." See Kleinfeld and Tambs, *Hitler's Spanish Legion*, p. 228.

[74] Major General Emilio Esteban-Infantes became the Blue Division commander upon Major General Muñoz-Grandes return to Spain in December 1942. He led the division until December 1943 when the division was recalled to Spain on orders from Franco. Like his predecessor, Muñoz-Grandes, Esteban-Infantes was awarded the Knight's Cross for his service to Germany.

[75] This UFO incident was in fact reported by hundreds of men assigned to the division in February 1943 and remains a mystery to this day. See Frank Joseph, *Military Encounters with Extraterrestrials: The Real War of the Worlds* (Rochester, VT: Bear & Company, 2018), pp. 66-67.

[76] Deschner states that "on November 8, 1941, the OKW instructed all commanders-in-chief of the German armies in the East to facilitate the missionary activities of the Catholic priests in the occupied territories... [by taking into consideration] the agreements with the Vatican. See Deschner, *God and the Fascists*, p. 178.

[77] Assigned to the Spanish division was a fighter squadron, known as the "Blue Squadron" (*Escuadrilla Azul*) it was equipped with the Me-109 and Fw-190 aircraft.

[78] See Henry L. de Zeng IV, "*Luftwaffe Airfields, 1935-45, Finland*, "available from http://www.ww2.dk/Airfields%20-%20Finland.pdf; Internet; accessed on 22 September 2017.

[79] Anti-aircraft gun, from the German FLUGABWEHRKANONE.

[80] Officer in Charge.

[81] Noncommissioned officer-in-charge.

[82] Nazi party district leaders. For example, Josef Goebbels, besides being Propaganda Minister, was also *Gauleiter* of Berlin.

[83] Cited in John Cornwell, *Hitler's Pope* (NY: Viking Press, 1999), p. 313.

[84] *SS Obergruppenführer* Reinhard Heydrich, the notorious "Hangman of Prague," who was assassinated in June 1942 by SOE-trained Czech commandos.

[85] Bishop Clemens von Galen was the Catholic bishop of Munster, Germany from 1933 till his death in 1946.

[86] This was part of a talk Hitler gave at a dinner on 4 July 1942. For purposes of this novel, I have him giving it a year later. For the entire monologue see *Hitler's Table Talk, 1941-1944* (NY: Enigma Books, 2000), pp. 553-555. The Concordat was the agreement signed between the Vatican and the Third Reich in 1933, giving the Catholic Church certain privileges within Germany.

[87] Hitler made this comment about the Pope's frailty on January 24, 1942. Cited in French L. MacLean, *2000 Quotes from Hitler's 1000-Year Reich* (Atglen, PA: Schiffer Military History, 2007), p. 150.

[88] Blet, *Pius XII and the Second World War*, p. 210.

[89] It is rather ironic to note that Bormann's son, Martin Bormann, Jr., whose godfather was Adolf Hitler, was ordained a Roman Catholic priest after the war. He later left the priesthood and married a former nun.

[90] In a document written by Wolff in 1972, the former SS general claimed that Hitler summoned him on September 13, 1943 and gave him the order cited above. For purposes of this novel, I have this exchange occurring in July rather than September 1943. See John Cornwell, *Hitler's Pope* (New York: Viking Press, 1999), pp. 313-315; Ronald J. Rychlak, *Hitler, the War, and the Pope* (Huntington, Indiana: Our Sunday Visitor, 2000), p. 265.

[91] Hitler mockingly referred to Victor Emmanuel as the "king nutcracker" because of his diminutive size. The Italians themselves also referred to their king as *Sciaboletta* or "Little sabre."

[92] 8th SS Cavalry Division commanded by Fegelein from 1941-43.

[93] *Generalmajor* Paul Conrath was the commanding general of the Hermann Goring Panzer Division from 21 May 1943 – 14 April 1944.

[94] In September 2012, the US National Archives and Records Administration (NARA) released some 1,000 pages of recently declassified documents showing that the US hushed up Soviet guilt over the Katyn massacre for the sake of maintaining its wartime alliance with Stalin. See "US 'Hushed up' Soviet Guilt Over Katyn," http://www.bbc.co.uk/news/world-europe-19552745?print=true. Accessed 11 September 2012; "New Katyn Massacre Documents May Cause Political Stir," http://www.en.ria.ru/features/20120911/175903560.html. Accessed 11 September 2012.

[95] Wolff's nickname amongst his intimates.

[96] On August 31, 1939, the Germans staged a phony attack on a radio station in Gleiwitz on the Polish-German border, as a *casus belli* for Hitler's invasion of Poland the very next day. The Germans shot and killed concentration camp inmates dressed in Polish army uniforms as proof-positive that the Poles had attacked Germany and that Germany was defending itself against Polish aggression. This "black flag" operation was put together by Himmler's deputy, *SS Obergruppenführer* Reinhard Heydrich.

[97] As a senior Prisoner of War in American custody in the aftermath of the Second World War, Erfurth wrote a study in 1947 for the US European Command's Historical Division, entitled, *Warfare in the Far North*, which was ultimately published as Department of the Army Pamphlet 20-292, in October 1951.

[98] Mikkeli is in the southern Savonia region in Finland's southeast. It was used as the army headquarters for the first time in the Spring of 1918 during Finland's war for independence from Russia. The next time Mikkeli served as the army headquarters was in the Winter War of 1939-40 and again during the Continuation War of 1941-44. It was chosen as the military headquarters site due to its favorable position away from the front, although it was bombed extensively by the Red Air Force during the war.

[99] For more on this bizarre arrangement, see Paul Kendall, "The Jews Who Fought for Hitler: We Did not Help the Germans. We Had a Common Enemy," *The Telegraph*, March 9, 2014.

[100] Eduard Dietl was commander of the German 20th Mountain Army in Finland until his death in a plane crash on June 23, 1944. He was succeeded by General Lothar Rendulic.

[101] The JU-52's were of German manufacture and sold to Sweden. The Swedes also used aircraft purchased from the US and Great Britain. Even though it was strictly neutral during the war, it was an armed neutrality, much like Switzerland. By war's end in 1945, the Swedish Air Force had well over 1,000 aircraft.

[102] Spanish word for embrace.

[103] Henry L. deZeng IV, *Luftwaffe Airfields 1935-45 (Russia)*, February 2020 p. 154. Internet, http://www.ww2.dk/Airfields%20-%20Russia%20and%20Ukraine.pdf. Accessed on September 23, 2020.

[104] During World War II, members of the German Armed Forces were regularly given Pervitin, a methamphetamine, to keep them awake during long periods of combat operations. See Norman Ohler, *Blitzed: Drugs in the Third Reich* (Boston: Houghton Mifflin Harcourt Publishers, 2017).

[105] *Reichsmarshall* Hermann Goring, head of the *Luftwaffe*.

[106] Henry L. deZeng IV, *Luftwaffe Airfields 1935-45 (Czechoslovakia)* September 2014, p. 30. Available from http://www.www2.dk/Airfields520-%20Czechoslovakia.pdf.; Internet; accessed on 25 September 2020.

[107] With the exception of this small training mission, until the summer of 1944, Slovakia was free of German troops. However, Soviet trained Partisans became active, and coupled with a failed uprising by elements of the Slovak National Army, brought about a massive influx of German troops, mainly *Waffen SS* formations, into the tiny nation.

[108] Originally signed between Tokyo and Berlin in 1936, Italy signed in 1937 and from 1939-41 the following nations would also become signatories: Hungary, Manchukuo, Spain, Finland, Romania, Bulgaria, Slovakia, China, Denmark, and the Independent State of Croatia.

[109] Carol Rittner, Stephen D. Smith & Irene Steinfeldt, *The Holocaust and the Christian World* (Jerusalem, Israel: Yad Vashem, 2000), p. 106.

[110] James Mace Ward, *Priest, Politician, Collaborator: Josef Tiso and the Making of Fascist Slovakia* (NY: Cornell University Press, 2013), p. 255. Ward writes that to a Slovak bishop, Michal Buzalka, Pius XII spoke of "secret forces that work against the Church. . . [which] often use

regimes [headed by] a priest...to attack [her]. See Ward, *Priest, Politician, Collaborator*, p. 194.

[111] Rittner, et. al., *The Holocaust and the Christian World*, p. 107.

[112] Concluding lines of the poem in *Das Schwarz Korps* (The Black Corps, the official newspaper of the SS) critical of Pius XI's efforts on behalf of the Jews. Cited in Coppa, *The Papacy, the Jews, and the Holocaust*, p. 142.

[113] This was part of a series of diplomatic deceptions known as Plan Graffham undertaken by the Allies prior to D-Day in 1944. For purposes of this novel, I have it occurring a year earlier.

[114] Operation Felix—the German plan for a joint German-Spanish assault and capture of British Gibraltar.

[115] Located just outside of Madrid; it appealed to Franco because of the palace's history and royal past, its security, and the hilly estate attached to it was ideal for hunting. See Paul Preston, *Franco* (NY: Basic Books, 1994), p. 345.

[116] Baron Eberhard von Strohrer.

[117] A battle that was part of the Seige of Leningrad

[118] Franco was only 5'4" in height, the same height as Stalin. Both men wore lifts in their military-style boots to make them appear taller.

[119] On September 26, 1943, a decision was made to withdraw the Blue Division from Russia. The troops would be home by the end of the year.

[120] Preston, *Franco*, p. 399.

[121] Cited in Kurzman, *A Special Mission*, p. 90.

[122] Paragraph 175 of the German Reich's Criminal Code made homosexual acts between males a crime and in early versions the provisions also criminalized bestiality as well as forms of prostitution and underage sexual abuse.

[123] Dirlewanger commanded a SS poacher unit—made up of convicts and other miscreants. Dirlewanger himself was a convicted child molester, but enjoyed the trust and confidence of Gotlieb Berger, an intimate of Himmler, who protected Dirlewanger and promoted his career within the SS. The unit was known as the "Dirlewanger Brigade" and by war's end had been given divisional status. Dirlewanger's unit was known for its brutality, especially during the Warsaw Uprising of 1944, when it carried out unspeakable crimes against captured members of the Home Army and against Polish civilians. See French L. MacLean, *The Cruel Hunters: SS-Sonderkommando Dirlewanger, Hitler's Most Notorious Anti-Partisan Unit* (Atglen, PA: Schiffer Publishers, 1998).

[124] V-Mann came from the German word "*Vertrauens-Mann*" or "person of trust." See Roger Moorhouse, *Berlin at War* (NY: Basic Books, 2010), pp. 225-226.

[125] A *Shtetl* was a poor, small village in Central and Eastern Europe populated mainly by Jewish inhabitants. The Nazis destroyed most of the Eastern European *Shtetl's* during the Second World War.

[126] Himmler himself sought treatment there for his often-debilitating stomach cramps.

[127] SS *Standartenführer* Herbert Kappler, Chief of German Security Police in Rome.

[128] Cited in Ruth Ben-Ghiat, *Strongmen*, p. 227.

[129] Italian word for "German."

[130] The German airborne units were under the command of the *Luftwaffe* rather than the Army as was with most western armies of the time. This unit had been moved from southern France to *Pratica di Mare* airfield in preparation for the rescue of Mussolini which would occur on September 12, 1943.

[131] The prison was located within sight of the Basilica of St. John Lateran in Rome. Also, the notorious *Regina Coeli* (Queen of Heaven) prison, located on the banks of the Tiber River, was run by the Italian Fascist government.

[132] For more on this action see Failmezger, *Rome City in Terror*, pp. 66-67.

[133] Pietro Koch was head of the special Fascist police unit in Rome known as "*Banda* Koch" Koch often spoke of his intent to torture O'Flaherty before executing him if the cleric was ever captured. For more on Koch see J.P. Gallagher, *The Scarlet and the Black* (San Francisco: Ignatius Press, 2009) and Robert Katz, *The Battle for Rome* (NY: Simon & Schuster Publishers, 2003). Another Fascist gang, this one in Florence, was led by Mario Carità, who post-war would be found guilty of murder, torture, and deportations in cooperation with German authorities.

[134] The Gestapo Chief in Rome, SS *Obersturmbannführer* Herbert Kappler, had a white line drawn around the 109-acre Vatican City state, clearly delineating the boundaries between the Vatican City and the city of Rome.

[135] Cited in Failmezger, *Rome City in Terror: The Nazi Occupation 1943-44*, p. 78. *Himmel* is the German word for "Heaven."

[136] The *Primo Notario* is the man who drafts all decisions of the Holy Office into their final form and signs them. See Gallagher, *The Scarlet and the Black*, p. 22.

[137] On 21 December 1943, the Koch Gang, aided by the German Gestapo, raided Vatican properties that were not extraterritorial to the Vatican, but were among Vatican properties recognized by treaty. The *Seminario* Lombardo, the Pontifical Institute of Oriental Studies and the *Russicum* Institute were all raided, and individuals arrested. See Katz, *The Battle for Rome*, pp. 133-135.

[138] According to Argentinian author Uki Goni, the Pontifical Institute of Oriental Studies would be used to assist in the escape of Nazi war criminals at the end of World War II as part of the Vatican's so-called "Rat Line." See Uki Goni, *The Real Odessa* (NY: Granta Books, 2002), p. 330.

[139] A Halberd is a pole-like weapon consisting of an axe-blade with a spike.

[140] The Swiss Guard's most significant military engagement occurred on 6 May 1527 when 190 guards died fighting troops of the Holy Roman Empire during their sack of Rome, allowing Pope Clement VII to flee to safety.

[141] Jerry Filteau, "Pope Pius XII Was Prepared to Resign as Pope," *National Catholic News Service*, January 28, 1988. http://ncronline.org/blogs/ncr-today/Pope-pius-xii-was-prepared-to-resign-Pope. Accessed on February 10, 2015.

[142]Sigismund von Braun was a career German diplomat and the older brother of German rocket scientist Werner von Braun. Although a Nazi party member, Sigismund von Braun worked quietly behind the scenes and at great personal risk, to assist cleric and other offices in hiding persecuted people and hindering their deportation to concentration camps.

[143] Cited in Kurzman, *A Special Mission*, p. 125.

[144] Colonel Eugen Dollmann was a senior SS officer assigned to Rome as Heinrich Himmler's personal representative.

[145] Greg Annussek, *Hitler's Raid to Save Mussolini* (Cambridge, MA: Da Capo Press, 2005), p. 169. For more on the rescue of Mussolini see, Robert Forczyk, *Rescuing Mussolini, Gran Sasso 1943* (NY: Osprey Publishing, 2014) and Otto Skorzeny, *My Commando Operations* (Atglen, PA: Schiffer Military History Publishers, 1995). Readers should be aware that Skorzeny's works are extremely self-serving.

[146] Otto Skorzeny, *My Commando Operations* (Atglen, PA: Schiffer Publishing, Ltd, 1995), p. 270.

[147] SS-Senior rifleman.

[148] Security Service

[149] For more on Priebke see Failmezger, *Rome City in Terror: The Nazi Occupation 1943-44;* Robert Katz, "The Last Nazi Trial," in *Military History Quarterly* (Summer 1996), Vol. 8, No. 4, pp. 74-79.

[150] It would not be until 2005 that German-born Cardinal Joseph Ratzinger, was elected Pope, taking the name of Pope Benedict XVI. He resigned in 2013. Prior to election as Pope, he held the important position of Prefect of the Congregation for the Doctrine of the Faith (1982-2005).

[151] Cited in Peter Eisner, *The Pope's Last Crusade* (New York: Harper Collins Publishers, 2013), p. 33.

[152] In German, a derogatory term for a homosexual. Dollmann was a closet homosexual and would more than likely have been stripped of his rank and thrown into a concentration camp had he been outted.

[153]Cited in Gallagher, *The Scarlet and the Black*, p. 10.

[154] Italian word for Excavation.

[155] The bulk of this quote is taken from Ines San Martin, "Peter is Here," *Columbia,* Vol. 99, Number 6 (June 2019), p. 10.

[156] German boxer, who was the former world heavyweight champion from 1930-32.

[157] The Lateran Treaty of 1929 between Mussolini's government and Pope Pius XI established the Vatican City State as an independent and sovereign state.

[158] Office of Strategic Services.

[159] Special Operations Executive.

[160] See Maria de Blasio Wilhelm, *The Other Italy,* pp. 180-185.

[161] Ibid., p. 178.

[162] Field Marshal Albert Kesselring, a *Luftwaffe* officer, was the senior German military commander for all of Italy.

[163] On October 1 1943, Mälzer was promoted to the rank of *Generalleutnant* and became the garrison commander and commandant of the occupied city of Rome (October 30, 1943).

[164] Major Mario Carità, head of an irregular pro-Fascist security force in the city of Florence, waged a ruthless war against Jews and other opponents of the Fascist regime. The band was responsible for conducting ruthless, sadistic, and bloody interrogations of its prisoners. At war's end, Carità was killed in a shootout with American troops at his mountain hideout in the *Alto Adige*.

[165] Cardinal Ildefonso Schuster, Archbishop of Milan.

[166] In Christian tradition, St. Peter flees from crucifixion in Rome at the hands of the government, and along the road outside the city, meets the risen Christ. Peter asks Jesus, *Quo Vadis?* and Jesus answers *Roman eo iterum crucifigi* (I am going to Rome to be crucified again). Peter regains the courage to return to Rome to preach and is ultimately arrested and crucified upside down. The Church of *Domine Quo Vadis* stands at the spot where the alleged meeting between Peter and Jesus took place. *Quo Vadis* was also a bestselling novel written in 1896 by Henryk Sienkiewicz, following on the heels of another great religious novel, *Ben-Hur: A Tale of the Christ* (1880), by former Union Army general, Lew Wallace, and is considered the most influential Christian book of the 19th Century.

[167] In 1945, a former Blue Division captain, Miguel Ezquerra, who had been promoted to the rank of colonel in the *Waffen SS*, commanded three companies of Spaniards and other European volunteers in the final battle of Berlin. The men of "Unit Ezquerra" were among the last troops engaged against the Red Army in the rubble around Hitler's Chancellery. See John Scurr, *Germany's Spanish Volunteers 1941-45*, p.30.

[168] At the time of this writing, The Washington Post published an article which stated that the newly opened wartime papers of Pius XII in the Vatican archives did not bode well for the late pontiff. Beginning March 2, 2020 and lasting only a week until the archives were closed due to the worldwide pandemic, researchers came across some disturbing documents that reflected badly on the pontiff, often accused of silence during the Holocaust. Further scholarly research will continue once the archives are reopened. See https://www.washingtonpost.com/history/2020/04/29/vatican-pope-pius-records-holocaust/

John R. Dabrowski

www.ingramcontent.com/pod-product-compliance
Lightning Source LLC
Chambersburg PA
CBHW051333020726
47501CB00007B/2064